JUBILEE

ALSO BY JACK DANN FROM TOM DOHERTY ASSOCIATES

High Steel
(with Jack C. Haldeman II)
Counting Coup

In the Fields of Fire
(edited with Jeanne Van Buren Dann)
Dreaming Down-Under
(edited with Janeen Webb)

JUBILEE

JACK DANN

A Tom Doherty Associates Book
New York

FOR NICK STATHOPOULOS

This is a work of fiction. All the characters and events portrayed in
these stories are either fictitious or are used fictitiously.

JUBILEE

Copyright © 2001 by Jack Dann

CONTENTS

The author would like to thank the following people for their help and support:

Theresa Anns, Jennifer Brehl, Ginger Clark, Sean Cotcher, Lorne Dann, Ellen Datlow, Gardner Dozois, Helen Doherty, Terry Dowling, Melanie and Lewis Downey, Sue Drakeford, Tom Dupree, Harlan and Susan Ellison, Andrew Enstice, Christine Farmer, Russell Farr, Edward Ferman, Keith Ferrell, Linda Funnell, Charles L. Grant, Martin H. Greenberg, Louise and Ron Harris, Merrilee Heifetz, Barrie Hitchon, Pat LoBrutto, Angelo Loukakis, Barry Malzberg, Shona Martyn, Midge McCall, Peter McNamara, Sean McMullen, Peter McNamara, Steve Paulsen, Robert and Opal Pemberton, Peter Schneider, Pamela Sargent, Carol Serling, Victoria Schochet, Bob Sheckley, John Silbersack, Nick Stathopoulos, Stephanie Smith, Jonathan Strahan, Dena Taylor, Kate Thomas, Norman Tilley, Gordon Van Gelder, John Wilkinson, Sheila Williams, Kaye Wright and George Zebrowski, and, of course, Janeen Webb.

JACK: OUT OF THE BOX

It seems an odd twist for me to be introducing Jack Dann's latest collection of short fiction, since when I was an aspiring writer in the early 1970s, Jack was one of my heroes, a man whose work I admired and sought to emulate.

Hark back with me to those storied days of yesteryear. In the United States, the New Wave debate that had rent the science fiction world of the 1960s still persisted, and there were signs of reaction. Despite the recognition that writers like Harlan Ellison and Ursula Le Guin had gained, for the most part science fiction writers were invisible outside of the genre. Peter Prescott, the book reviewer for *Newsweek*, called sf readers "a half million adult illiterates." Joanna Russ and Gene Wolfe, doing the most daring work in the U.S., were often scorned when they were recognised at all. If this was all the result that trying to write literary science fiction earned, what use was it?

But when has sense ever cancelled ambition? I was a science fiction freak from upstate New York with no conviction that I could ever sell a story. My role models were those writers on the literary edge of sf some few years older than I, writers in their twenties like Gardner Dozois, Edward Bryant, Joe Haldeman, and Jack Dann. They were the guys that I looked up to. Some day, might I be able to write as well as they? Could I ever speak to them as peers? Heaven forfend, might I ever come to call someone like Jack Dann my friend?

Jack held a special place because, like me, he was from upstate New York. You have to realise that since Grover Cleveland (U.S. President, 1885-89, 1893-97) *nobody* important came from upstate New York.

The more I read of Jack, the more I felt that he had some cable tapped into my soul. Jack's stories refused to admit that there was some inevitable divide between science fiction and literature. They showed evidence of wide

1

reading. They were written in a controlled prose that did not draw attention to itself. Most important to that young Kessel, they bespoke a dark existential angst. Jack was the complete modernist sf writer, owing as much to James Joyce as he did to Robert Heinlein. In the late seventies I saw him at conventions. He was tall and elegant and funny and dressed a lot better than I did. He was going to storm Parnassus and bring home the laurel crown not just for himself, but for all of us.

Of course, Steven Spielberg and George Lucas and Captain Kirk screwed it all up. They persuaded the literary world, which seemed for a brief time in the late 1970s to be on the brink of conceding that sf might be a legitimate form of fiction for adults, that stories of the future were for children. ("No soup for you! Back into the pulps!")

I left western New York, went to graduate school in literature, but still ran across Jack's fiction in *Omni*, in *F & SF*. If he was cowed by the media's dumbing down of sf, it did not change what he was writing one iota. In fact, the Dann of the late seventies and early eighties was writing better than ever. He had outgrown whatever self-consciousness might have marked his earliest stories and was producing completely assured work like "A Quiet Revolution for Death," "Bad Medicine," "Blind Shemmy," and "Going Under" (which knocked my socks off when I first read it in *Omni* in 1981 and still knocks them off today — perhaps I shouldn't bother wearing socks when I read Jack's fiction). His novel *The Man Who Melted* gained a lot of praise in the genre. For those of you who care about the debates of the time, both cyberpunks and humanists hailed him as an influence. Had the world been better arranged, this fiction would have drawn the attention of a non-genre audience as well.

It was about then, in the early 1980s, that I had the great good luck to get to know Jack personally. My parents still lived in Buffalo, and I would drive up from North Carolina to see them fairly often. Jack lived in Binghamton, New York (a town which appears in several of these stories). Before one of these trips I called him up and asked if I might stop by and say hello. Jack insisted that I stay for a visit, and after that I, and later my wife Sue, would stop to see him every time we came to New York.

In person, Jack demonstrates a weird sense of humour; T.S. Eliot becomes Groucho Marx. Acknowledging the pain of the world, he turns to goofiness, as surprising as an elegant young woman carrying her father's talking head in a box. I can't tell you how pleased I was to become Jack's friend. It was almost as if H.G. Wells had decided to hang out with me (though Jack is somewhat younger than H.G., and has more hair).

We would talk about writing and share manuscripts of work in progress. In the mid-eighties, those of us who read portions of his novel *Counting Coup* said, aha, here is the book that is going to break Jack out to a non-sf audience that could appreciate his work but had not had the opportunity to do so because of the world of category publishing. But a series of mishaps kept *Counting Coup* from seeing print then. Jack moved on to the years-long effort of writing *The Memory Cathedral*, and we saw little or no work from him through the second half of the 1980s.

Fortunately, the nineties have brought the Jack Dann renaissance. Jack left Binghamton for Australia. He won a Nebula for "Da Vinci Rising" and with the publication of *The Memory Cathedral* and *Dreaming Down Under* (co-edited by his wife, the esteemed scholar Janeen Webb) he has become a mover in Australian fiction, both within the world of science fiction and without. With 1998's *The Silent* and the belated appearance of *Counting Coup* (published in Australia as *Bad Medicine*), the evidence of Jack's continued vitality as a writer is everywhere with us.

The thing that first drew me to Jack's fictions was the theme of personal quest. His are stories of transcendence, spiritual exploration, harrowing psychological transformations. Rebirth and conceptual breakthrough. And yet they are grounded in a developed sense of personal relationships, the rag and bone shop of the human heart. Take a relatively simple story like "Kaddish", which tells of a man in spiritual crisis, carries him along a plotline as straight as an arrow to a confrontation with death, and ends on a note of ambiguous salvation. There are no false steps here. The story is quietly harrowing.

It's gratifying to see the rest of the world catch up with that perception of Jack I had in the 1970s. Jack always had the chops to be a mainstream writer, but the imagination to be a genre man, and you will find evidence of those skills everywhere in this collection. His novel-in-progress, *Second Chance*, promises to extend his reputation to a still larger audience. His work has deepened and grown over the last thirty years — has it been thirty years, Jack? — and he enters the new millennium poised to do the strongest writing of his career.

And so, this upstate New York boy gets to introduce this only slightly older upstate small town big city New York Australian boy (g'day, mate!). It's been a pleasure, Jack, and a learning experience, and I hope it goes on for another century or so.

John Kessel
Raleigh, North Carolina

John Kessel has taught fiction writing and American literature at North Carolina State University in Raleigh since 1982. He is a recipient of the Nebula Award and the Theodore Sturgeon Award. His play *Faustfeathers* won the 1994 Paul Green Playwrights' Competition and his audio play *A Clean Escape* was produced by the Seeing Ear Theater. His books include the novel *Good News from Outer Space* and the story collections *Meeting in Infinity* and *The Pure Product*.

He lives with his wife and daughter in Raleigh, North Carolina.

Introduction

OUT OF THE BLUE

I dreamed of being a writer when I was in high school, and I clearly remember thinking that once I became a writer, I'd be . . . rich, and I'd have a limousine and a driver. Ah, the delusions of youth.

I almost died when I was in my 20's. I was in hospital and was given a five percent chance of survival. The days and weeks and months were a series of stop-motion slides of agonizing pain and ice-blue Demerol dreams, pain, bliss, pain, bliss, and during the Demerol highs, I would ask my nurse for ice; I would place my hand in the ice and dream of "the blue country," a place of ice mountains and constant blue twilight, my own metaphor for lonely peace and death.

After months of fighting for my life on a terminal ward where my friends died and the patients formed a secret club of those traversing the blue country, I began to recover. On my tray table beside the bed, I kept a copy of Ernest Hemmingway's memoir of his youth in Paris, *A Moveable Feast*, and it became like a talisman for me. When I was too ill even to consider reading, I would put my hand on its cool covers . . . as if I could become a writer by osmosis. Later, I would read a passage or a page and enter Hemmingway's life, enter what the French author Jean Dutourd called the life of art. I associated books with life, with the juice and joy of being alive, and I felt . . . I felt that I had, in a sense, died and come back. I'd been given a second chance. And somehow that gave me the courage to take chances, live on the edge, live my dreams. I wasn't afraid of failure. For a while, I wasn't afraid of *anything*!

Thirty years later and I'm *still* living the dream, writing, stretching, reaching for that elusive, perfect image, living fast and hard and hot, and sometimes — when I'm sitting in front of the CRT screen and reaching for those images — I'm not afraid of anything.

* * *

The stories that follow are living bits of my experience and memory . . . alchemical distillations of my fantasies, dreams, and nightmares. They are the fictional flesh of my musings.

Magicks . . .

And if I've done something right, some of their magic might come alive for you . . . become part of *your experience and sense memory.*

Jack Dann,
Melbourne
March 2001

THE DIAMOND PIT

● ●

Homage to F. Scott . . .

I'd be flyin' to find!
My Miss One-of a kind!
If I could only get —
If only I could get —
out'a this jail! . . .

— Rumplemayer's Basement Blues, 1921

ONE

It was like being in a storm, except I heard the thunder first. That was the sound of a dozen anti-aircraft guns firing at us from the summit of a sheer butte that rose like a monolith above the cruel curls of the Montana Rockies.

The setting sun was wreathed with gauzy clouds, and it tinted the cliffs and crevasses below as pink as stained glass flamingos. We were flying a British Moth with a 60-hp de Havilland motor — those Brits could certainly make an airplane. The Moth was steady as a table and was Joel's and my favourite for wing walking and stepping off from one plane onto another.

I was in the front cockpit, this time, just along for the ride. It had been Joel's idea to borrow the boss's beaut and skip out after our last performance to investigate "something goofy" in the mountains near Hades, which was more bare rock than a village set in the saddle between a mountain that looked like a two-knuckled fist and the mountain that was shooting bullets at us.

Joel swore and shouted though the communication tube and tried to get us the hell out of there, as bullets tore into the fuselage. Another burst hit the upper wing just above my head, which was where the fuel tank was located. My face was spattered with gasoline and I figured then and there that I had just bought the farm; Joel was shouting through the tube to tell me that everything was okay — when we were hit again.

I heard a ping as a bullet hit the motor, and an instant later I could barely see through the oily smoke and fire. I gagged on the burnt exhalations of fuel and oil that smeared over my goggles as the Moth went into a dive. Reflexively, I took over the controls, which were linked to the front cockpit, God bless Mr Geoffrey de Havilland. I shouted back at Joel through the tube and pulled as hard as I could on the stick while working the rudder and aileron pedals. The compass was going all wacky, as though someone was playing over it with a magnet, pulling the needle this way and that. Although I couldn't see Joel, I *knew* that he had been hit. Another wave of heat swept over me, and I figured I'd be lucky to have another few seconds before the fuel tank blew Joel and me right out of the postcard pink and purple sky.

I always wondered what I'd be thinking about in my last moments. I'd wondered about it every time I climbed into a Spad during Bloody April of 1917; I could fly as well as most anybody, although I was no Rickenbacker. I had figured I was going to get it in '17 or '18, but I never even took a bullet, not a scratch — I had the proverbial angel on my wing — and now here I was, about to get it in 1923, which was *supposed* to be the best year of my life. I remembered Dr Coué's prayer, which everyone was saying: "Day by day in every way I am getting better and better."

Better and better.

"Joel," I shouted through the tube, "you're going to be okay. We're going to be okay." *Day by day in every fucking way*, and I felt that hot, sweaty tightness all over my face like I always do when I'm going to cry, but I slipped out of that because the old girl was making a whining keening sort of a noise, and then the motor sputtered and everything became summer afternoon quiet, except for the snapping of the wing wires . . .

And I found myself counting, counting slowly and the ground spun through the smoke, and I kept the nose up as the valley floor rose like an elevator the size of Manhattan, and I wasn't thinking about anything, not about dying or the tank exploding or the smoke or the smell of the oil . . . or my Mother, or Lisa, whom I had only dated twice, but she had gone down on the first date and said she loved me, and she had so many freckles, and three curly black hairs between her breasts, I remembered those three black hairs as I counted and by one-hundred-and-forty-seven I expected the giant hand of God to slap me right into the canyon floor and the fuel tank to explode like the sun and —

It was dark when they found me, but the moon was so big and bloated that everything looked like it was coated with silvery dust, except the shadows, where the moon dust couldn't settle. I don't know whether they woke me or whether it was the drip from the fuel tank, but once I realised I was alive and that this was certainly not heaven, I felt most every part of my body begin to ache. I moved my legs to make sure I still had them, and I tried to swat at the Negroes who were pulling me out of the cockpit. I don't know what was in my head because they were big men, and I was just swatting away, but they didn't throw me about or mistreat me or ask me any questions; it was as if they were just handling a fragile piece of merchandise, nothing that was alive, just merchandise. I started coughing as soon as they moved me, and I craned my neck for one last look at the plane . . . and at Joel, the poor dumb jake who just had to see if the stories were true about a grand castle on the mountain. Now Joel was dead, his face shot off, and I was being carried away by giants who were speaking a dialect like none I'd ever heard; in fact, I couldn't understand a word, although I couldn't help but think it was *some* form of Southern English.

And we hadn't even seen a castle.

Damn you, Joel.

I blacked out, and woke up as I was being thrown this way and that in the seat of some kind of souped-up, armoured suburban; but this beast hadn't rolled off any of Henry Ford's production lines. It was a chimerical combination of tank and automobile. Instead of windows, the passenger cab had thick glass portholes, and Lewis machine guns were mounted on the hood and trunk. I could hardly hear the motor as we sped and jostled into the long purple shadows of the mountains above, and my captors were as quiet as the mountains.

When I woke again, after dreaming that Joel was fine and we were back in the Moth gliding silently through the night over castles and fairy lights, I found myself in the air indeed. The suburban was being hoisted up the sheer face of a cliff, rising into the milky moonlight; and, startled, I bolted forward. The two black giants beside me pulled me back into the cushioned softness of the seat and held me there. I tried to talk to them, to ask them what was going on, but they just shook their heads as though they couldn't understand me.

Then with a bounce the suburban was lowered onto solid ground. Two men and a boy were waiting beside a crane used on aircraft carriers to hoist boats and planes; and as they removed the cables that had been attached to the hub-guards of the huge truck-tyred wheels, they spoke to each other in that peculiar dialect that was both familiar . . . and unfamiliar.

Once again we drove, only now we were that much closer to the sky. As I looked out through the porthole on my right, the moon looked green, radiating its wan, sickly light through filigrees of cloud; and the road made of tapestry brick was as straight and neat and ghostly as the fog and mist that clung to it.

We passed a lake that could have been a dark mirror misted with breath and reflecting the stars and bloated moon. I caught a sudden scent of pine, and then I saw it, a chateau — no, rather a moon-painted castle — with opalescent terraces, walkways, mosque-like towers, and outbuildings rising from broad, tree-lined lawns.

But my destination, alas, would be otherwise.

TWO

"Hell's bells, it's almost noon."

"Clarence, how would you know whether it was noon or what? Your wristwatch has stopped so many times, it could be midnight."

"Don't call me Clarence or I'll break your legs."

"You an' whose army?"

I snapped awake and looked around the room, which resolved around me. Walls, floor, ceiling seemed to be made of a piece, a smooth, translucent layer of opal, which glowed with light; but I could not discern the source of the suffusing light, nor could I see the inset marks of tile, only high, straight, iridescent planes that reached to a ceiling of the same substance. I was lying in a comfortable feather bed with a jewel-inlaid footboard; the bed and an ebony table and elbow chair were the only pieces of furniture in this smooth, glittering travesty of a monk's cell.

"Well, sleeping beauty has awoke," said Clarence. He had a pale, freckled complexion, red hair that was greying, and a pop-eyed look, no doubt because his eyebrows were so white that they seemed to disappear. "You're probably still feelin' dopey," he said to me. "The slaves drugged you so Old Jefferson could do his interrogation. Takes a while for it to wear off."

"Well, they didn't drug *me*," said the man who had been goading Clarence about his name. He was bald, tall, and aggressive; and he had a ruddy complexion like Clarence — it was as if both men were of the same Irish and Dutch ancestry. Both wore pants and shirts that looked like pyjamas, except Clarence wore an aviator's jacket and the bald man wore a cap. Eleven other men were standing in the room behind them, and a short wiry aviator — I was sure right then and there that they were *all* aviators — said, "Old man Jefferson drugged *everybody*. Even you, Monty. You just don't remember none of it, while we do."

"But none of us remembers much," said Clarence, who introduced himself as Skip, and then introduced me to Monty Kleeck and Farley James and Rick Moss and Carl Crocker and Eddie Barthelmet, Harry Talmadge, Keith Boardman, Gregory "Cissy" Schneck, "Snap" Samuel Geraldson, and Stephen Freeburg, who "was the only Jew in this mess of Protestants".

"You a Jew too?" asked the skinny, nervous upchuck who was called Cissy. There was a meanness in his voice, but he wasn't big enough to back it up, and I knew he was more dangerous than the three hundred pound hulk they called Snap.

I thought about saying yes, but I figured I might be here a while — maybe for life, from the look of them — and so I said, "No, I'm Catholic. You have a problem with that?"

"No, no," said Cissy, backing off. "I got no problem with Christians." Then in an undertone he said, "Long as they're Christians . . ."

"Where the hell am I?" I asked, some of the muzziness from the drugs finally clearing — if, indeed, I'd been drugged. I directed myself to Stephen Freeburg, who had the same kind of dark, sharp features as Rudolph Valentino, who last I heard had gone to prison for bigamy.

"You're in the Randolph Estes Jefferson Hotel," Freeburg said, smiling. "It's probably the fanciest, most comfortable jail in the world. And unless you can think of something we haven't, you're here for life."

"No, we'll get out," said Carl Crocker, a short, overweight, squarish chap with bristly brown hair — they must feed these guys pretty well, I thought; but everything was just words and thoughts wriggling like worms in sand. Nothing seemed real. My mouth felt like it was stuffed with wire. My eyes were burning. My head was pounding. Wake up, I told myself. Wake the hell up.

"Yeah, your tunnel," Freeburg said sarcastically. "Next, you and Snap will be drilling straight down." Everyone laughed at that.

I guess I looked bemused because Eddie Barthelmet, a reedy, yet muscular man with thinning black hair, whom I figured immediately as the sort who kept his own counsel, said, "It's solid diamond underneath us. Hardest substance in the world."

I shook my head and grinned. I could take being the butt of the joke.

"I'm not joshing you. The whole goddamn mountain is diamond, except for the rock and stone above. And it's all owned by the Old Man, who isn't too willing to share, which is why we're down here, and he's up there." Everyone laughed at that, and Eddie just nodded toward the ceiling, as if some omniscient being was standing right above us. Then after a pause, he asked, "Did you happen to notice if your compass seemed to go wild when you approached the mountain?"

"Yeah," I said. "But I figured it had been knocked out of whack."

"No, the same thing happened to me. None of the others remember anything being wrong with their compasses, so I figure that the Old Man concocted something new. An artificial magnetic field, or something like that."

"Well, if he could change the official maps of the United States, he could screw up our compasses, I suppose," Clarence said. I didn't figure him to be the brightest of the bunch, but I couldn't help but like him. He seemed genuinely concerned, and maybe it was the way he slouched or patted the chair, I don't know, but for some reason I had the feeling that really at home here. He turned to me and said, "Don't worry, you'll ___ing the Old Man soon enough. And when you're ready, I'll give ___ tour of the place and help you get set up. Now you think you're ___ tell us your name and how you came to be flyin' out here? You ___lyin' . . .?"

I nodded and told them my name — Paul Orsatti — and I told them that I was a mail pilot, which I'd been for a while, until I got myself fired from New York Chicago Air Transport for being self-righteous; and I wasn't going to tell them that I'd been kicking around for the past year as a roustabout stunt flier, working for crummy outfits like Pitkin's Circle-Q Flying Circus. Or that I'd been playing piano in cheapjack speakeasies for nothing more than drinks and whatever change the Doras and ossified lounge lizards could spare. I didn't tell them about Joel, and how he'd heard rumours about there being something strange in the mountain near Hades. I only told them I'd gotten a bit off-course — next thing I knew I was being shot at.

And as if I'd been caught telling a lie by the Lord God Almighty Himself, I heard a voice calling everyone to attention.

A broadcast from above.

"Well, boys," said God. "Don't you want to have a chat? My daughter's accompanying me, so y'all better be on your best behaviour, gentlemen. None of your usual filthy street patois. Now shake a leg!"

Everyone started swearing and complaining, but they obediently moved out of my room toward where the voice was probably coming from, and Skip pulled me along, telling me that I might as well know my keeper and get it in my head that I'm here and that's that and how it's not so bad, in fact, probably better than we'd ever have it back home in the *real* world.

We walked through a seamless corridor made of the same stuff as the walls, floor, and ceiling of the room where I'd awakened. Dim, pervasive light radiated wanly from the ceiling, and doorways were evenly spaced on both sides. I caught glimpses into other rooms, some larger than others, some dark, some brightly lit, and could see rooms that led into other corridors. I was in a polished, many-hued glass warren that could hold many more men than we who were here now. We crowded into an empty room, which was a high tower . . . a terminus of sorts.

I looked up at a large, brightly lit opening covered with grating an[...]
man looking down at us — I assumed he was Mr Randolph Estes Jeff[...]

Some sort of lens must have also covered the opening beca[...]
Jefferson seemed greatly magnified and also slightly distorted, as thou[...]
girth was being pulled toward the edges of the opening. He looked [...]
about forty-five and had one of those faces that always remind me of a p[...]
dog: jowly and fleshy, yet absolutely intent — the proverbial dog with a bone.
He stood erect, as though he was wearing military gear instead of a straw
boater, blue blazer, and white flannel Oxford bags. If it weren't for that face
and his bearing, he could have been a fashion plate. He was swinging what
I thought was a cane, swinging it back and forth over the opening to the
tower of our prison (but which was, in effect, just a grating in the grass from
his perspective). A girl of perhaps eighteen stood beside her pug dog father.
She wore a thin blue blouse with a pleated tennis skirt and a blue bandeau to
keep her hair in place. Her hair was blond, curly, and bobbed, and although
I couldn't see the colour of her eyes, I imagined they would be blue. Her
mouth was crimson, her face tan against the blue bandeau. Even with the
slight distortion, I could see that she was perfection — a pure vision of youth
and freshness and beauty.

"Hey, leave the old guy and come on down here."

"Push him through the grate, we'll take care of everything for you."

"They don't call me snugglepup for nottin'," Crocker shouted, and most
everyone was laughing . . . except Mr Jefferson. His daughter smiled warmly
at all of us and bowed, as though she was being presented at a cotillion in
New York or Chicago or Paris.

"Gentlemen," said Mr Jefferson, "remember your manners. If y'all
continue to embarrass me before my daughter, I shall be happy to instruct
my slaves to forget to supply you with your daily rations, which I presume
are to your expectations?"

"Slaves?" I asked Skip, who was standing beside me and rubbernecking, to
get a better look at the girl.

"Yeah," Skip said, "he's got hundreds of 'em, I guess."

"The rations are fine, except we could do without the fish eggs," said Rick
Moss, a short unshaven man, who was so muscular that he looked like he
might have been a weight lifter.

"So the rations of caviar are not appreciated," Jefferson said. "Well, we'll take that item off the menu." Randolph Estes Jefferson sounded cheerful, as if he were merely a waiter taking an order and listening to customers' complaints. "Now my Phoebe loves caviar," he said, putting his arm around his daughter, "so I, of course, just assumed y'all would too. I figured your generation with all your jazz and Wall Street savvy was more sophisticated than mine."

But Harry Talmadge and Keith Boardman, who were standing beside me and looking quietly bored, were not exactly what you'd call jazz babies — Harry looked to be in his middle-forties, but it would be difficult to guess whether Keith was in his fifties or sixties. He looked well fed and well exercised, as though he were someone who could afford to pamper himself and maintain his youth.

I thought it odd that our jailer Mr Jefferson used "y'all" like someone from the Deep South, yet he had no accent at all . . . which was probably the same thing as having a mid-west accent.

"Well, *I* don't mind the caviar," said fat Snap Geraldson. "I guess that makes me the only sophisticated guy down here." That got a laugh.

"Are you here to bait us like bears, or have you come up with a solution to our problem?" asked Freeburg.

"Ah, Mr Freeburg, you are always so angry and so ready to argue how many angels might rest on the head of a pin. Aren't you satisfied with the Talmud I provided for your studies?"

"I've simply taken the bait," Freeburg said.

"Well, good for you, then. But we've been over and over my predicament. I — being a man of conscience — must bear the burden of keeping y'all in prison because to free you would be harmful to my family and myself and my retainers. You'll soon come to understand that, too, Mr Orsatti."

I almost took a step back when he addressed me.

"I trust you're getting settled in comfortably," he continued. "The other boys will show you the ropes. If anyone mistreats you, just slip a note into the food slot. It'll reach me in due course. I've developed quite a paternalistic affection for all of you. Quite."

"We'd promise not to peach on you," cried Carl Crocker. "And that's the honest truth. Just let us go. Give us a chance."

"Ah, but you couldn't help yourself, could you, Mr Crocker," Jefferson said, as he pulled a lawn chair over for Phoebe and then disappeared for a few seconds to return with a chair for himself. "You'd have to tell *some*one. And if you could come back and get past my slaves and my guns, why then *you'd* be the richest man on earth. Would you like me to send some more gems down to you? You can have whatever you wish — diamonds, rubies, sapphires, a birthstone of your own weight."

"Won't do me any good down here," Carl said.

"Ah, you see, value is relative. But once you got away from here, these diamonds and rubies and sapphires would be worth as much as life itself. Surely you can see that?"

"No, I can't," said Carl.

"As I've asked you before, do you want me to have your wives and girlfriends brought here? I'll extend your accommodations. Y'all would have everything you could wish for."

"Except freedom," said Eddie Barthelmet. "What would it take to buy that?"

"You can't *buy* anything from me," said Mr Jefferson. "All that I give is as a gift. When last we spoke — how long ago was that? Perhaps a few months ago? — I asked if you could come up with a better solution. Well, this is your chance. Propose."

"So you can dispose," said Eddie.

"Very good, very good indeed. The newer members seem to be quicker than the rest of you. You'll need to study to keep up."

"Then let us have some newspapers," shouted Crocker.

"Yeah, is prohibition repealed yet?"

"What would you care?" Mr Jefferson said. "Whatever spirits you request are sent to you. What more could you ask for?"

That elicited shouting and swearing, and Mr Jefferson just smiled and held up his hands. "Well, gentlemen, I see that we're finished."

"We do care about whether prohibition has been repealed," Eddie shouted up to Mr Jefferson. "Just as we care about what the stock market is doing, what's the new dance, what's happening with the Fascists in Italy, what's the latest Zane Grey, is Dempsey still heavyweight champion, who won the World Series?"

"Giants over the Yankees, 5-3 in the fifth," I said in a low voice. Eddie nodded to me, and a few of the other boys started to argue the merits of the Giants and the Yankees.

"There's your answer," Mr Jefferson said. He could only have heard me if he had listening devices planted in here, which, of course, he would.

"We need access to newspapers . . . and the radio," Eddie said.

"It will only stir you up, son, and make you yearn for what you can't have," Jefferson said. "You've got a library of the great classics of literature. That should be edification enough."

"I want *The Saturday Evening Post*," Crocker said.

"I want *The Strand*."

"I want Phoebe."

"Goodbye, gentlemen," Jefferson said.

"Wait," shouted Eddie. "Why not at least give us leave? At least, let one or two of us out for a few days. You could have your slaves guard us to make sure we couldn't run for it. We could at least see a ball game, or a movie. Then you could bring us back, and take another group out. As you are always fond of telling us, 'Money's no object.'"

Jefferson made a clucking noise and said, "That's a new twist, Mr Barthelmet. Very good, indeed. Except my slaves would have to gag you and bind you so you wouldn't shout for help or make a run for it, and the constabulary might look askance at that. But even if you were a model parolee, you'd come back and yearn for what you'd seen. No, it would just deepen the pain of your circumstances. Allow me to bring your wives or lovers or friends to you."

"No," shouted Rick Moss, and he was echoed by the others.

"It's bad enough you've buried us."

"Let us the hell out of here, you bastid."

"Well, gentlemen, I think that's more than enough," Jefferson said. "Come on, Phoebe, enough diversion for you." He stood up, and I could see then that he had been holding a golf club, not a cane. We were buried under his golf course, and he and his daughter were just out playing eighteen holes. The sonovabitch!

There was a grating noise, and the opening above went black.

"Wait," I shouted reflexively.

The ceiling irised open, and Jefferson and his beautiful Phoebe looked down at us. "Yes, Mr Orsatti?" he asked.

"I'd like a piano."

Jefferson laughed and said, "Done."

"That's all we need, more noise —"

"We could use some of that —"

"You boys can dance with each other —"

"It beats what we're doin' now —"

But before the ceiling closed, I could see Phoebe looking down — right at *me* — and smiling.

THREE

The piano arrived, as promised. It was a special-edition, pearl-white Steinway grand, which produced a huge, full orchestral sound, yet the keys had such an incredibly fast action that I couldn't help but open up with a boogie-woogie medley. My feet stomped on the floor as my left hand flew over the keys beating out syncopated rhythms that were so tricky that I dared not watch what I was doing, lest I falter; and my right hand, weaving various melodies through the rhythms of my left, might as well have had a mind of its own.

I was a one-man band.

I was also, needless to say, half in the proverbial bag. But so was everyone else, except Cissy Schneck and Farley James, a nice British fellow who had been an Oxford don before the war. I found out from Skip that he had been an ace pilot. He'd come over here to compete in the ocean-to-ocean air race in '19, the same year the Cincinnati Reds beat the Sox in the eighth game, which was a miracle. So was Farley James, I guess, because he'd come in second place and decided to stay and start an air flying company with Charlie Lindbergh. That surprised the hell out of me because Joel, may God rest his soul, said he'd worked for Lindbergh for a while.

"Hey, Farley," I called, and he dutifully came over to the piano, where Skip formally introduced us.

"Fahley, z'ish is Pauhhzzotti . . ."

"Skip tells me you had some business with Charlie Lindbergh."

Farley nodded, smiling at Skip who then began to lead everyone in another chorus of another new song I had played for them.

"*Do you have any bananas?*"

"*Yes! We have no bananas!*"

"Do you know Charlie?" Farley asked.

"Yeah, I met him through a friend of mine, Joel Wagner. Ring any bells?"

"Small world. Sure, I remember Joel. Good aviator. Dependable. What's he doing with himself these days?"

"He's dead."

Farley looked shocked, and he stared down at his shoes, which were so highly polished he could probably see his face in them.

"Did you ever talk to him about . . . a castle up in the mountains?" I asked.

His thin, sensitive face was tight as shellacked paper. He looked straight at me and said, "No." After a pause, he said, "But he was shot down with you, wasn't he . . ."

I started playing "Look for the Silver Lining", which everyone knew, then "Wild Rose", and "Ma He's Making Eyes at Me" which Snap Geraldson sang in falsetto. That was something to hear . . . and see. Isn't often an elephant imitates a parrot being squeezed into a juicer. I played and sang Bessie Smith's "Downhearted Blues", and, of course, nobody knew who she was; but Rick Moss and Snap started dancing with each other. I taught them how to Charleston, which had just become all the rage, and all hell broke loose with everybody swaying back and forth, slapping their knees, swiveling around on the balls of their feet, and falling over like they'd been dancing in a marathon for two weeks. After a while I started playing slower tunes again like "All by Myself" and "Who's Sorry Now," and then even a little Lizst and Bach, and the party broke up, and —

"You can't sleep on the piana."

I don't know how he did it, but somehow Skip got me up and dragged me or walked me or rolled me toward my room. I remember seeing open doors that led into rooms with pool tables and ping-pong tables. I remember a kitchen and gymnasium and a room that was so bright that I could barely look into it. I passed the fabled library that God had provided with all the classics but no up-to-date Saturday Evening Posts, and I remember feeling a pressure around my temples; I imagined that Joel and I were back in the Moth, and the engine was on fire, and my forehead was hot, and then something squeezed my stomach, and from far away Joel or Skip or somebody said, "Hot damn," and I dreamed about beautiful Phoebe looking down at me from the perfect golf-course gardens and tennis courts of heaven. Her eyes, set in her sun-bronzed face like perfectly shaped transparent gems, were impossibly blue. Sky blue freedom.

And then I woke up in Skip's room.

"Drink this. Hair of the dog."

Skip probably looked worse than I did. I couldn't see him very well — my head was pulsing with pain. I guess I wasn't used to drinking real hooch. The rotgut I'd been drinking since '20 hadn't killed me, but it sure felt like the vintage Johnny Walker and Chivis Regal would.

I drank the tomato juice and brew, which Skip called "Virginia Dare". It went down like razor blades, and when I stopped being sick, I asked him why he'd decorated most every surface in the room with a towel — there was a white bath towel neatly tacked over his desk, a white dish towel on the bed table, a red face towel placed like a doily over the back of his stuffed chair, another added colour and warmth to a utilitarian tallboy, and towels of various sizes and hues decorated the inside of every drawer open to my view.

"I learned how to do that when I was a kid. I spent a few years in an orphanage." He grinned. "Well, not exactly an orphanage. A private school. But same difference. After Dad popped it, and Mom decided she'd follow by sticking her head in a stove, Dad's best friend kept me in the best schools for as long as my inheritance money held out, which wasn't long."

That was more than I wanted to know about Skip's schooldays, but he seemed cheerful about it all, even about finding his mother, who he said was "blue as a curtain". He said he'd learned about making things cozy in "the orphanage", and he'd got used to decorating with towels.

"Thanks for the bed," I said, "but you didn't have to sleep on the floor. You could've slept in my room, if you couldn't drag me that far."

"I could barely get you *this* far," Skip said. "You're heavier than you look. But I never sleep anywhere but right here. It's as much home as anything else. Some of the other guys move around. You know —"

I didn't, and I could feel the nausea working its way up to my throat.

"— sleep with each other, like that. No girls here, what else you going to do? Except get really friendly with Madam Palm and her five daughters." He grinned again, looking popeyed and childlike, and wagged his right hand at me. "I prefer Madam Palm."

"Can't God up there help you out with some women?"

Skip laughed and said, "Old Jefferson's very prim and proper. You heard him. The choice is wives or girlfriends, or nothin' — and he'd make you marry your girlfriend, sure as shit, not that it would matter, anyway, 'cause once they got here, they wouldn't have any choice. They'd be stuck here forever amen like we are. And who knows how dangerous it would be for them, what with all the other guys. We asked Jefferson if we could borrow some of his slave girls, although we never saw them, but he doesn't believe in whorin' and promiscuity, as he calls it, and, anyway, according to him, he wouldn't misuse his slaves."

"How does he keep slaves? It's 1923, for Chrissakes, not 1823."

Skip shrugged. "There's all kind of stories. George Bernard, who's been here the longest — over twenty years — probably knows, but he ain't saying. You didn't meet George. He's sort of a hermit, doesn't even go to the tower when the Old Man calls. He don't talk to no one. He wasn't no flier, that's for sure, but, like I said, he don't talk. You got to respect that, I figure. Anyway, none of us talk about the slaves since Lowell Legendre was poisoned — now he *was* a pilot, shot down just like the rest of us, only he could speak a couple of languages. He had your room, come to think of it. Anyway, he said he was learning how to talk slave-talk from one of the slaves who brung the food. That must have been some trick, 'cause I've never met any of the Old Man's slaves who could speak or understand one word of English. Lowell said he was getting the hang of it, though, and that once he'd figured it all out, he'd know what was going on and maybe we could figure a way out of here. But he got sick after eating dinner — it was terrible, worse than my mother — and we tried calling for someone to get us some help. But the Old Man and his slaves suddenly got deaf, dumb, and blind. We didn't get any food after that for a week. All we had was water. And after that, all the slaves that had anything to do with us were new. So probably best not to get too curious about them. You'll see your share."

"I want to meet this George Bernard," I said.

"I'll show you his room," Skip said, "but he won't let you in. I once —"

I made a dash for Skip's toilet, but didn't make it.

When I came around again, still hung-over with a blinding headache and a mouth that tasted like it was full of metal shavings and dirt, I was back in my room.

Old Skip must have found new reserves of strength. Or a few buddies.

* * *

George Bernard *did* receive me, as if he wasn't a prisoner like the rest of us, but a guest with special privileges. However, I waited before knocking on his door, which was a football field away from the rest of us. I got to know my fellow inmates. I spent time in the "sun room" with Snap Geraldson discussing Edward Egan and Sam Mosberg, who took gold in the Lightweight and Light Heavyweight categories respectively at the Antwerp Olympics in '20. It was like discussing boxing with the Buddha. I played ping-pong with Carl Crocker and pool with Keith Boardman and Harry Talmadge, who wanted to be brought up to date on current events; and we argued over the Sacco and Vanzetti convictions. I swam every day in the pool, usually with Skip, who did a couple of miles a day, when he wasn't coming off a hang-over, and I spent hours talking plays and movies and books with Farley James and Stephen Freeburg in the library. We discussed Conrad and Gide and Ibanez and Waley and Apollinaire, while we drank God's good whiskey until we were ossified. And every day I practised the piano. I played for hours, doing scales, working the life back into my fingers, which flew over the keyboard; and if I had to be here, if I was going to be trapped in this diamond pit with this ragtag group of swillers in this speakeasy prison, I'd get my hands back. I practised the sonatas of Scarlatti and Clementi and Mozart and Bach and Schumann and Brahms, and Liszt, of course; and it all came back to me; it was like I'd never left conservatory. I played Debussy's *Etudes for Piano*, Ravel's *Daphnis and Chloe*, Schoenberg's *Five Piano Pieces*, which I knew by heart, and Stravinsky's *Piano-Rag Music*. I played until I was exhausted, and there were no days or nights, just melody, counterpoint, rhythm, and drinking and talking.

Was I in prison? Or purgatory?

Or heaven, as it surely was for Skip — good food, whiskey, friends, a room tidied up with towels. But after Snap Geraldson threw a fit and hurt his back, I began to suspect that *everyone* was crazy . . .

That's when I decided to visit George Bernard.

"Welcome, Mr Orsatti."

A beefy man dressed in an old-fashioned military-style smoking jacket with silk cord frogging stood hulking like a costumed bouncer in the partially closed doorway. He was the same body type as Mr Randolph Estes

Jefferson — a bull-dog endomorph — and he was wearing flannel trousers that were so wrinkled they looked like he had been sleeping in them for weeks, which he might have been. His slippers were torn, and his sparse, curly brown hair appeared as though an electric current had passed through it only seconds before my arrival. But while the Lord God Jefferson above struck me as conceited, self-satisfied, and vital (as male members of the upper crust were trained to be), George Bernard seemed somehow incongruously tall and fat and fox-like. He sized me up, seemingly taking in every detail, and grinned.

"How do you know my name?" I asked, trying to place the ratchety noises that were emanating from all over his room. But I couldn't see past him.

Obligingly, he stepped aside.

"Skip Cinesky told me that —"

I suppose I was stopped dead in my tracks — so to speak! — because George's room was mostly a huge table covered with Lionel standard gauge HO track that ran over perfectly modelled hills and rills and suspension bridges, and through pastureland and woods and tunnels and realistic towns with main streets fronted by electrically lit municipal buildings, stores, and porched houses. It was like looking down from a cockpit, except there were too many trains chugging and spewing wisps of smoke as they rushed through miniature fields to miniature destinations. At least twenty brass trimmed Lionel and American Flyer locomotives pulled blue, green, and yellow enamel cattle cars, boxcars, oil tank cars, coal cars, day coaches, Pullmans, baggage cars, and bright red cabooses.

"You wanna try it?" George asked, as he pointed out a large black box that controlled the switching and speed; and I thought I said, "No," but there I was working the controls of the Blue Comet while George went into the kitchen to fix up drinks. Unlike the rest of his neighbours, he had a suite down here in the pit. I couldn't judge how many rooms he might have had.

For a few seconds, George's Blue Comet train set occupied all my attention because he had pushed all the rubber-tipped control levers over to No. 9, and the locomotives accelerated. They were chugging along so fast that they'd fly off the tracks when they hit the curves or smash into each other at the track switches. I pulled all the levers back, but not before a Cowen Comet Special locomotive pulling freight cars with their own magnetic lifting cranes jumped the track. Cars scattered across the table; although I prevented a few cars from falling, I couldn't reach the expensive, heavy black locomotive, which broke when it hit the floor.

"Good save," George said, returning with two whiskey glasses and a bottle.

"If that's your idea of a good save, you must have a lot of broken train sets."

George gestured toward two easy chairs placed around a table in the corner of the room. "What's the good of having things if you can't break them?"

There wasn't much I could say to that. We sat down, and he poured far too much whiskey into cut glass tumblers.

"That's why I'm down here. I broke too many things. So why give up a bad habit?"

"What did you break?" I asked.

"Ah . . . Confidences. The golden rule of silence. But only when I got drunk."

I tasted the whiskey, which was woody and bitter and good, and hefted the weight of the tumbler.

"You can *try* breaking that," George said, "but I'd drink up the contents first. You think it's crystal, don't you? Wrong, my boy. It's diamond . . . and probably enough to buy you the Ritz-Carlton in New York City, I would judge. But the boys have already told you that this mountain is one big diamond, didn't they? But that's probably about all they could tell you."

"What can *you* tell me?"

"Oh, probably everything."

"Can you tell me how to get out of here?" I asked.

"That's easy," he said, smiling and obviously enjoying himself hugely. "But you'll find out everything soon enough."

"How?"

He pointed upward, then poured himself another drink and topped mine up.

"For crying out loud, what are you getting at?"

"But don't break anything, 'cause he won't take you back."

"Who won't take me back where?"

"God won't take you back here."

Completely nuts, I thought.

After one more go-round with the trains, I left.

* * *

He probably was nuts.

But as I soon discovered, he was also probably right.

FOUR

It seemed like a dream, but, of course, it wasn't. I hadn't drunk very much, only a highball with Farley James and Keith Boardman in the library where we'd played a few games of Mah-jongg after dinner. That might not sound like a very manly thing to do, but then none of that mattered in the pit. I'd become a veteran.

We shouted "Pung!" and "Chow!" and "Kong!" and swore blue murder as we rolled the dice and tried to build winning hands out of the inlaid ivory tiles. But after about an hour, I started feeling queasy and headachy and cotton-mouthed, and so did Farley and Keith. We figured it was the food and blamed Snap Geraldson, who must have requested shit-on-a-shingle again — AKA tuna on toast — and the dumbwaiter in the dining room obliged.

So we dispersed and went to our rooms.

I fell asleep immediately, fell into the deep sleep of exhaustion, as though I was back in the war, flying mission after mission; and I dreamed that I was looking up at my ceiling, which glowed dimly like faraway neon; and it was like being a kid again and seeing faces and animals and buildings in the stucco ceiling of my bedroom. Only now part of the ceiling was slowly floating down towards me, and two slaves dressed in white uniforms were standing on what might have been a scaffold platform. They were black angels, and they carried me up to heaven. I smelled sweat and ambergris and roses and

I dreamed that I would float upwards forever . . .

As I woke up, blinking in the strong morning light, I could see ebony panels on tracks sliding open. Revealing formal gardens with stone hermae, geysering fountains, lamps, a marble wellhead, terra cotta jars tall as a man, and statues of sylphs and mythical animals so lifelike that they almost seemed to move through the boughs and terraced pathways. My new chamber was now open to the world, and I could smell perfume and the richness of loamy soil. Beyond the gardens lay a small village of cottages massed around a church; but it was no ordinary church; it rose into the brittle blue sky like it was all of a steeple; and it was transparent as glass, proof that man could rise up and tear into the very fabric of heaven.

"The gardens are indeed beautiful this morning, are they not, sir," said a man dressed in the same uniform as the men in my dream. He looked to be in his seventies, but he carried himself like an officer who was used to giving orders. His strong face and bald pate seemed polished; the wrinkles that radiated from his eyes and the corners of his thin mouth resembled fine scrolling chiseled into mahogany.

"Yeath," I said, my mouth dry and swollen and tasting of iron. My tongue didn't seem to be working right; it filled my entire mouth and wouldn't get out of the way of my teeth.

I'd surely been drugged.

"Whey am I an' ha'ad I get hea?"

The old man smiled, as one would at a child, and said, "You're in the north bedroom of the guest suite. You're a guest of the master, and it's my privilege to serve you, Mr Orsatti." I couldn't place his accent. It seemed Southern, but it had a certain crispness, a *wrongness*, as if an Englishman or German was speaking with a drawl.

I heard a rustling behind my bed, and although my head felt like it was half-filled with some vile-tasting, vile-smelling liquid, I managed to turn . . . and see a giant dressed in white like the old man.

"Don't give no never mind to Isaac, Mr Orsatti. You can think of him as your shadow . . . or your own personal bodyguard, if you prefer. Isaac won't be a bother, as he understands no English . . . Now, *you've* got a big day today, sir. A bath to start the morning right, sir?"

My head began to clear and I found my voice. "Tell me what the hell I'm doing here?"

"It's up to the master alone to explain his intentions, sir. But I believe you're to give a recital in an hour."

"The master?"

"Master Jefferson, sir. Surely you know —"

"And you, what do *you* know?" I asked Isaac, who stood as still as one of the statues in the garden and gazed at me disinterestedly.

"I told you, sir, he cannot understand you."

"Can't slaves understand English?"

"Sir, I am not in a position to advise . . . or to educate you. But I'm sure Master Jefferson will see to all your questions in his time."

"Are *you* a slave?" I asked. I would recite the Gettysburg Address to him if I had to.

"I have served Master Jefferson for many years, sir. Now would you prefer rosewater and a salt-water finish or a milk bath followed by warm water? Isaac will remove your pyjamas."

I wasn't letting Isaac or anyone else near me.

I heard the old man sigh and nod his head, and then the bed tilted, and before I could gather my wits to grab hold of something, I was sliding toward the wall, pyjamas and all. Drapes parted, as I slid down an incline into warm water. I heard myself shouting, but brought myself under control immediately. I watched the chute fold back into the wall. I was in a sunken bath, the water warm as a womb; but swimming all around me — and above and below — were salt-water fish of every description: spiny fire fish, huge groupers, barramundi, mackerel, cod, orange striped dragon fish, and there were jellyfish with long, almost transparent tentacles, a diamond-toothed moray eel, sea snakes, turtles, black spotted cuttlefish, and a hammerhead shark that was at least seven feet long.

The shark swam toward me, swam through the illuminated water.

Only a layer of crystal separated the shark from my feet, for my bathroom was inside an aquarium, and the great mass of water pressing against the walls cast shimmering, coruscating reflections everywhere. Then rain began to fall from the ceiling, and jets of rosewater and liquid soap bubbled into the bath while electric paddles churned the water into a blanket of sparkling soap bubbles. Music began playing, as if a chamber orchestra composed of mermaids were playing beside me.

The old man and Isaac stood on either side of the white marble sunken bath.

"My name is Robert," the old man said. "When you have completed your bath, Isaac will give you a rubdown and a shave and dress you. I will serve you breakfast in the sitting room," and with that he bowed and left.

Perhaps it was a combination of the drugs and warm bath, but — against my will — I found myself enjoying this warm, voluptuous kaleidoscope of a bath.

Nevertheless, I had the cold, dead feeling that I was being prepared for my last meal.

* * *

Washed, bathed, massaged, dressed, and fed steak fillet and eggs and hills of fried potatoes on plates shaped out of layers of emerald and diamond and ruby, I was led — like a royal prisoner — through corridors and rooms with walls created entirely of diamonds and other precious gems, through rooms where fire seemed to coruscate over walls and ceilings, through rooms composed of deep green crystal that could have held back the weight of an ocean with its dark, deep creatures, through elegant rooms, antique rooms, and rooms that might have been designed by Klee and Kandinsky to defy the normal rules of up and down. I walked over carpets of the rarest furs, glimpsed walls covered with paintings by Reubens, Caravaggio, da Vinci, Titian, Giotto, Manet, Monet, Poussin, Cézanne, and Miro, Picasso, Ernst, Gris, Demuth, and Modigliani. Marble creatures reached out to me: naiads, sylphs, satyrs, soldiers, gods, and goddesses by Michelangelo, Saint-Gaudens, Rodin, and Brancusi; and I was led up stairs cut into a huge, marble-veined extended hand.

Into a Baroque hall of mirrors that overlooked park like grounds.

Hundreds of mirrors were set opposite windows and into the scrolled columns and archways. The high ceiling was curved, and painted angels gazed down from clouds in heaven upon gold and silver chairs and bejewelled trees. A forest of gold. Glades of diamonds. In keeping with this stone and jewelled forest was a grand piano that looked to be cut from a gigantic block of jade. Our feet clacked on the inlaid floor of this formal hall that seemed to extend into a finger-width arched door in the distance as Robert and Isaac led me to the piano.

Robert bowed and said, "I will leave you now, sir."

Isaac stood over me, and I was sure that, should I stand up from the piano, he would force me back down onto the cushioned stool.

"And what am I to play?" I asked.

"I would think that would be up to you sir," Robert said, and, nodding to Isaac, he clattered away toward the far, perspective-shrunk doorway, his reflections creating an army of stiff, marching Roberts.

"And who am I to play to . . .?"

I sat before the translucent green piano, and began warming up by playing scales from Clementi's instruction book. I looked around the seemingly endless room, but I couldn't see anyone, except for Isaac reflected in a dozen mirrors, of course; he stood so still that I wondered if he even breathed. But I could *feel* other eyes watching me, and I remembered what crazy George Bernard had said about God not allowing me to return to my gilded prison. What was he planning for me, then? I wondered. Certainly Master Randolph Estes Jefferson wasn't going to take any chances with me, although I wondered . . . perhaps I *could* escape. I chuckled and looked around at this room constructed from dream and imagination. Would I *want* to escape?

But I could feel Isaac's presence pressing against me and knew I was freer in the pit. No matter, I was here to play, and if I failed Jefferson's test — if that's what it was — who knows what he might do. So I played, beginning with Chopin's *Waltz in G Flat*, then playing his preludes and nocturnes and etudes. I played Bach and Mozart and Beethoven. I expected *something* to happen. Someone besides Isaac to appear. Then I began playing Erik Satie's piano works, which I loved: *Gymnopédies, Gnossiennes, Pecadilles importunes* . . . Satie the joker, the dissonant, the genius; and I heard a giggle behind me.

Saw reflections.

Phoebe stood before me, big as life, just as she stood beside and behind me, reflections in myriad mirrors, a company of lovely, fragile, faun-like Phoebes looking awkward one instant and graceful the next. She wore a white gown, a silk scarf draped carelessly — or perhaps very carefully — over her shoulder, and a fetching bonnet with a red sash. Her eyes were indeed blue, and her face was freckled, and she was the most beautiful creature I'd ever seen.

She said something to Isaac, which sounded like, "*Ra'ase, nah'ye haingwine heaightmuh*," and then she stood right by the piano and said, "Well, Mr Paul Orsatti, you can certainly play, and I told Poppa that if he didn't bring you up out of that horrible place with those men, I'd never speak to him again. You're a genius, that's just what I told him, and I told him you'd be happy to teach me how to play the piano. I want to play as well as you, can you do that for me?"

I was about to tell her that I didn't know, but she said something else to Isaac, who looked sullenly down at the glassy floor.

"What did you say to him?" I asked.

"Just now, or before?" She looked steadily at me, and I could feel myself blushing. I don't know why, but she made me feel like I was sixteen and pimply and gawky and trying to get up the courage to ask out the prom queen. She was just a wisp of a thing, and her cheeks were freckled, and her curly blond hair stuck out from under her bonnet. Yet she seemed completely self-assured, as though she was accustomed to absolute obedience. And innocent. Perhaps it was the combination that unnerved me. Or perhaps I had just instantly fallen completely in love with her.

"I don't know," I said. "Both, I guess."

She giggled. "Well, I told him to calm himself down, that you probably weren't going to hurt me or kill me or anything like that." She backed away a step. "You're not, are you?"

"No, of course not."

"There, you see . . .? And then I told him . . ."

"Yes?"

"That's for me to know and you to find out," she said. "Now do you want to take me for a walk before you meet Poppa? He wants to have a talk with you."

"What about your friend Isaac?"

"Oh, don't worry about him. He'll keep out of the way," and she turned to him and glared. He quickly resumed looking at the floor.

"I'm Phoebe," she said as she led the way out of what she called the Mirror Gallery. Isaac followed, keeping a safe distance.

"I know your name."

"Ah, those awful men in the pit told you, did they." It wasn't a question. "I hate them."

"Why?"

"Because of what they say about me."

"And what is that?"

"That's for me to know."

I nodded. She was obviously younger than her years, but I couldn't help feeling attracted to her. I'd often been in the company of the rich and spoiled, and Phoebe was certainly the quintessential product of excess. Could she even imagine that there was another world out there, a world of people working twelve hours a day, haggling over pennies at the market, cooking their own food, sharing their possessions? Probably . . . no, definitely not.

"How did you know I could play the piano?" I asked.

"Well, because I heard you, that's how. Poppa can listen to everything those horrible men say down in the pit. And so can I, although if you tell Poppa that, I'll never speak to you again." We walked down a huge stone staircase and past the Neptune Pool that reflected the sun as a sheet of yellow light. "But you wouldn't care, would you?"

"About what?" I asked, overwhelmed by the sheer size of this place, by the formal gardens with statues as large as houses, by the pergola ahead, which was fashioned of crystal and gems and seemed to extend for a mile. And there was the chateau — the castle that connected to dozens of other buildings, each one of a different period, yet part of the perfect white, geometric whole — that was surrounded by pools the colour of terra cotta and marble constructions that resembled Greek and Roman ruins.

"You wouldn't care if I ever spoke to you again would you, Mr Paul Orsatti." She sniffled, turning her head from me. "Well?"

"Of course, I would care."

"Why?"

"I don't know!"

"There, you see?" she said, but, of course, I didn't see.

"I listened to you play, even the night you got so drunk that the dumbbell with no eyebrows had to drag you to his room. I listened to you snore. Do you know how loud you snore? I'd do something about that if I were you."

I chuckled and asked if her father was able to see his prisoners as well as hear them. But Phoebe ignored that question . . . as though she hadn't heard it.

We walked past tennis courts, a reservoir, greenhouses, barracks, a zoo surrounded by marble lions, and then through the pergola to the edge of the formal gardens. Phoebe glanced back at Isaac every few minutes, and he would respectfully drop back several feet.

"I think it's all a lie," Phoebe said.

"What?" I asked.

"That the servants can't understand English. I think they've been tricking Poppa about that for years, and so does Uncle George."

"Uncle George?"

"You met him and played with his trains. That's what Poppa told me."

"Your *uncle* is in the pit?"

"Oh, yes," Phoebe said. "George Bernard Jefferson. He didn't tell you his last name, I imagine." She giggled. "He's always been in there. Well, practically always. But Poppa will tell you all about that. He tells everybody."

Everybody . . .? I thought.

"Would you like to kiss me now?" Phoebe asked, as we looked out at a herd of Master Jefferson's zebras grazing on a hill beyond the gardens. I said something inane about Isaac lurking behind us — which he was . . . and the moment passed.

Of course I wanted to kiss her. But she looked so vulnerable . . . and she was so young.

"Do you hear that?"

"What?"

"Airplanes, I think. Listen —"

Sure enough, I could hear engines. But I couldn't see anything in that eggshell sky, which was the exact colour of Phoebe's eyes.

FIVE

An alarm sounded and a chill caught the air as we made our way back to the castle, which Phoebe called *Adamas*. She told me with breathless conviction that the King of France hadn't lived in anything half as nice, and she ought to know, she said, because Poppa had all the plans of the greatest castles in the world, and he made sure that his was the best. She was excited about reaching the roof garden so we could watch the airplanes through the telescope there.

Although she hurried to the castle, she was not in the least afraid. Isaac tried to say something to her, but she only had to shout something quick and guttural at him, and he fell back behind us, properly cowed.

Then a porcine, well-dressed young man flanked by what I took for two slaves caught up with us by the Roman ruins beside the pool. He was nervous and out of breath, and kept looking at the sky, as if lightning was going to strike him down at any second. Just ahead was a marble staircase that led to the western exposures of one of the buildings that adjoined the chateau. I could see a glint of metal: the telescope mounted on the embrasure.

"Father sent me to find you," he said, out of breath. "You won't believe how angry he is. You're supposed to be in the bunkers, and not legging around with *him*." He meant me, and his eyebrows knitted together and his face got all scrunched up when he said "him". I couldn't help but smile.

"You won't even get to keep him until September, if you act like that," the young man continued. "And that's *exactly* what Father said. I didn't make it up."

The alarm sounded again.

"Now come on, for crying out loud, or do you want to get killed out here?"

"Those airplanes are probably just mail carriers, like always," Phoebe said. "And mail carriers don't carry bombs. But they're all gone now."

She cocked her head, obviously listening for the sound of airplane engines. Everything was quiet, but for the wind.

"You see, false alarm. All that trouble for nothing . . . and I *was* coming back."

"Well, you can tell that to Father," the young man said.

"You're not my boss, Mr Near Beer."

The young man blushed at that, and Phoebe said, "Mr Orsatti, this is my brother Morgan."

Morgan gave me a slight nod, then shouted something at Isaac; but I couldn't understand a word.

"Isaac had nothing to do with it," Phoebe said. "It was my idea. And if you dare say one word —"

I heard the sudden drone of an engine, and then the deafening, bone-shaking *stucka-stucka* of anti-aircraft guns, which were mounted on the castle fortifications above.

There was another burst . . . and another.

"You see?" Morgan screamed at Phoebe, and he grabbed her. But she broke free. Isaac stepped over to her, as if to intervene. The guns fired again. I heard a distant explosion, but couldn't see any airplanes — the castle was blocking the view. One of George's slaves shouted something to Isaac, who looked nervously at Phoebe and then at me, before running after Morgan and his fellows.

"Morgan is such a flat tire," Phoebe said. "And I'll bet you ten thousand dollars right now that those enemy airplanes don't have any guns." She paused, then explained, "According to Poppa, everybody is the enemy. And so Morgan is always so-oh afraid we're going to get bombed. I know that Poppa scares the bunk out of him about it to make a man out of him, but Morgan is just a flat tire."

I followed her up the marble staircase, across a patio, and up several more staircases to the roof garden. I could see Jefferson's slaves manning the anti-aircraft guns, which were quiet now. Ghostly pink billowing clouds were filling up the sky like suds in a bathtub. From the position of the sun, I could see it was late afternoon. But how could that be? I must have slept through the morning.

I stared at an oily trail of black smoke left by a plane that had been shot out of the sky. But I could also hear the distant thrumming of an engine. Perhaps it was one of Jefferson's. Or perhaps one of the intruders had escaped into the swollen pink and purple curtain of storm clouds. Phoebe tossed her bonnet onto a wrought iron chair and looked through the brass telescope, swinging it around so hard, it was a wonder she could see *anything*.

"There it is," she said. "Right over . . . there . . . Poppa's guns got it. See the smoke in the canyon? Something's burning. Positively. But I can't make out very much. I can't see for jellybeans without my glasses. Here, you try." She pulled away from the telescope, brushing my face with her curly hair, and I could smell her perfume, lilac sweet and damp. I looked through the eyepiece. There was indeed a plane burning. I couldn't see it well through the smoke, but it looked like a Curtiss Jenny. I wondered if the pilot made it to safety and tried to cover the area by moving the telescope around, but Phoebe became impatient and insisted that I return it to her immediately. After a time she said, "I can't see anything. Do you want to bet on the pilot?"

"What do you mean?"

"A thousand dollars that Poppa's slaves find him alive and put him in the pit." She shrugged. "If he's dead, you win."

"I wouldn't make such a bet," I said. "And I certainly don't have a thousand dollars."

Phoebe pulled a magnificent diamond and ruby ring from her index finger and slipped it onto my pinkie. "That should cover your side of the bet." She smiled mischievously and said, "Now we're engaged."

"I can't accept this," I said, handing her back the ring.

"Perhaps I made a mistake about you, Mr Paul Orsatti."

"It's very beautiful, but I don't think your father —"

"He won't care. He's going to be too upset to care about anything, which means he won't be bothering too much about you." She took my hand, slipped the ring over my finger again.

"What do you mean?"

"There was another plane," Phoebe said. "Couldn't you hear it?"

"Yes, but I thought it might have been your father's."

Phoebe laughed at that, a soft, sexy, whispery laugh. "Not unless he was flying it. Or Morgan." She laughed again. "Or Uncle George."

"You've got plenty of . . . slaves."

She seemed astonished. "Why, you couldn't allow a slave to fly an airplane."

"Why not?"

"Because . . . you just couldn't. But it doesn't matter. Poppa will surely find out who was flying that plane and what company he worked for and fix it all up. He always fixes everything up."

"You mean he'll have him killed."

She shook her head and looked genuinely hurt. "Poppa's an honourable man. He'll have him brought back here to live and give him everything he could want. We don't just go around murdering people, you know." When I didn't say anything, she asked, "Are you sorry?"

"About what?"

"What you said about my father."

"Yes, of course. I'm sorry."

She turned back to me and asked, "Well, do you still want to kiss me?"

"I never said I wanted to kiss you."

But against all judgement — of course — I did.

Phoebe and I lay in bed. It was evening, and the garden was a fantasia of fairy lights. A sweetly scented breeze wafted in through the balcony, shadows and pale, milky lights played over a wall-sized Flemish tapestry of Neptune standing upon a shell and creating a horse of air with his trident. The walls were covered with blue brocade from Scalamandre, and the gilded wood ceiling glowed as if lit by fireflies. Phoebe was curled up beside me, and we were wrapped in smooth satin sheets as blue as the brocade.

"You see, everything is perfect," Phoebe said. "I knew it would be. I always know."

"Ah, so you always lure lonely prisoners into your den to have your way with them, is that it?"

"Exactly so." After a pause, she said, "How could you even imagine I would have anything to do with anyone else?"

There was nothing to say to that, so I enjoyed being close to her, feeling her smooth shoulder and slipping my hand down to caress her small breast. She was thin and long and smooth and as perfect as I had imagined.

"Well, just in case it might interest you, I've never had anything to do with anyone down there" — I knew she meant the pit — "or anyone who Poppa has brought to visit."

"So your father does have guests here," I said. "Doesn't he worry about security?" For an instant, Phoebe seemed to be nonplussed, but then she giggled and said, "Poppa worries about everything."

"What if they told their friends? Why —"

"They're very rich," Phoebe said. "Not nearly as rich as we are, of course, but they're worth a quite a boodle, you can count on that. And Poppa could just as easily make their shares in the stock market go up or down. He can make it do whatever he wants. But you, Mr Paul Rudolph Valentino Piano-player, you're like a big dog with a bone, aren't you? Now, do you *really* want to talk about Poppa's friends, or . . ."

She was quite persuasive; and I was indeed, in all respects, like a dog with a bone. "What was all that business about not getting to keep me until September?" I insisted. "What did your brother mean by that?"

She drew away from me and pulled the sheets up to her neck, as though she were wearing them as a nightgown. "You got what you want, so thanks for the buggy ride. And now you want to play twenty questions."

I tried to put my arm around her, but she turned away, taking most of the sheets with her. It suddenly felt cold in the room.

"I didn't mean to hurt your feelings," I said. "I —"

"Then say you're sorry."

"I'm sorry."

She unravelled herself from the sheets and turned toward me. "I'm coming out in London in September. I'll be presented at court, and I'll meet King George. He's also a friend of Poppa's. Now does *that* answer your question?"

Of course, it didn't; but I would bide my time. I nodded.

"Then you may have your way with me again."

But that wasn't to be either because there was a sharp knock on the door, followed by the booming voice of God.

"I'm not dressed, Poppa," Phoebe said sweetly, sitting up in the bed. She seemed to be talking to the polychrome sculpture of Saint John that was positioned beside the panelled door. "I'll meet you down in the library." She looked at me and shrugged.

"You'll open this door right now, young lady!"

"No I *won't*!"

I started to get up. I could grab my clothes, perhaps hide; but Phoebe said, "Don't be goofy. He'll go away in a minute. Absolutely-positively."

Then I heard Jefferson say something incomprehensible in a low voice — most likely, he was speaking to one of his slaves.

I was right.

I should have known better than to listen to Phoebe. Now it was too late.

A key turned in the lock, Robert pushed the great door open, and Master Randolph Estes Jefferson, dressed impeccably in formal eveningwear — white tie and tails — walked into the room. Phoebe was a blur rushing into the adjoining bathroom; it was a wonder she didn't slip on the blue, diamond-smooth floor. She slammed the door shut and left me to face the music by myself. There was nothing I could do but pull the sheets around me. My clothes were strewn across the floor.

Passion had certainly taken precedence over foresight.

"Do you see what happens, Robert, when you leave guests unattended?" Master Jefferson spoke to his slave in English.

Robert nodded and looked at me as if I were the wayward child and he was the parent.

"Well, good evening, Mr Orsatti," Jefferson said. "I see that you have already provided my daughter with her first lesson. I will expect you to attend to my daughter's musical education with as much ardor as you seem to have displayed here tonight." He lifted my undershorts with the toe of his polished leather spats and then kicked them across the room. "And I am expecting to see a marked improvement in her proficiency at the piano, Mr Orsatti. In September, she will give a recital at Carnegie Hall. It's all arranged."

"Sir, don't you think that's a bit, er, premature . . .?"

Jefferson gave me a genial smile, his ruddy, fleshy face the picture of cheerfulness, his eyes as hard as the diamond mountain below us. "Wouldn't you say *this* is premature, sir?" he said, looking around the room, indicating my situation with a simple turn of his head. Then he nodded to Robert, who picked up my scattered clothes and laid them out neatly on the corner of the bed.

"You look perplexed, Mr Orsatti," Jefferson continued. "Did you expect I would have you beaten? Or killed? Or thrown back into the pit with your colleagues? No, you're Phoebe's guest now. And Phoebe is a woman of the 20's. Why she's practically emancipated."

"*Practically* emancipated?" Phoebe asked, opening her bathroom door a crack and peering out. The light behind her transformed her curly hair into a halo.

"Well, maybe you'd prefer to leave school and go to work for Mrs Millie Scotch Barker and her suffragettes," Jefferson said. "But this is none of your business, young lady. You're taking your bath, are you not? while poor Mr Orsatti must make his own introductions."

"For your information, her name isn't Millie Scotch Barker. It's Abby Scott Baker, and in case you've been too busy to notice, Poppa, we've won the right to vote."

"*You* don't have the right to vote, nor do I think you'd care to be poor."

"I know poor people at school," Phoebe said.

"Ah, yes, those poor girlfriends of yours who can't afford to keep their own staffs of servants."

"Well, I know Mr Orsatti."

"Ah, yes, Mr Orsatti, whom you're going to make as rich as Croesus, isn't that so?"

"If you have no objections, Poppa," Phoebe said meekly, then closed the bathroom door.

Jefferson chuckled and said, "Well, Croesus had better dress for dinner, hadn't he? When Robert is finished with you, Mr Orsatti, he'll bring you to my library, and I will explain everything before we join the ladies. No, better yet, Robert, bring him to the theatre. Do you like moving pictures, Mr Orsatti . . .?"

Without waiting for an answer, Jefferson left, and Robert introduced me to my new bodyguard, Wordsworth, who had been waiting like a good foot soldier in the wood panelled lobby. I learned that Isaac was being punished for a dereliction of duty, and I would not see him again. I wondered if *anyone* would ever see him again.

As Robert and Wordsworth escorted me out of the room, I could hear the faint splashing of water and Phoebe singing in a sweet, yet raucous voice — "Who's Sorry Now?"

Scrubbed down like a horse after a race, perfumed, pomaded, and dressed in evening clothes, I sat in the richly cushioned, maroon seat beside Jefferson and watched Fatty Arbuckle and Buster Keaton slap each other across the screen.

Jefferson's "theatre" was more magnificent than any movie house I'd ever been in. The walls were lined with scarlet damask, and the thirty-foot ceiling was supported by huge gold caryatids holding dimly glowing ruby lamps. As the moving picture flickered before me like a dream, I sipped Napoleon brandy and smoked a sweet cigar rolled in the Haymarket district of New York City. But the butterfly collar that Robert had snapped around my neck was so heavily starched that I felt like I was wearing sandpaper.

"I think all that business about Fatty raping that actress and all is a lot of whooey," Jefferson said in a whisper, although there was no one but his manservants and us in the theatre. This was certainly a place that inspired awe, a church for the brightly lit images that towered before us in profound silence. This was the perfect temple for the new gods that were so much larger than life and above the sound and the fury, beyond boredom or smell or homely sound. We might laugh at their antics, but *they* would have the last laugh and live forever. However, being here, in this sumptuous palace atop a mountain of pure diamond, it would be easy to imagine that *we* were the new gods.

"Even if he did have a bit of fun with her," Jefferson continued, "it would have been her fault, not his. He didn't force her to stay at his hotel.

He didn't force her to stay there for two of God's long days. And now the poor soul is blacklisted and can't make a moving picture because that stupid woman ruptured her bladder, probably from being loaded to the Plimsoll."

"Well, she did die from it," I said, as we watched Buster Keaton being struck by a sack of flour. Keaton absorbed the shock as if he had been struck by a hanky. I'd seen *Butcher Boy*, although I can't say it was one of my favourites. But Jefferson howled with laughter.

After he calmed down he said, "The court cleared him of all charges, and the jury said that a great injustice had been done to him."

"It did take three trials."

"I wouldn't care if it took a hundred trials. He was completely exonerated."

"I'm not sure that —"

"Are you going to continue to argue with me?" Jefferson asked. His voice was soft, mellifluous, and menacing.

"No, of course not. I apologise."

"From what Phoebe tells me, you're good at that." He laughed, whether at me or Fatty Arbuckle's antics, I couldn't tell; but he patted my arm, thus preserving my . . . dignity. "Perhaps I should get into the film business. What do you think? Give Arbuckle a second chance?"

"The press and public seem to hate him," I said.

He pulled on his cigar, belched a huge cloud of smoke, and said, "I can fix the press. And I can guarantee that the public will love him. I'll bet you a thousand dollars. Is it a bet?"

"I've already had a conversation like this once with your daughter, sir. I don't really *have* a thousand dollars."

"Ah, but you've got a new ring, haven't you?"

"I think we'd both be in the doghouse if I lost her ring to you on a wager."

Jefferson seemed to like that because he put his arm around me, waved the porter over to fill my snifter with more brandy, insisted that I stop acting like a teetotaller, and told me the "improbable but true" story of the Jefferson family.

When he finished, I asked, "Why are you telling me all this?" I had become more and more nervous as he spoke because . . . I already knew too much.

But he just handed our crystal — or perhaps they were diamond — snifters to one of his servants and said, "Because you're part of the family now, Paul.

"Shall we join the ladies . . .?"

SIX

Randolph Estes Jefferson was no relative of Thomas Jefferson.

Nor was he the scion of any distinguished lineage. His father Frances Tiberio Jefferson did, however, settle in Shadwell, Albemarle County, Virginia, where the third president of the United States was born and grew up; and he claimed to be a distant cousin of "Thomas", who also had a reputation of being able to talk a tree out of its roots. Frances won a medal for "World's Greatest Liar" at the Great Albemarle Fair. Like Thomas, he was a states' rights man and distinguished himself in the War of Yankee Aggression by rising to the rank of colonel. He was too robust to succumb to the diseases that routed both the northern and southern armies, and rose quickly through the thinning ranks.

After the war, he took his pay and his gift of gab and became the most successful auctioneer in Albemarle County; but he was too restless for that.

It happened that he found twenty-five "orphans", ex-slaves still living on a played-out plantation. Their owners had put the plantation up for sale and left for Europe. The men and women left behind spoke high German, had developed their own, unique dialect, and didn't know that the North had won the war and that they were no longer . . . slaves. They were starving, and Frances fed them, gained their trust, and promised them wealth and a piece of land out west.

However, he neglected to explain that they were emancipated.

And so Frances left the Thomas Jefferson Auctioneers & Feed Company to his brother. His plan was to buy twenty parcels of cheap Montana land in the names of his new wards and start a cattle and sheep farm. But that was not to be because, after a series of misadventures, all he had left were his orphans; and they were starting to have doubts about the master who could do no wrong.

In fact, they would have probably killed him if he had not gotten lost in the mountains and shot a squirrel that happened to have a perfect diamond the size of a pebble in its mouth. That pebble would be worth a hundred thousand dollars. He went back to his camp and told his orphans that he had discovered a cache of "rhinestones" that could be mined "for a few dollars". Since none of the slaves had ever seen a diamond, much less owned one, they agreed that they could dig out enough stones to get back sufficient money to buy homesteads.

Leaving his miners to continue their work, he took a valise of diamonds to Billings; but he underestimated their value and a jeweller, flabbergasted at the size and quality of one of the smallest stones, tried to have Frances arrested. Frances went to New York, where he started another furor; this with only one stone, which a dealer of consequence believed might have been part of the Duvergier Diamond, said to have been stolen by a French soldier from the eye of an idol. The Duvergier had been cut into twenty-one stones, which ranged from less than a carat to eighty carats, and The World's Greatest Liar did not dispute the opinion that *his* diamond might have been cut from the same venerable stone.

After several weeks, Frances was several hundred thousand dollars richer. But he had to leave New York, as the metropolitan police were now looking for him. The diamond market was in chaos. Some said that the world's largest diamonds were somehow being cut up and "dumped by a 'syndicate'". These new stones *had* to be cut from great diamonds such as the Orloff, the Koh-i-nor, the Akbar Shah, the Dudley, and even the Cullinan — which became part of the crown jewels — because they were too big to be anything else. Madness had replaced logic. Would-be prospectors were rushing to Scranton, Pennsylvania and Southampton, Long Island — and the yellow rags kept proclaiming new locations where diamonds had "just been discovered".

Indeed, The World's Greatest Liar had found what was undoubtedly the world's largest diamond . . . a solid and perfect mountain of diamond; and he realised that he would have to be careful, lest he devalue the world market.

He sent for his brother to manage the mine and left for a tour of the world. Carefully, he sold his diamonds. He used pseudonyms, forged passports. He lived like a criminal on the lam, yet he sold his stones to emperors, kings, criminals, sultans, and mercantile barons; his diamonds became invested with their own history and myth, as if they had been in circulation for hundreds, if not thousands of years.

In a few years, Frances was worth millions.

In a few more years, he was worth billions.

And he married a Spanish beauty; had two sons, Randolph and George; convinced his slaves that the South had indeed won the war, and that all was once again right with the world; murdered his brother, who became too generous with the family fortune and "talked out of school"; and dedicated himself to protecting his family and consolidating his fortune.

Randolph, being a chip off the old block, also invested widely and wisely; saw to the construction of his castle on the mountain; married a woman from Braga, his mother's village near the west coast of Spain; sired a son and two daughters; and being kinder and gentler than Frances, he merely imprisoned his overly generous and voluble brother, rather than murdering him.

Thus was I introduced to the secrets of the family while titans who had assumed the shapes of Fatty Arbuckle and Buster Keaton beat and kicked each other in joyous, rapturous revenge.

SEVEN

It was like being invited to dinner in a cathedral, perhaps because great pennons hung from the high, gilded wood ceilings and paintings of winged cherubs and Rubenesque angels gazed down upon the guests, as though the heavenly host itself were in attendance. Perhaps it was the plundered sixteenth century choir stalls, or the flickering candles and the alter of a table spread with linen and silver and gold. The plates and glassware seemed to be composed of layers of ruby, sapphire, emerald, opal, and diamond. Muted colours and pure, prismatic reflections met my eyes wherever I looked, and the Persian tile upon which I stood seemed to have infinite depth, as if this great room was floating stock-steady upon extraordinarily deep water. Servants glided in and out, as though stepping through shadows, and I could hear the clear but distant strains of Vivaldi's *The Four Seasons*. I tried to locate the music, but could not.

Randolph Jefferson stood at the head of the long table and motioned me toward a chair beside Phoebe, who was dressed like a blond angel in white chiffon. Beside Phoebe, and facing Jefferson at the other end of the table, was a beautiful dark-haired woman wearing a black chiffon evening dress. I thought it particular that, except for a gold wedding band, she wore no jewellery. She looked like she could have been in mourning. To Jefferson's right was Morgan, and beside Morgan was a homely brown-haired girl in a stylish green evening outfit that somehow seemed larger than she was.

"Paul, allow me to introduce you to Giroma, my wife." I bowed, and she held out her hand to me. I wasn't sure whether I was expected to kiss it or formally shake it, so I decided upon the latter. She seemed pleased, but then she turned away from me, as though impatient to return to her own thoughts.

"And my son Morgan, who tells me y'all met under rather unexpected circumstances." Jefferson gave Morgan a cold, disapproving look and then introduced me to Marion, his eldest daughter, who was still being overwhelmed by her green evening dress. Perhaps I had been too hasty in describing Marion as homely. She had the same features as Phoebe, but they were slightly . . . crooked. What seemed like perfection in one sister was bland and uncomely in the other.

"Sit down," Phoebe whispered to me. "You look like you just stepped on your own foot." Marion giggled at that and, embarrassed, I sat down.

We made small talk throughout dinner, all seven courses, and Phoebe was winsome and witty and wickedly pressed her leg against my thigh. I asked about the music, wondering how many more musicians — indeed, how many other "guests" might be on the grounds — only to learn that the sweet music was being reproduced by an electrical phonograph that used a new Panatrope loud-speaker.

"It's the bass that fools you, Paul," Jefferson said. "It's big as life, don't you agree? The old orthophonic machines aren't a patch on this one. The diaphragm of the loudspeaker is coil-driven, the acetate records are finely grooved, and the stylus is diamond, of course. The Victor Talking Machine Company will be bringing out a version like this . . . sometime in the next four or five years, I would suppose." Jefferson seemed very pleased with himself.

I nodded, unsettled that I was the only guest. Phoebe's sister Marion must have been reading my mind because she complained, "It's not fair, Poppa, that Phoebe always receives special treatment. She's coming out before me, and I'm older. And you've allowed *her* to have company. I haven't had *any* company this summer." While Phoebe's voice was smooth, dulcet, Marion's was whiny.

"Phoebe has company for a reason," Jefferson said. "Would you have her give her concert unprepared?"

"She's never going to be prepared," Marion said, looking defiantly at Phoebe, who stared assiduously into her jewelled plate, as though she could move the broccoli by the mere power of her gaze. "She can't play the piano any better than I can, yet you've bought Carnegie Hall for her."

"I did no such thing," Jefferson said. "She was *invited* to play, as you might have been if you had applied yourself."

"She only wanted to play piano because I did. And y'all went gaga over *her* and couldn't even be bothered with me."

"That's not true."

"It is too. It's because Phoebe is a liar. She lies to all of you, and you believe everything she tells you. It's not fair, it's just not fair."

"Are you quite finished?"

"I'm sick of being here all by myself."

"You have your family here, or is that of no importance to you?"

Marion shook her head and said, "It's not fair."

"I'll spend time with her, Poppa," Phoebe said. "I will, Marion, I promise."

"That's the bunk!" Marion said to her father. "She's a liar."

"Morgan, what do you have to say?" Jefferson asked.

"Don't know, I —"

"She's your sister, and it's your responsibility to take care of her, isn't that right?"

"Yes . . . I suppose, but —"

"Well, I've decided that you should follow up our little problem with the pilot who got away from us," Jefferson said. "What do you think of that? It's time you proved yourself to be a man."

"What do you want me to do?" Morgan asked.

"More to the point, what do *you* think you should do?"

"I dunno . . . go find him, I guess."

"And what does that have to do with me?" Marion asked. "You see, that's just what I mean. I'm invisible."

"Not at all," Jefferson said. "You're the eldest. Perhaps I should send *you* out to test your mettle instead of Morgan."

"Perhaps you should send *me*," Phoebe said. "Mr Orsatti could protect me."

"Indeed he could," Jefferson said. "Indeed he could," and they exchanged teasing looks, as if they had rehearsed this little skit — as if Mother and Morgan and Marion were out, and only Poppa and Phoebe were in.

And I soon found out where I stood in their dangerous little universe.

"Oh, Poppa wouldn't send either one of them to the grocer for a loaf of bread," Phoebe confided to me as we stood on the artificially lit, glaucous-green lawn that seemed to roll on forever into the night.

Fireflies pulsed in the perfumed air. I held her cool hand; and I must admit that against all logic and experience and plain good sense, I was head over heels in love. It wasn't about what kind of a person Phoebe might be — how smart, immature, spoiled, and selfish she was. I knew her for a brat, and probably as dangerous as her father. Perhaps more dangerous. But she was . . . perfect. The sound of her voice was perfect, the way her eyes narrowed when she was thinking was perfect, her smell, the cast of her hair, the way her eyebrows arched, the curl of her mouth — all absolute perfection. I was smitten, but at least I had the presence of mind to conceal the extent of my ardor . . . or so I thought, anyway. In fact, I was as transparent as the goblet I had been drinking from at dinner.

"I'm surprised that he lets either one of them go to school," she continued.

"You don't like Morgan and Marion very much, do you?"

"*Au contraire*, I love them both to pieces. But would *you* let them out of your sight?"

"I'd rather not let you out of my sight."

She giggled and pulled me to a copse of trees that were silver and shadow in the dim, flickering lamplight. She sat down, her back against the bole of an elm.

"You'll catch cold on the damp ground," I said.

"Poppa will go alone," she said, as though talking to herself. "He won't take Morgan. I'll bet you a thousand —"

"Don't start that again."

"Did Poppa try to make a bet with you?"

"Why do you ask?"

She twirled the ring on my finger . . . the ring she had given me. "I expect he noticed my ring. Well, did he?"

"Did he notice . . .?"

"No, did he make you put it up for collateral?"

"I would never bet your ring."

"Good for you," Phoebe said. "Poppa likes you."

"He didn't suggest sending *me* to find your flier."

"But he did take you out of the pit."

"Because you asked him to."

"And you'd just better remember that," she said, and then allowed me to fumble with her clothes, caress her breasts, kiss her in all the delicious, unmentionable places, and finally make love to her. Everything was rustling and whispering and breathing, and when we were finished — and still half dressed — she said, "You haven't said you love me."

Caught off guard, I just smoked my cigarette.

"And you didn't offer *me* a cigarette."

I gave her the cigarette, which she smoked, inhaling deeply. She didn't cough . . . she just cleared her throat, as though she were about to give a formal speech. "Well, are you going to say it?"

"How could you be sure I'd mean it?"

"Because I know you do."

"And what about you?"

"Do you think I'd let you do what you just did if I didn't?"

I knew better than to fall into that trap.

"I love you," I said, trying to arouse her again.

"I know you do," Phoebe said, surrendering, or pretending to.

"But there is something else."

Phoebe pulled away and watched me.

"You've had company here before. Your sister said as much."

"Ah, so we're on that old stick again."

"Well, I still can't get what your father said out of my mind."

"And what would that be?" Phoebe sat up again and leaned against the tree. Her blouse was open, her hair was mussed, and I must admit I could not imagine anyone being more beautiful, alluring, and piquant.

"That unless you behave, you won't be able to keep me until September."

"Morgan said that, remember? And he lies."

"I need to know," I said, insistent.

"I've only had one friend from school ever visit me for vacation," Phoebe said. "A girlfriend. And you wouldn't have liked her, anyway."

"Why?"

"You just wouldn't. *I* didn't like her very much. I . . ."

"Yes . . .?"

"That's all. Now, are you done with your Twenty Questions?"

"Does your sister usually have guests?" I asked.

"So now it's Forty Questions, is it," Phoebe said, and she buttoned her blouse.

I felt the sudden distance between us, but I couldn't stop. "Well, does she?"

"Yes, this is the first summer she's been alone. Poppa's punishing her."

"Why?"

"Because she has a big mouth. She takes after Uncle George." She looked around, and although she didn't act nervous, I knew she was. I could feel it radiating from her.

"Your father doesn't let your guests return home, does he." That was a statement, not a question.

"What do you want from me?" Phoebe asked.

"The truth."

"Why? Will it make you free?"

I waited for an answer.

Phoebe looked directly at me as she spoke, as if the truth would be a reproach. "You're right . . . Father doesn't allow the guests to return home."

"Then he imprisons them, like he did me?"

"No," she whispered, watching, studying me. "That wouldn't be fair to the family."

"The family?"

"To us."

"Why?"

"Because we'd feel terrible. Mother would have a breakdown. She's had one already."

"So you *murder* them?"

She flinched at that, but kept looking at me, unafraid yet vulnerable. "There is no — there is really no other choice. Marion and Morgan need friends. And Poppa is too considerate to force them to be hermits."

"Considerate? I —"

"You'd think we starved and tortured them," Phoebe said. "Invited guests are shown every courtesy. They have the best time of their lives — good company, good food, the best quarters, and Marion and Morgan and Mother shower them with presents. Whatever they fancy they get, and when their time comes, they simply go to sleep. It's really very pleasant, I would imagine. It really is . . . It always happens in August or September, but Marion and Morgan never know exactly when. It's easier for them, that way."

"And what about their poor families?" I asked, aghast.

"We explain that they caught typhus and passed away, and Poppa *always* sends flowers."

"How lovely. And when is my time going to be, hey? This month or next."

"Well, you do have to give me lessons for my recital," Phoebe said. She was playing with me, yet I was convinced that she had told me the truth. Jefferson would never allow anyone to give up his secrets. It was a miracle that he allowed his brother George to live — perhaps he was a trifle sentimental.

I got up to leave, and she said, "If you go now, I'll never speak to you again."

"What's the difference?"

"What's the *difference* . . .? Do you seriously believe I would bring my friends here, knowing Poppa wasn't going to allow them to leave?"

"Well, you have. *I'm* your guest. Or rather your victim."

"Go fly a kite! You were going to rot down there in the pit."

"But I wouldn't be about to be murdered. Is it this week or next?"

"I wouldn't allow Poppa to murder you. He agreed that when you are finished tutoring me for my recital, you'll go back in the pit. So there! I wouldn't kill anybody. Not even you."

I could hear her breathing falter like she was going to cry, but I persisted. "But you have, haven't you? You've probably had as many guests as Marion. Or Morgan. Or your mother, for that matter."

"Mother never has guests, neither does Poppa," Phoebe said. "They allow us to have guests because there's no other choice. Mother stays by herself and barely speaks, or haven't you noticed? She lost her best friends, and couldn't stand to lose any more."

"It's disgusting."

"We're not like other people. We can't live like they do. If we could, we would. And for your information, Mister Know-it-all, when I found out what Poppa had to do, I refused to invite anybody else ever again. I'm content to read and enjoy music and walk in the gardens. Alone."

"That's very white of you."

"Thank you."

With that, I turned and walked away.

Half-dressed and shoeless, she caught up with me.

"Paul, do you really believe I could abide you being killed or put back with those other . . . men?"

"I don't really know," I said. "I would guess that you could."

"I love you. I didn't know that when I saw you in the pit, or when I heard you play the piano like a genius. And Poppa would never hurt anyone in the family."

"I'm your piano teacher, Phoebe. I'm not in the family."

"But you will be when we're married . . ."

EIGHT

Phoebe was, of course, correct. Her father left the mountain by himself to take care of business. It seemed that eight pilots had already been murdered by his agents, yet none of Jefferson's sources could be absolutely sure that the right pilot had been dispatched. Jefferson was going to take matters into his own hands and direct his army of spies, scouts, facilitators, lawyers, bankers, and mercenaries to find the "conspirators", wipe them out, and smooth over the facts so that no one would ever recollect that anything odd or untoward had ever occurred. Whether Jefferson was a good general, a coward, or just foolhardy, I couldn't say. But when the shooting started and all hell broke loose, he should have been present.

However, I'm getting a bit ahead of myself . . .

The next few weeks were bliss. Just Phoebe and me. There were long, languorous hours in the mirror gallery, the afternoon sun a dusty-golden mist filling the long, arched room as Phoebe concentrated on her music . . . and me. She was going to dedicate her recital to me and play a selection of my favourite piano works by Erik Satie. I tried to talk her into playing a selection of Chopin's waltzes and preludes and explained that Satie's music was absurdist and humourous and only seemingly simple, but she was not to be dissuaded. The hours of practice were punctuated by lovemaking and champagne lunches on the balcony. She disappeared the slaves. They were to be invisible, yet at her beck and call, as it should be, she said; and she was summer itself. Every day another Phoebe appeared, as though by magic. Sometimes she was an Egyptian queen in evening gown. Sometimes a chic matron wearing cloche hats and "Coco" Chanel skirts and pullovers and suits designed specifically for her and no one else. She could be "Flapper Jane" with heavy make-up and oiled hair and whiskey on her breath, or an athletic fresh-faced beauty in pleated skirt and blue bandeau.

And so the days passed, each delicious, each one only slightly different from those before. We swam in a green pool illuminated by ivory lamps under a ceiling of hammered gold. Surrounded by marble Roman sarcophagi and statues of Sekhmet, the Egyptian goddess of war and destruction, we made love. We had dinner with the family and made small talk; we hardly saw Morgan and Marion, who were sullen and secretive, as if they were privy to something we were not.

I found out what *that* was all about a few nights later.

Although Phoebe and I made love every night, we slept in our respective rooms. "When we're married, you can stay the night," she said; and, indeed, by midnight I would be so exhausted from the rigors of the night — and the day — that I would fall into a deep, satisfying sleep, only to be awakened by Robert with breakfast on a gold tray and the bright, pure light of another perfect morning.

But on the night when all hell broke loose, I was dreaming of the boys in the pit. I was back there with them, and so was Joel, who was dead, of course. But in the dream, we were all dead — except Phoebe and old man Jefferson and Morgan and Marion, who were all dressed in formal finery and standing on the golf course above us by the grated opening of the pit. Jefferson was praying for us and mixing up the part about dust to dust, and then Phoebe started crying while her brother and sister began shovelling dirt into the pit to bury us. There would be no more golden days and luminous nights with Phoebe, no more lovemaking in Jefferson's forests of gold and glades of diamonds, no more Bach or Beethoven, nor the ironic mockings of Satie. I could smell grass and rot and decay, the Paris perfume of Phoebe mixed with her sweet sweat as the clumps of black soil fell on top of us. Black rain. Phoebe's tears, tapping, dropping like soft leather heels on marble.

I choked. I couldn't breath. I —

Woke up to scuffing, whispering, creaking. Then the click of the diamond doorknob being turned, the sighing of the door. I didn't wait to determine who the intruders were because I was sure they were going to try to kill me, just as they killed all the other guests. But I couldn't escape without somehow getting past them. Unless . . .

I felt for the button on the wall beside my bed and pressed it hard. The bed tilted and drapes parted with hardly a sound as I slid down the shoot into the empty bath. The aquarium walls of the bathroom were a luminous green, and as I hastily made my way out, I could see the shadow of a ray swimming toward me. I turned the knob on the bathroom door. It wasn't locked, and I made my escape down the stairs. Indeed, my first thought was to go directly to Phoebe's room on the other side of the house. I certainly wanted to, but for all that I loved her, could I really trust her? She was, after all, a Jefferson; and I was, after all, just a guest, a guest who even now could not help but be awed by the pre-dawn magic of this house; by the cathedral walls covered with medieval tapestries; the loitering stone and marble fauns, naiads, satyrs, soldiers, gorgons, gods, and goddesses, all pale as moonlight and bigger than life; the carved ceilings so high above; the emerald and turquoise rooms that each opened into other, even more magnificent rooms. Tall, jewelled lamps cast a roseate light, and pitch-velvet shadows concealed treasures that could only be imagined.

I rushed toward the atrium, where I thought I would escape into the gardens.

And I heard Phoebe screaming hysterically. "You'd better not have killed him. He'd *better* be alive."

I retraced my steps and waited behind an archway near the ivory staircase. I wasn't surprised to see slaves pacing nervously on the landing above. Wordsworth and Isaac had obviously been sent to kill me, and perhaps Isaac had been given his chance to get back into the family's good graces.

But I *was* surprised to see Morgan step out of my room onto the landing; a very angry Phoebe was right behind him. I suppose Morgan had finally found his courage, although he seemed to have lost it again in Phoebe's presence.

"What the hell did you think you're doing, Morgan?" she shouted. Her voice seemed magnified by the dark, cavernous spaces. "He's my guest, you little twit, and what happens to him is *my* decision, not yours. Or Marion's."

"Marion has nothing to do with this," Morgan said. "It was all my idea. I just wanted to help you."

"Help me?"

"Anybody can see how much you're stuck on him, and you know father isn't going to let you keep him, no matter what. He told me that before he left."

"Did not."

"He did too, and he practically told me to take care of things for him while he's gone because the more you fall in love with him, the more you're going to be hurt. And Marion thought that —"

"That's just what I thought," Phoebe said, but she did not continue because at just that moment everyone looked up into the greyness above, as though we could see through the ceiling. We could hear the sound of aircraft overhead, and then there was a terrible concussion. I felt heat and was thrown backward. The ceiling shattered. The archway cracked and fell in a cloud of red dust and smoke before me.

More explosions.

Bombs falling, and I remembered my dream. Clumps of black soil falling. Black rain. Phoebe's tears. And, indeed, I was drenched. Water poured through cracks in what was left of the ceiling, which would soon give way; and the swimming sharks and rays and groupers and cuttlefish would fall onto the jewel-polished floor below.

Somehow, I had to rescue Phoebe, lest she be caught in the inevitable waterfall, a vertical tidal wave that would smash and splinter the balcony like balsa wood; but as I called out to her, my voice was swallowed by the staccato thunder-pumping of machine guns above. At least the slaves had the presence of mind to stand and fight. As I ran to the grand staircase, I met Marion and Morgan. We stopped for an instant, amid the cacophony of exploding bombs, machine guns, and the abdominal groaning of the castle. Water dripped like rain through the cracking and bulging ceiling high above. Morgan scowled at me, Marion called me a filthy something, and then I ran up the stairs to Phoebe while they, presumably, ran to the bunkers where they would be safe and sound and fitted out with champagne and caviar until the danger was over.

"Phoebe," I shouted, catching the back of her. She was running through the corridor, which curved around the inside of the house like a mullah's ledge on a minaret. She heard me over the firing of machine guns and the thrumming shaking deafening exploding of bombs.

She stopped and shouted, "Mother," which I understood as code for "I've got to find Mother," and then disappeared into one of the many branching corridors. I followed her, my eyes and nose burning from smoke.

"You've got to —"

I meant "You've got to get off this floor now immediately run," but I seemed to run right through my words. I was intent on grabbing her up and getting out of the house, into the bunkers, perhaps, off this mountain; and then, in those heart pounding exploding acrid smoke-smelling seconds I imagined that we'd somehow miraculously escaped from the mountain, from her father and family and everything associated with them, and I wondered whether she could live in the real world five minutes with me, without the insulation of millions — or billions — of dollars. It was idiocy even to dream of getting out, much less turning Phoebe into Suzy housewife. In spite of the smoke and sudden heat, for the house was certainly on fire, although I couldn't see flames . . . yet, I think I grinned at the thought. But if I had the chance, the split-second chance of a lifetime, I'd take Phoebe away, without a dime in my pocket, I'd take her away for as long as she'd stand me.

But there *was* a chance. I was, after all, a prisoner. If the air strike was successful, as I imagined it would be, then we would all be set free. The lads in the pit would vouch for me. Perhaps there was a way to escape. To hide Phoebe, take enough diamonds and rubies to keep us more than comfortable in our new life.

Nonsense madness lunacy, yet those words had little meaning deep in this castle of impossibility where ceilings were layered with gold and walls of diamond and ruby glowed translucently like dreams in the deepest sleep; where hammerhead sharks could fall like rain, and God's machines could play music as well as orchestras.

I found Phoebe in her mother's suite, which was the size of most people's houses, and Phoebe turned to me and said, "She wouldn't've gone to the bunkers on her own, how could Morgan and Marion leave without her?" Phoebe was wild-eyed. "They hate her, that's why."

"Why wouldn't your mother go to the bunkers?" I asked, trying to bring her back to reason.

"She's claustrophobic. She can't stand darkness, can't stand to be without windows and light and —"

The sound of gunfire, the ceiling cracking, the house groaning, and then the expected waterfall, complete with all manner of fishes. Water poured over us, for the aquarium was two stories high, an aquatic crystalline house within the house, and I grabbed Phoebe and ran through the rain and wriggling, flapping, slapping fishes as the floors and walls and ceilings collapsed behind me, ran until I found another staircase, a narrow *escalier dérobé*. The smell of wet ash was thick as we ran down the stairs, ran through the undecorated corridors used by servants, ran straight into blazing, blistering fire.

We found another way, which was blocked by the debris that had been ceiling and furniture, only moments ago. Coughing, panicking, we raced through darkness; now I was following Phoebe, who pulled me by the hand, down, down, into the damp stone cellars where we felt our way along the rough cold walls. Then an incline, the clanging of a heavy latch — Phoebe had found an exit. We pushed open a heavy door and looked up through the swirling smoke and soot to glimpse the dawn-pink sky.

The attack had been planned perfectly.

From an emplacement on the roof of an adjacent building . . . another burst of anti-aircraft guns. I could see only a few bodies of slaves scattered across the lawn; but in the dawn pinkness of this impossible morning, I couldn't see blood; nor could I smell the puke and faeces of dying men, thank God, for the reek of gasoline, the acrid smoke, and the thunderstorm and metal odor of machine guns firing on the roofs above were overpowering. I took a chance and stepped away from the castle to see what was in the sky; and you could've knocked me over with your pinky because the attackers-invaders-saviours, whatever they were, had just about everything in the air that could fly, all remainders from the war. Christ, there was a Vickers Gunbus, which hadn't been in service since 1916; and its gunner was strafing the slave quarters with his moveable Lewis machine gun. There were several Jennys in the sky, and from the sound of it, I guessed they had been fitted out with 7.7 mm machine guns, just like the Gunbus. The Jenny was the favourite of most barnstormers, and I was no exception. While everything was happening around me — all the crashing and burning and exploding, I daydreamed about whisking Phoebe away in a Jenny, saving her from all this death and destruction; and I felt a sudden, unexpected rush of happiness. I would be saved, wouldn't have to spend my life a prisoner, or worse, become another one of those poisoned or strangled guests buried in an unmarked grave in the shallow soil of the diamond mountain. All that in a second, just like when I'd been in combat in the *Toulouse-the-Wreck*, the Spad that got me through Bloody April without so much as a bullet tearing through its delicate frame. I was again smelling oil and gasoline, hearing the peculiar and particular chinking sound of machine guns, and daydreaming. Time stretching, then collapsing, while my body, my hands and eyes, made all the moves.

Phoebe caught my arm, as though she had just read my mind and discovered my true thoughts of escaping with the enemy, and that's when I saw the twin-engined Handley Page 400, a British bomber that could carry a bomb load of around 1,800 pounds — Lord knows how they got their hands on *that*, and again, daydreaming, I wondered who they were. The bomber made a wide circle, and I asked Phoebe where the bunkers were because once that Handley Page started dropping her guts, there wouldn't be much left to talk about.

"Look," Phoebe said, pointing, and, indeed, I saw slaves scrambling across the courtyard and leap-froging up the inlaid tile perrons of the castle. They moved like trained and disciplined soldiers; the strafing fire of machine guns didn't deter them, even when two slaves were hit and fell backward over the stone steps.

We had to get out of here. I could hear the Handley Page's engines change tune as the great plane turned to begin its bombing run.

And then Phoebe shouted "Momma", and ran into the courtyard.

Sure enough, there was Giroma Jefferson strolling absently in her black chiffon evening dress embroidered with tiny beads.

I followed, but was too late: the Gunbus was strafing the courtyard, and in that second I felt time stretch out like some terrible gasoline tainted, grey wodge of taffy, wrapping itself around me . . . suffocating me. I saw Phoebe's mother fall, hit by the strafing fire, and Phoebe screaming and falling on top of her; and then it was like being in the cockpit of my Spad again, feeling once again absolutely focussed yet numb, as I did during every dogfight. The numbness was fear, but it was a distant thing; and — as if I were a spectator still standing in the doorway of Jefferson's castle — I could see myself pulling Phoebe away from her mother and dragging her out of the courtyard. Phoebe screamed and tried to bite me before she came to her senses.

"I can't leave my mother," she said desperately. "She might be alive, mightn't she?"

"No, darling," I said, "but don't think about that right now. We'll think about everything once you're safe. Now tell me where the bunkers are."

"There," and she pointed toward a strand of rocks where goats were trying to hide in the surrounding brush. "But we can't leave without Mother." So I picked up Mrs Jefferson, who was just skin and bones, and we made our way under cover of the pine forest that was the west edge of Jefferson's zoo. I glimpsed zebras standing stock still, as if they were painted sculptures. Like Lot's wife, Phoebe looked back, seeking one last glimpse of paradise, and then we felt the concussion of an exploding bomb. For a few seconds, I could only hear a rushing, windy sound. I wasn't sure if the castle remained, as it was out of our sight from here; and we made our way, circuitously — keeping under cover — to the bunker. Phoebe pulled at an iron bar set cleverly into the rock — the camouflaged opening could only be detected if one already knew where it was — but nothing happened. I pulled the bar. Still nothing.

"They're in there, and they can hear us," Phoebe said to me. Turning to the cliff face of the bunker, she shouted, "Open the goddamn door, Morgan, you bastard. Mother's dead, and it's your fault."

But Morgan, if he was inside, was silent as the stone.

NINE

We laid Mrs Jefferson out in the family mausoleum between the marble sepulchers of her father-in-law, The World's Greatest Liar, and his brother, who was murdered for the family cause. The cacophony of machine guns and bombs was reduced to great sighs and groans; only the dead held sway in this great marble shrine at the end of the gardens, and they ruled

imperiously over the spiders and dust. Phoebe and I — and the cold and
stiffening Mrs Jefferson — were dwarfed by loggia of fifty-foot columns and
pavilions that supported hoards of stone beasts and angels; and a huge
equestrian statue of a Jefferson glowered down upon us like a marble god in
his adamantine heaven. But there were no glowing onyx or pearl walls here,
and not a diamond or a ruby or a sapphire in sight. This grand tomb might
well have been designed by Phoebe's mother, who defied her wealth by never
wearing a jewel. Perhaps she was the only one in the family who understood
that you couldn't take it with you.

"I can't leave her here like this," Phoebe said, her eyes glistening with
tears, and at that moment I felt I was more in love with her than ever before.

"It's not safe here."

"Pah! It's not safe anywhere," she said, suddenly gaining the weight and
wisdom of the world.

"I'm getting you away from here this very minute," I said, and she turned
to me, her face lit by anger and perhaps even hatred.

"That's my mother lying dead there, and you want to . . . you want to . . ."

"I want to get you to safety."

"You're as flat as my brother," she said, "and I'm not leaving."

"Then what *do* you propose to do?" I asked, trying to keep the frustration
out of my voice. She turned away from me, leaned over her mother's corpse,
and began to cry softly.

"It's all over. "

She allowed me to put my arms around her and pull her away from her
mother. "Poppa should have been here. He should have saved us. But he's too
interested in . . ." She looked up at me and said, "*You* should have saved us.
So what are we to do now, Mr Orsatti?"

She turned back to her mother, as though she could somehow find all the
answers behind those dead and closed eyes. She was shivering, trembling;
and then, by sheer act of will, I should imagine, she straightened up and
became absolutely calm. Her eyes narrowed in determination, and I saw her
father in her heart-shaped perfect face. I saw in that instant the inevitability
that she — and not her brother or sister or anyone else — would control
everything. She was her father's daughter; and love her as I did, I felt the
sudden panicky urge to flee.

"I'm *not* giving everything up," Phoebe said firmly to her dead mother.

"I won't, and they can't make me." Then she finally turned to me and said, "Well . . .?"

"Well, what?" I asked, and for that instant I felt like a nervous schoolboy. The muffled booming of bombs and the thick bursts of machine guns became louder. "We've got to get out of here right now!"

"Will you help me or not?" she asked, ignoring my last remark.

"Help you to do *what*?"

She stepped across the flawless marble floor and reached behind the stone sarcophagus of The World's Greatest Liar and strained as she pulled something. "Well, are you just going to stand there?"

She stepped back and allowed me to squeeze into the space behind the marble coffin. I felt the smooth metal bar she had been pulling at, which was ingeniously hidden under the curl of the coffin's lower rail, and released it without straining my back. The coffin slowly and smoothly slid down toward the wall, as if by magic, to reveal a dark catacomb fronted by dirty marble steps.

"Go on," Phoebe said; and when she saw my hesitation, she said, "Are you afraid I'd close you in?"

I must admit that a nervous thought had crossed my mind.

"Maybe I should, but I wouldn't," and she grinned at me, as if she'd forgotten everything for an instant; then she took a last look at her mother, and led me down the steps and into the pit. She picked up a lantern from a ledge and scratched a match. Once the lantern was radiating a halo of buttery light, she pulled at something in the wall. A rumbling echoed through what I imagined to be countless corridors, a hellish maze from which we would never escape; and I wanted to run back up the stone steps before the entrance was sealed. But the coffin fit into place like the last stone block of a pharaoh's tomb. The darkness seemed to sharpen my sense of smell. I breathed in the musty odors of the grave, and I was sure that this was a catacomb in the true sense — that bodies had been left to rot on shelves like the one where Phoebe had found her matches and lantern.

"Follow me," Phoebe said.

"What on earth is this place?" I asked

"You'll see."

"It's where your guests end up, isn't it?"

"Well, it's where *you* ended up."

"Answer me."

"I don't approve of overbearing men."

"Oh, I'm so very sorry," I said sarcastically. She hurried ahead, but I kept close to her. Our voices and movements echoed through the crudely cut corridor. "This place certainly wasn't cut out of diamond."

"Of course not, silly," Phoebe said. "The whole mountain isn't one big diamond."

"Your father said it was."

"Well, he's like my grandfather. He exaggerates. About two-thirds of the mountain is one big diamond. The rest is this stuff, regular stone, I would suppose."

"And where does it lead?"

"Well, you're going to find out now, aren't you?" Phoebe said peevishly. Perhaps she was as frightened as I was, although I doubted that. She had obviously been here before. Probably many times. I shivered, swore, and slapped at something that had dropped onto my neck. Phoebe waved her lantern, which was smoking.

"Lots of spiders in this part, I hate them, don't you?" Phoebe said, quickening the pace.

I heard a screeing sound.

"And bats," she continued.

Which meant that there was another opening. But I was not relieved yet. We came to a terminus of sorts, and I heard water dripping and the distant rumbling of machinery. Phoebe led me through another corridor, which became narrower and narrower; her lantern threw cascading shadows across the rough-cut walls . . . and the reinforced metal doorway ahead.

Turning a large combination lock, which would unbolt the heavy door, she said, "We'll be fine now." The door was three feet thick; I'd only seen its kind in bank vaults. I helped her pull it open, and we were bathed in the dim but steady light that emanated from the opalescent walls and ceiling. I felt like I was back in the pit. There were no shadows in this place. We had entered a two-dimensional realm.

Phoebe led me through a long corridor that opened into a large storeroom filled with rifles, machine guns, shotguns, pistols, flamethrowers, grenades and grenade launchers, all manner of knives and swords and bayonets, pull carts, sledge hammers, wire cutters, welding and carpenter's tools, cables, foodstuffs, canteens, medications, bandages, stretchers, gas masks, and canister weapons I didn't even recognise. "I think Poppa said this place is as secure as the bunker. Anyway, everything we need is right here."

"What are you looking for?" I asked warily, following her as she walked up one aisle and down another.

"You're the veteran of the Great War. You tell me." She walked on, then stopped and picked up what might have been a grenade. Behind her were shelves of gas masks and medicines: bleach ointments, clouded glass bottles of petrol, methylated spirits, kerosene, liquid paraffin, and carbon tetrachloride. There were swabs and eye drops and bandages and a metal mask with holes. I knew what *that* was for . . . what all that was for: mustard gas poisoning.

"No," I said, realizing that I had shouted. "No."

"We could gas them when they get out of their planes," Phoebe said excitedly, almost cheerfully. She walked a few paces down the aisle, stopped, and picked up what looked like an ordinary grenade launcher. Finding it unexpectedly heavy, she nearly dropped it. "Here, we can use these tubes to shoot them off with. I think these go with the gas grenades. Poppa showed me once, but I'm not so sure now."

"I won't have any part of cold-blooded murder."

Phoebe raised her eyebrow slightly, as if mystified. "I don't want to *kill* them, just put them to sleep for a while." Then her face reddened and she said, "What do you think they did to Mother . . . and our servants? Well . . .?"

I nodded — there was nothing I could say to that — and examined the canister she had been holding, and the others neatly laid out on the gunmetal shelves like condiments for a deadly banquet. "Well, you'll certainly put them to sleep for a good long while with this. It's phosgene, for Chrissakes. The German's used it at Ypres in 1915." I *thought* I could smell a faint odor of new mown hay, which is a dead giveaway for phosgene. "If I can smell it, something must be leaking. Let's get *out* of here now."

"I like the smell, don't you?" Phoebe said, teasing me.

"Phoebe!"

"Phoebe what, you flat tire. How could you believe for even one second that I would actually consider killing those men?" She seemed to be about to break into tears. "Well, I don't need your help, after all. I can do it myself."

"What? Kill all those aviators? And how do you propose to do that all alone? You could get a few of them, I'll admit, but not all of them."

"I told you I'm not going to kill *any* of them," Phoebe said, and she looked so angry that I thought she might actually stamp her foot. Or throw the canister at me. "Come over here."

"We need to get out of here," I said. "We've probably already poisoned ourselves."

"Well, I've been down here only about two hundred times, and it always smells like this, and I'm still alive, so stop being a stupid coward."

I felt my ears burn.

She walked over to me and asked in almost a whisper, "Are you going to trust me?"

After a time I said, "Yes" and put my arms around her.

"Then you'll help me?"

"Of course I will." I felt the last tuggings of my conscience and wondered if, indeed, I would be killing those aviators . . . For those few seconds as I held Phoebe close, I could hear her shallow breathing and the ever so faint booming of bombs.

And somehow I *knew* I was making a great mistake . . .

Then she kissed me, tenderly but without passion, and said, "Let's get ready. If you can pile up the little gas bombs and the tubes, I'll try to get us some more help."

"What do you mean?"

"I mean that I know the way to the servant's quarters," Phoebe said, "and I'll bet you dollars to doughnuts that some of the servants are using the tunnels like bunkers. If they're there, I'll find them."

"I should be with you."

"No, we've got to make sure the enemy doesn't land before we can get out there. If you just keep following the tunnels to your right, you'll come to the outside. Don't worry, I'll find you somewhere between here and there." Phoebe nodded toward a corridor that curved to the right. The light made the far wall and the branching corridors look flat, as though the tunnels, as Phoebe called them, had been lightly sketched with a charcoal pencil. Phoebe turned and looked back toward where we had come. She seemed to be staring at something only she could see, and her eyes were bright with tears.

"Phoebe . . ."

"They killed her," she said, meaning her mother, and then she disappeared into the flat light. I called after her, and her voice echoed back, "Make sure you take the right bombs."

And I wondered once again if the *right* bombs would be lethal.

I followed Phoebe's directions, kept turning to the right, and navigated the warren of corridors until I reached a camouflaged opening in the hill west of the château. Phoebe and I had spent many a perfect hour watching the zebras play and frolic through these gently inclined fields, and the sweet fragrances of spring flowers and Phoebe's perfume were cold memories as I looked out at the devastation before me. It was a clear morning with just a touch of chill . . . and the smells of oil and metal. Through the copses of evergreens and oak, I could see the blackened château and the ruined grounds of what the Old Man had called his enchanted hill. A streamer of smoke rose from the castle's west wing, yet, miraculously, most of the castle was untouched. A bomb had obliterated the Neptune pool and the great Grecian marble steps.

Above, in the blue, ceramic sky, planes circled like buzzing insects waiting their turn to land.

We were probably too late. At least half the planes would already be on the ground and the aviators, probably armed to the teeth, would be making their way to the château. I had enough gas canisters in the pull cart to asphyxiate half the population of Chicago. I waited for Phoebe and had begun to worry when I heard footsteps. Phoebe had indeed found a squad of servants, including Robert, who, surely, was too old and decrepit for this kind of operation. Yet he stood in front of the other slaves.

"We're ready," Phoebe said, looking at me determinedly, as if waiting for me to respond with the proper etiquette. She stood away from me, waiting, testing me, and I knew if I didn't respond properly, I would lose her forever.

I nodded to Robert and asked him if he knew how to launch the gas grenades.

"Yes, Mr Orsatti, I certainly do, and so do my men."

"Your men?" I asked, glancing at Phoebe, who did not seem disturbed, just anxious to get underway.

"Yes, I trained them. Under Mr Jefferson's orders, of course."

"And who trained you?" I asked.

"I believe he was an ordnance sergeant, whom Mr Jefferson invited for a visit. Miss Phoebe took quite a shine to him, if I remember correctly." There was an underlying meanness in his soft, pliant voice; and it was obvious that he viewed my condescension as intolerable. "Isn't that so, Miss Phoebe?"

Ignoring him, Phoebe asked me if I was ready.

I nodded and picked up a grenade. Robert did the same, and attached it to the launcher; indeed, he knew what he was doing. He then picked up a gas mask from the pull cart and pulled it over his face to be at the ready. The others followed in turn. Before Phoebe could pull her gas mask over her face, I said, "Phoebe, why don't you stay —"

"Don't even suggest it," she said.

Moving quickly, we made our way under cover toward the landing strip north of the château. I deployed the men along the way with orders to fire if they saw the enemy, even if there were other slaves nearby who might inhale the gas — after all, the grenades *should* not kill.

However, there was no time to wait and ponder.

By the time we reached the rocky outcrops near the landing strip, we were in the thick of it. Half a dozen pilots were already making their way toward the château, and they were armed and at the ready. They saw us at the same time we saw them, and we both took cover. They began firing, and Isaac calmly launched a grenade at them, which exploded with a low thumping sound. I watched through smeary goggles and heard my breath wheezing through the mask, which smelled of rubber and formaldehyde. After a few moments, the aviators stopped firing. We waited and then moved forward cautiously. I feared the worst, but when we examined them, they were indeed still breathing; one pilot was snoring, as if happily tucked into his bed. We wasted no time pulling the sleepers under cover so they could not be seen. Then we moved forward to keep an eye on the planes as they landed. They kept a tight formation. Impressive. As each plane taxied down the turf of the golf-course runway, the pilots that had just landed stayed close to provide possible covering fire. We waited behind copses of weeping willows. It was too easy to gas the aviators, take their weapons, and drag them under cover — we were shooting the proverbial ducks in a barrel — and like everything that seems too easy, there was a snag. We miscalculated.

One of the aviators had somehow managed to get past us and circle around to our rear. He was wearing one of our gas masks, which he must have taken from one of the servants on the way; and he shot three of our servants with his automatic rifle before we could retaliate. To my surprise, Phoebe shot him squarely through the forehead with a handgun.

Robert sprayed the area with machine gun fire and ordered his squad of servants to move forward.

More gunfire and the chuff chuffing of canister.

Then silence, a heavy awkward silence, as though some sort of geologic time or consensual dream had been replaced by a darker, more sinister reality.

As we moved forward, I could see faint wisps of gas roiling in the fetid air. Above me was a clear blue sky, as innocent as day. I looked around for Phoebe, but she had suddenly disappeared. "Robert, where's Phoebe?" I asked, and then I heard a series of shots from the trees behind us. Each shot seemed to be timed.

Robert just looked at me.

Of course, he knew . . .

And a moment later, so did I.

I found Phoebe beyond the landing strip near the cover of trees and brush. Facemask and goggles hid most of her perfect face . . . it was as if someone else was committing the terrible deed.

"Stop!" I shouted, my voice muffled by my own gasmask.

Phoebe looked up at me blankly, raised her rifle reflexively toward my chest . . . and I felt strong arms lift me into the air as my own rifle clattered to the ground.

Isaac — the slave who had been my "bodyguard" — didn't relax his hold on me, even while Phoebe calmly continued to execute the sleeping pilots.

TEN

"I can't believe that she has received any of my messages," I said.

Robert lowered his great wrinkled head and said, "All you have sent has been received by Miss Jefferson." He stood before my makeshift bed in the guest library where I'd been imprisoned . . . upon Miss Jefferson's orders.

Isaac stood by the door, his bulk taking up most of the doorway.

The North wing had survived intact, and I wondered why I was being kept here. Perhaps the other rooms, the bedrooms, had secret exits. Or perhaps Robert was right and Phoebe thought I'd keep myself occupied with her father's books and the Steinway grand piano that sat like a great white, gold-crested bird in the centre of the library. I'd practised most of the days and nights; the suppleness had returned to my fingers, and I indulged myself with Berg's atonalities and the cloying wretchedness of Mahler's *lieder*. Jefferson's collection of leather-bound volumes and first editions were, indeed, glorious, and it had taken me two weeks to replace the books back on the shelves in alphabetical order. It was as if an earthquake had struck the château, or what was left of it.

"Will there be anything else you wish this morning, Mr Orsatti?" Robert asked. "A bath, perhaps . . .? I've laid out your clothes, just in case." He bowed and smiled condescendingly.

"Just in case of what?" I asked.

"Why, in case you might wish to change, sir."

I waved him away. The door clicked shut, the key turned in the lock, and I was alone. I had not shaved, nor bathed. My hair needed trimming, my pyjamas smelled as sour as my breath, and I was wallowing in self-pity. I didn't feel like reading, studying, or even playing, which was most unusual. Instead I mused on the possibilities of escape. I had tried everything I could think of, from picking the door lock (impossible!), to working the bars loose on the high windows, to holding Robert hostage — but somehow the old servant had managed to break two of my ribs before Isaac overpowered me — and all I had accomplished trying to get past the bars was to break the window glass.

So Robert had won, and I had lost.

We both knew that he was not my servant. But I was certainly his prisoner.

To add insult to injury, it was yet another magnificent morning. Golden sunlight poured in from the gardens, and the grounds were alive with hammering and shouting and the grinding and creaking and groaning of heavy machinery. The château was being repaired . . . rebuilt, and I had been imprisoned in this room for almost two months.

At least when I was in the pit I had had company . . .

I padded back and forth barefoot on the Persian carpets. I examined

Jefferson's astonishing collection of Greek vases that were secured to the hand-carved bookcases in case there might be an earthquake. Well, there *was* an earthquake, and it originated in the skies! I plonked my fingers over the keys as I passed the piano. I took a bit of toast and bacon from the silver tray Isaac had laid on an overly ornate gilt bronze table designed by Pelagio Palagi. I picked up my rose porcelain coffee cup and paced.

I had ruined everything . . .

No, *Phoebe* had ruined everything.

I wolfed down breakfast and swore once again that if Phoebe ever had the gall to come anywhere near me, I would —

There was a light tapping on the door.

I knew who it was. I *knew* . . .

"Go away."

A key turned in the lock, the doorknob turned, and the door groaned open. Phoebe stood in the doorway, looking small, uncertain, and breathtakingly lovely. She wore a simple pleated blue skirt with a white pullover. Her blond hair was pulled back, rolled, and tied with a golden ribbon that was the same colour as the gilded trefoil arches over my prison bar windows. She stepped into the room, leaving the door ajar. Her face coloured as she looked at me. She lowered her eyes, then, as if catching herself, looked directly at me.

"Where are your bodyguards?" I asked, more harshly than I'd anticipated. "Surely they're waiting in the hall in case I try something funny."

"What could you try that would be funny?" she asked in a low voice, and for only an instant, there was merriment in her eyes, which were bright, as though she'd been crying.

"What do you want?"

"What do you think . . .?"

"Don't answer my question with a question. You at least owe me an explanation. I've been in here for . . . months."

"I don't owe anybody an explanation, and you've only been here for five weeks and a day," she said, then looked down at the carpet again. "I'm sorry, Paul. I'm getting this all wrong . . ."

"What are you talking about?" I asked, sitting down on the end of the long, gold brocade couch. My eggs were glassy-looking on the plate on the table before me. My coffee was cold, but I drank it anyway; I felt awkward, as

I always did around her, and I needed something to do with my hands. After the coffee, I lit a cigarette, and Phoebe asked if she could have one, too. She bent over me while I lit her cigarette, and I could smell her perfume, see the light in her hair, and I caught my breath.

"Please don't be angry with me," she said, standing behind the table, as though afraid to sit down beside me. I gestured her to do so, but she stood her ground, closed her eyes for a beat, then said, as if reciting, "I had no choice but . . . No, that's no good. None of it's any good." Then she sat down and against all my better judgement, I was caught by her . . . again. But she didn't seem to know. Her eyes filled with tears and she said, "How you must hate me."

I moved toward her, then caught myself. "I don't hate you."

"Yes, you do. I remember how you looked at me. I'll never forget the horror and disgust on your face. I — "

I didn't say anything.

"But I have to live with what I've done. Somehow . . ."

I could only nod.

"I've tried to come up with a way to tell you, to explain. Every day I prepared a speech, but I . . . I just couldn't."

"So you just left me here to rot."

"I told Robert to look after you."

"You know what *that* means," I said.

She nodded, and I saw that she had used too much rouge on her cheeks to give her colour; her perfect, dimpled face looked strained, and I detected worry lines on the corners of her pale blue eyes. "I know . . . I was selfish, but I couldn't think. I didn't want to lose you, so I —"

"Yes, Phoebe, we know what you did. Now what do you want to tell me." Those words sounded cruel, even to my ears, and I regretted them immediately. Foolishly, stupidly, impossibly, I didn't want to lose her. It didn't matter what she had done.

Too late. She stood up, as if I had slapped her. "Yes, of course, you're right."

"What do you want to tell me," I asked quickly, and I found myself standing too.

"I want to tell you that . . . I don't know. I can't do it now. It was a terrible mistake —" and she turned to run out the door.

I caught her, held her close, and although her breath was ragged, she didn't cry. She stiffened, then rested her face against mine and said, "All right, I can tell you now. I don't regret killing those men. I didn't then. I don't now. I know I was wrong, I know I'll burn in hell forever, God forgive me, but they *murdered* Momma. I couldn't help it. It was like someone else was killing them, even while I was doing it. Maybe it was because I found out about Father, maybe —"

"What about your father?" I asked.

She pulled away from me and sat back down on the couch. She took a puff on her cigarette, which was still burning in the ashtray, as was mine. The smoke roiled in the sunlight like clouds, or gas. "I'll tell you everything, but I need to know . . ."

"What . . .?"

"I know you can't forgive me, but will you listen?"

"Yes, I just told you that."

"I'll tell you everything," Phoebe repeated, "but . . ."

"But what?" I asked.

She shook her head, and tears stained her make up. Then she straightened up, composed herself, and said, "I kept you here because I love you. Selfishly. I knew you'd try to escape. I was even going to give you a choice. I was going to ask you whether you'd rather go back down to the Pit to be with your friends." She laughed, puffed her cigarette, and smashed it out in the ashtray.

"But you weren't going to let me be your confidant and stay with you."

"I . . . I needed time to —"

Instead of listening, I went on, caught up in my own anger. "And you certainly weren't going to let me leave the mountain."

"No," she said. "I'm crazy about you, but I'm not stupid. God help me, I'm my father's daughter." Before I could say anything, she continued. "I had to work things out. I told you . . . I needed time."

"You could have come to me any time," I said.

She nodded. "I've tried . . . every single day. I guess I can now. Now that Father is back."

I felt a chill tickle down my spine. It was over. All over. If Jefferson was back in charge, he'd figure a way to dispose of me sooner rather than later . . . once he got around Phoebe. Or perhaps he wouldn't even have to do that.

"No, Paul, you don't understand," Phoebe said. "Will you come with me? And then you can decide."

"Decide what?" I asked. "Whether to stay up here or go back to the pit?"

But Phoebe was waiting for me at the door . . . as were Robert and Isaac.

I must have been favouring my right side a bit as we walked because Phoebe asked me what was the matter. I glanced at Robert, then asked, "Didn't he tell you?"

"Tell me what?" Phoebe asked.

"Ask *him*."

"Well, Robert . . .?"

He started talking to her in dialect, but I interrupted. "In English, Robert."

So Robert explained that he had broken my ribs — by mistake — and Phoebe dismissed him then and there. Isaac, however, was retained, presumably to guard me from Phoebe. I couldn't help gloating, and defended Robert as my servant.

"You see, you're learning," Phoebe said to me as we climbed the servant's staircase to the third floor. She unlocked the door to old man Jefferson's bedroom and study, which was surprisingly modest . . . except for the wildly ornate Spanish ceiling crafted from gilded wood and an eighteenth century bed with a satin canopy and matching bedspread. There was a simple desk and cushioned chair beside the bed, a small fireplace that needed cleaning, and family portraits on the walls. The desk was piled with papers and an odd mechanism that seemed to sit on the desk but was supported by what looked like a drainpipe that disappeared into the floor. There were folders on the floor around the desk and the pipe, along with women's underclothing and various scattered skirts and dresses. Obviously Phoebe's. "I've taken Poppa's room," she continued. "It's a bit messy, but that's because I won't allow the servants in here." With that she pushed the door closed on Isaac. "You see, now I'm alone with you and at your mercy."

I nodded and she apologised.

"No need," I said, but she had already forgotten and was rummaging for something in the covers of her bed.

"Here they are," she said, finding what she was looking for: a large envelope containing photographs of her father and a dark haired, finely featured girl. "You see, she's younger than me. Can you beat that? It's the bunk. The fucking bunk."

I was surprised, as I'd never heard Phoebe swear before, but she just glared at those photographs and blinked back tears.

"Who is she?" I asked.

"Poppa's whore, that's who she is. Mother's dead because of her. Poppa promised that he'd make her a film star. Here, look for yourself," and she took a handful of letters from the desk and practically threw them at me.

"Easy," I said. "I'm not the enemy."

"Maybe you are . . . maybe you aren't. We'll see, won't we?"

As I glanced at the embarrassingly fraught yet boastful love letters, Phoebe continued. "Her name is Greta Gustafsson, but Poppa changed her name to Garbo because he thought Gustafsson sounded like it could be a Jew name, although anybody would know it was Scandinavian. And he hired his pervert friend Mauritz Stiller to pimp for her. Do you know who he is?"

I confessed I didn't.

"He made that sex film *Erotikon* back in 1920."

I shrugged.

"Poppa showed it to me in the theatre. He laughed all the way through it. It wasn't that bad, I suppose, but it was trash. Like her." Phoebe took the photographs from me. "Well, her career is down the drain. I've seen to *that.*"

"What have you done?"

"Taken Poppa back, the filthy snake in the grass double-crossing, double-dealing —"

"Phoebe . . ."

She hunched over the bed and wept. "He murdered Mother and sold us out. The dirty bastard." Then she shook her head, tried to smile at me, and said, "I found it all out from Uncle George."

"Uncle George?" I asked. "He's crazy . . . and he's in the pit."

"He knows more than you think. He's got ways of knowing everything, and the slaves trust him. It was Robert who passed on his messages, and because of you, I've probably lost a good slave forever."

"Because of *me?*"

"Well, slave or not, he shouldn't've broken your ribs and treated you like a bump."

"Phoebe, about your father?"

"He sold us all out. He brought in the planes and the bombs and the gunfire. After he changed his name and converted most of the money."

"I can't believe he'd do all that, just for a little bit of cheesecake."

"It was getting too dangerous to keep the mountain," Phoebe said. "Uncle George explained it all to me. It was so simple. Father allowed that pilot to get away from us, or could have allowed it, anyway. Once the mountain was found out, then the market for diamonds would crash, which is why Poppa started putting his money into . . . radium. Now he thought that would be perfectly safe, but he was wrong about that, too." She paused and stared at the contraption on the desk. "Poppa thought of most everything, I've got to hand him that. He'd even made sure that two of the aviators who tried to invade us were reporters, just to make certain that the word got out properly."

"It doesn't make sense that he would give up everything," I said.

"Did you read those letters?"

"Still . . ."

"And he wasn't giving up hardly anything. Only us. He'd end up with more money than he had, once the government clamped down on the diamond market, which Uncle George says would certainly happen. Poppa has hidden diamonds everywhere you could imagine."

"I can't imagine he'd harm his family. And family tradition was so important to him."

She chuckled. "So was his freedom, and he figured that we'd be let off. He probably also figured we'd all be safe in the bunkers. But he knew Mother wouldn't go to the bunker because of her claustrophobia. He *knew* that, and he killed her just as sure as if he pulled the trigger."

"But he came back," I said.

"Yes, Paul. I *brought* him back."

"How?"

"Uncle George. He knows everything Poppa knows. He and I . . . became Poppa, and used the slaves and his contacts to chase him down. We caught him buck naked with his mistress. I've got more photographs, but Uncle George is against letting the press have them."

"I should imagine he would be."

"And so am I . . . of course."

I nodded and watched her walk over to the desk and adjust the contraption.

"Come here, Paul, and I'll show you how Poppa kept an eye on everything."

I followed her to the desk, and she turned a switch that engaged gears below us — I could hear them shift. She directed me to look into the concave glass that covered the large pipe. For an instant everything looked ghostly and smeary, as if I were gazing at a crystal ball, and then my eyes got used to the images. I was looking into a room lit by uniform light. Looking down. Looking at Randolph Estes Jefferson, the Old Man himself. God.

"Can you see him?" Phoebe asked.

I nodded, fascinated. The room looked slightly askew, curved somehow, as if the edges were being pulled upward.

"It's hard to see sometimes."

"What's he *doing*?" I asked. He seemed to be kneeling beside his bed, except the bed was transparent as a diamond.

"That's the biggest diamond in the world . . . except for the mountain, of course," Phoebe said.

"Is he praying to it?"

Phoebe laughed mirthlessly. "He asked to have it sent down. It was all he wanted."

"Why?" I asked.

"Because it's perfect," Phoebe said. "Poppa has had I don't know how many diamond cutters working on it. They're all in the tunnels."

"You mean they're dead," I said.

She nodded.

I gazed at the stone, which seemed to be suffused with blue light.

"He calls it God's Blue, and I don't know what he's doing with it now. I eavesdropped on him when I first sent it down. He tried making some sort of deal with God. If God would turn everything around like it was before he left, he would give up all his sins and build God a diamond cathedral. Silly, but I guess he's quite mad." She looked at me — I could feel her staring at me — and said, "But no more mad than the rest of us, I suppose."

"Are you just going to leave him there?" I asked.

"Until he drops dead," Phoebe said quietly.

"Have you talked to him?"

"I'll never speak to him again, but Uncle George visits him regularly and makes sure he eats."

"The other men will kill him."

"No, they can't get to him. Poppa is perfectly safe." After a pause, Phoebe asked if I wanted to say hello to Uncle George. She turned one switch on and another off and said, "Hello, Uncle George."

I could see Uncle George looking straight up at us. He had been fiddling with his trains, which were all speeding around the miniature countryside with great electrical abandon.

"Hello, Phoebe."

"He can't see us," Phoebe said.

"Phoebe . . . are you there?" George asked.

"Yes, I'm here, and so is Paul Orsatti."

"Aha, so you've finally gotten up the courage to pop the question."

"Not yet, Uncle George," Phoebe said.

"Ah . . .? So why then are you calling me?"

"To ask you to come up and help us."

"You're doing just fine, Phoebe," George said. "You don't need me up there. You've got Paul . . . Hi, Paul."

"Hi, George," I said.

"No, I had more than enough of 'up there' when I was up there. Now stop watching me walk around in my underwear and fix things up with Paul. Bye, Paul."

"Bye, George," I said.

Phoebe clicked off the contraption.

"Well?" I asked. "What did George mean about popping the question?"

"What do you think he meant?"

"Stop it, Phoebe, and answer me."

"It's just what you probably think." She looked intently at the carpet and whispered, "Do you want to marry me?"

I was going to say yes immediately, but something caught in my throat. I wanted to rush to her, envelope her in my arms, and protect her. She was the pearl beyond price, the object of my desire. She looked perfect standing before me, her ribbon golden in the sunlight streaming through arched windows, her face flawless; and yet suddenly she seemed . . . flat, featureless like the denizens of dreams, dangerous creatures that suddenly appear, that *look* familiar, but are something else entirely.

Phoebe looked pale and white and fragile. She looked up at me and said, "You see . . .? There, I have your answer."

"I haven't said *anything* yet."

"Which says it all, doesn't it."

"No," I said. "I love you."

"But . . ."

"No buts."

"Then you'll marry me . . .?"

I nodded and started to move toward her, but she took a step backward.

"And you'd be willing to live here?" she asked.

"You mean as a prisoner?"

"No, as my husband."

"Would I be a prisoner?"

"You would be my husband," she said; and I felt a thrill of possibility . . . that I would be with her, but more than that . . . that I could change things, I could —

"And as my husband, you would respect the way things are," Phoebe said.

"What do you mean by that?"

"The way we live . . . the way we are."

"Of course, but we can make things better."

She looked away from me, as if considering. Then she said, "We *will* make things better. It's already happening. I'm rebuilding everything Poppa and those pilots destroyed. I hate pilots — except for you, darling." She smiled at me, as though I had provided her with all the answers. "We could make everything ever so much better. Poppa didn't think smart enough. We'll camouflage everything, so even if planes fly overhead, they won't see anything but rocks. Of course, it won't be rocks." She hugged me and said, "You're brilliant. I'll tell Uncle George about your idea, and he'll figure out how to do it. He won't want to stay down there in the pit anymore. He *loves* to solve problems . . ."

Phoebe must have seen something register on my face because she stopped talking and gave me a quizzical look. "But that wasn't what you meant, was it? So who *do* you want to make things better for?" she demanded. "The servants? The prisoners in the pit?"

"Both, for a start." I understood then that this mountain was the only thing that was real for Phoebe. She would never leave it for very long . . . or change it.

Her eyes suddenly became moist. "Poppa told me you'd be as selfish and greedy as all the rest of them." She turned away from me and walked out the door.

And I realised that I still loved her more than ever.

ELEVEN

I shouted "Pung" and concentrated on our game of mah-jongg while Uncle George's Lionel trains steamed and clattered around us. George was a good player . . . and he'd assured me that Phoebe would probably take me back once I saw the light of reason.

It was simply a matter of time . . . and conscience.

GOING UNDER

. . . .

She was beautiful, huge, as graceful as a racing liner. She was a floating Crystal Palace, as magnificent as anything J. P. Morgan could conceive. Designed by Alexander Carlisle and built by Harland and Wolff, she wore the golden band of the company along all nine hundred feet of her. She rose 175 feet like the side of a cliff, with nine steel decks, four sixty-two-foot funnels, over two thousand windows and side-lights to illuminate the luxurious cabins and suites and public rooms. She weighed 46,000 tons, and her reciprocating engines and Parsons-type turbines could generate over 50,000 horse-power and speed the ship over twenty knots. She had a gymnasium, a Turkish bath, squash and racquet courts, a swimming pool, libraries and lounges and sitting rooms. There were rooms and suites to accommodate 735 first-class passengers, 674 in second class, and over a thousand in steerage.

She was the RMS *Titanic,* and Stephen met Esme on her Promenade Deck as she pulled out of her Southampton dock, bound for New York City on her maiden voyage.

Esme stood beside him, resting what looked to be a cedar box on the rail, and gazed out over the cheering crowds on the docks below. Stephen was struck immediately by how beautiful she was. Actually, she was plain-featured, and quite young.

She had a high forehead, a small, straight nose, wet brown eyes that peeked out from under plucked, arched eyebrows, and a mouth that was a little too full. Her blond hair, though clean, was carelessly brushed and tangled in the back. Yet, to Stephen, she *seemed* beautiful.

"Hello," Stephen said, feeling slightly awkward. But coloured ribbons and confetti snakes were coiling through the air, and anything seemed possible.

Esme glanced at him. "Hello, you," she said.

"Pardon?" Stephen asked.

"I said, 'Hello, you.' That's an expression that was in vogue when this boat first sailed, if you'd like to know. It means 'Hello, I think you're interesting and would consider sleeping with you if I were so inclined.'"

"You must call it a ship," Stephen said.

She laughed and for an instant looked at him intently, as if in that second she could see everything about him — that he was taking this voyage because he was bored with his life, that nothing had ever *really* happened to him. He felt his face become hot. "Okay, 'ship', does that make you feel better?" she asked. "Anyway, I *want* to pretend that I'm living in the past. I don't ever want to return to the present, do you?"

"Well, I . . ."

"Yes, I suppose you do, want to return, that is."

"What makes you think that?"

"Look how you're dressed. You shouldn't be wearing modern clothes on this ship. You'll have to change later, you know." She was perfectly dressed in a powder-blue walking suit with matching jacket, a pleated, velvet-trimmed front blouse, and an ostrich feather hat. She looked as if she had stepped out of another century, and just now Stephen could believe she had.

"What's your name?" Stephen asked.

"Esme," she answered. Then she turned the box that she was resting on the rail and opened the side facing the dock. "You see," she said to the box, "we really are here."

"What did you say?" Stephen asked.

"I was just talking to Poppa," she said, closing and latching the box.

"Who?"

"I'll show you later, if you like," she promised. Then bells began to ring and the ship's whistles cut the air. There was a cheer from the dock and on board, and the ship moved slowly out to sea. To Stephen it seemed that the land, not the ship, was moving. The whole of England was just floating peacefully away, while the string band on the ship's bridge played Oscar Strauss's *The Chocolate Soldier.*

They watched until the land had dwindled to a thin line on the horizon, then Esme reached naturally for Stephen's hand, squeezed it for a moment, then hurried away. Before Stephen could speak, she had disappeared into the crowd, and he stood looking after her long after she had gone.

Stephen found her again in the Café Parisien, sitting in a large wicker chair beside an ornately trellised wall.

"Well, hello, *you,*" Esme said, smiling. She was the very model of a smart, stylish young lady.

"Does that mean you're still interested?" Stephen asked, standing before her. Her smile was infectious, and Stephen felt himself losing his poise, as he couldn't stop grinning.

"But *mais oui,*" she said. Then she relaxed in her chair, slumped down as if she could instantly revert to being a child — in fact, the dew was still on her — and she looked around the room as though Stephen had suddenly disappeared.

"I beg your pardon?" he asked.

"That's French, which *no one* uses anymore, but it was *the* language of the world when this ship first sailed."

"I believe it was English," Stephen said smoothly.

"Well," she said, looking up at him, "it means that I might be interested *if* you'd kindly sit down instead of looking down at me from the heights." Stephen sat down beside her and she said, "It took you long enough to find me."

"Well," Stephen said, "I had to dress. Remember? You didn't find my previous attire as —"

"I agree and I apologise," she said quickly, as if suddenly afraid of hurting his feelings. She folded her hands behind the box that she had centred perfectly on the damask-covered table. Her leg brushed against his; indeed, he did look fine, dressed in grey striped trousers, spats, black morning coat, blue vest, and a silk cravat tied under a butterfly collar. He fiddled with his hat, then placed it on the seat of the empty chair beside him. No doubt he would forget to take it.

"Now," she said, "don't you feel better?"

Stephen was completely taken with her; this had never happened to him before. He found it inexplicable. A tall and very English waiter disturbed him by asking if he wished to order cocktails, but Esme asked for a Narcodrine instead.

"I'm sorry, ma'am, but Narcodrines or inhalors are not publicly sold on the ship," the waiter said dryly.

"Well, that's what I *want*."

"One would have to ask the steward for the more modern refreshments."

"You did say you wanted to live in the past," Stephen said to Esme, and ordered a Campari for her and a Drambuie for himself.

"Right now I would prefer a robot to take my order," Esme said.

"I'm sorry, but we have no robots on the ship either," the waiter said before he turned away.

"Are you going to show me what's inside the box?" Stephen asked.

"I don't like that man," Esme said.

"Esme, the box . . ."

"It might cause a stir if I opened it here."

"I would think you'd like that," Stephen said.

"You see, you know me intimately already." Then she smiled and winked at someone four tables away. "Isn't he cute?"

"Who?"

"The little boy with the black hair parted in the middle." She waved at him, but he ignored her and made an obscene gesture at a woman who looked to be his nanny. Then Esme opened the box, which drew the little boy's attention. She pulled out a full-sized head of man and placed it gently beside the box.

"Jesus," Stephen said.

"Stephen, I'd like you to meet Poppa. Poppa, this is Stephen."

"I'm pleased to meetcha, Stephen," said the head in a full, resonant voice.

"Speak properly, Poppa," Esme said. "Meet *you*."

"Don't correct your father." The head rolled his eyes toward Stephen and then said to Esme, "Turn me a bit, so I can see your friend without eyestrain." The head had white hair, which was a bit yellowed on the ends. It was neatly trimmed at the sides and combed up into a pompadour in the front. The face was strong, although already gone to seed. It was the face of a man in his late sixties, lined and suntanned.

"What shall I call, uh, him?" Stephen asked.

"You may speak to me directly, son," said the head. "My given name is Elliot."

"Pleased to meetcha," Stephen said, recouping. He had heard of such things, but had never seen one before.

"These are going to be all the rage in the next few months," Esme said. "They aren't on the mass market yet, but you can imagine their potential for both adults and children. They can be programmed to talk and react very realistically."

"So I see," Stephen said.

The head smiled, accepting the compliment.

"He also learns and thinks quite well," Esme continued.

"I should hope so," said the head.

The room was buzzing with conversation. At the other end, a small dance band was playing a waltz. Only a few Europeans and Americans openly stared at the head; the Africans and Asians, who were in the majority, pretended to ignore it. The little boy was staring unabashedly.

"Is your father alive?" Stephen asked.

"I *am* her father," the head said, its face betraying its impatience. "At least give me *some* respect."

"Be civil, or I'll close you," Esme said, piqued. She looked at Stephen. "Yes, he died recently. That's the reason I'm taking this trip, and that's the reason for this . . ." She nodded to the head. "He's marvellous, though. He *is* my father in every way." Then, mischievously, she said, "Well, I did make a few changes. Poppa was very demanding, you know."

"You ungrateful —"

"Shut up, Poppa."

And Poppa simply shut his eyes.

"That's all I have to say," Esme said, "and he turns himself off. In case you aren't as perceptive as I think you are, I love Poppa very much."

The little boy, unable to control his curiosity any longer, came over to the table, just as Esme was putting Poppa back in the box. In his rush to get to the table, he knocked over one of the ivy pots along the wall. "Why'd you put him away?" he asked. "I want to talk to him. Take him out, just for a minute."

"No," Esme said firmly, "he's asleep just for now. And what's *your* name?"

"Michael, and please don't be condescending."

"I'm sorry, Michael."

"Apology accepted. Now, please, can I see the head, just for a minute?"

"If you like, Michael, you can have a private audience with Poppa tomorrow," Esme said. "How's that?"

"But —"

"Shouldn't you be getting back to your nanny now?" Stephen asked, standing up and nodding to Esme to do the same. They would have no privacy here.

"Stuff it," Michael said. "And she's not my nanny, she's my sister." Then he pulled a face at Stephen; he was able to contort his lips, drawing the right side toward the left and left toward the right, as if they were made of rubber. Michael followed Stephen and Esme out of the cafe and up the staircase to the Boat Deck.

The Boat Deck was not too crowded; it was brisk out, and the breeze had a chill to it. Looking forward, Stephen and Esme could see the ship's four huge smokestacks to their left and a cluster of four lifeboats to their right. The ocean was a smooth, deep green expanse turning to blue toward the horizon. The sky was empty, except for a huge, nuclear-powered airship that floated high over the *Titanic* — the dirigible *California,* a French luxury liner capable of carrying 2,000 passengers.

"Are you two married?" Michael asked, after pointing out the airship above. He trailed a few steps behind him.

"No, we are not," Esme said impatiently. "Not yet, at least," and Stephen felt exhilarated at the thought of her really wanting him. Actually, it made no sense, for he could have any young woman he wanted. Why Esme? Simply because just now she was perfect.

"You're quite pretty," Michael said to Esme.

"Well, thank you," Esme replied, warming to him. "I like you too."

"Watch it," said the boy. "Are you going to stay on the ship and die when it sinks?"

"No!" Esme said, as if taken aback.

"What about your friend?"

"You mean Poppa?"

Vexed, the boy said, "No, *him*", giving Stephen a nasty look.

"Well, I don't know," Esme said. Her face was flushed. "Have you opted for a lifeboat, Stephen?"

"Yes, of course I have."

"Well, *we're* going to die on the ship," Michael said.

"Don't be silly," Esme said.

"Well, we are."

"Who's 'we'?" Stephen asked.

"My sister and I. We've made a pact to go down with the ship."

"I don't believe it," Esme said. She stopped beside one of the lifeboats, rested the box containing Poppa on the rail, and gazed downward at the ocean spume curling away from the side of the ship.

"He's just baiting us," Stephen said, growing tired of the game. "Anyway, he's too young to make such a decision, and his sister, if she is his sister, could not decide such a thing for him, even if she were his guardian. It would be illegal."

"We're at sea," Michael said in the nagging tone of voice children use. "I'll discuss the ramifications of my demise with Poppa tomorrow. I'm sure *he's* more conversant with such things than you are."

"Shouldn't you be getting back to your sister now?" Stephen asked. Michael responded by making the rubber-lips face at him, and then walked away, tugging at the back of his shorts, as if his undergarments had bunched up beneath. He only turned around to wave goodbye to Esme, who blew him a kiss.

"Intelligent little brat," Stephen said.

But Esme looked as if she had just forgotten all about Stephen and the little boy. She stared at the box as tears rolled from her eyes.

"Esme?"

"I love him and he's dead," she said, and then she seemed to brighten. She took Stephen's hand and they went inside, down the stairs, through several noisy corridors — state-room parties were in full swing — to her suite. Stephen was a bit nervous, but all things considered, everything was progressing at a proper pace.

Esme's suite had a parlour and a private promenade deck with Elizabethan half-timbered walls. She led him right into the plush-carpeted, velour-papered bedroom, which contained a huge four-poster bed, an antique night table, and a desk and a stuffed chair beside the door. The ornate, harp-sculpture desk lamp was on, as was the lamp just inside the bed curtains. A porthole gave a view of sea and sky. But to Stephen it seemed that the bed overpowered the room.

Esme pushed the desk lamp aside, and then took Poppa out of the box and placed him carefully in the centre of the desk. "There." Then she undressed quickly, looking shyly away from Stephen, who was taking his time. She slipped between the parted curtains of the bed and complained that she could hear the damn engines thrumming right through these itchy pillows — she didn't like silk. After a moment she sat up in bed and asked him if he intended to get undressed or just stand there.

"I'm sorry," Stephen said, "but it's just —" He nodded toward the head.

"Poppa *is* turned off, you know."

Afterward, reaching for an inhalor, taking a long pull, and then finally opening her eyes, she said, "I love you too." Stephen only moved in his sleep.

"That's very nice, dear," Poppa said, opening his eyes and smiling at her from the desk.

Little Michael knocked on Esme's door at seven-thirty the next morning.

"Good morning," Michael said, looking Esme up and down. She had not bothered to put anything on before answering the door. "I came to see Poppa. I won't disturb you."

"Jesus, Mitchell —"

"Michael."

"Jesus, Michael, it's too early for —"

"Early bird gets the worm."

"Oh, right," Esme said. "And what the hell does that mean?"

"I calculated that my best chance of talking with Poppa was if I woke you up. You'll go back to bed and I can talk with him in peace. My chances would be greatly diminished if —"

"Awright, come in."

"The steward in the hall just saw you naked."

"Big deal. Look, why don't you come back later, I'm not ready for this, and I don't know why I let you in the room."

"You see, it worked." Michael looked around the room. "He's in the bedroom, right?"

Esme nodded and followed him into the bedroom. Michael was wearing the same wrinkled shirt and shorts that he had on yesterday; his hair was not combed, just tousled.

"Is *he* with you, too?" Michael asked.

"If you mean Stephen, yes."

"I thought so," said Michael. Then he sat down at the desk and talked to Poppa.

"Can't we have *any* privacy?" Stephen asked when Esme came back to bed. She shrugged and took a pull at her inhalor. Drugged, she looked even softer, more vulnerable. "I thought you told me that Poppa was turned off all night," he continued angrily.

"But he *was* turned off," Esme said. "I just now turned him back on for Michael." Then she cuddled up to Stephen, as intimately as if they had been in love for days. That seemed to mollify him.

"Do you have a spare Narcodrine in there?" Michael shouted.

Stephen looked at Esme and laughed. "No," Esme said, "you're too young for such things." She opened the curtain so they could watch Michael. He made the rubber-lips face at Stephen and then said, "I might as well try everything. I'll be dead soon."

"You know," Esme said to Stephen, "I believe him."

"I'm going to talk to his sister, or whoever she is, about this."

"I heard what you said." Michael turned away from Poppa, who seemed lost in thought. "I have very good hearing, I heard everything you said. Go ahead and talk to her, talk to the captain, if you like. It won't do you any good. I'm an international hero, if you'd like to know. The girl who wears the camera in her hair already did an interview for me for the poll." Then he gave them his back and resumed his hushed conversation with Poppa.

"Who does he mean?" asked Esme.

"The woman reporter from *Interfax*," Stephen said.

"Her job is to guess which passengers will opt to die, and why," interrupted Michael, who turned around in his chair. "She interviews the *most* interesting passengers, then gives her predictions to her viewers — and they are considerable. They respond immediately to a poll taken several times a day. Keeps us in their minds, and everybody loves the smell of death." Michael turned back to Poppa.

"Well, she hasn't tried to interview *me*."

"Do you really want her to?" Stephen asked.

"And why not? I'm for conspicuous consumption, and I want so much for this experience to be a success. Goodness, let the whole world watch us sink, if they want. They might just as well take bets." Then, in a conspiratorial whisper, she said, "None of us really knows who's opted to die. *That's* part of the excitement. Isn't it?"

"I suppose," Stephen said.

"Oh, you're such a prig," Esme said. "One would think you're a doer."

"What?"

"A doer. All of us are either doers or voyeurs, isn't that right? But the doers mean business," and to illustrate she cocked her head, stuck out her tongue, and made gurgling noises as if she were drowning. "The voyeurs, however, are just along for the ride. Are you *sure* you're not a doer?"

Michael, who had been eavesdropping again, said, referring to Stephen, "He's not a doer, you can bet on that! He's a voyeur of the worst sort. *He* takes it all seriously."

"Mitchell, that's not a very nice thing to say. Apologise or I'll turn Poppa off and you can go right —"

"I told you before, its Michael. M-I-C-H-A-"

"Now that's enough disrespect from both of you," Poppa said. "Michael, stop goading Stephen. Esme says she loves him. Esme, be nice to Michael. He just made my day. And you don't have to threaten to turn me off. I'm turning myself off. I've got some thinking to do." Poppa closed his eyes and nothing Esme said would awaken him.

"Well, he's never done *that* before," Esme said to Michael, who was now standing before the bed and trying to place his feet as wide apart as he could. "What did you say to him?"

"Nothing much."

"Come on, Michael, *I* let you into the room, remember?"

"I remember. Can I come into bed with you?"

"Hell, no," Stephen said.

"He's only a child," Esme said as she moved over to make room for Michael, who climbed in between her and Stephen. "Be a sport. *You're* the man I love."

"Do you believe in transmigration of souls?" Michael asked Esme.

"What?"

"Well, I asked Poppa if he remembered any of his past lives, that is, if he had any. Poppa's conscious, you know, even if he is a machine."

"Did your sister put such ideas in your head?" Esme asked.

"Now you're being condescending." However, Michael made the rubber-lips face at Stephen, rather than at Esme, Stephen made a face back at him, and Michael howled in appreciation, then became quite serious and said, "On the contrary, *I* helped my sister to remember. It wasn't easy, either, because she hasn't lived as many lives as I have. *She's* younger than me. I bet I could help *you* to remember," he said to Esme.

"And what about me?" asked Stephen, playing along, enjoying the game a little now.

"You're a nice man, but you're too filled up with philosophy and rationalizations. You wouldn't grasp any of it; it's too simple. Anyway, you're in love and distracted."

"Well, I'm in love too," Esme said petulantly.

"But you're in love with everything. He's only in love with one thing at a time."

"Am I a thing to you?" Esme asked Stephen.

"Certainly not."

But Michael would not be closed out. "I can teach you how to meditate," he said to Esme. "It's easy, once you know how. You just watch things in a different way."

"Then would I see all my past lives?" Esme asked.

"Maybe."

"Is that what you do?"

"I started when I was six," Michael said. "I don't *do* anything anymore, I just see differently. It's something like dreaming." Then he said to Esme, "You two are like a dream, and I'm outside it. Can I come in?"

Delighted, Esme asked, "You mean, become a family?"

"Until the end," Michael said.

"I think it's wonderful, what do you think, Stephen?"

Stephen lay back against the wall, impatient, ignoring them.

"Come on, be a sport," Michael said. "I'll even teach you how to make the rubber-lips face."

Stephen and Esme finally managed to lose Michael by lunchtime. Esme seemed happy enough to be rid of the boy, and they spent the rest of the day discovering the ship. They took a quick dip in the pool, but the water was too cold and it was chilly outside. If the dirigible was floating above, they did not see it because the sky was covered with heavy grey clouds. They changed clothes, strolled along the glass-enclosed lower Promenade Deck, looked for the occasional flying fish, and spent an interesting half hour being interviewed by the woman from *Interfax*. Then they took a snack in the opulent first-class smoking room. Esme loved the mirrors and stained-glass windows. After they explored cabin and tourist class, Esme talked Stephen into a quick game of squash, which he played rather well. By dinnertime they found their way into the garish, blue-tiled Turkish bath. It was empty and hot, and they made gentle but exhausting love on one of the Caesar couches. Then they changed clothes again, danced in the lounge, and took a late supper in the Café.

He spent the night with Esme in her suite. It was about four o'clock in the morning when he was awakened by a hushed conversation. Rather than make himself known, Stephen feigned sleep and listened.

"I can't make a decision," Esme said as she carefully paced back and forth beside the desk upon which Poppa rested.

"You've told me over and over what you know you must do," said Poppa. "And now you change your mind?"

"I think things have changed."

"And how is that?"

"Stephen, he . . ."

"Ah," Poppa said, "so now *love* is the escape. But do you know how long that will last?"

"I didn't expect to meet him, to feel better about everything."

"It will pass."

"But right now I don't want to die."

"You've spent a fortune on this trip, and on me. And now you want to throw it away. Look, the way you feel about Stephen is all for the better, don't you understand? It will make your passing away all the sweeter because you're happy, in love, whatever you want to claim for it. But now you want to throw everything away that we've planned and take your life some other time, probably when you're desperate and unhappy and don't have me around to help you. You wish to die as mindlessly as you were born."

"That's not so, Poppa. But it's up to *me* to choose."

"You've made your choice, now stick to it, or you'll drop dead like I did."

Stephen opened his eyes; he could not stand this any longer. "Esme, what the hell are you talking about?"

She looked startled and then said to Poppa, "You were purposely talking loudly to wake him up, weren't you?"

"*You* had me programmed to help you. I love you and I care about you. You can't undo that!"

"I can do whatever I wish," she said petulantly.

"Then let me help you, as I always have. If I were alive and had my body, I would tell you exactly what I'm telling you now."

"What is going on?" Stephen asked.

"She's fooling you," Poppa said gently to Stephen. "She's using you because she's frightened."

"I am not!"

"She's grasping at anyone she can find."

"I am not!" she shouted.

"What the hell is he telling you?" Stephen asked.

"The truth," Poppa said.

Esme sat down beside Stephen on the bed and began to cry, then, as if sliding easily into a new role, she looked at him and said, "I did program Poppa to help me die."

Disgusted, Stephen drew away from her.

"Poppa and I talked everything over very carefully, we even discussed what to do if something like this came about."

"You mean if you fell in love and wanted to live."

"Yes."

"And she decided that under no circumstances would she undo what she had done," Poppa said. "She has planned the best possible death for herself, a death to be experienced and savoured. She's given everything up and spent all her money to do it. She's broke. She can't go back now, isn't that right, Esme?"

Esme looked at Stephen and nodded.

"But you're not sure, I can see that," Stephen insisted.

"I will help her, as I always have," said Poppa.

"Jesus, shut that thing up," Stephen shouted.

"He's not a —"

"Please, at least give us a chance," Stephen said to Esme. "You're the first authentic experience I've ever had, I love you, I don't want it to end . . ."

Poppa pleaded his case eloquently, but Esme told him to go to sleep.

He obediently closed his eyes.

* * *

The great ship hit an iceberg on the fourth night of her voyage, exactly one day earlier than scheduled. It was Saturday, 11.40 p.m. and the air was full of coloured lights from tiny splinters of ice floating like motes of dust. "Whiskers 'round the light" they used to be called by sailors. The sky was a panoply of twinkling stars, and it was so cold that one might imagine they were fragments of ice floating in a cold, dark, inverted sea overhead.

Stephen and Esme were again standing by the rail of the Promenade Deck. Both were dressed in the early-twentieth-century accouterments provided by the ship: he in woollen trousers, jacket, motoring cap, and caped overcoat with a long scarf; she in a fur coat, a stylish Merry Widow hat, high-button shoes, and a black velvet, two-piece suit edged with white silk. She looked ravishing, and very young, despite the clothes.

"Throw it away," Stephen said in an authoritative voice. "Now!"

Esme brought the cedar box containing Poppa to her chest, as if she were about to throw it forward, then slowly placed it atop the rail again. "I *can't*."

"Do you want me to do it?" Stephen asked.

"I don't see why I must throw him away."

"Because we're starting a new life together. We want to live, not —"

Just then someone shouted and, as if in the distance, a bell rang three times.

"Could there be another ship nearby?" Esme asked.

"Esme, throw the box away!" Stephen snapped; and then he saw it. He pulled Esme backward, away from the rail. An iceberg as high as the forecastle deck scraped against the side of the ship; it almost seemed that the bluish, glistening mountain of ice was another ship passing, that the ice rather than the ship was moving. Pieces of ice rained upon the deck, slid across the varnished wood, and then the iceberg was lost in the darkness astern. It must have been at least one hundred feet high.

"Omygod!" Esme screamed, rushing to the rail and leaning over it.

"What it is?"

"Poppa, I dropped him, when you pulled me away from the iceberg. I didn't mean to . . ."

Stephen put his arms around her, but she pulled away. "If you didn't mean to throw it away —"

"Him, not it!"

"— him away, then why did you bring him up here?"

"To satisfy you, to . . . I don't know, Stephen. I suppose I was going to *try* to do it."

"Well, it's done, and you're going to feel better, I promise. I love you, Esme."

"I love *you*, Stephen," she said distractedly. A noisy crowd gathered on the deck around them. Some were quite drunk and were kicking large chunks of ice about, as if they were playing soccer.

"Come on, then," Stephen said, "let's get heavy coats and blankets, and we'll wait on deck for a lifeboat. We'll take the first one out and watch the ship sink together."

"No, I'll meet you right here in an hour."

"Esme, it's too dangerous, I don't think we should separate." Stephen glimpsed the woman from *Interfax* standing alone on the elevated sun deck, recording this event for her millions of viewers.

"We've got time before *anything* is going to happen."

"We don't know that," Stephen insisted. "Don't you realise that we're off schedule? We are supposed to hit that iceberg *tomorrow*."

But Esme had disappeared into the crowd.

It was bitter cold, and the Boat Deck was filled with people, all rushing about, shouting, scrambling for the lifeboats, and inevitably, those who had changed their minds at the last moment about going down with the ship were shouting the loudest, trying the hardest to be permitted into the boats, not one of which had been lowered yet. There were sixteen wooden lifeboats and four canvas Englehardts, the collapsibles. But they could not be lowered away until the davits were cleared of the two forward boats. The crew was quiet, each man busy with the boats and davits. All the boats were now swinging free of the ship, hanging just beside the Boat Deck.

"We'll let you know when it's time to board," shouted an officer to the families crowding around him.

The floor was listing. Esme was late, and Stephen wasn't going to wait. At this rate, the ship would be bow-down in the water in no time.

She must be with Michael, he thought. The little bastard must have talked her into dying.

* * *

Michael had a stateroom on C Deck.

Stephen knocked, called to Michael and Esme, tried to open the door, and finally kicked the lock free.

Michael was sitting on the bed, which was a Pullman berth. His sister lay beside him, dead.

"Where's Esme?" Stephen demanded, repelled by the sight of Michael sitting so calmly beside his dead sister.

"Not here. Obviously." Michael smiled, then made the rubber-lips face at Stephen.

"Jesus," Stephen said. "Put your coat on, you're coming with me."

Michael laughed and patted his hair down. "I'm already dead, just like my sister, almost. I took a pill too, see?" and he held up a small brown bottle. "Anyway, they wouldn't let me on a lifeboat. I didn't sign up for one, remember?"

"You're a baby, they —"

"I thought Poppa explained that to you," Michael lay down beside his sister and watched Stephen like a puppy with its head cocked at an odd angle.

"You do know where Esme is, now tell me."

"You never understood her. She came here to die."

"That's all changed," Stephen said, wanting to wring the boy's neck.

"Nothing's changed. Esme loves me, too. And everything else."

"Tell me where she is."

"It's too late for me to teach *you* how to meditate. In a way, you're *already* dead. No memory, or maybe you've just been born. No past lives. A baby." Again, Michael made the rubber-lips face. Then he closed his eyes. He whispered, "She's doing what I'm doing."

An instant later, he stopped breathing.

Stephen searched the ship, level by level, broke in on the parties, where those who had opted for death were having a last fling, looked into the lounges where many old couples sat, waiting for the end. He made his way down to F Deck, where he had made love to Esme in the Turkish bath. The water was up to his knees; it was green and soapy. He was afraid, for the list was becoming worse minute by minute; everything was happening so fast.

The water rose, even as he walked.

He had to get to the stairs, had to get up and out, onto a lifeboat, away from the ship, but on he walked, looking for Esme, unable to stop. He had to find her. She might even be on the Boat Deck right now, he thought, wading as best he could through a corridor.

But he had to satisfy himself that she wasn't down there.

The Turkish bath was filling with water, and the lights were still on, giving the room a ghostly illumination. Oddments floated in the room: blue slippers, a comb, scraps of paper, cigarettes, and several seamless plastic packages.

On the farthest couch, Esme sat meditating, her eyes closed and hands folded on her lap. She wore a simple white dress. Relieved and overjoyed, he shouted to her. She jerked awake, looking disoriented, shocked to see him. She stood up and, without a word, waded toward the other exit, dipping her hands into the water, as if to speed her on her way.

"Esme, where are you going?" Stephen called, following. "Don't run away from *me*."

Just then an explosion pitched them both into the water, and a wall gave way. A solid sheet of water seemed to be crashing into the room, smashing Stephen, pulling him under and sweeping him away. He fought to reach the surface and tried to swim back, to find Esme. A lamp broke away from the ceiling, just missing him. "Esme!" he shouted, but he couldn't see her, and then he found himself choking, swimming, as the water carried him through a corridor and away from her.

Finally, Stephen was able to grab the iron curl of a railing and pull himself onto a dry step. There was another explosion, the floor pitched, yet still the lights glowed. He looked down at the water that filled the corridor, the Turkish bath, the entire deck, and he screamed for Esme.

The ship shuddered, then everything was dead quiet. In the great rooms, chandeliers hung at angles; tables and chairs had skidded across the floors and seemed to squat against the walls like wooden beasts. Still the lights burned, as if all were quite correct, except gravity, which was misbehaving.

Stephen walked and climbed, followed by the sea, as if in a dream.

Numbed, he found himself back on the Boat Deck. But part of the deck was already submerged. Almost everyone had moved aft, climbing uphill as the bow dipped farther into the water.

The lifeboats were gone, as were the crew. Even now he looked for Esme, still hoping that she had somehow survived. Men and women were screaming "I don't want to die," while others clung together in small groups, some crying, others praying, while there were those who were very calm, enjoying the disaster. They stood by the rail, looking out toward the lifeboats or at the dirigible, which floated above. Many had changed their clothes and looked resplendent in their early twentieth-century costumes. One man, dressed in pyjama bottoms and a blue and gold smoking jacket, climbed over the rail and just stepped into the frigid water.

But there were a few men and women atop the officers' quarters. They were working hard, trying to launch collapsible lifeboats C and D, their only chance of getting safely away from the ship.

"Hey!" Stephen called to them, just now coming to his senses. "Do you need any help up there?" He realised that he was really going to die unless he did something.

He was ignored by those who were pushing one of the freed collapsibles off the port side of the roof. Someone shouted, "Damn!" The boat had landed upside down in the water.

"It's better than nothing," shouted a woman, and she and her friends jumped after the boat.

Stephen shivered; he was not yet ready to leap into the twenty-eight-degree water, although he knew there wasn't much time left, and he had to get away from the ship before it went down. Everyone on or close to the ship would be sucked under. He crossed to the starboard side, where some other men were trying to push the boat "up" to the edge of the deck. The great ship was listing heavily to port.

This time Stephen didn't ask; he just joined the work. No one complained. They were trying to slide the boat over the edge on planks. All these people looked to be in top physical shape; Stephen noticed that about half of them were women wearing the same warm coats as the men. This was a game to all of them, he suspected, and they were enjoying it. Each one was going to beat the odds, one way or another; the very thrill was to outwit fate, opt to die and yet survive.

But then the bridge was underwater.

There was a terrible crashing, and Stephen slid along the float as everything tilted.

Everyone was shouting; Stephen saw more people than he thought possible to be left on the ship. People were jumping overboard. They ran before a great wave that washed along the deck. Water swirled around Stephen and the others nearby.

"She's going down," someone shouted. Indeed, the stern of the ship was swinging upward. The lights flickered. There was a roar as the entrails of the ship broke loose: anchor chains, the huge engines and boilers. One of the huge black funnels fell, smashing into the water amid sparks. But still the ship was brilliantly lit, every porthole afire.

The crow's nest before him was almost submerged, but Stephen swam for it nevertheless. Then he caught himself and tried to swim away from the ship, but it was too late. He felt himself being sucked back, pulled under. He was being sucked into the ventilator, which was in front of the forward funnel.

Down into sudden darkness . . .

He gasped, swallowed water, and felt the wire mesh, the airshaft grating that prevented him from being sucked under. He held his breath until he thought his lungs would burst; he called in his mind to Esme and his dead mother. Water was surging all around him, and then there was another explosion. Stephen felt warmth on his back, as a blast of hot air pushed him upward. Then he broke out into the freezing air. He swam for his life, away from the ship, away from the crashing and thudding of glass and wood, away from the debris of deck chairs, planking, and ropes, and especially away from the other people who were moaning, screaming at him, and trying to grab him as buoy, trying to pull him down.

Still, he felt the suction of the ship, and he swam, even though his arms were numb and his head was aching as if it were about to break. He took a last look behind him, and saw the *Titanic* slide into the water, into its own eerie pool of light. Then he swam harder. In the distance were other lifeboats, for he could see lights flashing. But none of the boats would come in to rescue him; that he knew.

He heard voices nearby and saw a dark shape. For a moment it didn't register, then he realised that he was swimming toward an overturned lifeboat, the collapsible he had seen pushed into the water. There were almost thirty men and women standing on it. Stephen tried to climb aboard and someone shouted, "You'll sink us, we've too many already."

"Find somewhere else."

A woman tried to hit Stephen with an oar, just missing his head. Stephen swam around to the other side of the boat. He grabbed hold again, found someone's foot, and was kicked back into the water.

"Come on," a man said, his voice gravelly. "Take my arm and I'll pull you up."

"There's no *room!*" someone else said.

"There's enough room for one more."

"No, there's not."

A fight threatened, and the boat began to rock.

"We'll all be in the water if we don't stop this," shouted the man who was holding Stephen afloat. Then he pulled Stephen aboard.

"But no more, he's the last one!"

Stephen stood with the others; there was barely enough room. Everyone had formed a double line now, facing the bow, and leaned in the opposite direction of the swells. Slowly the boat inched away from the site where the ship had gone down, away from the people in the water, all begging for life, for one last chance. As he looked back to where the ship had once been, Stephen thought of Esme. He couldn't bear to think of her as dead, floating through the corridors of the ship. Desperately he wanted her, wanted to take her in his arms.

Those in the water could easily be heard; in fact, the calls seemed magnified, as if meant to be heard clearly by everyone who was safe, as a punishment for past sins.

"We're all deaders," said a woman standing beside Stephen. "I'm sure no one's coming to get us before dawn, when they have to pick up survivors."

"We'll be the last pickup, that's for sure, that's if they intend to pick us up at all."

"Those in the water have to get their money's worth."

"And since we opted for death . . ."

"I didn't," Stephen said, almost to himself.

"Well, you've got it anyway."

Stephen was numb, but no longer cold. As if from far away, he heard the splash of someone falling from the boat, which was very slowly sinking as air was lost from under the hull. At times the water was up to Stephen's knees, yet he wasn't even shivering. Time distended, or contracted. He measured it by the splashing of his companions as they fell overboard. He heard himself calling Esme, as if to say goodbye, or perhaps to greet her.

By dawn, Stephen was so muddled by the cold that he thought he was on land, for the sea was full of debris: cork, steamer chairs, boxes, pilasters, rugs, carved wood, clothes, and of course the bodies of those unfortunates who could not or would not survive; and the great icebergs and the smaller ones called growlers looked like cliffs and mountainsides. The icebergs were sparkling and many-hued, all brilliant in the light, as if painted by some cheerless Gauguin of the north.

"There," someone said, a woman's hoarse voice. "It's coming down, it's coming down!" The dirigible, looking like a huge white whale, seemed to be descending through its more natural element, water, rather than the thin, cold air. Its electric engines could not even be heard.

In the distance, Stephen could see the other lifeboats. Soon the airship would begin to rescue those in the boats, which were now tied together in a cluster. As Stephen's thoughts wandered and his eyes watered from the reflected morning sunlight, he saw a piece of carved wood bobbing up and down near the boat, and noticed a familiar face in the debris that seemed to surround the lifeboat.

There, just below the surface, in his box, the lid open, eyes closed, floated Poppa. Poppa opened his eyes then and looked at Stephen, who screamed, lost his balance on the hull, and plunged headlong into the cold black water.

The Laurel Lounge of the dirigible *California* was dark and filled with survivors. Some sat in the flowered, stuffed chairs; others just milled about. But they were all watching the lifelike holographic tapes of the sinking of the *Titanic*. The images filled the large room with the ghostly past.

Stephen stood in the back of the room, away from the others, who cheered each time there was a close-up of someone jumping overboard or slipping under the water. He pulled the scratchy woollen blanket around him, and shivered. He had been on the dirigible for more than twenty-four hours, and he was still chilled. A crewman had told him it was because of the injections he had received when he boarded the airship.

There was another cheer and, horrified, he saw that they were cheering for *him*. He watched himself being sucked into the ventilator, and then blown upward to the surface. His body ached from being battered. But he had saved himself. He *had* survived, and that had been an actual experience. It was worth it for that, but poor Esme . . .

"You had one of the *most* exciting experiences," a woman said to him, as she touched his hand. He recoiled from her, and she shrugged, then moved on.

"I wish to register a complaint," said a stocky man dressed in period clothing to one of the *Titanic's* officers, who was standing beside Stephen and sipping a cocktail.

"Yes?" asked the officer.

"I was saved against my wishes. I specifically took this voyage that I might pit myself against the elements."

"Did you sign one of our protection waivers?" asked the officer.

"I was not aware that we were required to sign any such thing."

"All such information was provided," the officer said, looking uninterested. "Those passengers who are truly committed to taking their chances sign, and we leave them to their own devices. Otherwise, we are responsible for every passenger's life."

"I might just as well have jumped into the ocean early and gotten pulled out," the passenger said sarcastically.

The officer smiled. "Most people want to test themselves out as long as they can. Of course, if you want to register a formal complaint, then . . ."

But the passenger stomped away.

"The man's trying to save face," the officer said to Stephen, who had been eavesdropping. "We see quite a bit of that. But *you* seemed to have an interesting ride. You gave us quite a start; we thought you were going to take a lifeboat with the others, but you disappeared below decks. It was a bit more difficult to monitor you, but we managed — that's the fun for *us*. You were never in any danger, of course. Well, maybe a *little*."

Stephen was shaken. He had felt that his experiences had been authentic, that he had really saved himself. But none of that had been *real*. Only Esme . . .

And then he saw her step into the room.

"Esme?" He couldn't believe it. "Esme?"

She walked over to him and smiled, as she had the first time they'd met. She was holding a water-damaged cedar box.

"Hello, Stephen. Wasn't it exciting?"

Stephen threw his arms around her, but she didn't respond. She waited a proper time, then disengaged herself.

"And look," she said, "they've even found Poppa." She opened the box and held it up to him.

Poppa's eyes fluttered open. For a moment his eyes were vague and unfocussed, then they fastened on Esme and sharpened. "Esme . . ." Poppa said uncertainly, and then he smiled. "Esme, I've had the strangest dream." He laughed. "I dreamed I was a head in a box . . ."

Esme snapped the box closed. "Isn't he marvellous," she said. She patted the box and smiled. "He almost had me talked into going through with it this time."

VOICES

. . . .

I was carefully papering the balsa-wood wing struts of my scale-model *Gotha G-V Bomber* when Crocker asked me if I ever spoke to dead people.

Although Crocker is a member of the Susquehanna River Model-makers and Sex Fiends Association (which doesn't say much because all you have to do to become a member is hang-out in the shack by the river and make models), everybody thinks he's right off his nut. One of the guys nicknamed him "Crock-a-shit" because of all the stupid stories he told — and the stupid questions he asked — and the name stuck. Hell, he seemed to like it. But nobody broke his arms or his legs or smashed up his models, and so he stayed on, sort of like a mascot. He was fat, freckled, and wore his white-blond hair in a brush-cut. But he was also smart, in his way. He was twelve, a year younger than me, and was in seventh grade honours.

"Steve, you hear me or what?" he asked me, turning down the volume on the club's battery-powered radio. It was playing the Big Bopper's "Chantilly Lace". Since Buddy Holly, Ritchie Valens, and the Big Bopper had died in a plane crash back in February, the radio stations were still playing their stuff all the time — and here it was August! "You ever talk to a dead person or not."

"No, Bobby," I said. I was trying to work the air-bubbles out of the paper: this Gotha was the only model of its kind and would have a wingspan of over six feet. My step-father had given me the kit for my birthday. "I never talked to anybody who's dead . . . except maybe you. Now turn the volume back up." But the song was over and the disk-jockey was saying something about Lou Costello being dead. I couldn't remember if he was the fat comedian or the skinny one; but I only liked the fat one and hoped it wasn't him.

Anyway, this was frustrating work, and Crock-a-shit was, as usual, fouling everything up. I have to admit, though, that he had made me curious; but just thinking about dead people made me feel jittery, and sad, too. It made me think of my Dad, my real Dad, who died in the hospital when I was seven. Funny, the things you remember. I used to play a game with him when he came home from the office every night. We had a leather couch in the den — Dad called it "The Library" — and I would slide my hand back and forth on the cushion while he would try to catch it. And then when he did, he would hold it tight and we'd laugh. Dad had grey hair, and everybody said he was handsome. But when he was in the hospital, he didn't even know who Mom and I were. He thought Mom was *his* mother! She cried when he got mixed up, and I just felt weird about it. Especially when he had an attack and then talked in a language that sounded like Op-talk. Mom said it was because his brain wasn't working right. I knew that if I could only understand it, everything would be all right. It was like he was trying to tell me what to do in some secret language; and if I could only figure out the words, I'd be able to help him get well. But then he died, and I never got to say goodbye in a way he could understand because his brain never did get right again.

Crocker didn't say anything more for a while, which was unusual for him.

When I had finished the wings, which weren't right and would have to be redone again, I looked up and said, "Crock-a-shit, what are you looking at?"

"Nothin'."

"What's with all this dead people stuff?" I asked, trying to treat him like a human being.

"I just wanted to know if you have ever done it, that's all."

"Done what?"

"I just told you! Talk to dead people."

"Have *you*?" I asked, knowing for sure I would get one of his bullshit answers.

"Yeah, I do it a few times a week. When I don't come down here."

"Oh, sure, and where do you do that?"

"Every day I check the paper to see if there's anything going on at the funeral home on the corner of Allen and Main. If there is, I just sort of walk in and talk to the corpse in the casket. If not, I come over here."

"And nobody says nothing to you? They just let you walk in and talk to the dead people?"

"They ain't bothered me yet." After a pause, he said, "You wanna go with me today? They got somebody in there," and he showed me the obituary column from today's *Sun-Bulletin*. I glanced at what he was trying to show me and shook out the sports section. Patterson was fighting Ingemar Johansson on Friday. I was rooting for Patterson, who had KO'd Archie Moore in '56.

"You wanna go with me and see for yourself or not?" Crocker asked, indignantly ripping the paper out of my hands. "Or are you afraid?"

"Screw you!"

"You probably never been to a funeral in your life."

"I've been to funerals before," I said. "Everybody has."

"But did you ever *see* a dead person?"

I had to say no to that. "I never even saw my own father after he died."

That certainly shut him up, but he had such a sorrowful look on his face that I felt sorry for him.

"I'm Jewish," I said, "and Jews can't have open caskets. Of course, there must be a reason for that, but I don't know what it is."

"How'd he die?" Crocker asked, fumbling around with his hands as if he wasn't used to having them.

"Something wrong with his liver."

"Like from drinking?" he asked.

"No, it was nothing like that," I said. But I had heard my mother talking to the doctor; maybe he did get sick from drinking, although I swear I can't remember ever seeing him drunk or anything. And I had just about had it with Crocker's questions; he was acting like Jack Webb on *Dragnet*. You'd think he would have shut up after I told him about my father. But not Crocker. He was a nosy little bastard.

After a pause, Crocker asked, "Did you ever talk to him after he died?"

"You're out of your freaking gourd, Crocker. Nobody but an A-hole thinks he can talk to people after they're dead."

"If you come with me today, I'll prove it to you."

"No way, sucker. I got better things to do than act like a nimblenarm."

"With your father being dead and all, I can't blame you for being afraid," Crocker said. "I'd be, too."

"Crocker, get the hell out of my life," I said. I guess I shouted at him because he looked real nervous. But I didn't need him spreading it all over the place that I was afraid to look at a dead person. Christ, Crock-a-shit had a bigger mouth than my mother.

"Okay," I said, "but if I don't hear this dead person talk like you say, I'm going to break your head." I said it as if I meant it.

I guess I did.

But that only seemed to make Crocker happy, for he nodded and helped me put away my Gotha Bomber.

The worst part of it was that I had to sneak into my house and put on a suit and tie, for Crocker said you can't just walk in with jeans and a tee-shirt.

But a deal was a deal.

I met him back at the clubhouse, and we walked to the funeral home.

It had been a hot, humid summer, and boring as hell. There was never anything to do, and even going down to the club and smoking and working on models was boring. And to make matters worse, I thought about Marie Dickson all the time. She was so . . . *beautiful*! I would see her around once in a while, but I never said anything to her. I was waiting for the right time.

Not a good way to get through a summer.

Anyway, she was always with a girl friend, and I was most times by myself. No way I was going to walk up to her and make a complete asshole of myself in front of her and her girl friend. She hung around with a fat girl, probably because it made her look even better; it seemed all the good-looking girls did that.

"Okay, you ready?" Crocker asked as we approached the front stairs to the building, which was grey and white, with lots of gingerbread like my parent's house.

"I was born ready. Let's go."

I hated this place already.

"We'll go in right after these people," Crocker said, nodding in the direction of a crowd waiting to get past the door into the parlour. "Pretend like you're with them."

So we followed them inside. I was all sweaty and the sharp blast of the air-conditioning felt good.

The old people ahead of us all stopped to write in a book that rested on what looked like a music stand; but Crocker really knew his way around here and led me right into a large, dimly-lit, carpeted room with high windows covered with heavy blue drapes. People were standing around and talking, soft organ music was playing, and there was a line of people filing past an ornate casket that was surrounded with great bushes of flowers.

"Let's go see it and get the hell out of here," I said, feeling uncomfortable. I looked around. Even though this room was certainly big enough, I felt as if I was being closed up in a closet. And I figured it had to be just a matter of time before someone would see we weren't supposed to be here and kick us out.

"Wait till the line gets through," Crocker said.

But a woman wearing a silky black dress and one of those round pillbox hats with a veil put her hand on my shoulder and asked, "Did you go to school with Matt?"

I looked at her, and I've got to say I was scared, although I don't really know why I should have been. "Uh, yes, ma'am," I said, looking to Crocker — who was supposed to be the professional — to pull us out of this.

"I'm his Aunt Leona. You should meet his Mom and Dad, they're right there." She pointed to a tall, balding man and a skinny woman who made me think of some sort of bird. "Stay right here and I'll get them," Aunt Leona said. "I'm sure they'll want to talk to you."

I could only nod. When the woman walked away, I said, "What the hell did you get us into?"

Crocker looked nervous, too; but he said, "Didn't you read the obituary?"

"Piss off, Crocker."

"Well, it was a kid who used to live in Endicott. His family moved to Virginia. I can't remember the rest."

"You should have told me it was a kid. Christ Almighty!"

"You should'a read what I gave you," he said in a singsong voice that made me want to crown him.

"How'd he die?" I asked.

"I dunno," Crocker said. "They don't tell you that kind of stuff in the paper."

"Well, did he go to our school?" I asked.

"I can't remember," Crocker said; but it was too late, anyway, because Aunt Leona brought a whole crowd to talk to us.

I was really nervous now.

What were we supposed to say to the dead kid's parents?

Although it surprised the living hell right out of me, Crocker and I managed to hold our own. We said how sorry we were and what a nice guy he was, how he played a mean stickball and was a regular nut for Bill Haley and the Comets and Jackie Williams — you know, "Lonely Teardrops"; and it was the craziest damn thing because it was almost as if we did know this kid. With all the crying and hugging going on around us, I started to get that thunder sound in my ears, which I always used to hear before I was going to cry.

I haven't heard *that* sound in a long time.

I didn't even hear it at my Dad's funeral, or at the house when everyone stood around and told me I had to be a big boy and all that crap. It wasn't until months later that I heard the thunder sound, when I was in the house alone and practising the piano. I looked up and saw Dad's photograph on the piano; and suddenly, like I was crazy all of a sudden, I heard the thunder and then I started to cry. It made me feel sick. But after that, I didn't cry again.

Until now.

Everybody was crying, including me, and Crock-a-shit excused both of us so we could pay our respects to the departed (that's just what he said). As soon as we were out of their reach, he said, "Steve, you're *good* at this."

"So are you," I said, pretending that it was all an act. "Now let's get it over with."

"Okay," Crocker said, and we stood right before the casket and looked into it. I could smell the flowers — the ones with the long wormy things inside them, but they didn't smell bad. The kid in the casket was wearing a suit and tie . . . just like us. He looked like Pug Flanders, who lived down the block from me: the corpse had black hair, which was greased back: he had probably worn it in a D.A. with an elephant's trunk in the front, but whoever did him up probably thought a flat-top was the height of coolness. It looked like he had had pimples, too, but his face was coated with makeup; and it looked too white, like someone had gone crazy with the powder or something. The expression on his face was kind of snarly: I guess they couldn't wipe it off.

I had a strong feeling that I would have liked this guy.

But looking down at this corpse made me feel sort of weird. Not that I was scared anymore, but this kid didn't really seem to be dead. It was like this was some sort of a play, and everybody was acting, just as we were.

This guy just *couldn't* be dead.

He looked like he was going to sit up any second.

I blinked then because it was almost as if he was glowing like one of those religious paintings I've seen in churches. It was as if I could see the stuff of his soul, or something like that. Christ, I almost fell backward.

I knew that was all bullshit, but I saw it just the same.

Crocker didn't seem to see it; at least he didn't say anything. So it must have just been me.

And then I remembered something about my father that scared me. It just sort of came out of nowhere!

I remembered the nurse taking my arm and trying to pull me out of the hospital room. Mom was crying and screaming, and she fell right on top of Dad on the bed. But I got one last look at Dad; and he looked like he was made up of light, sort of like a halo was around him and all over him.

How could I have forgotten something like that?

But I did. I must have just pushed it right out of my mind.

"How d'you think he died?" I asked Crocker. Hearing my own voice made me feel normal again. And that was important right now.

"Who knows? Probably some sort of accident."

"Nah, he looks too good."

"That don't mean nothin,'" Crocker said. "They can make anybody look good as new . . . almost. He could have even had cancer."

Crocker looked up in the air.

I called his name, but he ignored me. It was as if he was listening to something. He had his head cocked like the RCA dog.

"Crocker, come *on*," I said after a while. I was starting to get worried. "Hey, you . . . Crock-a-shit."

"Shut-up!" Crocker snapped. "Can't you hear him?"

"Hear what?"

"Just listen."

I listened, I really did, but I couldn't hear a damn thing. Crocker is probably off his nut, plain and simple. But I wasn't much better; not after I had just seen the corpse glowing like the hands on a watch.

Who knows, maybe the dead guy could talk. And maybe Crocker could hear him.

But I just wanted to get out of here.

I was already feeling like the walls and everything were going to close in on me.

"He's leaving," Crocker said. "He's saying goodbye to everybody. Cool!"

"Okay, then let's go," I said; but I couldn't help but look at the spot where Crocker seemed to be staring; and I got the strangest feeling. Then I saw it: a pool of light like a cloud that seemed to be connected to the body that was now glowing softly again.

And the light was bleeding out of the corpse like it was the guy's spirit or something.

A few seconds later the light just blinked out, as if someone had thrown a switch; and the body looked different, too, as if something vital had just drained out of it. Now it was nothing more than a shell; it looked like it was made of plastic. It was dull, lifeless.

We left then . . . Crocker and I just left at the same time, as if we both knew something.

And I heard thunder and remembered my father talking in the language only he could understand; and I felt as if I was drowning in something as deep and as big as the ocean.

When we got out of the funeral home, and past all the men standing around and smoking cigarettes, Crocker said, "You heard him, didn't you? I could tell."

"I didn't hear nothin'," I said, protecting my ass.

"Bullshit," Crocker said.

"Bullshit on you," I said.

"Well, you were acting . . . different," Crocker said.

I admitted that maybe I saw something that was a little weird, but it was probably just in my head. That bent Crocker all out of shape; he seemed happier than a kid with a box of *Ju Ju Bees*, and I got worried that he'd shoot off his mouth to everyone he saw.

I warned him about that.

"Give me a break," he said. "It's enough that the guys in the club think of me as some sort of asshole as it is. You're the only one I feel I can talk to — and I don't even really *know* you."

"Okay," I said, worried that maybe there was something wrong with *me*. Why else would Crocker feel that way? It also worried me that first I saw the dead guy glowing like my aunt's Sylvania "Halolight" teevee, and then I saw his soul (or whatever it was) pass right out of him, leaving nothing but a body that was more like a statue or something made out of plaster-of-Paris. But I put those thoughts away and asked, "What did the guy say?"

"His name is Matt . . . remember? He said he was scared out of his gourd until he found his grandmother."

"What?"

"His grandmother's dead. She'll show him around."

"Around? Around where?"

"How the hell should I know?" Crocker said. "Heaven, probably."

"You got to be kidding." I couldn't help but laugh. "You're making that stuff up." But somehow I really wanted to believe it.

"I thought you said you saw something," Crocker said, hanging his head. "And I believed you . . . I wanted to know what you saw —"

"I said I *thought* I saw something." I punched him hard on the arm to make him feel better. "And it wasn't nothing but a glowing like a teevee tube when you turn it off."

"I never saw that."

"Now tell me what else did Matt say?" I asked.

"He *hates* Bill Haley, but we got Jackie Williams right."

"Uh, huh," I said.

"Well, that's what I thought I heard," Crocker said.

"Why'd you say 'cool'?" I asked.

"Whaddyamean?"

"When you were looking up in the air, you said, 'Cool.' Don't you remember?"

"Yeah."

"Well?"

And Crocker started laughing. It was like he couldn't stop. He kept leaning forward and stumbling and then laughing even louder. I couldn't help but smile, and I kept knuckling his arm until he told me.

"He said he was going to visit the Big Bopper."

"What?"

"That's what he said. And Ritchie Valens."

"You're *so* full of crap," I said.

But now I couldn't stop laughing either.

"Then maybe dying's not so bad," I said; and we fell down right there on the sidewalk on Ackley Avenue in front of a brown, shingled house that belonged to Mrs Campbell, my third grade teacher.

I don't know what it was, but I just couldn't stop laughing and crying.

Neither could Crocker.

And who knows, maybe I really *did* see something flickering in the air above Matt's dead body while he was floating around in heaven somewhere meeting his grandmother.

And maybe he did get to see the Big Bopper.

Just like the Big Bopper probably got to see Valens and Holly... and probably Mozart and Beethoven, too.

And maybe the Big Bopper also got to meet my Dad.

Why not? Dad would be there, standing right on line; he always liked to play the piano, all that beebop and boogie-woogie stuff. So maybe he became a musician, just like all the others.

Now *that* would be something . . .

FAIRY TALE

. . . .

This is a fairy story. Not that kind, *Shtumie.* Fairies, as in goblins and glashtins and shellycoats; or, for the rest of you non-Jews, as in leprechaun.

I've seen them all and almost died in the doing. That's what this story is all about. Moishe Dayan was not the only Jewish hero, you might note.

My name is Moishe Mencken (not related to the H.L. of the same surname) and I'm a comedian by trade. I'm kind of a permanent fixture at the Rachmones Resort. That's in the heart of the Borscht Belt, near Liberty, and right off old Route Seventeen.

Noo-oo? Do I detect some little condescension back there?

Well, let me tell you, this isn't such a bad place, as resorts go. It's not like it was in the old days, of course, when we had the Concord and Grossingers. But this is the best you get now. I make a living wage here, which is better than most of my peers can muster.

In the old days we could use good material. We could be funny then. (I mean really funny. Not what *you* call funny.) Now everything's so uptight that even the Jews can't take a joke. Everyone's afraid. God forbid they should laugh at themselves.

So we give the *shleppers* what they want.

Like Polish and frog jokes. (Yes, the Poles are the true heroes of America. They can take a joke and prosper.)

But you always want one more Polish joke, right?

Okay, *shtumie*. Everybody knows that European and South American banks have taken over the country. You see them everywhere, right? But have you ever been to a Polish bank? They have a new policy: You give them a *toaster* and they refund you three hundred dollars.

Ha-ha.

That's what you pay for. You deserve it.

The frog joke. The oldest one still gets a laugh. Can you believe that? *Oy*, someone doesn't know the frog joke. What's green and red and goes sixty miles an hour?

Go figure it out.

Okay, now I'll tell you about Shearjashub Mills. He's the one who got me into all the fairy trouble in the first place.

Nobody knows what Shearjashub means, or how he got the name because he's not telling. He likes to be called Hub, and he's as Jewish as bacon — pure Wasp, yet he smells from herring and speaks a passable Yiddish, which is mostly a *shtik*.

He was born on a shtetl in Galacia; that's how come the Yiddish.* Hub is not quite six feet tall (but he lies about his height and his age), has grey frizzy hair, a pot belly, and a beautiful girl always on his arm. How he does that is beyond me. He says it's the meat *and* the motion. It certainly couldn't be the money.

For your information, I'm five-feet-two and three-quarters. Let's get that out of the way. And I do not have frizzy hair and a pot belly. I'm tough, scrappy, and told that I'm quite handsome in a goyish way: big blue eyes, squarish, strong face, cleft in my chin, you get the picture.

Hub still works and lives at the Graubs Resort, a third-rate club with some decent skiing, which has kept it alive. At one time, the Graubs did quite well, as attested by its many bungalows and central houses, all stone — the old wooden barn, where stores used to be kept, caved in years ago, and still sits there in a field like an old grey hat.

Every few months I get the urge to see Hub. He's like lumpfish caviar: good once in a while, but every day — *feh*. So last month I got the urge and called and this is what I got:

---

* It occurs to me that some of you were not brought up in a shtetl in Galacia and cannot understand Yiddish, which is to miss most of the important dirty words in the English language. For you there is a Yinglish glossary at the end of the story.

"Hello, Diana, this is Moishe Mencken, connect me with Hub Mills' room, I love you."

Silence on the line. Perhaps she was overwhelmed.

"Hello? Diana?"

"I'm sorry, but we're closed" — that said in a voice that was unmistakably Diana's, but so cold I felt a chill. "If you would like to leave your address, we will —"

"What are you, a recording?" I asked. "Cut the crap. Diana, this is Moishe, your little Moishe, now let me speak to Hub."

Click.

That's all, just like that, and I stood there with the phone still to my ear as the chills went up and down. That wasn't Diana, I knew that. The Graubs couldn't be closed. When a resort closes, everybody knows. It's like a telepathic hotline. And certainly Hub would have told *me*, if such a thing had happened.

It wouldn't take me but five minutes to reach the Graubs and find out what was what. I had a few hours before I had to perform at eight.

"Nobody screws around with Moishe Mencken," I said into the dead phone. "Just wait!"

So put the phone down, already, I told myself. But I couldn't move, not a muscle. I was in some kind of trance, like a dream. Until seven-thirty I stood there.

Later I couldn't remember a thing. But, *oy*, did my right arm ache!

I had just enough time to dress and get downstairs and do the show, tuxedo and studs and all; but I had a splitting headache like I sometimes get from drinking Wild Turkey (good stuff, mind you, but always gives me a migraine on the left side). I wondered why my right arm was numb; maybe it had fallen asleep.

Because the crowd was small (what else is new?), I had to perform in the Bronze Room. Can you imagine a room with tin walls and red velvet chairs? It was enough to embarrass even the *nouveau riche*. Then I shot an hour at the bar with Finney the barkeep (who looks like everyone's bald uncle who plays the stockmarket) and a bellboy, talking about the old days. The bellboy wasn't old enough to remember the Manhattan Riots, much less the good times, but we always made a show of impressing him with how good it was. (Ah, it wasn't that good then, either; just better than now.)

No, I still didn't remember the phone call business. Wasn't it enough that the crowd was a bunch of *pishers* and all the demons of *Gehennà* were banging on my skull?

After a while, Finney asked about Hub — he was the only person I ever met who called him Shearjashub.

Gottenyu, it was like waking from a dream. Suddenly I could remember! But everything wasn't all right. I was still *farchadat*, a little *meshugge*, ready for the funny farm.

I could not speak Hub's name. *Gott*, did I try, over and over! But every time I tried, I had a terrible compulsion to say all the Yiddish words that start with *S*, which is akin to listing the nine billion names of God:

Shabbos	*Schmuck*
Sachel	*Schneider*
Schatchen	*Schnook*
Shlack	*Shaygets*
Schlemiehl	*Shaytl*
Schlep	*Shekel*
Schlok	*Shlemozzl*
Schloomp	*Shikk* —
Schmo	

"Hey Moishe," Finney said, reaching across the bar and shaking my shoulder.

— er
Shikseh
Shmachel
Shmatehs

"Moishe, hey, enough, already. Are you all right? Come on."

"I'm all right," I said. "I'm all right." But I wasn't, as you can see. I was under some kind of spell. But how could this be? This was New York, not Moravia! I took the hint: if I started trying to talk about Hub, I would only start with the list again. So with great presence of mind, I excused myself (after liberating Finney of some more of his Wild Turkey — screw the headache) and went out to my car.

Of course, my lousy luck, it wouldn't start.

Back inside. It took a good half-hour to convince Finney that, indeed, I was all right, had not been drinking *that* much, and, yes, I would gas up his *farshtinkener* car and take good care of it. I'll be back in less than an hour, if you please.

I took old Seventeen, the Winding Way, as it was nicknamed. There was no one else on the road, which was unusual, but not that unusual. Finney had a convertible, a real antique, and the top was down. It was the kind of night to look up at the stars while a beautiful girl did unmentionable things to you in the front seat.

The main house of the Graubs, which I could see when I was off the highway, was lit up like a bingo parlour.

Something fishy on Mott Street.

Everywhere else it was dark. Except for a flickering light near the old wooden barn. I stopped the car and watched. It was most certainly the phenomenon known as Ignis Fatuus (you see, I'm no dummy), otherwise known as will-o'-the-wisp. But who knows from will-o'-the-wisp in Kerhonkson, New York?

Something about all this bothered me. The directions didn't seem right. Everything seemed, somehow, placed wrong. It was what my mother, may she live many more good years, would call a *goslin* night.

But I was wasting time here. If Hub was around, he'd be at the bar in the Main House.

Then a voice called my name.

"Hub?" I answered. It sure as hell sounded like him, but I was wary after that Diana business. Maybe I was talking to spooks again. Ah! I couldn't believe that, either. I'd been under a lot of strain lately. Maybe the whole damn thing was a loose cog in my head.

Again the voice called my name. It *was* Hub's voice. I wasn't so delirious that I couldn't recognise the voice of my best friend. The dumb sonovabitch had probably bought himself a bottle of cheap wine and was getting bent up in the woods. It didn't take much to get Hub drunk. He had emphysema and still smoked like hell and took pills, which dried out his lungs. Mix the booze with the pills and you have a cheap drunk.

Maybe he was out here getting laid. Out of the question: he always said that he was born in a bed and not in a bush. He didn't want any of that country-bumpkin prickers-in-your-ass stuff.

But how could he tell it was me? I was driving Finney's car. It was dark.

So what would you have done? Sit like a *schlemiehl*? Tell yourself you were hearing things again?

So you have no *chutzpa*.

I went to investigate.

And found a very drunk Shearjashub sitting like a toad on a rock in front of a dying fire. (So I was wrong about the will-o'-the-wisp. Sue me.) Behind him were two huge oak trees, their branches grotesquely twisted together. There was a log for the fire beside him. Nearby was another log and some kindling. Remember that, it's important.

"Hello, diminutive person," Hub said, slurring his words. He leered at me as if I were jailbait. "What brings you here?"

"I wanted to see you, dummy. How did you know it was me?"

"I didn't."

"Well, you called my name. You must have known something."

"Nope."

"You didn't call my name?"

"Uh-uh. But I'm glad you're here." Then he offered me his bottle, which I politely refused. "Come on. They'll be none left soon."

That wasn't like Hub. The Hub I knew and loved wouldn't drink out of a glass that had been used by his mother, much less share a bottle with me.

"Okay, that's enough," I said. "I'm taking you home."

"Don't come near me," Hub said, rocking back and forth on his rock — *shuckling*, my mother calls that: it's what the old men do when they pray next to you in *shul*. It's Jewish machismo, who can rock back and forth the fastest. Maybe it helps shoot the prayers up to heaven.

Anyway, I stopped where I was. He had said it like he meant it. Then he stopped *shuckling*, picked up the log that he had kept beside him, and then broke it in half over his knees.

I didn't believe it either, but seeing is believing.

"What are you, training to be a masher?" I asked.

He placed the log on the fire, which soon came alive. It was getting a little cool and the warmth and light and crackling of the fire felt good — almost reassuring.

"Not bad, huh?" Hub asked, taking another sip. "It's a trick, like tearing telephone books. The log was rotten."

"Very good," I said, impatient to get out of there. "Now let's —"

"Sit down and be humble and I'll tell you a story."

"I've heard enough stories for one day. When I called the hotel, Diana of the big boobs didn't know who I was and told me the place had closed and wouldn't let me speak to —"

"It's all true, the place is done, but we did have some good old times here, didn't we?"

I was about to remonstrate and tell him why the Graubs could not possibly be closed when, *feh*, he drooled all over his chin. Like my uncle used to do, may he rest in peace.

"Come on, sit down beside me like a good little person, and I'll tell you about the fairies."

"What? I asked.

"Remember when you talked to Diana?"

"Well?"

"It wasn't Diana."

"Then who was it?" I asked. I knew what Diana's voice sounded like. Hub always referred to her as a sexy frog — as good a description as any. I wanted to get out of there. Even though the fire was warm (too warm), I didn't like being out here in the middle of nowhere.

"A bogle," Hub said. "You talked to a bogle."

"A what?"

"If you want to find out more, sit here by me and I will tell you." He patted the rock and said, "There's enough room."

So I sat down beside him.

"A bogle, my son, is a goblin. And very evil tempered."

Not only was he drunk, but completely *meshugge* — blotto, crazy, off the wall — exactly what you thought about me when I told you what kind of story this was going to be.

"And you're *shikker*, let's get coffee," I said.

"No, sit a minute. Believe me, bogles are notorious for playing with telephones and disguising their voices."

Maybe this bogle cast a spell over me on the telephone, I thought, but I told myself to think straight like a person; otherwise, I would become a *draykop* like Hub, if I wasn't one already.

"The fairies are taking everything over," Hub said, looking around at the trees as if he was talking to them. *Nu?* Maybe he was. "And a good thing, too," he continued. "The Catskills are as dead as Dublin. Maybe we should go back to Miami Beach."

Heaven forbid!

"Okay, Hub," I said, standing up now. "I'm going down to the Main House where I will ask the bogle if I can use his phone for a minute and call the zipzip boys in the white coats."

"Fine. Go ahead. But first, maybe, you could get me that log on the pile of kindling over there."

"You just put a log on the fire," I said. But lo and *gevalt*, it was true. Burned through and through. Only glowing embers remained. "It couldn't burn that fast!"

"Get me the log and I'll show you the trick to break it," Hub said.

"Get the log yourself, *putz*. You want a fire, get your own log."

"I'm drunk, you want I should fall? Anyway, you're already standing."

But I refused to budge.

Then, without warning, he lunged at me. The Hub I knew couldn't move that fast if his life depended on it. He hit me hard, and we grappled. This was no drunkard; this boy was all muscle.

Maybe a *dybbuk*, God forbid, was inhabiting my friend.

He locked his arms around my chest and started dragging me toward the log and pile of kindling. All the while, he was laughing like hell.

Suddenly everything changed. Again it was like waking up from a dream. Nothing was as it should be. The trees had disappeared, as had the fire and log and kindling. I had thought I was in the backwoods of the Graubs; instead, I found myself on Fishkill Craig. About a foot away from us, where the log and kindling had been, was a four-hundred-foot-drop — straight down.

And I saw now that it wasn't Hub who was squeezing the life out of me, but a dwarfish person with a scraggly beard, sloped forehead, and hooked nose.

I'd been tricked, duped, the same old thing all over again. I'd fallen under another spell.

But, *gottenyu*, what fear can do to a man!

I started kicking and screaming and making such a *tummel* that this *dybbuk*, or whatever it was, twisted around and slipped on a smooth rock. Even as he fell over the cliff, he was grabbing at me to pull me over with him.

* * *

No, *Shtumie*, it doesn't end there. What comes next is the heroic part, but first let me tell you what it was that tried to seal my doom. It was a duergar using glamour, which is a fairy spell, to make me think I was talking to my friend. Nu? So what's a duergar, you may rightly ask. A duergar is a dwarf, very nasty, not well disposed to humankind, and originally from the North of England.

Remember when I talked to Diana and fell under a spell? Well, I really had been talking to a bogle, which is a goblin. Bogles and duergars always work together. The bogle casts a spell to lure a human to the duergar, and the duergar kills him. Very neat. It seems they've been doing this sort of thing for years.

How do I know that? My wife explained it to me later. She's had trouble with duergars and bogles, too.

For your information, my wife is a water fairy. Don't worry, it all fits in. Believe me.

Whenever I was about to do something crazy, my mother would say: "Moishe, if you had another brain, you'd be a halfwit."

If she had known what I was about to do, she would say it again. "Leave well enough alone, Moishe." Moma was smart. She understood that bravery was the other side of stupidity, and didn't approve of either. (Neither would she approve if she knew that my wife turns into a serpent at the touch of a drop of water.)

But she also used to say that God works in mysterious ways. God made me a comedian; now maybe he was working in a mysterious way to find me a wife. I'm a deeply religious man about these things.

Anyway, I drove down to the Main House to find out what had become of my friend.

Well, there might as well have been a bar mitzvah going on. If that's what happens when a place goes out of business, it should only happen at my resort! The place was crowded as an Irish bar on St Patrick's Day. Outside, Cadillacs as thick as cockroaches; inside . . .

It was like walking into a Las Vegas club. Like the Concord in the old days. Like heaven. It was opulent. It was filled with beautiful people, with blond Galitzianers and dark Litvaks, all sitting together at long, lavishly laid-out tables,

as if they didn't know about the Jewish pecking order. (*Nudnik! You* must be a
Litvak, you with the blank face. A Galitz is a Jew whose ancestors came from
Poland, but he likes to think they came from Austria. A Lit knows his ancestors
came from Lithuania, but he's sceptical, nevertheless. Me? I'm a Galitzvak: blue
eyes and swarthy skin, you should note.)

But the room was filled with strangers. Not one face did I recognise.
A waiter passed me with a tray of champagne (this was no cheapskate party)
and I lifted two glasses. Before I could touch glass to lips, a girl with blond,
frizzy hair, who, at first glance, didn't look more than thirteen or fourteen,
said, "Don't drink that!"

"And why not?" I asked, surprised. Maybe this was a bas mitzvah, and it
was her party, and she didn't like strangers. Look again! She was no child,
just childlike. She was a woman, as delicate as a spiderweb, with eyes that
made me think of being nineteen again and falling in love. (And I like *zoftig*
women! This one was positively skinny.)

"If you drink or eat anything, you'll never leave this place," she said.
"What?"

"It's fairy food, and not for you. You must leave. You have enemies here."

"How can I have enemies when I don't even know anybody here?"

"You just killed a duergar," she said, and she told me what a duergar
was, just as I told you. Of course, I didn't believe her, even after what
happened on the hill with Hub. I had to try to maintain some modicum of
sanity. "Half of the Unseelie Court was watching you," she continued. "And
they're all here."

"Who're the Unseelie Court?" I asked, suddenly feeling a bit claustrophobic,
even in this large room, as if I really was being watched. Something else, too:
I noticed that everything was wonderfully lit, as if ceiling, floor, and walls were
glowing. It was like a dream.

"You can think of the Unseelie as the duergar's family," and then she
reached up and put something sticky into my eyes — first one eye and then
the other.

Gottenyu! What a family!

It was a spell — glamour, as the girl called it. (Her name, incidentally, was
Asrai.) I looked around. It was like seeing with new eyes. Instead of being
opulent, this place was a mess, a real dive. Everything was dirty. What had
looked like a terrific meal turned out to be plates filled with yellow weeds

and lumpy gruel. And the light was coming from a large fire right in the centre of the room, which cast jumping shadows all over the walls.

But even in the shadows, I saw things too ugly to be human:

I saw men with webbed feet and goat's hooves and noses without nostrils. I saw water bogles, called shellycoats, festooned with shells and women with squinty eyes and back-to-front feet and long hoselike breasts. (One woman-thing had such long dugs that she carried them over her shoulders.) Every humanlike form had some deformity.

There were goblins with protruding stomachs and large ears and long slit mouths, and dirt-crusted kobolds that looked as if they had just risen up from the bowels of the earth; there were duergars with malicious grins and phookas with horns and shaggy black pelts and yellow eyes; there were shape-shifting bogles, and trows with octopoidal limbs, and fachians, which had only one eye and one arm and one leg (and one foot, of course), and there were glastig hags (part woman, part goat) with beautiful grey faces and insect-infested pubes; there was a killmoulis with a huge nose and no mouth and a fenoderee with its man-killing sickle. And there were evil-looking vampire fairies, and pretty girls with snakes instead of hair, and the dour, ugly, rockskinned spriggans that kidnap children and burn down houses.

This was the Host, the Unseelie Court, the evil ones . . .

And they were all closing in on me and chanting, "Flax on the floor, death at the door."

Oy!

I turned to run, but they were all around me. I screamed and closed my eyes (you thought maybe I would draw a sword and start hacking away like Douglas Fairbanks?) and dropped both of the drinks I was holding like a grand rabbi about to make a blessing.

Then this little girl standing beside me, this *mazik*, who was not even five feet tall, made a noise like water on the burner and turned into a dragon, maybe nine feet high, complete with green scales, a tail, and protruding eyes.

(I only closed my eyes for a second; a coward I'm not.)

She made a terrible noise and knocked over the front rank of monsters with her tail. Then she turned around, gave the wall a swat, and I could see outside.

The dragon didn't wait around; she bolted through the hole. I followed. (What else?)

I didn't have to look behind to imagine what various monsters were *shpatsing* after me.

Let's get two things out of the way.

First of all, the stuff my little Asrai put into my eyes was fairy ointment, which, if you haven't guessed by now, has the power to break the spell of glamour, which, *nudnik*, I already explained.

But now, you may ask, how did Asrai suddenly turn from a faunlike young thing into a ferocious — albeit relatively small — dragon?

Remember, I gave you a clue: it only takes a drop of water to change a water fairy into a dragon. Well, I was *dershrokn*, as Moma would say — afraid, ready to make weewee — and I spilled the champagne, which was really pishwater, on her feet.

That saved my life, although I'm sure Asrai would have done something, anyway. She's a nice girl.

So I was running after a dragon, who was cutting quite a swath through back lawns, fields, and woods. Behind me were the Unseelie monsters, all shrieking and making unearthly noises, inspiring me to run all the faster.

Then, pop, just like that, Asrai turned back into a girl and kept running. Her feet hardly seemed to touch the ground. I *grepsed* and followed as best I could, but I felt that any second a cold hand would grab me by the neck and drag me into hell. (Modern Jews might not believe in hell, but then most of them aren't chased by monsters in Kerhonkson at one o'clock in the morning, either.)

"We're safe now," Asrai said, stopping at the northern edge of the woods. I looked around, still huffing for breath, and didn't see anything strange or terrible. Even the trees looked normal, instead of like trolls.

"Good," I said, regaining my composure. "Thanks for making like a dragon." No, I didn't ask her right away how she turned into a dragon. Sometimes it's better to leave well enough alone.

"Do you like me better as a dragon?"

"No, I like you fine the way you are." *Gevalt!*

"I'm not really a dragon."

"What, then?"

"A serpent — a worm, really."

Feh, I thought, but then I looked into those eyes, green as some primordial pond. What lovely eyes, what a child of the morning. Terrific, I didn't have enough trouble with the family, now I was falling in love with a worm. And it wasn't even Jewish.

"What about all those monsters that were behind us?" I asked.

"The Unseelie?" Asrai asked, then answered: "They won't cross out of the woods, it isn't their territory, it's ours. So don't worry."

Why be worried? Let the monsters take over. Maybe the killmoulis can become a comedian.

Asrai explained that the Unseelie were originally the guardians of the gold; they were the troops, and they've always followed the Seelie Court, of which she was a member. But times changed, and the Unseelie became resentful and destructive. Although the Seelie Court bore humankind no great love, by comparison with the Unseelie, they were saints — you should excuse the expression.

"But why are *you* here?" I asked.

"We never live where we're not wanted," Asrai said, looking at me with those eyes that didn't need light to make them shine. (Normally, I would be afraid of such eyes; tonight was not normal.) "You humans have been calling us again in your dreams. You dreamed us up."

"So you mean we're stuck with you and your Unseelie friends?"

"If you want me to leave . . ."

"No," I said quickly. "But I could do without the monsters."

"Then go tell you friends to stop dreaming terrible things and think nice thoughts."

"What's happened to my friend Hub?" I asked.

"He's on Unseelie territory, with the others, probably in a fairy ring."

"A what?"

"He'll dance his life away in a few minutes," Asrai said. "But that's subjective time — time is different for fairyfolk, if we wish it so — but I assure you he'll have a good time."

"Terrific. Can he be rescued?"

"Only a human can help him," Asrai said. "But he would risk falling into the ring himself. Would you be willing to take such a chance to help your friend?"

Of course not! It's a miracle that I've survived for my thirty-odd years, already. But as I stood by the edge of the forest with this lovely girl, my thoughts were pinwheels inside my head. Of *course* I would risk my life for my friend and make the world a better place.

"Can you help me?" I asked. But I was thinking libidinous thoughts.

"Maybe, if you ask my father." She smiled mischievously. "But, remember, you get nothing for nothing, as your mother says, Moishe."

"How do *you* know what *my* mother says?" I asked.

"I read your mind."

Now I was in trouble!

We made our way to Asrai's camp, which was in the hills beyond the forest. I wasn't afraid now — duergars and bogles and spriggans might as well have been a thousand miles away — such is the effect safety has on me.

The fairy hillsides, you should note, were beautiful, covered with twinkling lights, as if thousands upon thousands of fireflies were resting in the grass. And there were doorways into the hills, wherein banquets as lavish as bar mitzvahs in Westchester were being held. And the music . . .

But I would not be fooled so easily now; I had seen one such banquet before.

"*Shtumie*, you've still got ointment in your eyes," Asrai said. "What you're seeing now is real, no glamour."

Oy vay, now she speaks Yiddish by reading my mind.

"Don't read my mind," I said.

"It's hard not to," she replied. Again that mischievous smile.

"A man needs some privacy, would you watch me go *kacken*, too?" She did not reply to that, and I felt ashamed of myself. "So what should I say to your father?" I asked.

"What do you want to say?"

"Okay, I want to help my friend, get rid of the Unseelie monsters, make the Graubs — dive that it was — kosher again, so my friend should live and have work." As usual, I was getting carried away with myself.

"So you want us to help *you* get rid of the Unseelie host? That's a big order." Two dimples she had when she smiled.

And diarrhoea of the mouth I got. Now I was taking on, almost single-handedly, all the forces of darkness. That wasn't exactly what I had had in mind, but I nodded, anyway.

Remember what Moma said about stupidity and bravery?

"Who's your father?" I asked, changing the subject.

"He's head of the Daoine Sidhe — that's our family — and High King of the Hills. His name is Oberon. But he's very short, you should note, so make sure that you're always lower than he."

"I'm from the family of Mencken," I said, and she giggled as we walked in the moonlight toward her father's hill. Fairy-folk gave us curious stares as we passed.

I felt a bit better now and walked tall. Moma used to say, "In the land of the blind, the one-eyed man is king." King Moishe of Mencken the Tall.

Not bad.

Good-looking the great king was not (how could such an ugly man produce such a darling daughter?), but he was attended by a livery of pages dressed in scarlet and yellow, who, if such a thing was possible, were even smaller than he.

From killmoulis to king in a matter of minutes. My head was spinning. From king to *krenk* I was going.

The little king, with his bird's nest of a beard and owl eyes sunk into sourdough skin, wore a bejewelled crown and sat on a throne atop the highest hill. He used gargoyles (I'm sure they were alive) as armrests.

"Hello, king," I said, forgetting the "great". Asrai gave me a little kick and whispered, "Kneel!" I kneeled. *Feh.* Moishe Mencken could certainly not be doing such a thing.

"Howdy-doo, what do you want, Jewboy?" asked the *gonif* king. Enraged (you see, you can't get away from anti-Semites), I started to stand up; but Asrai rested her hand on my shoulder — a hand as light as down, and as strong as handcuffs. So I told the king that I wanted to save my friend from the Unseelie.

"That's all?" he asked, and Asrai explained that I had wanted to vanquish the Unseelie host myself, but she had talked me into coming here for a little help.

So what was I to do? Admit to being a coward? They'd give me back to the Unseelie, who would bake me for bread.

"Okay, you lead the fight," the king said, "and, maybe, with luck, we'll send them to New York City for a while. But they'll be back. You're starting a big *tummel*. Fighting and *tsuris*, that's what's in store for all of us."

"Maybe they'll like New York," I said. My knees were beginning to ache.

"Nah. Too much cement." After a considerable pause, he said, "Now, what are you going to do in return for *us*?"

"What do you mean?" I asked, raising my voice. "I'm supposed to be leading the fight."

"Big deal."

"Then what do you want?" — this time I added, "Great King."

"You like my daughter who saved you from the Unseelie, which she had no right to do." The king glared at his daughter. "Well . . .?"

"Yes," I said. "I like her fine." This meant trouble; I could feel it.

"Then it's all arranged. You marry my daughter, and make sure you keep her away from water when your *shlepper* friends are around. And if you mistreat her, I'll turn you into a cockaroach and send you home to your mother, so she should step on you."

For effect, the king said a bad word, waved his hand, and suddenly I *was* a cockroach, complete with feelers, barfbrown chitin, everything. I was too scared to be scared, but I can tell you one thing: Kafka had it all wrong, but that's another story.

"Well?" asked the king, after transforming me back into a normal person. "Is it a deal?"

What kind of a deal was that? Did he want to get rid of her so bad? *Gottenyu!* If I kiss her, will my saliva turn her into a worm? I told myself not to think about it. "What about this gold business?" I asked the king.

"Don't even think it," the king said, as he squeezed the ear of his gargoyle. "We keep the Unseelie's gold and maybe make a deal here and there, but you should know from the literature that gold makes trouble. If you want to make a deal, you have to live reasonably like the lower middle class, without temptation, so my daughter should have a nice life. Of course, if you don't want to make a deal with us, I'm sure the Unseelie would be interested in such a nice boy to bake into bagels.

"It's a terrible thing for a father to have to let his daughter marry a mortal," the king continued, "but you're all that's left." Father gave daughter a sneer. "Fairyfolk won't have her, you should be pleased to know."

"Why not?" I asked, not very pleased at all. But she certainly was pretty, and she had saved my life, and I would get out of this somehow . . .

"Because everything's on straight. My Asrai has no deformities, poor child. Look" — and he proudly lifted up his kirtle and showed me his chickenfeet. I looked at the page standing beside him and saw that his feet were backwards.

"All right, then," said the king. "It's done. One more thing, Mister Smartass. I can read your mind in Yiddish, Hebrew, Ladino, you name it. So if you even think bad thoughts about my little Asrai, it'll be cockaroach time."

This was some set-up. I stood up and turned toward Asrai. I was ready with a dirty look, cockroach or not, believe me.

Then I looked into her eyes. Who would not have fallen under such a spell? What loveliness! What perfection! (Better her spell than the bogle's.)

I immediately asked her to marry me.

Such is the mystery of love. *Oy*, Moma.

I spent such a night with Asrai that I won't even tell you about it. (The Great King was very cosmopolitan and had no objections to his daughter having premarital sex.)

Okay, this much I'll tell: fairyfolk are kinky. Me? I was doing a sacred duty, for it is written that whosoever does not unite with a woman in this life (providing he is a man) must return in the next and get the job done.

This way I wouldn't have to make a special trip later.

No rest for the weary! I was awakened at dawn by a bunch of chattering pixies and given what looked to me like a hockey stick.

Moma, sometimes half-wits make out, you should know. Your idealistic Moishe did not know that the Daoine Sidhe (and the whole Seelie Court) were the goody-goodies of fairydom. They weren't hot on killing, although they had a sinful weakness for turning human beings they didn't like into abominable things. I'm still afraid to step on a cockroach. Nu? It might be my Uncle Herman.

Instead of killing, they hurled. Hurling, I found out, was also very popular with the Unseelie. It's a bloody sport, a way of beating your opponent's brains out and still living to fight another day. Something like hockey.

It's really just a nice excuse to start a fight.

Which we did.

* * *

So there I was, Moishe Mencken, riding a fairyhorse shod with silver and leading the minions of goodness. Behind me were fairy knights decked out with all manner of jewels; their greaves and helmets were made of beaten gold, and they rode huge, beautiful horses.

Of course, I was scared, *Plotzing*, more like it. But Asrai was riding beside me like a queen, and I had no choice but to be a *mench*.

We met the enemy in a clearing by the edge of the forest. Even in the daylight, the Unseelie host looked dark and terrible. I could hear Moma's voice inside my head whispering, "He who runs away lives to fight another day." But I wasn't running. Not me. A moment such as this is a gift. Unfortunately, at the moment — I must admit — the thought that crossed my mind was that this was something right out of a Cecil B. DeMille film. And in colour, too.

The Unseelie host cried out (in unison, no less), "We're ready."

And our king, who was now sitting astride his horse beside Asrai, shouted, "Out with ye all."

Then the *tummel* began.

The Unseelie threw a golden ball toward me, which I struck with my stick (what a civilised way to resolve differences), and then with a great shout both sides ran to meet each other. My horse jumped forward with the others.

But no one, neither Seelie or Unseelie, made even a pretense of trying to hit the ball and play the game. They started, right off, to club one another.

I had enough to contend with: a balding witch was determined to bash my brains out with a stick.

Sometime during all his shouting and heavy breathing, I realised that maybe fairyfolk couldn't get killed at this game, but I could. Later, I found out that it's considered mandatory for fairyfolk to include at least one human in their wars. The good king had probably been looking for an excuse to grab the Unseelie's gold, all the while.

They were all *gonifs* and *gozlins*. While they were attacking each other, and probably having a helluva time, I was having enough trouble just staying alive.

Gottenyu, did the blood flow! Limbs were lost, maidens deflowered (probably for the umpteenth time!), and it all looked very real to me.

So how did I survive all this, you may ask?

Just as you thought: Asrai had turned herself back into a dragon and was felling the beasties and trows and bogles around me like a woodcutter working to a deadline. Her green scales were spattered with blood.

So she protected me (although I fought like a demon, you should know). For most of the day, I hid out on the edge of the field. Don't be so quick with the sneers. Remember what my mother said.

The carnage went on until dark, and then the Unseelie finally began to lose. The battlefield looked like something Dante would think up. Maybe all these spirit things could just go home and grow new heads and limbs, like worms. It was enough to make even a strong person such as myself want to *varf*.

What was left of the Unseelie began to make a buzzing noise. Then, just like that, they turned into a horde of insects — every kind you could think of, but mostly locusts.

They flew around and away, eating anything that was green, from grass to leaf, cutting a swath from here to New York City.

That locust business is a Jewish bit, you know.

Go read about it in the *Haggadah*.

Of course, everybody (except the locusts) was happy. The Seelie folk were milling about, shaking hands, hugging, and making a great roar, the Unseelie had flown away. Good riddance!

But my real work was still to be done. Even though the good fairies won, any mortal (remember Hub?) left in the Unseelie's fairy ring would become old and shrivel up and turn to dust like the bad witch in the Wizard of Oz. (*Shtumie*, where do you think Frank Baum got it from?)

As I said before, fairy time is different from human time. (Where do you think Washington Irving got the idea for Rip Van Winkle?) Even now, I might be too late. Hub might have aged sixty years in the last few hours.

Asrai and I made our way to Fishkill Craig, past the old barn, to the scraggly wood below the cliffs, where the fairy ring was lit by will-o'-the-wisp. A motley group of curious pixies and fairychildren followed us. The pixies were green as grass, and the fairychildren were all babyfat, blond hair, and hummingbird wings.

The ring was between two huge blackthorn trees, and it looked like a soap bubble — it had a shimmering, transparent surface, and inside I could see lithe figures dancing wildly. I could almost hear the fairy music, but we were still a safe distance from the ring.

"You'll be first inside the ring," Asrai said to me. "I'll follow, and we'll all make a chain" — she waved her hand at the pixies and fairychildren.

"What about *that?*" I asked, pointing to what I thought was a pair of eyes in the forest dark.

"Don't worry, Poppa's already made a spell for those on the outside of the ring. What's left of the Unseelie won't be aware of us, and those inside the ring won't notice, anyhow. They're too busy dancing."

I wondered what the king, my future father-in-law, was up to. Probably negotiating a contract with the Unseelie. I didn't trust him, but didn't dwell on the thought. If he happened to be reading my mind, it would be, as he said, cockroach time.

As we neared the ring, I could hear the most beautiful music that was ever played. Bach was boogie compared to this. All I wanted to do was dance, and Fred Astaire I'm not. (Indeed, that's the way humans are trapped in fairy rings. You hear the music, and then you're dancing with all the creatures from *Gehennà* until you fall apart.)

I saw all manner of horned and winged creatures hopping about with naked human beings. Such a frenzy!

And there was Hub! His pot belly jiggled like jello as he danced with a beautiful, blue-eyed goblin girl. She had primroses in her long, black hair.

"That's not so bad," I mumbled, developing a yen for that goblin girl, and then Asrai was daubing fairy ointment on my eyelids and in my ears. She used too much, and it stung like hell. (Maybe she was reading my mind again and got a little jealous.) But the music suddenly sounded like chalk rubbing across a blackboard. Now I could see that the dancers — monsters and humans alike — were filthy. And what a smell! Next to that, herring was perfume. The whole forest seemed to stink.

"All right, Mister Ladies' Man," Asrai said, "get into the ring and pull out your friends." She took hold of my belt and the waistband of my pants. "I'll hold onto you, but you must keep one foot outside the circle. If you fall completely into the circle, none of us can help you."

I was more than a little nervous about all this, but I crawled into the fairy ring like a natural-born, thank you, Moma, hero. The bubble-surface of the ring felt like wet cellophane: slippery and slimy.

Even with the fairy ointment in my eyes and ears and Asrai holding me by the pants, I felt a wild urge to break away and dance with the naked folk. But I have will power. I grabbed Hub — *feh!* he was as sweaty and slippery as a horse — and with a jerk pulled him out.

He promptly fell asleep. The bags under his eyes looked like windowshades, but he had not aged very much.

So I went back into the fairy ring to do the good deed. One by one, I pulled out every man, woman, and child. Each one fell asleep immediately. This was hard work, you should note, and seemed to take all night. Now you know: even heroism involves drudgery.

There were a few close calls, of course. Several times when I grabbed someone dancing with a kobald or a gnome, I was almost pulled completely into the ring — foot and all. But Asrai and the pixies and fairychildren held fast: they were stronger than I thought.

When I finally pulled out the last person, there was a great hue and cry. It was as if only now had the Unseelie seen what I had done. The gnomes and goblins and dwarfs — all the various demons — danced and spun even more wildly, and turned into goats and cats and dogs and creatures of the woods.

Asrai pulled me out, and I promptly fell asleep in her arms, ready to rest, at least for a while, on my laurels.

I deserved it!

You want the loose ends tied up now, right?

Okay, the Daoine Sidhe are still in the Jewish Hills, and Asrai and I visit them once a week. We got married, of course — a nicer girl you couldn't find — although we had some trouble at the wedding when the rabbi spilled some wine on Asrai. But she made it to the girl's room before she turned into a dragon; she waited there until she changed back into a girl again and then returned to the wedding. It worked out: Everyone thought she ran away because she was shy and afraid to marry such a worldly person as I.

We also visit Moma. Asrai sounds Jewish, doesn't it? Such a nice girl, my mother should complain? Anyway, Moma wants to be Grandma. So I'll be Moishe, the sower of dragons.

Of course, Hub's all right. If he wasn't, don't you think I would have mentioned it before? Asrai's father placed a cleaning spell over the Graubs and mixed up the fabric of time. When Hub and the others woke up, everything was as it was before. Nobody was lost, and all the hotel guests left on time to make their various appointments.

The gold I try not to think about. Asrai has been helping me with a few routines, and her father told me if I keep his daughter happy (which I do!), he'll book me in Vegas for a few weeks — the pixies need a vacation, anyway, he said. But any funny business with the showgirls and go forage for food with the other cockroaches.

So much for his liberal attitude.

New York City is still having trouble with the Unseelie, but that couldn't be avoided. (Better them than us!)

My father-in-law, the king, tells me they'll be back.

That I try not to think about.

There's a little of Scarlett O'Hara in every heroic type.

Just as I thought. Someone doesn't know the frog joke. Okay, just to prove to you that I'm not a mean person, here it is:

What's green and red and goes sixty miles an hour?

Shtumie! A frog in a blender.

No, I don't tell dragon jokes!

Moishe Mencken's
Yinglish-Yiddish Glossary: *
A Guide for the Perplexed

bar mitzvah/bas mitzvah — the ceremony signifying and celebrating passage
     into Jewish adulthood and responsibility. The *bar mitzvah* is for boys,
     the *bas mitzvah* for girls.

chutzpa — guts, nerve, presumptuousness. For example, it takes *chutzpa* to
     write this glossary.

dershrokn — the German word for *afraid*. Linguists might argue, but as far as
     I'm concerned, if my mother uses *dershrokn*, it's Yiddish!

---

* *Yinglish*: a term coined by Leo Rosten to mean Yiddish words used in colloquial English. Bagel is a Yinglish word. While I'm at it, I would like to acknowledge my debt to Mr Rosten's wonderful sourcebook, *The Joys of Yiddish* (McGraw-Hill, 1968). Go ahead, buy the book: you'll be a better person for it. Credit also goes to Harlan Ellison, he should live and be well. It was his glossary at the end of his story "I'm Looking for Kadak" that gave *me* the idea to do such a thing. You should read that story, too. You'll find it in an anthology by Jack Dann (who?) entitled *Wandering Stars: an Anthology of Jewish Fantasy and Science Fiction* (Harper & Row, 1974; Jewish Lights Publishing, 1998).

draykop — a confused or addled person. (See *meshugge*.)

dybbuk — a demon that possesses a person and makes him or her do terrible and crazy things.

farchadat — punchy, dizzy.

farshtinkener — stinky, stunk-up. Stick this word on anything you don't like.

feh! — a Jewish way of saying "phooey!" Say it loud and with gusto.

Gehennà — hell.

gevalt — a very versatile word. Use it as an exclamation when you're surprised or in trouble. What does your date say to the waiter when he brings the cheque? "*Gevalt*, I forgot my wallet!"

gonif — see gozlin.

goslin — some sort of demon. (But see *gozlin*.) According to Avram Davidson, *goslins* come "leaping through the vimveil to nimblesnitch, torment, buffet, burden, ugly-look, poke, makestumble, maltreat, and quickshmiggy back again to geezle guzzle goslinland." If you want to find out about goslins, you must read Davidson's perfect short story "Goslin Day". It can be found in *Wandering Stars*.

Gott — God. Frequently used as an exclamation.

Gottenyu — "Dear God." Use it like *gevalt* when you're surprised or in trouble. (See *gevalt* and *oy*.)

gozlin — a thief or swindler: a nonprofessional *gonif*. A *gonif*? He's the real McCoy — like the mafioso who lives next door.

grepse — when your mother picks up something heavy and makes that funny breathing sound — that's *grepsing*.

Haggadah — the narrative which recounts the bondage and exodus of the Jews from Egypt. It is read aloud at the table on Passover.

kacken — defecate. What all Jewish mothers refer to as "Number Two."

kosher — food that is considered "clean" according to the Jewish dietary laws. Certain meat and fish (such as pork and shellfish) cannot be eaten at all; beef, to be *kosher*, must be blessed according to ritual and slaughtered a certain way. In Yinglish, *kosher* means that someone or something is okay, authentic.

krenk — means sick in German; hence, an illness. *Krenk* can be used sarcastically to good effect: "Oh, so you want a tip for such lousy service? A *krenk* I'll give you."

mazik — a clever, devilish child.

mench — a real person, someone you can depend on, someone to be proud of. But don't tell your wife that she's a real *mench*. It's a masculine noun. Tell *her* she's a real *baleboosteh*. That's a feminine noun, and it means someone who's got it together, an owner, a runner of things — whether it's a job or the home. Got that?

meshugge — crazy. (See *draykop*.) A *draykop* looks at you funny and maybe he can't quite focus; a person who is *meshugge* (a *meshuggener*) hits you over the head with a Q-tip.

nu? — always say this with a question mark. Use it when you're surprised, disgusted, or questioning anything. Use it anytime: you can't louse this one up. "*Nu*, how's by you?" "*Nu*, again you need money?" "*Nu?* So all right already, I'll go look for a job." See what I mean? So *nu?* Go practise.

nudnik — a person who is a pain in the *tuchis* (ass) and, maybe, boring, too. Such a person you would not fix up with your sister.

oy — now this is a word you can use! Use it to indicate happiness, dismay, *tsuris* (See *tsuris.*), ecstasy, fatigue, pain, etc. It can be used anytime, with any emotion. Don't be afraid: you can't make a mistake. Try it: "*Oy*, am I (happy, sad, etc.)" If you're *really* happy, sad, etc., then say, "*Oy-oy-oy*, am I —" See how easy?

oy vay — it means "Oh, pain." It's used like *oy* (see *oy*), but it's even more emphatic than *oy-oy-oy*.

pisher — one who pees; a young, inexperienced person; a nobody.

plotz — to explode. "From such aggravation I could *plotz!*"

putz — the male reproductive organ. When you refer to someone as a *putz*, you're saying he's a jerk, a real idiot.

schlemiehl — a jerk, an unlucky fool.

shikker — drunk. Can be used either as a noun or an adjective. "He's a real *shikker*, that one," or, "Is he *shikker* again?"

shlepper — a jerk who is also a slob. (See *schlemiehl.*)

shtik — from German: piece. Often used to describe any distinctive or showy behaviour. "Picking his nose in public is a *shtik* with him." One can also say, "I'll have a *shtik* bread (piece of)." Notice I didn't say *shtik of* bread. That's bad form. So what's your *shtik*?

shtumie — use it as you would "dummy", and with some affection.

shul — synagogue.

shpatsing — from the Yiddish word *spatzier,* which means to walk, stroll, amble. Blame this on my mother, all you scholars who say you can't use the word this way. She makes up her own Yinglish. Wanna make something of it?

tsuris — trouble. That we all got.

tummel — means tumult in German. So it's any big noise or commotion.

varf — vomit.

zoftig — pleasingly plump. Only used to describe certain members of the fairer sex.

MARILYN

. . . .

I was fourteen, and she was stone white and naked and blond.

She was hazed in the pale cold light pouring in from the frost-shrouded windows of my bedroom, and I remember the dustmotes floating in the mid-afternoon sunshine, I remember the luminous living clouds of dust swirling around her great diaphanous wings, which seemed to shudder as she stepped toward the bed . . . my bed.

Those wings were white as tissue and seemed as fragile, as if they would break or crack or tear with the merest motion or gust of wind, and I remember her green-flecked eyes staring at me as she moved across my bedroom, which was filled with books and magazines and forty-five rpm records and pre-cut balsa models of World War II fighter planes (including a British Supermarine Spitfire MK XII that would be fitted with radio control) in various stages of completion, and I couldn't help myself, I looked at her breasts and at her naturally dark mat of pubic hair, and I was so terrified that I closed my eyes.

I remember, as if it had happened last month, rather than forty years ago.

It was the year that Buddy Holly, the Big Bopper, and Richie Valens were killed in a plane crash in Iowa. Alaska became the 49th State, which brought Texas down a peg, and Hawaii became the 50th. *Rio Bravo* and *Ben Hur* came out that year; Navy beat Army 43–12, and Mafia boss Joseph Barbara and forty of his "delegates" got busted at his house in Appalachian, which was about fifteen miles away from my home town in upstate New York.

I found the old book after my father died in 1987.

I was searching through the bedroom closet that he had always locked, and I was lost in the smells of cedar and old clothes — there were old leather key rings and wallets, a lifetime member Playboy card, a stiletto knife that he had taken away from me when I was sixteen, a taped envelope that contained an old black and white Polaroid photograph of a dark haired buxom woman — certainly not my mother — wearing the skimpy outfit of a belly dancer, and there were tuxedo studs and cufflinks and silver pens and penknives, playing cards backed with photographs of nude women, white plastic collar stays of varied size, cheque registers, an old will in a manila envelope, letters tied with a black ribbon, expired insurance policies, a woman's red silk handkerchief, and my paperback edition of *The Fundamentals of Self-Hypnosis and Yoga: Theory, Practice, and Application by Julian Rammurti, MA, MD.* Its spine was broken and pages fell out as I held it open in my palm.

Dad had never told me he had taken the book. Nor had he ever told me that he had taken the stiletto.

I remember how keenly I had felt the loss of the book at the time, But that was only because it was mine . . . because it was the first book I'd found on the subject . . . and because it worked. I could find other books on yoga and hypnotism, which I did. I lived in libraries and learned clinical theories and models and techniques, and I'd even developed a flair for stage hypnotism, which was the antithesis of the careful, quiet clinical process. For an instant — standing there in my father's closet, a grown man discovering the secrets of his youth, savouring the presence of the living past — I saw myself, as if in a mirror: a thin, gangly, pimply-faced boy of fourteen once again, straight brown hair greased back with pomade, red button-down shirt, collar raised, leather jacket, black pegged pants. The boy sneered into those books, indeed, as if he were looking into a mirror. A poor reflection of Elvis.

Reading . . . reading about posthypnotic suggestion and methods for creating the state of yoganidra. The powers of tratakam. Lucid Dreaming. The state of somnambulism. Hypermnesia. Prana and Pranayama. The story of the man and the bear.

I've often remembered that story of the man and the bear. It went something like this: There was a psychiatrist who was wounded in France during the Second World War. As he recuperated in a military hospital in Cornwall, he grew bored and occupied himself with a posthypnotic suggestion. He'd hypnotised himself and conjured up a great bear to provide some comic relief from the day to day boredom. All he had to do was say "Bear" and count to five and miraculously, a huge white polar bear with a long, flexible neck would stroll upright into the ward, leap about in the aisles, try to mount the nurses, frolic around the other patients, or hunch against the psychiatrist's bed and allow himself to be petted. So the bear cavorted in the mornings and afternoon, and likewise all the psychiatrist had to do was count to five and the bear would disappear. The bear had no weight, made no noise, could somersault in the air, walk on the ceiling, deftly unbutton nurses' blouses with its curved yellow claws, remove bras, and dance with any of the variously undressed doctors, nurses, patients, and visitors, who were never the wiser. The psychiatrist also conjured up the bear every night as an antidote to counting sheep, but the apparition soon began to take on a different, more ominous aspect in the dark. It became more aggressive, would not always obey commands, and when it leered, a feat the psychiatrist was certain no other bear could manage, its fangs seemed much longer than they had been during the day. So the psychiatrist mumbled "Bear", counted to five, and disappeared his ill-conceived creation.

But the bear was not so easily dismissed.

It appeared the next night, unbidden, and the next day it snapped at the nurses and bit the psychiatrist on the forearm. A warning. Although it left no marks, of course, the psychiatrist was in excruciating pain for hours.

The psychiatrist had to hypnotise himself three times to get rid of it.

Nor did that work . . . entirely; and years later, the bear would oftimes appear — a vague, threatening form in the distance — and follow the psychiatrist, who developed the disconcerting habit of always looking behind him.

So I lay on top of the prickly wool blankets of my neatly made bed and waited for Marilyn Monroe to come to me, to change me completely — change me from an awkward, pimply-faced adolescent into a full-blooded man who knew the moist secrets of women, who'd actually and really been laid, even if through the devices and snares of an altered state of consciousness known only to hypnotists and young dabblers in the arcane such as myself.

It didn't matter how I did it. What mattered was that I *did* it.

I had floated, fallen, drifted, breathed myself into the deepest, most profound state of hypnosis. I had imagined myself rowing a boat on a calm, shallow, infinite sea, every breath took me farther out upon the placid ocean, breathing in, breathing out, skiffing in smooth clockwork motion, each breath out, each breath in taking me farther, farther into a calm azure place without depth, without horizon; yet I could feel everything around me: the wool of the blanket itching my neck, the cold smoothness of the pillowcase as I moved my head, the cold chill seeping in through the windows, and I saw her in that instant as I blinked open my eyes and shut them tight again. The woman who inhabited every adolescent male's dream. Walking toward me, a look of blond rapture on her painted full-lipped face — six shades of lipstick, I knew about that, Marilyn I love you, and I waited for her, waited in the dark bosom of my self-directed dream, waited for her to come upon me, slip beside me, touch me, guide me, sail me across the sea of my quickening breathing, sail me out of my virginity.

I would lose my cherry to an apparition, a ghost, a hallucination, but at thirteen, in North Leistershire, New York, population 16,000, in 1959, that was the best I could hope for.

With my eyes closed — I do believe they were closed, but perhaps they were not — I could feel her walking toward me, past the built-in, beige-painted bookshelves that housed my father's mystery collection, which he'd always kept in my room, past the door that connected to my parents' bedroom . . . walking under all the mobiles and models that floated just below the ceiling and defied gravity by mere threads; and then she was standing over me, standing beside the bed, standing beside my slippers and sneakers and cordovan dress shoes, and I *knew* that she was leaning, leaning over me now — I could hear her shallow, patient breathing and the rustling whispering of her wings, smell her overly sweet perfume mixed with a more acrid, damp odour — and all I would have to do was take her in my arms, she would fall into my arms like pillows and soft toys and cushions; and all I had to do was open my eyes to see her breasts and I could raise my hands to touch them.

All I had to do was open my eyes.

I tried. I *had* to see her. I had memorised her from a hundred photographs: the mole above her swelled lips, the eyelashes heavy as cardboard, the eyelids white as chalk, the earings dangling, everything about her swollen and curved and fleshy and full of promises —

But in that instant, in that terrible instant of realization or proffered possibility, I felt everything change. I know it was my own fault, my own perverse nature, but somehow I suddenly changed the rules. Much as I desired to bring Marilyn's warm body close to my own, to enter her and lose everything I hated and instantly gain my manhood, I imagined something else instead.

In that terrifying, transforming instant I imagined that whatever I was most afraid of now stood in Marilyn's place, and I dared not open my eyes for fear of what I would see, yet I was afraid to keep them closed because it was unbearable *not* to see what was looming over me, suffocating me, watching me; and I remember the slow-motion tossing and turning and shaking, as the sea I had drifted too far upon began to rage and rise; and, in fact, I was caught between fear and desire. I could not tell how long the convulsion lasted, but once I awakened to the world of slanting sunlight and the familiar smell of bedsheets and air-freshener, I vowed never to hypnotise myself again.

After that Marilyn never came to me in my dreams, but the dark thing that I had conjured in her place shadowed me.

Like the psychiatrist who kept looking over his shoulder to check whether his great white bear was tailing him, so did I feel the presence of my apparition. But unlike the psychiatrist, who at least knew his enemy, I could only sense this manifestation of my fears. In my teens I thought of it as a monster shaped something like a bear, and I imagined its claws tapping on macadam or sidewalks, and I would turn quickly, just to check, and, of course, there would never be anything there, at least not anything untoward. Over the years, I gave up on monsters, for they, too, ceased to inhabit my dreams. My dreams had one recurrent element, and that was more an experience of synthesthesia: they would all, at one stage or another, take on the colour of deep purple, yet the colour would be more like damp mist, which felt thick and ominous and signalled danger, but the mist was the stuff of the world in my dreams, and it would bleed out of the sky and buildings and people — just as it would bleed out of myself — dying my monochrome dreams with purple fear and anxiety and uncertainty.

But I wasn't the beast entirely. Only part of it.

The dreams coalesced into reality one numbingly cold dark morning in Vietnam.

It was January 1969. We'd been stuffed into a deuce-and-a-half, one of three trucks going out of Phu Bai down south where the fighting was supposed to be heating up. Everybody was shivering, and I remember sitting perfectly still because it was warmer that way, and Joey Mantaneo was pushed against me like four o'clock on the D-train going to Brooklyn, and even in the cold he smelled like cordite and rot and piss (and that cordite smell should have alerted me that something bad was crawling toward me), and he had his war name SCARED SHITLESS painted across his flack jacket and stenciled on his helmet like he was military police, and I knew the story about how he got his name — but he was the only one in Bravo who'd never been wounded or sick, not even an infection when he cut his finger. He claimed he was a street-fighter and his gang was called "The Road Gents", even though nobody in the gang had a car, and he said he knew as much about killing before he came out here as he did after, but he always looked scared — he just had that kind of a face — and when he was green somebody said he was scared shitless and so he took that name for himself. The guy who named him was dead, but SCARED SHITLESS wasn't. Neither was BURNT COP and CALL ME WHITE, and they'd been brought up in a black bopping gang in Philadelphia called "The Flicks", whatever the hell that meant, and the rest of the guys were farmers or factory workers or mechanics — I was the only college boy, and they called me "Professor" — and they named themselves BORN TO DIE, BORN TO KILL, KILL OR BE KILLED, KILLER ANGEL, and if you believed everybody, every one of them was a stoned killer street-fighter and a drug-dealer and a hustler and a pussy-magnet, but we were all just kids. Full of piss and vinegar eight months ago, but now exhausted and sick with the shits and fungus and getting bald and everything else. And while the goddamn truck rocked and jittered in the muddy craters that was supposed to be the convoy route — I was black and blue from being thrown around in that can — everybody was singing and whistling "Reach Out, I'll be There", and then "Mellow Yellow", and Cop and

Mantaneo and Sammy Chitester were singing in falsetto, so it sounded like we had women in the chorus, and then everybody did Otis Redding's "Sittin' on the Dock of the Bay", and they were pretty good.

We sounded like a rock band without microphones coming through the storm that had kept up for days, and it seemed like the world was going to stay dark and moonlit forever; and everything was covered with leaves that blew all over like home in October, but nothing else was like home: the houses along the way that were still standing were burned and pitted from shells, and there were refugees that looked like they ought to be dead and buried walking along the road; some were wounded, and although the old people didn't seem to pay any attention to us, the rest looked at us like we were the enemy; they hated us, even though they were too afraid to say word one; and we just crashed and bounced and sang and whistled through the dark, through the rain and fog, and you would have thought you were at the South Pole or something where it was twilight all the time, and then we blew out our transmission, and although a few of the guys got on the other two trucks, the rest of us marched.

We went twenty clicks before we finally bivouacked in a deserted village that wasn't far from the Citadel of Hue.

It was cold and wet and dark and I couldn't stop shivering.

Viet Cong could have been all around us, for all we could tell, even though we'd caught up with our trucks and guards were posted and the place was secured, but I didn't care about anything. None of us who'd done the marching copped guard duty, and I would have fallen asleep if I had; it was as if someone had pushed a button and all the life just went out of me. I couldn't even eat or relieve myself. I just wrapped myself up in my poncho liner and fell asleep in an empty hooch. There were bits of glass all over the floor that would sometimes catch the light like little green and yellow and orange and blue gems, the kind sold in the hobby stores along with crystals and beads, but I didn't dream about that . . . I didn't dream about jewels and beads and velvet and cold empty darkness.

I didn't dream at all.

But dreams or no dreams, we were up before first light; and our orders were to go the rest of the way, wherever that was going to be, on foot because they needed the trucks up north (where it was safe), and so we watched the deuces drive off and then we walked to paradise. That's what it looked like, anyway, and before we realised what was happening, most of us were dead. Only Joey Mantaneo and I survived, and Joey, of course, didn't even get a scratch, but he suffered later, went half-crazy with recurring nightmares; at least that was what I heard, only I can't to this day remember who I heard that from.

I didn't suffer any nightmares . . . after that I couldn't remember my dreams.

We were approaching the south bank of the Perfume River, and there were the smashed walls of what had once been beautiful French-style villas of the southern sector of Hue; and spread out before us was lush grass and fog swirling like we were walking on a carpet through clouds — the grass was deep green from all the rain, but there was a metal smell to the air; and although that mist didn't look purple, like in my childhood dreams, I sensed that this place was wrong, that it was hazy and purple and that the purple was about to bleed out from the sky and me and everyone else, but I just couldn't quite see it yet.

For all that I just said, this place was picture-perfect: a lone sampan on the river, an old man riding a bicycle up the avenue that ran along the park, for we were walking through a park. I remember breathing in and looking around, and then I saw a flash and heard an explosion, and Mantaneo screamed "Motherfuckers!" or maybe that was me, but it didn't matter because there was another explosion and I realised that I was lying flat on the ground and looking up at the sky and watching watching watching for the purple, watching waiting for the change, please God make this just a dream, and I heard a gurgling noise and a wheezing noise, and I remembered the training film I'd seen on sucking chest wounds, and I just figured my chest had been blown out and I was dying, but I didn't think "Oh my God I'm dying" or "Mamma".

Everything was still and cold and quiet as a winter morning, and Marilyn came to me, just like she did the first time.

I could smell her damp perfume and then I could feel her coming toward me and studying me like she was a doctor and I was a patient, and then she lay down on top of me, straddling me; her pale face pressed against my neck, her stiff blond hair tickling my chin and lips; and I could feel her body moving against mine, and her wings, feathered white, layers and layers of down, covered us, sheltered us, and I felt myself inside her, felt the cold ether wetness, felt myself being drawn into her, into down, into feathers, into the swirling mists of cloud, drawn into a silent, cold heaven.

* * *

Mantaneo saved my ass that day by pulling me into one of the VC's tunnels, and we hid in a dark, damp, earthy room. By all rights, we should have met up with its owner; but, as I said earlier, Mantaneo always had the right luck and never got hurt. The way I heard it later, he just waited until the VC left and somehow managed to keep me alive.

I never saw him again to thank him.

And, of course, I don't *remember* what happened.

After I came back to the World, as we called coming home in those days, I waited for Marilyn. I liked to think that she came to me every night in my dreams. But since I couldn't remember dreaming, it was moot.

My shrink told me that once I'd worked everything out and regained my health, I'd remember my dreams again. The shrink, of course, attributed everything to Post-traumatic Stress Disorder, which had become the fashionable diagnosis for everything that had happened to every grunt in 'Nam. I argued that I didn't exhibit any of the other symptoms of PTSD: diminished interest in activities, feelings of detachment from others, exaggerated startle responses, sleep disturbances, survivor guilt, memory impairment, recurrent dreams of a traumatic event, or trouble concentrating. I'd put myself through law school — memorised the Uniform Commercial Code and fifty cases a night, and I won't believe you can do *that* without concentration and a good memory. But he was not to be dissuaded. He figured that I was having nightly traumas; I just couldn't remember them.

I couldn't argue that kind of logic, so I stopped seeing him.

Eventually, of course, I started dreaming again, and I was, indeed, having recurrent dreams, but whether or not they were traumatic, I couldn't tell you because all I could remember was that they were about wings — gauzy, translucent wings that sometimes looked like feathers, sometimes like down, and sometimes like the surface of a soap bubble. I suppose I became obsessed by the very idea, obsessed with flying frogs and flying dragons and flying fish, with horseshoe bats and redwings and griffon vultures and hummingbirds, with hawk moths and wasps and hovel flies . . . and with those who like me couldn't fly. I spent hours at the botanical gardens watching the swans and remembering Marilyn's wings fanning and spreading; and I wondered, I tried to remember: were they white and feathery or were they gossamer rainbows settling around me like silken sheets, billowing, as alive as the surface of the sea?

I usually remembered them as white and feathery.

The wings of angels.

I started dating blond women — how I yearned for pale skin and white-bleached hair — and then I married a petite, dark haired woman, may she rest in peace, and we had children and lay in bed every night, and some nights she knew I wasn't with her. I would dream pretend that she was someone else, and then for an instant the sheets would become wings.

Josiane died of ovarian cancer under cool white sheets.

I had always thought that the next time — if there were ever to be a next time — I would find myself looking at the monster that was unseen but terrifyingly present when I'd first conjured Marilyn out of an old book about hypnosis.

Every night I lived with the anticipation, with the desire and the fear — waiting for Marilyn, or the monster, Marilyn, monster; and my bones grew, my hormones changed, as did the colour of my hair — from blond to brown to grey, as the years passed me through Binghamton Central High School, Broome Community College, Vietnam with its smells of cordite and damp familiar colours of fear, Hofstra University in Hempstead, Long Island, where I drove a Buick Le Sabre and wore tie-dyed tee-shirts, Brooklyn Law School, clerking for Bernstein, Haversham, Lunquist, Esqs — from associate to junior to senior partner, from Brooklyn to Brooklyn Heights to Manhattan to Connecticut; marriage, children, vacations, fourteen-hour days, weekends on Fire Island, divorce, reconciliation, death, Josiane's dead, say it, admit it, there, fact, and through it all, through all the empty and disconnected nights, all that was left were desire and fear. My whole life a moment wrapped around anticipations of dreams . . . or nightmares.

Marilyn or the monster.

I did finally find them.

I'd received an invitation from my old unit to attend a reunion. It had been thirty years. I looked for Joey Mantaneo in the columns of names and addresses between the grainy photographs, but he wasn't mentioned. I was listed alphabetically, home address, home phone, business phone, just like all the other officers and noncoms and grunts. There I was, a ghost in black letter type, but Joey had disappeared.

That night I dreamed about him.

While the little black and white television blinked ghostly light into my bedroom I allowed myself to follow him, skipping around time like it was an old neighbourhood, and I found him in Bayonne, New Jersey, where he was working as an electrician for the building firm of Calley & La Cross, or so I dreamed; and Joey's wife was named Louise, and he had three daughters, Marsha, Missie, and Mave, and in that dream I'd forgotten the names of my own daughters, but didn't follow that trail, lest I dwell upon how I'd failed my children and my wife, and how I — but that wasn't important; I was following Joey. I'd always be safe with Joey because he was a survivor; he survived, survived the bopping gangs and the drugs and everything else and I wouldn't let myself drift back into Vietnam, but Joey led me right back. He took me through his father's candy store and showed me how he'd grown up. He took me to Larry's Bar, which was across the street from his three bedroom apartment on Stadler Avenue, and we sat at the bar, which had a brass rail to rest your feet on, and we drank boilermakers, dropping the shot-glasses filled with Johnny Red right into the beer mugs — all the regulars had their own personal mug at Larry's. We drank three shots and beers, and I felt an overwhelming sadness as I looked at Joey, an overwhelming longing. He had lost most of his hair, had put on weight, which changed the shape of his face — took out the definition and sharp, clean good looks and replaced them with a softness that was somehow repellent; and Joey smelled bad; he was dressed in jeans and a faded shirt, and he leaned over and told me that he was still in Hue, still in Vietnam — that *we* were still in Hue — and that's when the dream broke apart.

It had been so real, as not to be a dream, although I knew that bits and pieces were wrong, that there was no company called Calley & La Cross; those were just names from the war, but Joey leaned toward me, then grabbed me by the shoulders and —

We tumbled into the VC's tunnel, back into that cold, damp morning near the Perfume River, and I was lying against the dirt wall, sitting up, while Joey pressed his hand against my chest and said, "Jesus Christ, Jesus Christ," and there were a few rays of light coming in from the entrance above, and they were golden and seemed as solid as the blades of ancient bronze swords, and I watched the dust swirling through them, swirling swirling and I remembered my room in Leistershire, remembered lying on the bed and counting myself into a hypnotic trance, into a deep state of somnambulism, and I was fourteen and about to conjure up Marilyn out of my adolescent desires and the light pouring in through my windows, light filled with dustmotes dancing swirling, promise, everything filled with promise and —

Then Joey stopped fussing with me, and we could hear someone scraping around above. Somebody shouted *"Chew hoi, chew hoi,"* which meant surrender, but we could tell it was our own boys; we were all taught *Chew hoi, Yuh tie len, lie day* — surrender, come out with your hands up, and then concussion, blinding light, the cracking of thunder, and then silence as my ears popped, and I felt sudden wetness all over me, sonovabitch whoever was up there couldn't wait to take prisoners, or find out who the hell we were, and I wiped my face, everything smeared with blood, Joey, Joey was all over me. I looked around, light now pouring in from the entrance that was forward and above, pouring in like mist, which swirled, turning everything to blood, and I was holding Joey's torso, but his arms and legs and head had been blown off, and I was a liar, he wasn't lucky, or maybe he was.

I closed my eyes, but the blood and light and mist could not be closed out; rather everything slowly darkened to purple, and I could feel myself tossing and shaking in slow-motion, and I remembered having convulsions before, but now it didn't matter if I closed my eyes or opened them, I'd found the monster — Joey, Joey, goddamn it, and I screamed and opened my eyes and the mist and the fog cleared and I could see her, standing in the entrance that was flooded with light, pure blazing sunlight, cold winter morning light. She was moonlight white, and naked, and her eyes were drawn in black and her lips were smeared with blood and as she reached toward me, coaxing me out of the earth, her wings spread out reflexively; they were butterfly blue fans, deep azure, darkening, darkening into purple black, and they quivered, trembling to the meter of her perfectly measured pulse, and I remember

I remember

I whispered "Mamma"

Just like every other grunt who thought he was about to die.

THE BLACK HORN

• •

From his oceanfront room on the tenth floor of the Hotel Casablanca, Judge Stephen Steiner saw the unicorn standing in the shallow end of the swimming pool below. It was almost four in the morning, and most of the Christmas tree lights of the gambling ships three miles out on the ocean had been turned off. The expanse of beach ahead was dark and ominous, except for a single light that burned to the left on the beach that belonged to the Fontainebleau Hotel. But the Casablanca pool was illuminated by green and red underwater lights, giving the breeze-blown surface of the water an almost luminary quality, as of melted, rippling gems.

The unicorn looked greyish in the light, although surely it was white, and large, at least eighteen hands high from poll to hoof. Its mane was dark and shaggy; and at first Steiner thought it was a horse. But how strange to see a horse running loose on the beach at such an hour. There must be *laws* prohibiting animals from running loose, he thought. Miami Beach is a densely populated area . . . surely there must be a law. Perhaps this horse had run away from its owner . . . perhaps it was part of a road show . . . a circus.

My God, Steiner mused, how long has it been since *I've* been to a circus . . .?

It was then that Steiner noticed that the horse had a horn protruding from its wide forehead. He hadn't noticed it before because the horn was black . . . and also perhaps he didn't see it because he'd *assumed* he was looking at a horse, and horses didn't have horns. But now Steiner could see that horn. It looked like black marble. It was long and fluted and would make a vicious weapon. The horn reflected the green and red light as if the light were oil flowing along its conchlike spirals.

The unicorn dipped its horn into the pool, as if to neutralise some chlorine poison in the water, and then drank.

Steiner reached for his glasses, although he didn't really need them for distance. It couldn't be, he thought, yet there it was. Perhaps it was some advertising gimmick, but Steiner discounted that thought immediately. No one would let an animal run loose at this time of night, horned or otherwise.

Then the animal raised its head, as if sensing that it was being watched. It blew air through its muzzle and looked up at the building, slowly turning its head, scanning the windows on one story, then going on to another, until finally it seemed that the unicorn had found him. It seemed to be looking right *at* him, and Steiner felt transfixed, even through the thick, protective pane of glass. The unicorn knew he was there.

It was looking at *him*.

Steiner felt drawn to it . . . it was as beautiful as a childhood fantasy. Yet there was something dangerous and even sinister about it; its very being challenged Steiner's reason, and Steiner himself. Steiner felt an almost uncontrollable urge to smash through the window and jump . . . as if by some sort of television magic he'd be able to leap through the glass and land on the unicorn's back.

He found himself pressing dangerously hard against the plate-glass window as he stared down at the animal below that was still as stone, watching him.

Suddenly he *wanted* to jump.

"No!" he cried, feeling sudden, reeling terror, for he knew in that instant that if he could have jumped, he would have. It was as if he had glimpsed his own death deep in the eyes of that beautiful horned stallion staring up at him from the pool.

He turned away from the window and closed his eyes tightly, so tightly that everything turned purple for an instant. Then, slowly, he turned back toward the window. There was nothing there, just the metal lounge chairs situated around the illuminated pool, and the dark beach and ocean stretching into flat darkness. He looked to his left, toward the dimly lit Fontainebleau beach, but there was no sign of anything there, either.

Steiner closed the curtains and sat down on his uncomfortable double bed. His hands were shaking. He reached for a bottle of kosher brandy on the nightstand beside him and took a shot right out of the tinted green bottle. The stuff tasted like hell; it was coarse, not made as well as in the past — or perhaps he just remembered the past as being better in all respects.

He suddenly thought of his wife, Grace, who had died six months ago, God rest her sweet soul. Although he had been separated from her for over ten years, she had waited . . . waited for him to come back home. But he just couldn't have gone back. Grace would have been a constant reminder of everything Steiner feared. He needed younger women to feed his ego . . . to be in awe of him. They all probably thought he had money, but they were his only barricade against the fustiness of old age . . . against death itself. They kept him feeling young.

He felt the old guilt weighing down upon him. Grace, I'm sorry . . .

The air-conditioner was on; it suddenly felt cold in the room. The graft on Steiner's back, where he had had a melanoma removed, hurt him tonight.

He'd inquire tomorrow at the desk whether there were any reports of a horse running loose. It *was* a horse, Steiner told himself, as he lay his head against the lumpy, overlarge pillow.

But he couldn't fall back to sleep.

After morning prayers in the makeshift synagogue on the fourth floor of the hotel, Steiner met his three sisters for breakfast. He escorted them to their table on the eastern side of the grand old dining room, which overlooked the beach and the perfectly blue ocean beyond. The table was prepared, and their waitress was waiting to attend them. Behind each setting was a glass of borsch mixed with sour cream. An unopened box of egg matzoth stood in the centre of the table, as prominent as a bouquet of freshly cut flowers.

Steiner sat each of his sisters and then himself.

It was Passover, and Cele and Kate and Mollie had decided it would be better for Steiner if they all spent the holiday together at a hotel. Steiner could not disappoint them . . . somehow he would get through it. Although Cele was quite well off, she lived with her two sisters in Flatbush. Those two counted their pennies as if they were all being chased by the specter of relief.

But Cele would spend her money for a good cause, especially if it involved family and religion . . . so this was a real vacation for them. And who knew how long Steiner might have them, anyway? Cele was the youngest, and she was seventy-seven.

Steiner was five years her junior . . .

"It's another *beautiful* day," Cele said brightly, placing her green linen napkin on her lap. She wore a crisp red flowerpot hat that matched her square-shouldered jacket with patch pockets. It was as if she had never left the 1940s. Her dyed blond hair was combed down smoothly, and tightly rolled up at the ends, and she was growing a bit thin on top. She had a long, oval face with great blue eyes, the same lively eyes that used to tease Steiner sixty years ago. Cele was going to make the best of her vacation in the sun. "Don't you think so, Stephen? Isn't it a beautiful day? Of course, you *live* here in Florida, so sunshine is probably old hat to you."

Steiner managed a smile, but he was in a disagreeable mood. Two hours of sitting and standing and praying with a congregation of evil-smelling, doddering old men had sapped him of all *joie de vivre* . . . had soured his morning. Although Steiner had always prided himself on being a religious man — he donned his prayer shawl and phylacteries every morning to pray toward the east, and it was to just that habit that he attributed what wealth and fame and good fortune he had acquired over the years — he couldn't *stand* being around old people. It was as simple as that. Steiner glanced uncomfortably around the room. Just sitting in the dining room made his flesh crawl — this entire hotel seemed to be filled with the most Orthodox and the oldest of Jews. Association could kill you . . . *would* kill you. Make your flesh shrivel right up. That was another reason why Steiner had never gone back home; even before his beloved Grace had died, she smelled of the grave. Her skin had turned wrinkled and dry, and she exhuded an odor that could not be concealed by even the most expensive perfume.

He turned to Mariana, his waitress, who was ready to take their orders. Her very presence lightened his mood. She was Brazilian, dark, strong-featured, with full lips and tilted green eyes; her wiry black hair, though disguised in a bun, was long. She couldn't be more than twenty-one, the epitome of youth itself. Steiner flashed her a smile and ordered breakfast for his sisters and himself. He felt as if he were swelling up, regaining everything he had lost upstairs in the synagogue; and he heard a pompous affectation come into his voice, which was rather loud and bombastic, but he couldn't help himself... and anyway, a fine, articulated sentence had *always* impressed the young ladies.

When Mariana left and the busboy was out of earshot, Steiner's sister Kate said, "You know, Stephen, you make a fool out of yourself talking like that to the waitress." Kate was two years older than Cele, and she seemed to bear a grudge against any woman under sixty... or so Steiner thought. Kate had once been beautiful, high-breasted and thin-waisted, but now she had become puffy. She dyed her hair orange-red. Steiner nicknamed her "the Flying Nun" because she wrapped paper around her hair every night so it wouldn't muss.

"I'll thank you to mind your own business, ma'am," Steiner said stiffly, still using the artificial inflection he used with people he wished to impress. Cele gave Kate a nasty look and shook her head. Mollie, who was the oldest, didn't seem to be listening; instead she began talking about her children, who were supposed to visit her the week after Passover.

"Well, he *does* make a fool out of himself," Kate said to Cele.

"Stephen's right," Cele said, speaking sharply but in a low voice. "Mind your business."

"We can't even talk to each other around here," Kate said petulantly, as she smoothed out the napkin on her lap. Kate was overdressed in a silk gauze summer dress trimmed with black; she also wore a small pillbox hat with a veil.

"Why are you wearing a veil this morning?" Steiner asked. "You look like you're still in mourning."

"Well, I am ... and you should be, too!" Then she caught herself. "I'm sorry, Stephen. I'm just not myself this morning —"

"On the contrary, you're very much yourself this morning," Mollie interrupted. Mollie wore a tan suit and blouse. Her hair was grey and frizzy, and she had a crinkly, Irish-looking face.

"Mollie, shut up," Kate said, and then continued talking to Steiner. "I didn't sleep well last night at all. I have a canker sore or something in my mouth, and my whole jaw's killing me. I don't even think I'll be able to eat."

"Oh, she'll eat," Mollie said sarcastically.

"And for your information" — Kate was still talking to Steiner — "I'm wearing a hat because this is a religious hotel, and religious women are supposed to wear hats. I can't help it if the hat has a veil."

"She's right, Stephen," Cele said. "Look around, all the women are wearing hats." She self-consciously adjusted her own hat.

"Of course I'm right," Kate said softly, indicating by her tone of voice that she was willing to drop the argument.

Mariana brought the food, purposely serving Stephen first, which stimulated a *tss*ing from Kate. Steiner teased the waitress by telling her how beautiful she looked, and she blushed and backed away.

Cele changed the subject by saying, "I think we should all sit by the pool when we're finished with breakfast. That would be nice, wouldn't it?"

"I'm going upstairs," Kate said. "I'm not feeling at all well."

"Kitty, you can take me upstairs with you," Mollie said. She was slightly infirm, and had trouble navigating stairs by herself.

"I think we should *all* spend at least a few minutes together in the sun," Cele said firmly — although she was the youngest, except for Steiner, *she* made all the decisions for her sisters.

"He shouldn't be out in the sun with his cancer," Kate said petulantly.

"You see, there she goes again," Mollie said to Cele. "Always starting *some*thing."

Cele flashed Kate a nasty look, and Mollie seemed pleased with herself. Then Cele said in a calm, quiet voice, "The morning sun in not dangerous, I'm told . . . it's the afternoon sun that has the dangerous rays."

Steiner nodded without paying much attention, but he always sided with Cele. She had enough of a cross to bear, living with and supporting her two sisters. He looked up and smiled generously at Mariana as she cleared the table. He could see the tiny dark hairs bristling on her arms, and could smell her slightly pungent musk-like odor. She returned his smile, her cheeks dimpling, and for an instant their eyes met. Steiner felt his heart pump faster . . . felt his glands open up. He imagined making love to her . . . imagined her naked and holding him like a baby in a dimly lit bedroom. She would be beautiful naked, he thought, daydreaming about how she would look with her hair undone and hanging loose down her bare back. She would look like a wild animal . . .

She's a perfect madonna, he thought . . . but then he had thought that about every waitress and shop clerk and hatcheck and typist he had ever dated. Perhaps later, when his sisters went upstairs for their afternoon nap, he'd work up the courage to go into the hotel kitchen and ask her out. He could buy her a tall, lemony drink by the pool, talk to her in whispers, caress her, and then take her back to her apartment . . .

That thought alone gave him the strength to take his sisters outside to the pool, where they could gab and complain and gossip in Yiddish with their newfound octogenarian friends and neighbours.

Steiner did not go upstairs with his sisters, but made the excuse that he wished to take some more sun and maybe a walk before going inside. Cele seemed a bit agitated that he would get sick from *too* much sun, but he promised to sit in the shade near the cabanas. Steiner felt nothing but claustrophobic in the presence of his sisters.

"I wouldn't mind taking a walk myself," Cele said, standing over him and looking forlornly out to sea. "Come, we'll take a walk now down Collins Avenue, and then you can sit in the sun if you really want to."

"Well, *I* have to go upstairs," Mollie said. "My feet are *killing* me."

Kate, who had wanted to go upstairs earlier, now said, "I wouldn't mind taking a walk and doing some window-shopping. It might be good for me, make me forget how much my jaw is aching me."

"Well, I can take Mollie upstairs and —" Cele said, but she gave up in mid-sentence, accepting her responsibility to her sisters. Steiner could see the trapped frustration in her face. "All right," she said resignedly, "I suppose we should just go upstairs . . ."

"I'll take a walk with you, Stephen," Kate said.

"Either we'll *all* take a walk or we'll all go upstairs together," Cele said, her hands gently shaking, whether from age or anger, Steiner didn't know. But he felt guilty, for he had sacrificed Cele to them just so he could be alone . . . Cele deserved better than that. The poor old girl . . .

But Steiner was on his feet as soon as his sisters disappeared into the side entrance of the hotel. It's too hot out here anyway, he told himself, sweating under his polyester powder-blue shirt and matching slacks. He wore a white jacket and white loafers. As he passed, the gossips and wrinkled sunbathers nodded to him and said, "Good morning, Judge."

Steiner hadn't been a judge for thirty years, and even then had served only one term. But Steiner like the title — it opened "doors" for him. Everyone called him "Judge" at the very exclusive Boca Club, where he was a member. In fact, he had had the heraldic blue and white gold emblem sewed on all his sports jackets. Of course, he didn't attend very many functions there, as they were very expensive. But he had been known to take his dates to the club for swanky luncheons. Perhaps Mariana would visit him at his home in Fort Lauderdale, and he could take her, too . . .

He was immersed in that daydream as he stepped through the coffee shop beside the pool area and into the large kitchen behind. There were busboys and waiters and waitresses bustling around, carrying large aluminum trays in and out of the two wide swinging doors that led into the dining area. Cooks and helpers were working at sinks and long wooden tables. Squashed prunes and apples and matzo brie and puddles of soup and juice and coffee discoloured the white tile floor.

Mariana stepped backward into the kitchen, pushing the door open. She was holding a tray filled with glasses and dishes and silverware.

"Mariana!" Steiner said, overly loud. She turned to him, looking surprised, but no one else seemed to notice his presence . . . or care.

She put the heavy tray down on one of the tables and said, "Yes, Judge? Is something wrong?" She tilted her head in a most attractive manner, Steiner thought.

"Yes . . . I just thought —" and suddenly the words left him. He felt awkward and foolish . . . and suddenly paranoid that she would think he was a "dirty old man". But that was plain stupid! He told himself. She doesn't even know why I'm here yet. "Do you have any plans for this evening?" he blurted out. But even as he spoke, he realised that he had lost the advantage entirely . . . that now *she* was in the position of power.

"I'm not sure what you mean, Judge," she said, looking uncomfortable. "I'll be taking care of your table tonight, is that —"

"No . . . I mean, would you care to have a drink with me *after* dinner, after you've finished working. Perhaps we could meet at the Fontainebleau . . . by the bar. It's very nice there."

"Well . . . I don't know." She was actually blushing. *That's* a good sign.

"I'll be waiting for you at poolside at ten o'clock," Stainer said with authority, feeling much better about the venture now.

"I'm really not supposed to be going out with the guests," she said coyly, her eyes averted from his. "I could get fired, and —"

"Well . . . *I'll* be waiting for you at" — Steiner looked at his thin gold watch for effect — "ten o'clock sharp."

"I've really got to get back to work, please . . ."

"Ten o'clock," Steiner said smartly, using his best judicial tone. Mariana nodded once, shyly, her eyes still averted from his.

Steiner turned heel back to the pool area.

Once outside, back in the sun, he felt relieved and full of nervous energy. He felt like a schoolboy dreaming about the girl he was going to take to the senior prom. He couldn't stand the thought of going back to his room or sitting in the hotel lobby, which smelled of old age and was filled with urns of fake flowers and plants. He couldn't bear to look at another old man or woman. He couldn't sleep, and he had just eaten.

He just wanted to be alone and daydream . . .

He found himself walking along the sand toward the ocean. Perhaps he'd walk along the beach to the Fontainebleau. Have a drink, and then return down Collins Avenue, thus making a circle. But once he reached the Fontainebleau and saw the pool and bar to his left, he just didn't feel like stopping. He was too filled with energy to stop and sit, so he continued walking, enjoying the brisk breeze coming off the ocean, the healthy smell of the salt air, and the pounding of the surf just inches away from his sand-encrusted white loafers. He dreamed about Mariana . . . and imagined himself as a young man courting her, a young man with thick black hair and a strong, handsome face. A strong man eyed by every bikini-clad woman he passed . . .

But Steiner was beginning to swelter in the afternoon heat. The sun was unbearable, and Steiner had misjudged how much of it he could take. The ocean breeze, which was at first cool and refreshing, now felt hot and muggy. He turned around and started back to his hotel.

Thank goodness he didn't have far to go.

Steiner wouldn't have seen the unicorn if it hadn't made a snorting noise as he passed. It stood behind a dozen one-man red and white sailboats leaning against an old pier that was in disrepair. It stood in the shadows, as if to cool off.

The unicorn carefully stepped out from the boats and gazed at Steiner with its ocean-blue eyes. It pawed the sand with its heel, sending ribbons of sand into the air to be carried away on the wind.

Steiner stopped, transfixed again by the unicorn. He broke out in a sweat, but it was cold sweat, and from fear rather than heat. "What do you *want*?" he asked, feeling foolish talking to an animal like this, but he had to break the spell with *something* . . . a word, the sound of his voice. Suddenly Steiner was aware of a myriad of tiny details: the soft pinkness of the unicorn's muzzle; the white whiskers growing out of its chin and nostrils; its coarse, shaggy white mane and fetlocks; its cloven hooves worn from the sand; and the strange, ridged black horn that looked as if it had somehow erupted from the animal's forehead. In fact, it looked glassy, as if it might have indeed been formed from lava. In the bright sunlight it took on a reddish sheen, which seemed to deepen at the tip. Steiner was acutely aware of the splashing and gurgling of the surf, but he couldn't make out any *human* sounds, except for his own quickened breathing. This was an empty stretch of beach. Steiner was shaking, and he felt weak. The animal was so *large*. It looked like a huge Morgan, with its muscular back, strong neck, and large head. It stood square, its legs right under its shoulders. The unicorn was overpowering . . . yet it *seemed* to be gentle. It didn't move, but seemed to be made of porcelain and coal. It just stared at Steiner; and it was as if the unicorn's eyes were blue magnets pulling him closer . . . and Steiner imagined how it would be to ride this great beast, to feel its bulk beneath him and the wind whistling in his ears and the salt spray biting his chest and face. He could ride it along the beach . . . along the ocean.

The unicorn took a cautious step toward Steiner.

Suddenly Steiner remembered last night and broke the reverie. He stepped back in terror, almost falling over his own feet. The unicorn took on an entirely different guise as Steiner remembered how he had wanted to jump from his window at the mere sight of the beast. The unicorn — as if reading Steiner's thoughts — whinnied and pawed the sand. Then, ready to charge, it lowered its head.

The sharp black horn was pointed directly at Steiner.

And Steiner saw the unicorn for what it was: death. Death in its simplest, most beautiful guise. "No," he whispered to the beast. "No!" he screamed, hating it. He turned from the unicorn and ran, his narrow-toed Italian white loafers heeling into the soft sand. His eyes burned and seemed to go out of focus as he ran. His heart felt as if it were pounding in his throat. He could *hear* the unicorn behind him. He could *feel* the unicorn's horn at his back, ready to slash him wide open.

But Steiner wasn't ready for death. He wanted to live. He *had* to live. If death was going to take him, it would have to take him on the run. Steiner wasn't going to make it easy. He wasn't going to slip into any eternal slumber with a toothless goodbye. Not Steiner.

He ran as hard as he could, the blood pulsing in his chest and head, making him dizzy, until he tripped over a tangled, polished piece of driftwood and fell headlong into the sand. He turned backward, resolved to face death with his eyes open.

But the unicorn was gone . . . disappeared. There were no tracks, except for his own, no outline of equine heel or bar or furrow in the soft white sand. Steiner tried to catch his breath. He felt at once relieved and anxious. He *had* been chased by something. His breathing began to return to normal, but he had a flash of searing pain in his abdomen, and his arms and shoulders felt heavy and began to ache. He broke out into a cold sweat. He felt clammy and chilled and nauseated. It was the fall, he told himself . . . and the exercise. He hadn't run like that in forty years.

But one thing was certain: he *had* seen a horse with a horn. It might have been some sort of publicity trick, but it was no hallucination. Steiner wasn't the type to hallucinate. He might have had some crazy thoughts when the beast was chasing him, but then, who wouldn't? He felt foolish, running as he had. The damned thing obviously hadn't been chasing him, or he would have seen it when he had turned around. Actually, if it had *really* been chasing him it would have run him through with that horn in no time flat.

Still . . . it *had* to be some sort of publicity stunt, Steiner thought.

Steiner told his sisters he wasn't feeling very well and stayed in his room. He forced himself to take a swallow of brandy and tried to sleep, but he felt feverish. Frenzied, unconnected thoughts flashed through his mind. He tucked himself under the covers. The pain seemed to lift.

I'm *not* crazy, he thought, raising himself up on his right elbow to gaze below. The ocean was turquoise green in the shallows and deep cyan blue farther out. The sun was bright and warm and reassuring. Although no one was swimming in the pool, there were over thirty people sitting in deck chairs and chatting while others walked about. Everything was perfectly all right, exactly as it should be, as ordinary as bread.

Then Steiner saw the unicorn lift its head out of the ocean.

At first, he thought he was seeing a wave, a distant whitecap, but there was no mistaking that black fluted horn. There were those blue eyes and thick white mane and muscular neck. The unicorn rose out of the water, revealing itself little by little as it moved into the shallows, until the water was only up to its knees and it walked forward, kicking, lifting its long legs out of the water, onto the beach. The unicorn was dripping wet and as big as life. It stood on the edge of the empty beach and looked up at Steiner, as foamy water purled past its hooves. It *knew* Steiner was there. It had come for him again.

"Go away!" he shouted, as he shakily got up from his bed. As the pain began to radiate into his shoulders and arms and chest, he pulled the curtains closed.

But he knew the unicorn was still out there, waiting . . .

Stainer felt much better by dinnertime. He had rested, and the aching in his arms and chest was gone, as were the sweats and fever. Steiner was prone to night sweats, anyway. He was apprehensive about opening the heavy curtains, so he left well enough alone . . . he had had enough excitement for one day.

He dressed informally in tan shirt and slacks and went downstairs to pick up a newspaper in the lobby. He leafed through it outside the shabby hotel shop that sold magazines, newspapers, aspirin, suntan lotions, cheap trinkets, and sunglasses. He was disappointed — there wasn't even a mention of a circus, or a carnival, or a runaway horse . . . or a unicorn. Well, *someone* must have seen the damn thing, too, he thought. Surely, it will be in *tomorrow's* papers.

He put the newspaper back on the rack and met his sisters for dinner in the dining room. He felt a bit hesitant about seeing Mariana before their forthcoming tryst at the Fontainebleau, but it couldn't be avoided. If he *didn't* show up for dinner, she might think he was ill or not interested, and she might not meet him later. Still, he felt uncomfortable. But when she took his order, and Steiner smiled at her, she returned it. She even blushed. That made Steiner feel very good indeed.

Everything else went along as it had for the past five days. Cele and Kate and Mollie discussed the menu and chose each dish with care, but when the food actually came, each one complained bitterly that she should have ordered a different entrée. Kate complained about her sore mouth. Mollie talked about her children and "the grandkids" and told Cele that the veal was the wrong colour.

After dinner and a wink at Mariana, Steiner accompanied his sisters to the obligatory 7:30 show in the ballroom, where the hotel rabbi — a slick stand-up comedian, who had made records and played the Catskills every year — was performing. Steiner didn't listen to the stale jokes. He kept glancing at his watch. After the show, he kissed his sisters good night and went to his room to change into fresh, more formal clothes for his date with Mariana. He felt a bit weak and dizzy, but he was determined to go out tonight, as if he had to prove something to himself.

As he entered the room, he examined himself in the full-length mirror on the bathroom door. He had a shock of white hair, which was yellowed a bit in the back; deep brown eyes; a thin nose; and a full, sensual mouth — it was a strong, angular face that had loosened with age. Although the face-lift two years ago had helped, lines still mapped his face. But he certainly didn't look his age.

He began to feel anxious here in the room, but he made a point of not going near the closed curtains. He could hear the faint murmur of the surf; it was like gentle white noise. He wondered if the unicorn was still out there as he changed into a smart-looking chocolate brown suit with a matching tie and a white-on-white shirt. His brogues were a bit scuffed; he reminded himself to buy polish. He concentrated on small details.

But he couldn't leave the room this time without finding out if the unicorn was still out there. He pulled open the drapes and looked out the salt-stained window ... he looked by the pool and on the beaches ... he looked at the white-crested black waves of the ocean.

The pool area and the beach were empty.

There was not a unicorn to be seen.

Steiner took a small table in front of the enclosed driftwood bar poolside at the Fontainebleau. The pool was huge and kidney-shaped, and Steiner enjoyed a tall whiskey and soda while he watched floodlit water cascading down a stonework waterfall into the pool. Palms were spaced around the pool area, and green and blue lights gave the place a festive, romantic atmosphere. To his left were the glass doors that led into the Fontainebleau shopping centre; to his right, across an expanse of lawn, was the new ten-story addition to the hotel. Cozy paths wound their way between palmettos and hibiscuses, and the ocean was a dull, dark pounding behind him. Guests in evening clothes, in jeans and tubetops, in bathing suits and clogs, in gaudy slacks and Hawaiian shirts promenaded past him. Two callow-looking, teenaged lovers walked by, hand in hand, followed by a small group of executives and their wives. The whole world seemed to be carved into *twos*. But Steiner felt strong with excitement and anticipation; he felt dashing, good-looking, if just a trifle tired.

As he sat, waiting, two women who looked to be in their late thirties sat down at the wooden table beside him. One was dumpy-looking and plump; she wore clogs, white Bermuda shorts that were too tight for her, and a very revealing pink halter top. Her hair was blond and coarse, obviously bleached. Her companion, in contrast, looked quite demure. She was tall and skinny, with short-cropped brown hair and a long, hollow-cheeked face. She wore a blue outfit — a blue blazer and a pleated white and blue skirt — which was actually quite stylish. But she had the worst teeth that Steiner had ever seen. Her two front teeth were long and crooked and widely spaced, and one protruded beyond the other. Obviously, they should have been pulled long ago. She must be a country girl, Steiner thought. Country people don't take care of their teeth . . . they hate dentists.

Steiner ignored the women and waited for Mariana. He gazed at the path that led from the shopping centre: the direction that Mariana should be coming from. He sipped his drink and eavesdropped on the conversation of the men at the bar. From what he could overhear, they were microprocessor executives from Atlanta here on a convention. They talked mostly about getting laid.

The blond woman kept smiling at the men at the bar. To Steiner's surprise, the ploy worked, because when the waitress came to take her order, one of the men insisted on buying the blond woman a drink. He was rather good-looking in an athletic sort of way . . . what the hell would he want with someone like *that*? Steiner mused. Steiner couldn't help but stare. The man sat down, winked at his friends at the bar, and put his arm around the back of the blond woman's chair. She was cooing and shifting about, smiling and nuzzling closer to the man as introductions were made. The other woman craned her long neck slightly to join in the conversation, but she looked uncomfortable, although she was the type who *always* looks uncomfortable. Steiner watched the executive lean forward to get a better look at the blond's breasts; but Steiner was caught staring by the tall woman, who was looking directly at him. She smiled at him without revealing her teeth. Steiner nodded curtly and turned away.

That's *all* I need, he told himself. But he was getting anxious. Where *was* Mariana, anyway? It's ten o'clock already. I was a fool not to have gotten her home phone number. Dammit! Perhaps I can call the hotel . . . she just might be working late. Steiner called from the bar, where the rest of the men were taking bets on whether their friend would get laid or not. Steiner watched the burly executive making his pass at the blond. Then Mr Lareina, the maître d', came to the phone and told Steiner that Mariana had left shortly after nine. "All right, thanks," Steiner said and hung up. He wasn't going to abase himself by asking for her home phone — Lareina wouldn't give it out, anyway.

Stainer sat back down at his table. He felt dazed. He brooded and stared out at the pastel-lit path leading to the Fontainebleau. Perhaps Mariana went home first to change.

Then he saw her. He straightened up in his chair, and waved excitedly to the dark-haired woman approaching the pool area. She was walking quickly on high heels, as if late for an appointment. Steiner felt a warm rush of anticipation. He started to get up as she approached . . . and only then realised that she *wasn't* Mariana. Up close, she didn't look like Mariana at all. She looked quizzically at Steiner, who was half out of his chair.

Steiner was mortified. He sat down reflexively. How could I have made such a mistake? He asked himself. He thought about going home, slinking away, crawling into his cool, uncomfortable bed, but he just *couldn't* leave. Mariana *had* to show. He *wouldn't* be stood up! Pain began to radiate once again throughout his arms and shoulders, then down into his chest.

"Girl troubles? Asked the skinny woman sitting at the table beside Steiner. She had a thin, reedy voice.

Steiner turned toward her. "I *beg* your pardon," he said, annoyed.

The woman tried to smile without revealing her teeth. "Your friend . . . she might just be late, that's all," she said nervously. But she was persistent. "Why don't you have a drink with *us*? We'll cheer you up, we're good company . . . and here I am a third wheel. Help us out."

"Thank you kindly, but I don't think so," Steiner said. The skinny woman pouted, an exaggerated moue.

"Oh, c'mon, buddy *I'll* buy you a drink," the executive said as he self-consciously ran his hand through his short-cropped hair. But Steiner knew his type, all right. He had probably been a bully when he was a kid, and a ROTC lieutenant in the army, and now he's some sort of zipperhead IBM-type manager who makes life hell for everyone under him. He was obviously looking for a way to cut the blond away from her friend, and he was trying to use Steiner as a foil. "C'mon, what the hell," the man said, flashing a boyish smile, and he jumped his chair toward Steiner and then pulled his table over until it was touching Steiner's. The blond woman laughed when the drinks spilled, and then she and her friend moved their chairs closer, too. Steiner was too embarrassed to do anything but accept the situation. He felt even more uncomfortable with the skinny woman pressing close to his elbow.

The executive waved down the waitress, and Steiner ordered another drink, which he didn't need . . . he was achy and dizzy as it was, and his right arm felt numb. "So, friend, where do you hail from?" the man asked Steiner as he massaged the blond's arm, purposely letting his fingers brush against her breast. The skinny woman leaned closer to Steiner, as if expecting him to answer in a whisper.

"I'm from upstate New York," Steiner said. "Binghamton." He felt his skin crawl. The woman was *too* close to him. She smelled of cheap perfume, and she had chicken skin. God . . . he could imagine what she *really* smelled like.

"Is that so," the skinny woman said. "I've been through there. I used to live in Milford, Pennsylvania. Small world, isn't it?"

Steiner didn't have anything to say to that; he just leaned away from her and nodded glumly.

"I'm from Detroit," the executive said. "I'm in systems management . . . mostly consultation work for engineering firms. What's your line?"

"I'm a judge . . . was a judge, I'm retired now," Steiner replied.

"A *judge!*" the skinny woman said, brightening. "Jeeze, we don't have *any* manners here at this table. I'm Joline, and my friend here is Sandy, and he's . . . *oops*" — she said, turning to the man from Detroit — "I've forgotten your name."

"Frank," the man said, paying the waitress for the new round of drinks.

"I'll take care of that," Steiner said stiffly, automatically, but Frank wouldn't hear of it.

"You haven't told us *your* name," Joline said.

God, she has a chalkboard voice, Steiner thought. "Stephen," he mumbled.

"That's a very nice name," Joline said, warming to her role as Steiner's new companion. "It fits you, somehow."

Stephen felt trapped at his own table. He began to perspire. Joline primly sipped her drink — something white and frothy in a tall, frosted glass — through two short narrow cocktail straws. Steiner was of the opinion that sipping a drink through those straws, which were made for decoration, was like drinking coffee out of a cup without removing the spoon. Joline wriggled toward him. Every one of her movements seemed exaggerated. "I think you take life very seriously," she said, looking at him intently, as if she were working her way into something profound.

I've *got* to get out of here! Steiner thought. He looked at his watch, making it very apparent that he had other things to do. Frank and Sandy certainly didn't take any notice; they were kissing each other right there at the table like two high school kids on a bench at a roller-skating rink. I *can't* be seen with these people, Steiner told himself. Jesus Christ . . . He glanced at Joline, who smiled and blushed a little and then firmly pressed her leg against his. She looked somehow limp, as if waiting to be embraced. Oh, Jesus . . . Steiner thought.

Frank whispered something to Sandy and then said to Steiner: "Steve, if you've no objections, we're going to take a little walk . . . we'll be right back. Give you two a chance to talk. Nice meeting you."

"See you soon honey," Sandy said to Joline, smiling warmly as she stood up.

"We'll hold down the fort," Joline said shyly, her knee still wedged woodenly against Steiner's.

"Would you care for another drink?" Steiner asked Joline after the others had left. He had to say *something* to her. Her silence was oppressive, and he was uncomfortable enough as it was.

"Yes . . . thank you." Joline didn't seem to be able to look at Steiner now that her friend had left, but she leaned against him until he said, "Excuse me," and tried to disengage himself.

"You aren't going to leave me here alone, are you?" Joline asked. There was a pleading in her voice, and suddenly Steiner felt sorry for her . . . she was lonely and ugly and past her prime. He felt both loathing and pity. "No . . . I'll be right back," he said as he stood up.

"Promise?" Joline asked coyly, trying to smile again without revealing her crooked teeth.

"I promise," Steiner said. Jesus, Mary . . . he thought as he walked away. Is *that* the way Mariana saw *me* . . . the way I see that poor girl at the table? Could I be *that* repulsive to her? He knew the answer . . . he was an old man wearing old man's pastel clothes. He was an old man carrying a Jewish bankroll. No! he insisted. His skin might be like old clothes, but *he* wasn't old. Suddenly he understood why his wife, Grace, may she rest in peace, had become obsessed with butterflies. She had *filled* her house with butterfly-shaped bric-a-brac before she died.

He walked to the far end of the bar, as if he were going to the men's room, then ducked under the rope that separated deck from beach. Joline would be sitting back there alone, waiting. But I *can't* go back, he thought. He shivered at the thought of kissing that mouth . . . feeling that long, protruding tooth with the tip of his tongue . . . smelling her odor.

He walked along the surf's edge, shoes squishing in the wet sand, and he became lost to the sound of waves pummeling the shell-strewn beach . . . lost to the waiting darkness ahead . . . lost below the clear sky filled with clusters of silent stars.

He passed a small hotel, which had one beachlamp on overhead, and standing upon the shadow line was the unicorn. It had been waiting for Steiner. It stood tall and gazed at him, only its great horned head clearly visible. The unicorn's blue eyes seemed to glow, the same melting, beautiful colour of the water in the Blue Grotto in Capri. Steiner stopped, and suddenly remembered being in Europe as a young man, suddenly felt the selfsame awe of the world he had once felt. He also felt lost and empty. He grieved for himself and for the poor woman waiting for him at the Fontainebleau. What would she tell her friends when they returned? Would she, indeed, even wait for them?

Steiner gazed back at the unicorn, trying to make certain it was real and not just the play of shadows, or his imagination. It was *not* his imagination, he told himself. Staring into the unicorn's eyes seemed to stimulate memories he had forgotten for years:

He remembered swimming in the Mediterranean. He remembered a two-week vacation in Atlantic City with Grace and his two sons. He remembered riding bicycles on the boardwalk with his family. He remembered cooking eggs at four o'clock in the morning after a party and permitting the kids to come down and eat, too. He remembered his first trial . . . as a lawyer and as a judge. He remembered uneventful days with Grace . . . beautiful, precious, never-to-be-recovered days. He remembered coming home to problems with the boys and sharing dinnertime conversation across the table with Grace.

And he suddenly, desperately missed it all. He wanted the days back!

He also remembered the nameless women, and how Grace had begged him to come back. She had waited, but couldn't wait long enough. He wanted to go home . . . to Grace. He looked into the unicorn's sad eyes and saw himself, as if in a mirror. He was an empty old man who had lost his life to foolishness. He had wasted all of Grace's love . . . and now it was too late to make reparation.

Tears trembled and worked their way down his face, and the unicorn stepped toward him. It walked slowly, as if not to frighten him. Steiner stepped to the side, but did not try to run. The beast lay down beside him and rested its head in the sand, a gesture of submission. Steiner nervously extended his hand towards the unicorn's muzzle. The unicorn didn't flinch or move, and Steiner stroked its forehead. He touched its fluted black horn and saw that is tip looked red, as if dipped in blood.

He felt a contentment radiate through him as he stroked the unicorn. He also felt the throbbing return of the pain in his chest and arms, yet as the pain became greater, so did his sense of being removed from it. As he rested against the unicorn, he felt it quiver, then begin to move. It raised its head, all the while watching Steiner, but before it stood up, Steiner pulled himself upon its back. I *can* ride the beast, Steiner thought as he held onto its coarse mane as the unicorn brought itself to full height.

"Come on, boy," Steiner whispered, feeling an almost forgotten heart-pounding joy. The unicorn sensed it, too, because it broke into a playful canter. It shook its head, as if miming laughter, and kicked its hind legs into the air. Steiner held the horse tightly with his legs. He felt his youthful strength returning. He felt at one with the unicorn. The unicorn jumped, galloped, and stopped short, only to sprint forward again. It ran full-out, edging closer to the sea, until it was splashing *in* the water. Steiner was shouting and laughing, unmindful of anything but the perfect joy of the moment. Steiner felt wonderful. For the first time in his life, everything was *right*. He felt he could do *anything*. He was at one with the world . . . and he rode and balanced on the back of the unicorn as if he had spent the past forty years of his life riding the wind.

Suddenly the unicorn turned and headed straight out into the ocean. Waves broke against its knees and chest. Steiner's legs were immersed in water. "What are you *doing?*" Steiner shouted joyfully, unafraid but holding on tightly to its neck. The unicorn walked deeper into the sea, past the breakers, until it was swimming smoothly and quickly through the warm, salty water. The sea was like a sheet of black glass, made of the same stuff as the unicorn's horn. It seemed to go on forever.

As the dark water rose over Steiner, he finally accepted the wreck of his life.

The unicorn lifted its great head as it descended into the sea. Steiner took hold of its red-tipped horn, and the unicorn carried him gently down into the ocean's cool, waiting depths.

BAD MEDICINE

He woke up coughing, pushing his way out of the dream and into the secure and familiar darkness of his bedroom. His wife Helen stirred beside him, then turned over, pushing her rump against him. He looked over at the digital clock on the nightstand: it was five-thirty in the morning.

He sat up in bed. He had a long drive ahead of him, and he was nervous about going. That was why he had slept fitfully during the night. It was a relief to be awake, to be *going*. The morning darkness made everything seem unreal now that he was sitting up in bed, already removed from the security of everything he knew and loved. He felt like a ghost in his own house.

Who the hell would have thought that he, of all people, would be getting into this kind of stuff? Into religion, and Indian religion at that . . . as if his own wouldn't do. Christ, being a Jew was hard *enough*. Well, he thought, if I hadn't met John, then it probably would have been something else. He was looking for *something* . . . some kind of meaning, something that rang true. An authentic religious experience. He'd smoked the pipe with John, who rented the furnished room under Stephen's real estate office, smoked it out of curiosity, or perhaps just to do something he could talk about. But when he smoked that pipe in the woods with John, he felt . . . something, something that breathed power and truth. It was as if Stephen could somehow *feel* everything the earth felt . . . he couldn't verbalise it. He still couldn't say if he really believed. But he was *willing* to believe.

He smiled to himself. He was a realtor turned mystic.

"Steve?" Helen mumbled, then, as if finding her voice, she said, "What are you doing up at this hour?"

"I told you, I'm going with John to that guy's vision-quest ceremony."

"Oh, Jesus . . . why don't you just take us to the Temple? The kids would like that. It *is* Saturday."

"We've been over this a million times," Stephen said. "I know how you feel, but this is something I want to do. Please try to understand. Think of it as a passing phase, male menopause, something like that."

She reached toward him, but he was too geared up to make love. His mind was on the ceremonies, on the vision-quest and the sweat-lodge. Some guy was going to sit naked on top of a hill without eating or drinking for four days . . . just to have a vision. Screaming for a vision, they called it. And he, Stephen, was going to sit in a sweat-lodge . . . if he could survive it.

He wished he could just make love to Helen and make everything right. But he *couldn't*. He just couldn't turn himself on and off.

She drew away from him; he knew she was hurt and angry. "First it was all that Zen-Buddhism business at the college," she said, "and then that pseudo-Jungian philosopher, that self-styled guru, what was his name?"

Stephen winced, and shook his head. "I don't remember . . ."

"And then there was the Transcendental Meditation kick, and that goddamn EST, which you dragged *me* into. Christ, that was the worst. They wouldn't even let you go to the bathroom during those stupid meetings. And now it's something else. Do you really believe in all this Indian business?"

"I don't know *what* I believe in."

"And I don't know why I converted . . . you don't seem to want to have anything to do with your own religion."

"We did it for the family," Stephen said lamely. Helen had always been a religious woman; she *knew* that God existed. Perhaps He'd made Himself known to her in the operating room, amidst all the cancer and broken bones and smashed skulls. She was an operating-room nurse. She had told him that it didn't matter whether she was Christian or Jewish. God was God. But Stephen shouldn't have asked her to convert. Now he had a responsibility to her which he couldn't live up to. He was a hypocrite . . . and now Helen had nothing. She wasn't comfortable in the synagogue without him; it was a foreign place to her.

"I did it for you," she said softly. She always looked the best to Stephen in the morning, her thick long black hair framing her childlike face, "I don't know what you think you can find with those Indians. I think you're getting into something dangerous. You're not an Indian."

"Just bear with me a little bit longer," Stephen said. "I feel I have to do this." He kissed her and stood up. "Go back to sleep, I'll be back tonight and we'll talk about it."

"I'll be here," Helen said, yawning. She'd been on call all last night and had only slept for a few hours. "I do love you . . . I hope you find whatever it is you're looking for . . ."

John was waiting for him on the metal steps which led up to Stephen's real estate office. He was wearing a woollen shirt over a torn white tee-shirt, faded dungarees, worn boots, and a vest with lines of bright beads worked in geometrical patterns. He was in his early sixties, and he wore his coarse white hair long in the Indian fashion. His face was craggy and deeply-lined. That face looked as cracked and baked as the earth itself, as if it were some undecipherable roadmap of the man's past. On his lap he held a soft white and blue rolled-up blanket. Inside the blanket, protected, was his ancient pipe and an eagle's wing.

The morning light was grey, and the air was still full of the night's dampness.

John stood up when he saw Stephen, but he paused, looking at the sky as if something was written there that he couldn't read. Then he got into the car and said, "I stopped being *wrong* today." Stephen looked perplexed. "You know," John continued, and then he raised his hand to his mouth as if he were drinking from an invisible bottle. "Gonna lay off the booze. Gonna stay straight . . . I figure I owe it to Sam, the guy we're going to see, to help him out with his ceremony."

Stephen got onto Route Seventeen easily; there was hardly any traffic at this time of the morning, especially on a Saturday. Those who were going to the Catskills for the week-end had already left last night or would be leaving later today. The light fog and slanting morning sunshine gave the mountains a dreamlike appearance, as if they'd been painted by Maxfield Parrish.

John kept his window open, even though there was a chill to the air. The breeze made Stephen uncomfortable, but he didn't say anything to John.

John seemed to be looking for something, for he kept leaning forward to look upwards out of the windshield. "What are you looking for?" Stephen asked.

"Eagles."

"What?" Stephen asked.

"When I became a medicine man," John explained, "I was given the gift of eagles."

"I didn't know you were a medicine man."

"A sweat-lodge man can also be a medicine man . . . and vice versa. But I'm a good sweat-lodge man; that's probably why Sam wants me to help him out with his sweat."

"You never talked about being a medicine man," Stephen said. He wasn't going to give John the chance to change the subject so easily.

"I haven't been a medicine man for a while. Booze and medicine don't mix."

"What did you do when you were a medicine man?" Stephen asked.

"Same things I do now, mostly . . . except for the drinking. I used to help people out."

"How do you mean?"

"Just help out."

"Like a doctor or a minister?"

John laughed at that. "Maybe like both."

"What do the eagles have to do with it?" Stephen asked.

"They're my medicine."

"You're talking in circles."

John chuckled, then said, "I always went on binges. My downfall was always the booze and the broads, but then I'd pray my ass off and try to be right again and sooner or later the eagles would come back, I'd look up and there'd always be one or two just circling around, way the hell up, and, man, those eagles would keep me on the straight path, keep me good, until I just couldn't stand being right and I'd go and get messed up and leave all my responsibilities behind, and I'd lose the eagles again. I haven't had them for a couple of years now, since I've been on the booze. And I've been paying for *that*, you'd better believe it. Now I'm right again, I think maybe they'll come back."

"I still don't understand," Stephen said. "Are you telling me that wherever you go, there are eagles flying around . . . even in the city?"

"I've seen them in the city . . . once. It way my first time in New York, and I was scared shitless of all those cars and concrete and people. One of the people I was with . . . we went to do some politics and ceremonies . . . pointed up to the sky, and sure as shit there was an eagle making a circle. I wasn't afraid to be in that city anymore . . . I mean I was no more afraid than the next guy."

"No disrespect," Stephen said, "but I'll believe it when I see it."

"Maybe when we do the sweat . . . maybe one will fly into the sweat lodge and bite your pecker off," John said. "Then would you believe?"

Stephen laughed. "Yes, *then* I'd believe."

They reached the outskirts of Binghamton in the early afternoon. It was a clear sunny day, dry, with the softest touch of fall. Stephen turned onto a rough road flanked by white cement gas stations, and they drove uphill, over a bridge that overlooked an automobile graveyard, and followed the turns as the road narrowed.

"I've been here before," John said, "so I'll remember the house."

"Is it your friend's house?" Stephen asked.

"Sam's parents own it. It's a farm, and Sam is sort of living there now."

"How do you come to know him?"

"Sam came to learn some things from me when I was living in South Dakota," John said. "He was hoping to become a medicine man."

"Is he?"

"Never quite came around that way. Like most of us, he got sidetracked. Fell in with some kinds of people."

"What do you mean?" Stephen asked, slowing down for a turn. There were trees thick on both sides of the road. This was good country, gnarly and wild, and, although close to the city, thinly populated.

"He got medicine things mixed up with human things," John said. "All the people he was with were blaming everything on bad medicine instead of on themselves. When anything had happened, they thought that somebody had done something to them."

"What do you mean?" Stephen asked nervously, remembering what Helen had said to him this morning . . . that they were dangerous. Maybe he *was* getting in over his head.

"They blamed everything on sorcery."

"Sorcery? Do *you* believe in that?" Stephen was a non-believer, but just the idea that magic could be real, that there was more than just getting up in the morning and going to bed at night, excited him.

"Sorcery's real," John said flatly, quietly. "Medicine is just there, it can be used in good ways or bad ways. But I think that Sam just got himself messed up. He came out west for a sun dance, and stayed with me for almost a year. He started to become a pretty good sweat-lodge man, but he wanted to go too fast, he wasn't ready to be a healer, and I thought he should work and learn from someone younger for a while. So I sent him to Virginia, where a Sioux guy I know lives . . . Joseph Whiteshirt. He's a young medicine man with a good talent. Anyway, Sam needed to study in a different place. Different places have different medicine, different powers. Well . . . he ended up screwing the guy's wife and almost got himself a knife in the belly for that. Was a lot of bad blood between Sam and Whiteshirt . . . maybe some bad medicine, too. Anyway, Whiteshirt blamed me for what happened with Sam and his wife. He thought I put Sam up to it or something. Everybody got sick . . . I guess I was responsible. When they needed help, I was drinking and didn't have any power to help anybody, including myself. But that's no excuse . . ."

"So where's this Whiteshirt now?" Stephen asked. Christ, he *was* getting into something over his head.

"He's at Sam's . . . so is his wife, they got back together."

"What?"

"There's still a lot of bad blood," John said, "but Whiteshirt has to help Sam out on his vision-quest whether he likes Sam or not . . . if he's a real medicine man. Maybe doing some ceremonies together will help them all out."

"What about you?" Stephen asked. He was nervous about this whole thing now, but he couldn't back out. He knew it was foolish, but it was a matter of male pride. Helen would have laughed at the idea of him still being macho, here in the quiche-eating eighties, but there it was.

"Maybe it'll help me out, too," John said, smiling faintly. "But then again maybe the ceremonies won't change Sam and Whiteshirt and the other people mixed up in this, maybe their hearts will stay hard. You sure you still want to go along? If you're nervous, you can drop me at the house. I'll get back. No trouble."

"I came to do a sweat and I'm going to do it," Stephen said.

John laughed. "Don't worry, I won't let you die in there . . . You'd better start slowing down now," he said as Stephen came to another sharp curve in the road.

On Stephen's side of the car were hayfields stretching back to smooth, fir-covered hills. The fields were still green, but beginning to brown. An old cannibalised mowing machine was rusting in the middle of one of the fields. On the other side of the road, on John's side, were a few modern, expensive houses owned by executives who worked in town, but they were outnumbered by farms and the everpresent country shacks, their front yards littered with old car hulks and ancient appliances, their porches filled with mildewed mattresses and torn couches and broken cabinets.

"There's the house," John said, pointing. It was red clapboard, set about fifty feet from the road. Behind it on higher ground was a dilapidated red barn and several storage sheds. The sheds were unpainted, and one was caving in.

Stephen pulled into the driveway, behind a green Ford truck, which had a poster in the rear-view window proclaiming that it was an Official Indian Car. On the back of the truck was painted AKWESASNE in large block letters.

"What does that mean?" Stephen asked.

"It's a Mohawk reservation, not far from here," John said. "It got invaded, you might say, by white folk . . . poachers, and the Indian people had it out with the state police. Sam was there, so was Whiteshirt. But there ain't no more poachers."

"What about you?" Stephen asked.

"I was home getting blind." Then, after a beat, John said, "There might be people here who are really against me . . . do you still want to come?"

"Christ, I'm already *here*," Stephen hoped he would not regret it.

"Anyway, you don't believe in any of that superstitious nonsense like we were talking about, do you?" John asked, grinning, his demeanour suddenly changed, as if he had just put on a mask, or taken one off.

"You're crazy," Stephen said. Yet he felt a chill run down the back of his neck . . . or perhaps it was just sweat.

They crossed the road and cut across a field, passing the rusting mowing machine. On the western edge of the field was woodland. They walked through the woods, which opened up into a clearing. A man in his late twenties with jet-black shoulder-length hair waved at them as they approached him.

Stephen knew it was too late to turn back now.

"Steve, this is Sam Starts-to-Dance," John said.

He doesn't *look* like an Indian, Stephen thought as he shook hands with Sam. Sam's features were fine and thin, almost nordic; but he wore a beaded shirt and a headband . . . and he did have that black hair.

"I'm glad you came," Sam said to John, as they all walked over the stones of a dry riverbed onto a well-worn path that wound up a gentle incline. "I didn't think you were going to make it."

"I told you I'd be here," John said flatly.

"We got the sweat-lodge ready," Sam said, "and the women went and got the meat; they're preparing it now. Are you going to take flesh?"

"Didn't Whiteshirt take flesh?" John asked. He stopped walking just before they reached the crest of the hill.

"He said he thought it was proper for you to do that."

John nodded. "That's good . . . how are things going? Still bad blood?"

"Whiteshirt's doing what he's supposed to," Sam said. "He's helping me to do this thing. But it feels very bad between us. Most of the people that were with him in Virginia have left. He's got new people, too many Wannabees."

"What's that?" Stephen asked.

But John laughed. "A Wannabee is a white who wants to be an Indian." Stephen felt his face grow hot. "Don't worry about that," John said.

"Anyway," Sam said, "I hear that there's some bad stuff going down there at Whiteshirt's place."

"Is he back together with Janet?" John asked.

"Yeah, she's here with him. She's taking care of the other women."

"Well . . . that's good."

"She did a lot of sweats, and vision-quested, and the spirits told her to stay with Whiteshirt and help him out. That's what she says. But it's over between us. Even though she says she doesn't love Whiteshirt, what we did was wrong. It was my fault, and you were right, it was a human thing."

"Happens," John said. "Maybe it can be put behind all of you."

"But I still think something's going on."

"Bad blood doesn't mean there has to be bad medicine," John said.

Sam didn't say anything; he looked down at the ground. Then he said, "Janet told me some things... that Whiteshirt blames you for what happened. He thinks you sent me to him to bring him trouble."

"Why would he think that?" John asked.

"He says the spirits told him that you were using bad medicine on him because you'd lost your power... because you'd stopped being a medicine man. He thinks *you're* a witch." After an awkward pause, Sam said, "I think Whiteshirt's jealous of you."

"Why?"

"Because most people come to see you when they have problems, even when you're drinking... most traditional Indian people don't have much respect for Whiteshirt. They call him a white man's medicine man."

"Maybe we'll talk about that," John said, "or pray about it."

"I think you should be very careful, anyway," Sam said. "Whiteshirt's changed. He's not the man you used to know."

"I'll think right about him until I see otherwise."

"I'm glad you're here," Sam said. "It's going to be right for me now, I can *feel* it."

"Well, we're soon going to find out," John said; and then he turned to Stephen and asked, "You know how Sam got his name?" John had put on another one of his masks and switched moods. "He touched a rock in the sweat-lodge once and jumped around so much that he got a new name."

"It certainly beats being called Sam Smith," Sam said, and then he went on ahead to let everyone know John was here and going to take flesh.

"Sam likes you, I can tell," John said.

"How can you tell that?" Stephen asked, distracted. He was uneasy about all this. Sam and John talked about magic as if it were a given. They didn't even question it!

"You think he'd talk like that if he didn't?" John asked. "You can feel right about Sam."

"What's this taking flesh business?" Stephen asked. If it's what I think it is, then I *will* have to leave, he told himself. It was almost a relief to think about leaving... to have a valid excuse.

"You got that bad face on again," John said. "You don't have to come along on this, I told you. If you're worried and —"

"Just tell me about this flesh business. What do you do, cut somebody up?" Although he'd committed himself to trying to find God or *something* inside the burning steam of the sweat-lodge, Stephen would not stand by and watch someone get mutilated.

"It's a ceremony," John said. "It's a kind of prayer, a gift . . . the only thing we really have to give of our own is our flesh. That's the only thing that's really ours. So everyone who wants to make a gift for Sam, that he should have a good vision-quest and find what he's looking for, everyone gives a little of himself. I usually take flesh off the arm, with a needle. I don't carve out steaks, if that's what you think."

"Are you going to do this to yourself, too?"

"I might have Whiteshirt take my flesh after Sam's vision-quest is over . . . if everything is okay. But not now, people might think I was following my ego and not my heart. After the vision-quest is a good time to do that; also, there'll be lots of food, Indian food . . . a good time. You'll see . . . maybe I'll even take flesh from *you.*"

"The hell you will!" Stephen said, and they walked down the hill toward the ceremonial grounds below. Stephen glanced up at the sky; there were certainly enough birds flapping around up there. Maybe some of those *were* John's eagles, swooping around, waiting for John to get to be a medicine man again.

Maybe they weren't, either.

John introduced Stephen to several people, one of whom was white: a young guy with shoulder-length dirty-blond hair who was wearing a headband, faded dungarees, and a tee-shirt. He asked Stephen if he wanted to smoke his pipe. Stephen politely declined and sat down under a large oak to watch John take flesh from the men and women standing around him.

Although he felt awkward and out of his depth, Stephen could not help but be awed by this place. It seemed to be completely secluded, a grotto. The sun filtered through trees, giving the place a dusty, soft quality, and the blanket of leaves on the ground made Stephen feel somehow secure here . . . and it *seemed* quiet, even though children were running around, shouting, playing games, and men and women and adolescents were all busy doing something: attending the large fire, which would heat the rocks for the sweat-lodge; tearing pieces of cloth; carrying stones and blankets; or just sitting around talking in huddled groups, passing pipes back and forth.

But sitting under that tree, feeling the cool dampness of the ground, smelling grass and sage and the burning of the fire, Stephen felt as he had when he smoked the pipe with John.

He watched John as he talked to a young woman wearing a sleeveless flower-patterned blouse. She had curly reddish hair and looked Mexican. She held John's pipe in both hands upon her lap and stared at it. Her mouth moved. She must be praying, Stephen thought. Then John began making lines down her arm with a razorblade. He gave her a yellow piece of cloth to hold in her palm, and with a needle began to remove tiny pieces of her flesh. She didn't flinch as John cut her, and Stephen noticed that she had scar-lines from previous cuttings . . . neat little indentations, pieces of flesh removed. They made Stephen think of tattoos.

To Stephen's right, about thirty feet away from him, was the sweat-lodge, a small, squat, round frame of willow shoots covered with old blankets. A dark-skinned woman with wiry hair pulled back from her face was piling up blankets and tarpaulins beside the lodge. About ten feet east of the sweat-lodge several men were attending a large, crackling fire, which had been prepared in a special way under the supervision of a scowling heavy-set man. Rocks for the sweat-lodge had been placed on the fire, and the heavy-set man squinted at them, as if he was reading the entrails of some sacred beast.

"These rocks should be just about ready now," one of the men shouted to John, who nodded.

Stephen just looked at the sweat-lodge nervously and wondered how the hell anybody was going to fit in there. It was so *small*.

The woman who had been piling up the blankets said something to the heavy-set man and walked over to Stephen. She couldn't have been more than five feet tall; she had a dark, flat face, high cheekbones, dark large almond eyes, and a thin mouth. She was missing a tooth, but there was a feral beauty about her; it was as if she, like John, had come from the earth. She carried a different map etched across her face, but the lines were there, even though she looked to be only in her mid-thirties. There were laugh lines and worry-lines on that face, which looked like it had never been touched by make-up. There was also a smell to her, the smell of the fire mixed with perspiration, a perfume like grass and mud, sweet and sour. "You came with John, didn't you?" she asked.

"Yes . . . although I feel like a fish out of water."

She chuckled. "I'm Janet, Joe Whiteshirt's woman. This is a good place, been some good ceremonies here, good feelings, before . . . before a lot of things turned sour and people's hearts became hard to each other. But John is a good man . . . and so was . . . is Joe. Maybe Sam's vision-quest will bring them close again. I know Sam told you about . . . us. He liked you."

"That's what John told me," Stephen said, "but you couldn't prove anything by me. He hasn't said anything to me — he was talking to John."

"Before a vision-quest is a quiet time, you're not supposed to talk much or mingle around. A vision-quest is dangerous. Sam's getting ready. Sometimes people who go up on the hill don't come back . . . people have been known to just disappear."

"Do you *believe* that?"

"Yes," Janet said, "I do."

More bullshit, Stephen thought with a sudden flash of renewed scepticism, but he kept his mouth shut about that. "Why do they do it, then?" he asked almost embarrassedly.

"We go to have a vision, sometimes find a name . . . the spirits give us things there . . . medicine. You find out who your spirits are, where you came from. Hasn't John told you *anything* about this?"

"A little," Stephen said. "I guess I never felt right about asking."

"I can see why he likes you. I once heard John tell Joe that we're like trees, all of us. But when you look at a tree you only see the trunk and branches and leaves, but deep down in the roots is where we take our life from, that's where the dreams and visions are . . . that's where our life *comes* from. That's why we vision-quest . . . to go back to the roots . . . and don't you worry while you're in the sweat, no matter how hot it gets," she said, changing the subject. She gave him a sprig of sage, pressed it into his hand. "Use this in the sweat-lodge, it'll help you breathe easier. You breathe through it like this" — and she showed him — "so you won't feel the heat so bad. It really helps."

"Thanks," Stephen said, feeling awkward.

"Everyone will take care of you," Janet continued. "No matter what's between John and Joe, neither one will let any harm come to you." But she averted her eyes from his when she said that, as if she wanted to believe it, but somehow couldn't.

"Which one is your husband?" Stephen asked. He was on edge — soon he would be in the sweat-lodge with them all, helpless.

"The big one, tending the rocks on the fire."

Stephen looked towards the fire and saw Whiteshirt, the same heavyset man he had seen before. Whiteshirt had a large belly and huge arms. His black hair was long, and for an instant, when their eyes met, Stephen felt a chill feather up his spine. The man seemed to be looking right through him.

"Those rocks have to be hot for the sweat-lodge; they glow like coals," Janet said.

Then there was a loud crack, and something hit the tree just above Stephen. Stephen and Janet jumped away from the tree.

"It's those damn river rocks." Janet said apologetically. "They explode sometimes like that. The next time, if there is a next time, we're going to bring our own rocks."

But Stephen had the uneasy feeling that Whiteshirt had somehow *willed* that rock to explode . . . as surely and as certainly as if he had fired a warning shot from a pistol.

The women brought out bowls of raw heart and raw liver. Everyone took a piece, even the children. When it was Stephen's turn, John said, "Eat just a little, It's good for you, give you strength." Then John bit down on a large piece of raw liver.

Stephen ate a piece of the chewy, slippery meat quickly, not knowing whether he was eating heart or liver, hoping he wouldn't gag. God knows what kind of germs are crawling around on this meat, he thought. He wondered if he'd get sick on it, or develop worms . . .

It was time to go into the sweat. The willow-stick skeleton of the lodge had been covered with old blankets and large tarpaulins.

John and Stephen took off their clothes behind a tree and left them in a pile. Stephen hadn't brought a towel or blanket for himself, but John got one for him. They walked around the sweat-lodge, careful not to walk between the altar and the lodge. The altar was a mound of dirt set back from the opening of the sweat-lodge; the ceremonial pipes were propped against it. John told Stephen to wait, that Janet — who was keeping the door, as he called it — would tell him when to enter. Then John crawled in through the low, narrow opening, and said, "*Pila miya*, thank you." Whiteshirt crawled in after him, but not before giving Stephen a look of pure hatred, as if he hated Stephen just because he was with John. But the others would no doubt interpret it as simply Whiteshirt's dislike for honkies. Two young whites and two Indians, who looked like brothers, followed Whiteshirt into the sweat-lodge.

Stephen stood back, feeling anxious and also foolish wrapped in a blanket and holding the sprig of sage that Janet had given him. He didn't want to sweat . . . not with Whiteshirt in there.

Sam walked over to Stephen and said, "Come on, your turn next." Then he smiled and said, "Don't worry, it'll be a good sweat, good ceremony. Jim and George, they're brothers, they know some old songs, and John, he's one of the best sweat-lodge men around. He says you and he are a lot alike." Sam laughed. "Both fucked up."

Stephen forced a smile and crawled into the sweat-lodge, trying not to crawl on his blanket and trying to keep it around his waist. Sage and sweetgrass had been scattered over the earthen floor, and their smell was overpowering. He already felt claustrophobic, even though the door of the lodge was still open, letting in some light. But he felt locked in — the blankets and tarpaulins and willow sticks of the sweat-lodge might as well have been made of steel. He could hear the women standing and chatting outside. They would listen to the prayers and watch for the eagles to dive out of the sky into the top of the sweat-lodge.

"Did John ever tell you about his eagles?" Sam asked Stephen in a whisper. He was sitting on John's right. "Those eagles can really be something. We've had them right here inside the sweat-lodge . . ."

What the hell am I *doing* here? Stephen asked himself as he grunted something back to Sam. He sat back against one of the willows, but the sweat-lodge was so small that he couldn't sit up straight. He looked at John, who looked back at him, but didn't say a word; then he looked at Whiteshirt, who was gazing into the pit in the centre of the sweat-lodge, where the rocks would be placed. Everyone sat with his legs crossed, but even then, toes were almost touching the pit. Stephen would have to watch himself, lest he burn his feet.

There was a tension in here, palpable, growing stronger. Stephen felt a pressure on his eyes, and he looked up. He caught Whiteshirt glowering at him. Whiteshirt averted his eyes and stared once again into the pit.

But Stephen was certain that Whiteshirt was going to make trouble . . . for all of them. He felt the hair on the back of his neck rise. It was too late to get out now.

"Okay," John said, "let me have a small rock," and Janet handed in a glowing coal on the end of a shovel. John used a forked stick to push it into the hole. He asked for his pipe, which he purified over the coal. He sprinkled sweetgrass on the rock, and the sweetgrass sparkled like fireflies.

John passed the pipe around, and everyone made a prayer. Stephen just asked that he get out of here alive. Then John asked for more rocks, and Janet brought in a shovelful. John took a large rock and placed it in the centre of the hole with his stick, and said "*Ho Tunkashila*," which everyone repeated . . . everyone except Whiteshirt, who seemed to be praying on his own, as if *he* had to purify the lodge himself, as if *John* was making them impure. But John ignored Whiteshirt and scraped the rocks from the shovel. Stephen could feel the heat already, and then John said, "Okay, close the door," and everything was darkness, except for the reddish glowing rocks. Every bit of light was blotted out, for the women outside stamped down the blankets wherever the men saw any light.

"Aha," John said, "we thank the rock people, the rock nation, for these good rocks which are sacred, we pray they will not break and kill us in the darkness. It is from your sacred breath, the breath of life, that we inhale, that our people will live. Oh, rocks, you have no eyes, no ears, and you cannot walk, yet you are life itself, alive as we are."

Then John explained the ceremony. He talked about how the *Inipi*, the sweat-bath, was probably the oldest ceremony in Indian religion. "The steam brings friends and families and even enemies together. It heals. It is the strongest medicine. The sweat is a way to make ourselves pure, and it gives us much of our power. No matter what the ceremony — sun-dance or vision-quest — we do this first. It binds us. Even though Sam here is going to vision-quest alone on the hill, we all sweat with him now. We pray together and suffer together. We'll help him now, and he'll remember when he's alone on the hill tonight facing the dreams and spirits." Everyone agreed, and there was much yeaing in the darkness. Only Whiteshirt was silent.

John prayed to the Grandfathers and the Four Directions. He prayed to *Wakan-Tanka*, he prayed for the two-leggeds and four-leggeds and wingeds and everything else on the earth, but he also seemed to be talking to God as if He were a presence in the sweat-lodge. He prayed for everyone in the sweat-lodge, for Stephen who he said was walking a different path, yet they were all walking together . . . whatever the hell that meant, Stephen thought.

But in the blackness, you couldn't tell if you were cramped in a small space, or whether you were somehow suspended in eternity. Stephen felt as if everything was being pushed up right against him, yet paradoxically, he had no sense of breadth or width or height here. He felt dizzy. He could hear the others beside him . . . he could smell them. It was already getting too hot. It was difficult to breathe. He stared at the glowing rocks, and heard the water swishing in the bucket as John stirred it with the dipper . . . and he *felt* Whiteshirt's glowering presence, even though he couldn't see him in the dark. He felt that same pressure against his eyes and knew that Whiteshirt was watching him.

It was then that Stephen realised how frightened he was.

John prayed, but Whiteshirt was praying louder, trying to drown him out.

John poured a dipperful of water onto the rocks.

It was as if a gun had been fired. Suddenly, Stephen couldn't breathe. He was screaming, bending forward to get away from the searing steam. Everyone was shouting, "*Hi-ye, Pilamaya*, thank you, thank you," and Stephen found himself shouting, too, but he didn't know what he was saying.

He had to get out of here. He was going to die. He pressed the sage to his mouth, but it was still like breathing fire. He didn't know where he was; it was as if part of his mind knew, but another part was soaring, taking him miles into darkness, from where he might not return.

Another retort, as more water was poured on the rocks. This time, though, it didn't seem so bad. Stephen heard the brothers singing. The melody was strange and harsh and ancient; through what seemed to be a hole in Stephen's consciousness, he could hear John's prayers for them all.

"If anybody has to eliminate, that's okay," John said. "This is a place to get purified, to get out all the evil, to get all the garbage picked up from the world outside out of your system."

Stephen started coughing. He couldn't get his breath, but he heard Whiteshirt say, "The evil's right here, *inside* the sweat-lodge."

"Well, if it is, then we'll just have to burn it right out," John said in an even, cutting voice.

George laughed at that. "Don't worry, John . . . if you get burned, I'll take over the ceremony for you."

After a pause, John said, "We came here to pray, remember? And to sweat." Then he poured water on the rocks.

Stephen felt the pain as a searing wave. He pressed his blanket to his face, trying to breathe, trying to find respite from the rising heat. After a few seconds, he could breathe again. He removed the blanket from his face and stared into the darkness. He could swear that he could see something flickering in the blackness. John would have called them spirits.

Sam handed Stephen a bucket to cool him off, and automatically Stephen ran his hands through his hair. It was hot to the touch, as if on fire. He splashed water on his face. I'm not going to last, he thought. John had told them all that if anyone had to get out to say, "All my relatives," and the door would be opened for them.

Stephen would try a little longer.

More rocks were brought in, glowing red, and Stephen burned in the darkness. But he thought he was beginning to understand something about this ceremony, that if he was going to pray — and he really wasn't sure if there *was* anyone or anything to pray to — he had to do it like this. Prayers had to be somehow *earned.* You had to go through the pain and sit with your ass in the mud like an animal.

He felt the mud beneath him. He was part of the earth. He was connected.

As the steam exploded again, Stephen thought of Helen and his children, and he started crying for them, for the pain he had caused them . . . and he hallucinated that he was not drenched in sweat, but in blood.

John told everyone not to wrap their towels and blankets around themselves, but to let the steam sink into their bodies. "The pain is good," he said as he ladled more water on the rocks. Stephen heard the hiss of steam and felt the hot blast burn over him.

"The pain is only good if it comes from the spirits," Whiteshirt said loudly, belligerently. "Only the spirits can burn away bad medicine . . . only *they* can drive a witch out of the sweat-lodge . . ."

John began to pray, as if nothing had been said, as if nothing had gone sour. "Oh, Grandfather, *Wakan-Tanka,* we're sending you a voice. Please hear us . . . pity us for we are weak. Give us the strength and wisdom so that our hearts may soften."

Whiteshirt began praying, too. But he was praying as if he was fighting. He was mocking. He was accusing. He was trying to drown out John.

But John didn't raise his voice.

The tension was electrifying the steaming, boiling darkness.

Then John decreed that the first round was over and called for the door to be opened. Janet, who looked distraught, pulled the blankets and tarpaulins away from the sweat-lodge . . . letting in the blessed light and air and a cool, chilling breeze.

John explained that this was going to be a "hot" round. He also told everyone that this was going to be a "spirit round", and that anyone could ask the spirits for help, or ask them to answer questions, but they'd better be sure they really wanted an answer.

Then Whiteshirt said, "Just as long as it's really the spirits that's doing the talking."

John ignored the remark, as he had the others, and called for the "door" to be closed. Once again the women draped the blankets and tarpaulins over the lodge and it was pitch-dark inside.

Maybe John hadn't ignored Whiteshirt's remark, after all, for he ladled enough water onto the rocks to melt iron. Stephen buried himself in his blanket to escape the burning steam, and everyone shouted thanks.

Stephen gagged and coughed. For an instant, everything went blank. Then Stephen found himself praying and crying for his family, for every family, for everyone. He was praying and crying *because* of the heat and the pain. He believed in the spirits flickering all around him, and yet at the same time he disbelieved. Part of his mind seemed to shrink back, and he was left with the part that believed what was happening to him. He was in the centre, he was praying for his own, for himself, for his family . . . and for the trees and the rocks and birds and animals and every other goddamn thing in the world. Words were *things*. They could *do* things. They could help or harm. Magic was real.

And praying was something that was as practical as cooking food.

Then he caught himself . . . he was thinking crazy.

His lungs were raw, but he wasn't coughing. He saw things in the darkness; maybe they were words or spirits or just something like the patterns you see behind your eyes when you press them hard with your palms.

One part of him saw the trails of spirits. Another part dismissed them. He was fighting with himself, believing and disbelieving, and just trying to breathe . . . to stay alive so he could get out and know that he had done it.

The spirits flickered in the dark and left trails like particles in a cloud chamber.

John poured more water onto the rocks, and everyone screamed with pain. Time seemed to slow down for Stephen, contracting hours and events into instants. In these flashing beads of time were buried hours of mistakes and cruelty, all the memories of his life. He screamed out against himself, for everything wrong he had done, for his failures as a man, as a father and a son and a husband, and he saw blood . . . he was breathing it . . . he was tasting it . . . it was the very steam itself . . . it was the rocks, which were of the same stuff, coagulated.

Then the questions began.

Everyone had a question for the spirits, and John seemed to be talking, but it wasn't quite his voice. It was somehow shrill, and it certainly wasn't John's personality. He was laughing at almost everything; he was cutting, witty, nasty. But always laughing . . . and Stephen began to believe that it really *wasn't* John who was speaking. He heard different voices, yet he didn't hear what the spirits were telling the individual people in the sweat-lodge. The words seemed mostly garbled, except for a phrase or sentence here or there. John had told him that usually happened . . . that you only heard what you were meant to hear . . . what was important for *you*. This was a private place, even with the others sitting and groaning and sweating beside you.

But when it came to Stephen's turn, he didn't ask the spirits any questions. Once the spirits gave you an answer, you had to follow what they told you to do, and Stephen wasn't taking any chances. John, however, asked for him. He seemed to appear in the middle of those spirit voices, and he asked that Stephen be helped to find himself with his family. The spirits thought that was funnier than hell, and it gave Stephen a chill to hear those laughing voices and see those flickerings in the dark. He wondered what had happened to John. He felt naked and alone. Vulnerable.

Did John just disappear? Or was he just talking funny . . . of course, *that* was it.

It was . . . and it wasn't. Something else seemed strange in Stephen's mind. Even if the flickerings and the voices were phoney, he found that he somehow didn't care. It was real even if it wasn't. That felt true, but it didn't make a bit of sense. Still . . .

Then it was Whiteshirt's turn. Stephen had blanked everyone else out, just as John had told him to do. But he was going to listen now. He supposed everyone else felt the same way because the tension returned to the darkness like a storm.

It was then that Stephen saw the coal move in the pit.

Whiteshirt picked up the glowing coal, hot as it was, and put it in his mouth. It illuminated his face in red, as if that face was hanging in the darkness, disconnected. It was as if Whiteshirt had become a spirit himself . . . or maybe the spirits were *inside* him. Whiteshirt turned toward John and grinned; the coal was clenched between his teeth, its glow illuminated the hatred and frustration and sickness on his face. Whiteshirt was making a funny keening noise as if the spirits were speaking through him.

It's a trick! Stephen thought. It's got to be . . .

Then the coal moved toward John, as if Whiteshirt were embracing him. John screamed, an animal scream of pure agony, and the smell of burning flesh pervaded the sweat-lodge.

"Open the door, for Christ's sake," Sam shouted. "All my relatives. Goddammit, open the door!"

The women pulled down the blankets and tarpaulins from the willow framework of the sweat-lodge. The light was blinding. Everyone was silent, stunned. John had fallen forward. Blood oozed from large ugly gashes in his back. It wasn't the glowing coal that had burned and cracked John's flesh; the coal was just a symbol of Whiteshirt's power. It was the heat that had torn him open . . . the heat contained in Whiteshirt's burning heart.

John groaned and sat up, shaking his head as if warding off something invisible. Whiteshirt stared at him in hard satisfaction. He didn't say a word, but his wife, Janet, applied sage moistened with her spittle to the gashes in John's back. John flinched every time she touched him.

"You were wrong to do this thing," she said to her husband.

"*I* didn't do it," Whiteshirt said flatly. "It was the spirits."

"You were *wrong*," Janet said again, and Stephen could see in her face how much she hated this man . . . or perhaps the intensity of her hatred was fuelled by love and guilt.

"This can't go on," Sam said. "I'll vision-quest another time. I need to pray about all this . . . let's forget it all for now."

"No," John said, a quaver in his voice, "we're going to do the last round . . .

and you're going to keep your promise to the spirits and make your vision-quest. Today. But first there's something between Joe Whiteshirt and me that has to be finished. Everybody, get out of the sweat-lodge. We're going to let the spirits decide about this bad thing that has come between us."

"The spirits *already* decided," Whiteshirt said. "They made their mark on your back. Do you want them to burn you again?"

"That was *you*, Joe," John said. "So you *are* using medicine to get what you want. But you won't get it. Nobody will follow you . . . you're a witch, not a medicine man." John spoke in low, even tones, as if he were simply reciting facts. But he was trembling, exposing his rage and humiliation . . . and perhaps his fear.

"This time you'll die," Whiteshirt said. "That will be proof enough."

"We'll see . . ."

"You're not going to do this thing," Janet said to Whiteshirt, but it was already as good as done because the men were leaving the sweat-lodge.

"What's going *on*?" Stephen asked John, but John wouldn't answer him. He just nodded his head, indicating that Stephen should get out with the others.

When everyone was out, John said, "Close it up." The blankets and tarps were thrown back on the lodge, and one of the men handed in a shovelful of glowing rocks. Janet had refused to act as keeper of the door.

John asked for another shovelful . . . enough for *two* rounds.

"More rocks aren't going to help you," Whiteshirt said.

John didn't answer. He was praying in Sioux.

Stephen tried to approach Sam and Janet and ask them to try and stop John and Whiteshirt from sweating. Sam just shook his head, and Janet gently told him not to interfere in matters he didn't understand. So Stephen went back to the sweat-lodge and stood with the others. An older woman in a cotton print housedress stood beside him. Every once in a while, she would nervously look up at the sky, as if watching for eagles . . . waiting. Even the children were quiet. Everyone was listening, waiting to hear what was going to happen inside the sweat-lodge. There was a communal sense that what was about to happen was out of human control. The next few minutes would, indeed, be decided by the spirits.

"Close the door," John said, and the keeper of the door closed the last opening of the sweat-lodge with a tarp.

Stephen could hear John stirring the water with the aluminum ladle. Then there was a hissing of steam as John poured some water on the rocks. Both men prayed in Sioux. Once again Whiteshirt prayed louder than John, drowning him out. But then he switched to English. He called John a witch . . . a spy for the white world. He blamed John for what had happened between Sam and Janet. He blamed John for sending Sam with a disease . . . bad medicine, a disease that had afflicted everyone at Whiteshirt's camp. But now the spirits were going to put things to right. He called them down from the heavens to destroy his enemy.

Whiteshirt worked himself into a frenzy.

When Whiteshirt paused to catch his breath, John said, "Okay, we *will* let the spirits decide. We'll make this a short round." Then there was an ear-splitting cracking sound like an explosion inside the sweat-lodge. Everyone outside jumped back. John must have thrown most of the bucket onto those rocks. And right after that there was another explosion.

"You bastard," Whiteshirt screamed. "You're going to die for this."

But now John was praying . . . it was his turn to scream for the spirits. "Oh, Grandfather, *Wakan-Tanka*, *Tunkashila*, send down the eagle to guard the sacred pipe and the life of the People. Send *Wakinyan-Tanka*, the great thunderbird to scourge out the evil." He intoned, "Send us the one that has wings, but no shape. Send us the one that has an eye of lightning. Send us the one that has no head, yet has a beak filled with the teeth of the wolf. Send us the winged one to devour whatever is bad inside us, just as it devours its own young."

Stephen listened, his hands resting on the outside of the sweat-lodge. He heard a flapping noise like the working of wings. It sounded as if there was a huge bellows inside the sweat-lodge. The noise grew louder. Something was beating against the inside of the sweat-lodge. Stephen could hear and *feel* it slapping against the blankets and tarpaulins. It was as if a great bird was trapped in there with John and Whiteshirt, and it was thrashing its wings, beating to get out of the darkness . . . to find the cold blue of the upper air.

But that's impossible, Stephen thought, even as he felt the sweat-lodge shake.

There was scuffling inside . . . and screaming.

Then there was sudden silence.

Stephen pressed the side of his face against the rough canvas of the sweat-lodge to hear better, but all he could hear was his own heart beating in his throat . . . a tiny trapped eagle.

"Open the door," John said in a voice that was hardly more than a whisper. "It's over . . ."

They quickly pulled the tarpaulins and blankets away from the willow frame of the sweat-lodge . . . and found John sitting by himself. He blinked in the bright sunlight. His pipe rested on his lap. He didn't seem to notice that he was sitting stark naked, his blanket underneath him. He looked pale and drawn, as if he had just sweated away part of his life. The dead coal that had been in Whiteshirt's mouth lay in the dirt before him. It was all that was left of Whiteshirt.

Whiteshirt had disappeared . . .

"Do you believe in the eagles now?" John asked Stephen.

Stephen could only shrug. It was all some sort of a trick, he told himself, even though the hairs on the back of his neck were still standing up. Whiteshirt couldn't have just disappeared . . . he had to have sneaked away somehow.

John smiled weakly. "Next time, maybe the eagles *will* bite your pecker off." Then he raised his head and gazed into the sky. He was still smiling.

Stephen looked uneasily upward at the eagles circling high overhead, and he thought about Helen and his children and the blood he had tasted inside the sweat-lodge. There wouldn't be a next time, he told himself. He was certain of that. He was ready to go home.

Perhaps John understood because he started laughing like a spirit.

TATTOOS

. . . .

We are never like the angels till our passion dies.

— Decker

For the past few years we'd been going to a small fair, which wasn't really much more than a road show, in Trout Creek, a small village near Walton in upstate New York. The fair was always held in late September, when the nights were chilly and the leaves had turned red and orange and dandelion yellow.

We were in the foothills of the Catskills. We drove past the Cannonsville Reservoir, which provides drinking water for New York City. My wife Laura remarked that this was as close to dry as she'd ever seen the reservoir; she had grown up in this part of the country and knew it intimately. My son Ben, who is fourteen, didn't seem to notice anything. He was listening to hard rock music through the headphones of his portable radio-cassette player.

Then we were on the fairgrounds, driving through a field of parked cars. Ben had the headphones off and was excited. I felt a surge of freedom and happiness. I wanted to ride the rides and lose myself in the arcades and exhibitions; I wanted crowds and the noise and smells of the midway. I wanted to forget my job and my recent heart attack.

We met Laura's family in the church tent. Then Laura and her Mom and sister went to look at saddles, for her sister showed horses, and Dad and Ben and I walked in the other direction.

As we walked past concession stands and through the arcade of shooting galleries, antique wooden horse race games, slots, and topple-the-milk bottle games, hawkers shouted and gesticulated at us. We waited for Ben to lose his change at the shooting gallery and the loop-toss where all the spindles floated on water; and we all went into the funhouse, which was mostly blind alleys and a few tarnished distorting mirrors. Then we walked by the tents of the freak-show: the Palace of Wonders with the original Lobster Man, Velda the Half-Lady, and "The Most Unusual Case in Medical History: Babies Born Chest to Chest."

"Come on," Dad said, "let's go inside and see the freaks."

"Nah," I said. "These places depress me. I don't feel right about staring at these people."

"That's how they make their money," Dad said. "Keeps 'em off social services."

I wasn't going to get into *that* with him.

"Well, then Bennie and me'll go in," Dad said. "If that's all right with you."

It wasn't, but I wasn't going to argue, so I reached into my pocket to give Ben some money, but Dad just shook his head and paid the woman sitting in a chair outside the tent. She gave him two tickets. "I'll meet you back here in about ten minutes," I said, glad to get away by myself.

I walked through the crowds, enjoying the rattle and shake of the concessionaires, all trying to grab a buck, the filthy, but brightly painted oil canvas, the sweet smell of cotton candy, the peppery smell of potatoes frying, and the coarse shouting of the kids. I bought some french fries, which were all the more delicious because I wasn't allowed to have them. Two young girls smiled and giggled as they passed me. Goddamn if this wasn't like being sixteen again.

Then something caught my eye.

I saw a group that looked completely out of place. Bikers, punkers, and well-dressed, yuppy-looking people were standing around a tattoo parlour and conversing with each other. The long-haired bikers flaunted their tattoos by wearing cut-off jean jackets to expose their arms and chests; the women who rode with them had taken off their jackets and had delicate tattoo wristlets and red and orange butterflies and flowers worked into their arms or between their breasts. In contrast, most of the yuppies, whom I assumed to be from the city, wore long-sleeved shirts or tailored jackets, including the women, who looked like they had just walked out of a New England clothes catalogue. There was also a stout woman who looked to be in her seventies. She had grey hair pulled back into a tight bun and she wore a dark pleated dress. I couldn't help but think that she should be home in some Jewish neighbourhood in Brooklyn, sitting with friends in front of her apartment building, instead of standing here in the dust before a tattoo parlour.

I was transfixed. What had brought all these people here to the boonies? Who the hell knew, maybe they were all from here. But I couldn't believe that for a minute. And I wondered if they were *all* tattooed.

I walked over to them to hear snatches of conversation and to investigate the tattoo parlour, which wasn't a tent, as were most of the other concessions, but a small, modern mobile home with the words TAROT TATTOO STUDIO — ORIGINAL DESIGNS, EXPERT COVER-UPS painted across the side in large letters with red serifs through the stems. Then the door opened, and a heavy-set man with a bald head and a full black beard walked out. Everyone, including the yuppies, were admiring him. His entire head was tattooed in a Japanese design of a flaming dragon; the dragon's head was high on his forehead, and a stream of flame reached down to the bridge of his nose. The dragon was beautifully executed. How the hell could someone disfigure his face like that? I wondered.

Behind the dragon man was a man of about five feet-six wearing a clean, but bloodied, white tee-shirt. He had brown curly hair, which was long overdue to be cut, a rather large nose, and a full mouth. He looked familiar, very familiar, yet I couldn't place him. This man was emaciated, as if he had given up nourishment for some cultish religious reason. Even his long, well-formed hands looked skeletal, the veins standing out like blue tattoos.

Then I remembered. He looked like Nathan Rivlin, an artist I had not seen in several years. A dear friend I had lost touch with. This man looked like Nathan, but he looked all wrong. I remembered Nathan as filled-out and full of life, an orthodox Jew who wouldn't answer the phone on *Shabbos* — from Friday night until sundown on Saturday, a man who loved to stay up all night and talk and drink beer and smoke strong cigars. His wife's name was Ruth, and she was a highly-paid medical textbook illustrator. They had both lived in Israel for some time, and came from Chicago. But the man standing before me was ethereal-looking, as if he were made out of ectoplasm instead of flesh and blood. God forbid he should be Nathan Rivlin.

Yet I couldn't keep myself from shouting, "Nate? Nate, is it you?"

He looked around, and when he saw me, a pained grin passed across his face. I stepped toward him through the crowd. Several other people were trying to gain Nathan's attention. A woman told me to wait my turn, and a few nasty stares and comments were directed at me. I ignored them. "What the hell *is* all this?" I asked Nathan after we embraced.

"What should it be, it's a business," he said. Just then he seemed like the old Nathan I remembered. He had an impish face, a mobile face capable of great expression.

"Not what I'd expect, though," I said. I could see that his arms and neck were scarred; tiny whitish welts crisscrossed his shaved skin. Perhaps he had some sort of a skin rash, I told myself, but that didn't seem right to me. I was certain that Nathan had deliberately made those hairline scars. But why . . .? "Nate, what the hell happened to you?" I asked. "You just disappeared off the face of the earth. And Ruth too. How is Ruth?"

Nathan looked away from me, as if I had opened a recent wound. The stout, older woman who was standing a few feet away from us tried to get Nathan's attention. "Excuse me, but could I *please* talk to you?" she asked, a trace of foreign accent in her voice. "It's very important." She looked agitated and tired, and I noticed dark shadows under her eyes. But Nathan didn't seem to hear her. "It's a long story," he said to me, "and I don't think you'd want to hear it." He seemed suddenly cold and distant.

"Of course I would," I insisted.

"Excuse me, please," interrupted the older woman. "I've come a long way to see you," she said to Nathan, "and you've been talking to everyone else but me. And I've been waiting . . ."

Nathan tried to ignore her, but she stepped right up to him and took his arm. He jerked away, as if he'd been shocked. I saw the faded, tattooed numbers just above her wrist. "Please . . ." she asked.

"Are you here for a cover-up?" Nathan asked her, glancing down at her arm.

"No," she said. "It wouldn't do any good."

"You shouldn't be here," Nathan said gently. "You should be home."

"I know you can help me."

Nathan nodded, as if accepting the inevitable. "I'll talk to you for a moment, but that's all," he said to her. "That's all." Then he looked up at me, smiled wanly, and led the woman into his trailer.

"You thinkin' about getting a tattoo?" Dad asked, catching me staring at the trailer. Ben was looking around at the punkers, sizing them up. He had persuaded his mother to let him have a "rat-tail" when he went for his last haircut. It was just a small clump of hair that hung down in the back, but it gave him the appearance of rebelliousness; the real thing would be here soon enough. He turned his back to the punkers with their orange hair and long bleach-white rat-tails, probably to exhibit his own.

"Nah, just waiting for you," I said, lying, trying to ignore my feelings of loss and depression. Seeing Nathan had unnerved me. I felt suddenly old, as if Nathan's wasting had become my own.

We spent the rest of the day at the fair, had dinner at Mom and Dad's, watched television, and left at about eleven o'clock. We were all exhausted. I hadn't said anything to Laura about seeing Nathan. I knew she would want to see him, and I didn't want her upset, at least that's what I told myself.

Ben fell asleep in the back seat. Laura watched for deer along the road while I drove, as my night-vision is poor. She should be the one to drive, but it hurts her legs to sit — she has arthritis. Most of the time her legs are stretched out as far as possible in the foot well or she'll prop her feet against the dashboard. I fought the numbing hypnosis of the road. Every mile felt like ten. I kept thinking about Nathan, how he looked, what he had become.

"David, what's the matter?" Laura asked when we were about half-way home. "You're so quiet tonight. Is anything wrong. Did we do anything to upset you?"

"No, I'm just tired," I said, lying. Seeing Nathan had shocked and depressed me. But there was a selfish edge to my feelings. It was as though I had looked in one of the distorting mirrors in the fun-house. I had seen something of myself in Nathan.

Ben yelped, lurching out of a particularly bad nightmare. He leaned forward, hugging the back of the front seat, and asked us if we were home yet.

"We've got a way to go," I said. "Sit back, you'll fall asleep."

"I'm cold back here."

I turned up the heat; the temperature had dropped at least fifteen degrees since this afternoon. "The freak show probably gave you nightmares; it always did me."

"That wasn't it," Ben insisted.

"I don't know what's wrong with your grandfather," Laura said. "He had no business taking you in there. He should have his head examined."

"I told you," Ben said, "it had nothing to do with that."

"You want to talk about it?" I asked.

"No," Ben said, but he didn't sit back in his seat; he kept his face just behind us.

"You should sit back," Laura said. "If we got into an accident —"

"*Okay*," Ben said. There was silence for a minute, and then he said, "You know who I dreamed about?"

"Who?" I asked.

"Uncle Nathan."

I straightened up, automatically looking into the rear-view mirror to see Ben, but it was too dark. I felt a chill and turned up the heat another notch.

"We haven't seen him in about four years," Laura said. "Whatever made you dream about him?"

"I dunno," Ben said. "But I dreamed he was all different colours, all painted, like a monster."

I felt the hairs on the back of my neck prickle.

"You were dreaming about the freak show," Laura told him. "Sometimes old memories of people we know get mixed up with new memories."

"It wasn't just Uncle Nathan looking like that that scared me."

"What was it?" I asked.

He pulled himself toward us again. But he spoke to Laura. "He was doing something to Dad," Ben said, meaning me.

"What was he doing?" Laura asked.

"I dunno," Ben said, "but it was horrible, like he was pulling out Dad's heart or something."

"Jesus Christ," Laura said. "Look, honey, it was only a dream," she said to him. "Forget about it and try to go back to sleep."

I tried to visualise the lines on Nathan's arms and neck and keep the car on the road.

I knew that I had to go back and see him . . .

Monday morning I finished an overdue fund-raising report for the Binghamton Symphony with the help of my secretary. The three o'clock meeting with the board of directors went well; I was congratulated for a job well done, and my future seemed secure for another six months. I called Laura at home, told her I had another meeting, and that I would be home later than usual. Laura had a deadline of her own — she was writing an article for a travel magazine — and was happy for the stretch of work-time. She was only going to send out for a pizza anyway.

The drive to the fairgrounds seemed to take longer than usual, but that was probably because I was impatient and tense about seeing Nathan. Ben's crazy dream had spooked me; I also felt guilty about lying to Laura. We had a thing about not lying to each other, although there were some things we didn't talk about, radioactive spots from the past which still burned, but which we pretended were dead.

There weren't as many people on the fairgrounds as last night, but that was to be expected, and I was glad for it.

I parked close to the arcades, walked through the huckster's alley and came to Nathan Rivlin's trailer. It was dusk, and there was a chill in the air — a harbinger of the hard winter that was to come. A few kids wearing army jackets were loitering, looking at the designs of tattoos on paper, called flash, which were displayed under Plexiglas on a table secured to the trailer. The designs were nicely executed, but ordinary stuff to attract the passers-by: anchors, hearts, butterflies, stylised women in profile, eagles, dragons, stars, various military insignia, cartoon characters, death-heads, flags, black panthers and lions, snakes, spiders; nothing to indicate the kind of fine work that had been sported by the people hanging around the trailer yesterday.

I knocked on the door. Nathan didn't seem surprised to see me; he welcomed me inside. It was warm inside the trailer, close, and Nathan was wearing a sixties hippy-style white gauze shirt; the sleeves were long and the cuffs buttoned, hiding the scars I had seen on his arms yesterday. Once again

I felt a shock at seeing him so gaunt, at seeing the webbed scars on his neck. Was I returning to my friend's out of just a morbid fascination to see what he had become? I felt guilty and ashamed. Why hadn't I sought out Nathan before this? If I had been a better friend, I probably would have.

Walking into his studio was like stepping into one of his paintings, which covered most of the available wall space. Nathan was known for working on large canvases, and some of his best work was in here — paintings I had seen in process years ago. On the wall opposite the door was a painting of a nude man weaving a cat's cradle. The light was directed from behind, highlighting shoulders and arms and the large peasant hands. The features of the face were blurred, but unmistakably Nathan's. Beside it was a huge painting of three circus people, two jugglers standing beside a woman. Behind them, in large red letters was the word CIRCUS. The faces were ordinary, and disturbing, perhaps because of that. There was another painting on the wall where Nathan had set up his tattoo studio. A self-portrait. Nathan wearing a blue worker's hat, red shirt, and apron, and standing beside a laboratory skeleton. And there were many paintings I had never seen, a whole series of tattoo paintings, which at first glance looked to be nonrepresentational, until the designs of figures on flesh came into focus. There were several paintings of gypsies. One, in particular, seemed to be staring directly at me over tarot cards, which were laid out on a table strewn with glasses. There was another painting of an old man being carried from his death-bed by a sad-faced demon. Nathan had a luminous technique, an execution like that of the old masters. Between the paintings, and covering every available space, was flash; not the flash that I had seen outside, but detailed coloured designs and drawings of men and animals and mythical beasts, as grotesque as anything by Goya. I was staring into my own nightmares.

The bluish light that comes just before dark suffused the trailer, and the shadows seemed to become more concrete than the walls or paintings.

The older woman I had seen on Sunday was back. She was sitting in Nathan's studio, in what looked like a variation of a dentist chair. Beside the chair was a cabinet and a sink with a high, elongated faucet, the kind usually seen in examination rooms. Pigments, dyes, paper towels, napkins, bandages, charcoal for stencils, needle tubes and bottles of soap and alcohol were neatly displayed beside an autoclave. I was surprised to see this woman in the chair, even though I knew she had been desperate to see Nathan. But she just didn't seem the sort to be getting a tattoo, although that probably didn't mean a thing: anyone could have hidden tattoos: old ladies, senators, presidents. Didn't Barry Goldwater brag that he had two dots tattooed on his hand to represent the bite of a snake? Who the hell knew why.

"I'll be done in a few minutes," Nathan said to me. "Sit down. Would you like a drink? I've got some beer, I think. If you're hungry, I've got soup on the stove." Nathan was a vegetarian; he always used to make the same miso soup, which he'd start when he got up in the morning, every morning.

"If you don't mind, I'll just sit," I said, and I sat down on an old green Art Deco couch. The living room was made up of the couch, two slat-back chairs, and a television set on a battered oak desk. The kitchenette behind Nathan's work area had a stove, a small refrigerator, and a table attached to the wall. And, indeed, I could smell the familiar aroma of Nathan's soup.

"David, this is Mrs Stramm," Nathan said, and he seemed to be drawn toward me, away from Mrs Stramm, who looked nervous. I wanted to talk with him . . . connect with him . . . find the man I used to know again.

"Mister Tarot," the woman said, "I'm ready now, you can go ahead."

Nathan sat down in the chair beside her and switched on a gooseneck adjustable lamp, which produced a strong, intense white light. The flash and paintings in the room lost their fire and brilliance, as the darkness in the trailer seemed to gain substance.

"Do you think you can help me?" she asked. "Do you think it will work?"

"If you wish to believe in it," Nathan said. He picked up his electrical tattoo machine, examined it, and then examined her wrist, where the concentration camp tattoo had faded into seven smudgy blue letters.

"You know, when I got these numbers at the camp, it was a doctor who put them on. He was a prisoner, like I was. He didn't have a machine like yours. He worked for Dr Mengele." She looked away from Nathan while she spoke, just as many people look away from a nurse about to stick a needle in their vein. But she seemed to have a need to talk. Perhaps it was just nerves.

Nathan turned on his instrument, which made a staticky, electric noise, and began tattooing her wrist. I watched him work; he didn't seem to have heard a word she said. He looked tense and bit his lip, as if it was his own wrist that was being tattooed. "I knew Mengele," the woman continued. "Do you know who he was?" she asked Nathan. Nathan didn't answer. "Of course you do," she said. "He was such a nice-looking man. Kept his hair very neat, clipped his moustache, and he had blue eyes. Like the sky. Everything else in the camp was grey, and the sky would get black from the furnaces, like the world was turned upside down." She continued to talk while Nathan worked. She grimaced from the pain of the tattoo needle.

I tried to imagine what she might have looked like when she was young, when she was in the camp. It would have been Auschwitz, I surmised, if Mengele was there.

But why was a Jew getting a tattoo?

Perhaps she wasn't Jewish.

And then I noticed that Nathan's wrist was bleeding. Tiny beads of blood soaked through his shirt, which was like a blotter.

"Nathan —" I said, as I reflexively stood up.

But Nathan looked at me sharply and shook his head, indicating that I should stay where I was. "It's all right, David. We'll talk about it later."

I sat back down and watched them, mesmerised.

Mrs Stramm stopped talking; she seemed calmer now. There was only the sound of the machine, and the background noise of the fair. The air seemed heavier in the darkness, almost smothering. "Yesterday you told me that you came here to see me to find out about your husband," Nathan said to her. "You lied to me, didn't you."

"I had to know if he was alive," she said. "He was a strong man, he could have survived. I left messages through the agencies for him when I was in Italy. I couldn't stand to go back to Germany. I thought to go to South America, I had friends in Sao Paulo."

"You came to America to cut yourself off from the past," Nathan said in a low voice. "You knew your husband had died. I can feel that you buried him . . . in your heart. But you couldn't bury everything. The tattoo is changing. Do you want me to stop? I have covered the numbers."

I couldn't see what design he had made. Her wrist was bleeding, though . . . as was his.

Then she began to cry, and suddenly seemed angry. But she was directing her pain and anger at herself. Nathan stopped working, but made no move to comfort her. When Mrs Stramm's crying subsided and she regained control of her breathing, she said, "I murdered my infant. I had help from another, who thought she was saving my life." She seemed surprised at her own words.

"Do you want me to stop," Nathan asked again, but his voice was gentle.

"You do what you think, you're the tattooist."

Nathan began again. The noise of his machine was teeth-jarring. Mrs Stramm continued talking to him, even though she still looked away from the machine. But she talked in a low voice now. I had to lean forward and strain to hear her. My eyes were fixed on Nathan's wrist; the dots of blood had connected into a large bright stain on his shirt cuff.

"I was only seventeen," Mrs Stramm continued. "Just married and pregnant. I had my baby in the camp and Dr Mengele delivered it himself. It wasn't so bad in the hospital. I was taken care of as if I were in a hospital in Berlin. Everything was nice, clean. I even pretended that what was going on outside the hospital in the camp, in the ovens, wasn't true. When I had the baby — his name was Stefan — everything was perfect. Dr Mengele was very careful when he cut the cord; and another doctor assisted him, a Jewish doctor from the camp. Ach!" she said, flinching; she looked down at her wrist, where Nathan was working, but she didn't say a word about the blood soaking through his shirtsleeve. She seemed to accept it as part of the process. Nathan must have told her what to expect. He stopped, and refilled his instrument with another ink pigment.

"But then I was sent to a barracks, which was filthy, but not terribly crowded," she continued. "There were other children in there, mutilated. One set of twins had been sewn together, back to back, arm to arm, and they smelled terrible. They were an experiment, of course. I knew that my baby and I were going to be an experiment. There was a woman in the barracks looking after us. She couldn't do much but watch the children die. She felt sorry for me. She told me that nothing could be done for my baby. And after they had finished their experiment and killed my son, then I would be killed also; it was the way it was done. Dr Mengele killed all surviving parents and healthy siblings for comparison. My only hope, she said, was to kill my baby myself. If my baby died "naturally" before Mengele began his experiment, then he might let me live. I remember thinking to myself that it was the only way I could save my baby the agony of a terrible death at the hands of Mengele.

"So I suffocated my baby. I pinched his nose and held his mouth shut while my friend held us both and cried for us. I remember that very well. Dr Mengele learned of my baby's death and came to the barracks himself. He said he was very sorry, and, you know, I believed him. I took comfort from the man who had made me kill my child. I should have begged him to kill *me*. But I said nothing."

"What could you have done?" Nathan asked, as he was working. "Your child would have died no matter what. You saved yourself, that's all you could do under the circumstances."

"Is that how *you* would have felt, if you were me?"

"No," Nathan said, and a sad smile appeared for an instant, an inappropriate response, yet somehow telling.

Mrs Stramm stopped talking and had closed her eyes. It was as if she and Nathan were praying together. I could feel that, and I sensed that something else was happening between them. Something seemed to be passing out of her, a dark, palpable spirit. I could feel its presence in the room. And Nathan looked somehow different, more defined. It was the light from the lamp, no doubt, but some kind of exchange seemed to be taking place. Stolid, solid Mrs Stramm looked softer, as if lighter, while Nathan looked as ravaged as an internee. It was as if he were becoming defined by this woman's past.

When Nathan was finished, he put his instrument down on the cabinet, and taped some gauze over his own bleeding wrist. Then he just stared at his work on Mrs Stramm. I couldn't see the tattoo from where I was sitting, so I stood up and walked over. "Is it all right if I take a look?" I asked, but neither one answered me . . . neither one seemed to notice me.

The tattoo was beautiful, lifelike in a way I had not thought possible for a marking on the flesh. It was the cherubic face of an angel with thin, curly hair. One of the numbers had now become the shading for the angel's fine, straight nose. Surrounding the face were dark feathered wings that crossed each other; an impossible figure, but a hauntingly sad and beautiful one. The eyes seemed to be looking upward and out, as if contemplating a high station of paradise. The numbers were lost in the blue-blackness of lifting wings. This figure looked familiar, which was not surprising, as Nathan had studied the work of the masters. I remembered a Madonna, which was attributed to the Renaissance artist Lorenzo di Credi, that had two angels with wings such as those on the tattoo. But the tattooed wings were so dark they reminded me of death; and they were bleeding, an incongruous testament to life.

I thought about Nathan's bleeding wrist, and wondered . . .

"It's beautiful," Mrs Stramm said, staring at her tattoo. "It's the right face, it's the way his face would have looked . . . had he lived." Then she stood up abruptly. Nathan sat where he was; he looked exhausted, which was how I suddenly felt.

"I must put a gauze wrap over it," Nathan said.

"No, I wish to look at him."

"Can you see the old numbers?" Nathan asked.

"No," she said at first, then, "Yes, I can see them."

"Good," Nathan said.

She stood before Nathan, and I could now see that she had once been beautiful: big-boned, proud, full-bodied, with a strong chin and regal face. Her fine grey hair had probably been blond, as her eyebrows were light. And she looked relieved, released. I couldn't help but think that she seemed now like a woman who had just given birth. The strain was gone. She no longer seemed gravid with the burden of sorrow. But the heaviness had not disappeared from the room, for I could feel the psychic closeness of grief like stale, humid air. Nathan looked wasted in the sharp, cleansing, focussed light.

"Would you mind if I looked at *your* tattoo?" Mrs Stramm asked.

"I'm sorry," Nathan said.

Mrs Stramm nodded, then picked up her handbag and took out her chequebook. She moved toward the light and began to scribble out a cheque. "Will you accept three hundred dollars?"

"No, I cannot. Consider it paid."

She started to argue, but Nathan turned away from her. "Thank you," she said, and walked to the door.

Nathan didn't answer.

Nathan turned on the overhead light; the sudden change from darkness to light unnerved me.

"Tell me what the hell's going on," I said. "Why did your wrist start bleeding when you were tattooing that woman?"

"It's part of the process," Nathan said vaguely. "Do you want coffee?" he asked, changing the subject — Nathan had a way of talking around any subject, peeling away layers as if conversation was an onion; he eschewed directness. Perhaps it was his rabbinical heritage. At any rate, he wasn't going to tell me anything until he was ready. I nodded, and he took a bag of ground coffee out of his freezer, and dripped a pot in the Melitta. Someone knocked at the door and demanded a tattoo, and Nathan told him that he would have to wait until tomorrow.

We sat at the table and sipped coffee. I felt an overwhelming lassitude come over me. My shoulder began to ache . . . to throb. I worried that this might be the onset of another heart-attack (I try not to pay attention to my hypochondria, but those thoughts still flash through my mind, no matter how rational I try to be). Surely it was muscular, I told myself: I had been wrestling with my son last night. I needed to start swimming again at the "Y". I was out of shape, and right now I felt more like sixty-two that forty-two. After a while, the coffee cleared my head a bit — it was a very, very strong blend, Pico, I think — but the atmosphere inside the trailer was still oppressive, even with the overhead light turned on. It was as if I could *feel* the shadows.

"I saw Mrs Stramm here yesterday afternoon," I said, trying to lead Nathan. "She seems Jewish, strange that she should be getting a tattoo. Although maybe not so strange, since she came to a Jewish tattooist." I forced a laugh and tried not to stare at the thin webbing of scars on his neck.

"She's not Jewish," Nathan said. "Catholic. She was interred in the camp for political reasons. Her family was caught hiding Jews."

"It seems odd that she'd come to you for a tattoo to cover up her numbers," I said. "She could have had surgery. You would hardly be able to tell they'd ever been there."

"That's not why she came."

"Nathan . . ."

"Most of the people just want tattoos," Nathan said. He seemed slightly defensive, and then he sighed and said, "But sometimes I get people like Mrs Stramm. Word gets around, word-of-mouth. Sometimes I can sense things, see things about people when I'm tattooing. It's something like automatic writing, maybe. Then the tattoo takes on a life of its own, and sometimes it changes the person I tattoo."

"This whole thing . . . it seems completely crazy," I said, remembering his paintings, the large canvases of circus people, carny people. He had made his reputation with those melancholy, poignant oil paintings. He had travelled, followed the carnies. Ruth didn't seem to mind. She was independent, and used to travel quite a bit by herself also; she was fond of taking grueling, long day-trips. Like Nathan, she was full of energy. I remember that Nathan had been drawn to tattooing through circus people. He visited tattoo studios, and used them for his settings. The paintings he produced then were haunted, and he became interested in the idea of living art, the relationship of art to society, the numinous, symbolic quality of primitive art. It was only natural that he'd want to try tattooing, which he did. He had even tattooed himself: a tiny raven that seemed to be forever nestled in his palm. But that had been a phase, and once he had had his big New York show, he went on to paint ordinary people in parks and shopping malls and in movies houses, and his paintings were selling at over five thousand dollars apiece. I remembered ribbing him for tattooing himself. I had told him he couldn't be buried in a Jewish cemetery. He had said that he had already bought his plot. Money talks.

"How's Ruth?" I asked, afraid of what he would tell me. He would never be here, he would never look like this, if everything was all right between them.

"She's dead," he whispered, and he took a sip of his coffee.

"What?" I asked, shocked. "How?"

"Cancer, as she was always afraid of."

The pain in my shoulder became worse, and I started to sweat. It seemed to be getting warmer; he must have turned the heat up.

"How could all this happen without Laura or me knowing about it?" I asked. "I just can't believe it."

"Ruth went back to Connecticut to stay with her parents."

"Why?"

"David," Nathan said, "I knew she had cancer, even when she went in for tests and they all turned out negative. I kept dreaming about it, and I could *see* it burning inside her. I thought I was going crazy . . . I probably was. I couldn't stand it. I couldn't be near her. I couldn't help her. I couldn't do anything. So I started travelling, got back into the tattoo culture. The paintings were selling, especially the tattoo stuff — I did a lot of close-up work, you wouldn't even know it was tattoos I was painting, I got into some beautiful Oriental stuff — so I stayed away."

"And she died without you?" I asked, incredulous.

"In Stamford. The dreams got worse. It got so I couldn't even talk to her over the phone. I could see what was happening inside her and I was helpless. And I was a coward. I'm paying for it now."

"What do you mean?" I asked. Goddammit, it was hot.

He didn't answer.

"Tell me about the scars on your neck and your arms."

"And my chest, everywhere," Nathan confessed. "They're tattoos. It started when I ran away, when I left Ruth, I started tattooing myself. I used the tattoo gun, but no ink."

"Why?" I asked.

"At first, I guess I did it as practice, but then it became a sort of punishment. It was painful. I was painting without pigments. I was inflicting my own punishment. Sometimes I can see the tattoos, as if they were paintings. I'm a map of what I've done to my wife, to my family; and then around that time I discovered I could see into other people, and sort of draw their lives differently. Most people I'd just give a tattoo, good work, sometimes even great work, maybe, but every once in a while I'd see something when I was working. I could see if someone was sick, I could see what was wrong with him. I was going the carny route, and living with some gypsy people. A woman, a friend of mine, saw my 'talent'" — he laughed when he said that — "and helped me develop it. That's when I started bleeding when I worked. As my friend used to tell me, 'Everything has a price.'"

I looked at Nathan. His life was draining away. He was turning into a ghost, or a shadow. Not even his tattoos had colour.

My whole arm was aching. I couldn't ignore it any longer. And it was so close in the trailer that I couldn't *breathe*. "I've got to get some air," I said as I forced myself to get up. I felt as if I hadn't slept in days. Then I felt a burning in my neck and a stabbing pain in my chest. I tried to shout to Nathan, who was standing up, who looked shocked, who was coming toward me.

But I couldn't move; I was as leaden as a statue.

I could only see Nathan, and it was as if he were lit by a tensor lamp. The pigments of living tattoos glowed under his shirt, and resolved themselves like paintings under a stage scrim. He was a living, radiant landscape of scenes and figures, terrestrial and heavenly and demonic. I could see a grotesque caricature of Mrs Stramm's tattoo on Nathan's wrist. It was a howling, tortured, winged child. Most of the other tattoos expressed the ugly, minor sins of people Nathan had tattooed, but there were also figures of Nathan and Ruth. All of Ruth's faces were Madonna-like, but Nathan was rendered perfectly, and terribly; he was a monster portrayed in entirely human terms, a visage of greed and cowardice and hardness. But there was a central tattoo on Nathan's chest that looked like a Dürer engraving — such was the sureness and delicacy of the work. Ruth lay upon the ground, amid grasses and plants and flowers, which seemed surreal in their juxtaposition. She had opened her arms, as if begging for Nathan, who was depicted also, to return. Her chest and stomach and neck were bleeding, and one could look into the cavities of the open wounds. And marching away, descending under the nipple of Nathan's chest, was the figure of Nathan. He was followed by cherubs riding fabulous beasts, some of which were the skeletons of horses and dogs and goats with feathery wings . . . wings such as Nathan had tattooed on Mrs Stramm. But the figure of Nathan was running away. His face, which had always seemed askew — a large nose, deep-set engaging eyes, tousled hair, the combination of features that made him look like a seedy Puck, the very embodiment of generous friendliness — was rendered formally. His nose was straight and long, rather than crooked, as it was in real life, and his eyes were narrow and tilted, rather than wide and roundish; and his mouth, which in real life, even now, was full, was drawn as a mere line. In his hands, Nathan was carrying Ruth's heart and other organs, while a child riding a skeleton Pegasus was waving a thighbone.

The colours were like an explosion, and the tattoos filled my entire field of vision; and then the pain took me, wrapped like a snake around my chest. My heart was pounding. It seemed to be echoing in a huge hall. It was all I could hear. The burning in my chest increased and I felt myself screaming, even if it might be soundless. I felt my entire being straining in fright, and then the colours dimmed. Fainting, falling, I caught one last glimpse of the walls and ceiling, all pulsing, glowing, all coalescing into one grand tattoo, which was all around me, and I followed those inky pigment paths into greyness and then darkness. I thought of Laura and Ben, and I felt an overwhelming sense of sorrow for Nathan.

For once, I didn't seem to matter, and my sense of rushing sadness became a universe in which I was suspended.

I thought I was dying, but it seemed that it would take an eternity, an eternity to think, to worry back over my life, to relive it once more, but from a higher perspective, from an aerial view. But then I felt a pressure, as if I were under water and a faraway explosion had fomented a strong current. I was being pulled away, jostled, and I felt the tearing of pain and saw bright light and heard an electrical sparking, a sawing. And I saw Nathan's face, as large as a continent gazing down upon me.

I woke up on his couch. My head was pounding, but I was breathing naturally, evenly. My arm and shoulder and chest no longer ached, although I felt a needle-like burning over my heart. Reflexively, I touched the spot where I had felt the tearing pain, and found it had been bandaged. "What the hell's this?" I asked Nathan, who was sitting beside me. Although I could make out the scars on his neck, I could no longer find the outlines of the tattoos I had seen, nor could I make out the brilliant pigments that I had imagined or hallucinated. "Why do I have a bandage on?" I felt panic.

"Do you remember what happened?" he asked. Nathan looked ill. Even more wasted. His face was shiny with sweat. But it wasn't warm in here now; it was comfortable. Yet when Mrs Stramm was sitting for her tattoo, it was stifling. I had felt the closeness of dead air like claustrophobia.

"Christ, I thought I was having a heart attack. I blacked out. I fell."

"I caught you. You did have a heart attack."

"Then why the hell am I here instead of in a hospital?" I asked, remembering how it felt to be completely helpless in the emergency room, machines whirring and making ticking and just audible beeping noises as they monitored vital signs.

"It could have been very bad," Nathan said, ignoring my question.

"Then what am I doing here?" I asked again. I sat up. This was all wrong. Goddammit, it was wrong. I felt a rush in my head, and the headache became sharp and then withdrew back into dull pain.

"I took care of it," he said.

"How?"

"How do you feel?"

"I have a headache, that's all," I said, "and I want to know what you did on my chest."

"Don't worry, I didn't use pigment. They'll let you into a Jewish cemetery." Nathan smiled.

"I want to know what you did." I started to pull off the gauze, but he stopped me.

"Let it heal for a few days. Change the bandage. That's all."

"And what the hell am I supposed to tell Laura?" I asked.

"That you're alive."

I felt weak, yet it was as if I had sloughed something off, something heavy and deadening.

And I just walked out the door.

After I was outside, shivering, for the weather had turned unseasonably cold, I realised that I had not said goodbye. I had left, as if in a daze. Yet I could not turn around and go back. This whole night was crazy, I told myself. I'd come back tomorrow and apologise . . . and try to find out what had really happened.

I drove home, and it began to snow, a freakish wet, heavy snow that turned everything bluish-white, luminescent.

My chest began to itch under the bandage.

I didn't get home until after twelve. Understandably, Laura was worried and anxious. We both sat down to talk in the upholstered chairs in front of the fireplace in the living room, facing each other; that was where we always sat when we were arguing or working out problems. Normally, we'd sit on the sofa and chat and watch the fire. Laura had a fire crackling in the fireplace; and, as there were only a few small lamps on downstairs, the ruddy light from the fire flickered in our large white carpeted living room. Laura wore a robe with large cuffs on the sleeves and her thick black hair was long and shiny, still damp from a shower. Her small face was tight, as she was upset, and she wore her glasses, another giveaway that she was going to get to the bottom of this. She almost never wore her glasses, and the lenses were scratched from being tossed here and there and being banged about in various drawers; she only used them when she had to "focus her thoughts".

I looked a sight: my once starched white shirt was wrinkled and grimy, and I smelled rancid, the particular odor of nervous sweat. My trousers were dirty, especially at the knees, where I had fallen to the floor, and I had somehow torn out the hem of my right pantleg.

I told Laura the whole story, what had happened from the time I had seen Nathan Sunday until tonight. At first she seemed relieved that I had been with Nathan — she had never been entirely sure of me, and I'm certain she thought I'd had a rendezvous with some twenty-two-year-old receptionist or perhaps the woman who played the French horn in the orchestra — I had once made a remark about her to Laura. But she was more upset than I had expected when I told her that Ruth had died. We were friends, certainly, although I was much closer to Nathan than she was to Ruth.

We moved over to the couch and I held her until she stopped crying. I got up, fixed us both a drink, and finished the story.

"How could you let him tattoo your skin?" Laura asked; and then, exposing what she was really thinking about, she said in a whisper, "I can't believe Ruth's gone. We were good friends, you didn't know that, did you?"

"I guess I didn't." After a pause, I said, "I didn't *let* Nathan tattoo me. I told you, I was unconscious. I'd had an attack or something." I don't know if Laura really believed that. She had been a nurse for fifteen years.

"Well, let me take a look at what's under the gauze."

I let her unbutton my shirt; with one quick motion, she tore the gauze away. Looking down, I just saw the crisscrossings and curlicues and random lines that were thin raised welts over my heart.

"What the hell did he *do* to you? This whole area could get infected. Who knows if his needle was even clean. You could get hepatitis, or AIDS, considering the kinds of people who go in for tattoos."

"No, he kept everything clean," I said.

"Did he have an autoclave?" she asked.

"Yes, I think he did."

Laura went to the downstairs bathroom and came back with Betadine and a clean bandage. Her fuzzy blue bathrobe was slightly open, and I felt myself becoming excited. She was a tiny woman, small boned and delicate-featured, yet big-busted, which I liked. When we first lived together, before we married, she was extremely shy in bed, even though she'd already been married before; yet she soon became aggressive, open, and frank, and to my astonishment I found that *I* had grown more conservative.

I touched her breasts as she cleaned the tattoo, or more precisely, the welts, for he used no pigment. The Betadine and the touch of her hands felt cool on my chest.

"Can you make anything out of this?" she asked, meaning the marks Nathan had made.

I looked down, but couldn't make anything more out of them than she could. I wanted to look at the marks closely in the mirror, but Laura had become excited, as I was, and we started making love on the couch. She was on top of me, we still had our clothes on, and we were kissing each other so hard that we ground our teeth. I pressed myself inside her. Our lovemaking was urgent and cleansing. It was as if we had recovered something, and I felt my heart beating, clear and strong. After we came and lay locked together, still intimate, she whispered, "Poor Nathan."

I dreamed about him that night. I dreamed of the tattoo I had seen on his chest, the parade of demons and fabulous creatures. I was inside his tattoo, watching him walking off with Ruth's heart. I could hear the demon angels shouting and snarling and waving pieces of bone as they rode atop unicorns and skeleton dragons flapping canvasd-skinned pterodactyl wings. Then Nathan saw me, and he stopped. He looked as skeletal as the creatures around him, as if his life and musculature and fat had been worn away, leaving nothing but bones to be buried.

He smiled at me and gave me Ruth's heart.

It was warm and still beating. I could feel the blood clotting in my hand.

I woke up with a jolt. I was shaking and sweating. Although I had turned up the thermostat before going to bed, it was cold in the bedroom. Laura was turned away from me, moving restlessly, her legs raised toward her chest in a semi-foetal position. All the lights were off, and as it was a moonlit night, the snow reflected a wan light; everything in the room looked shadowy blue. And I felt my heart pumping fast.

I got up and went into the bathroom. Two large dormer windows over the tub to my left let in the dim light of a streetlight near the southern corner of the house. I looked in the mirror at my chest and could see my tattoo. The lines were etched in blue, as if my body were snow reflecting moonlight. I could see a heart; it was luminescent. I saw an angel wrapped in deathly wings, an angel such as the one Nathan had put on Mrs Stramm's wrist to heal her; but this angel, who seemed to have some of Nathan's features — his crooked nose and full mouth, had spread his wings, and his perfect infant hands held out Ruth's heart to me.

Staring, I leaned on the white porcelain sink. I felt a surging of life, as if I was being given a gift, and then the living image of the tattoo died. I shivered naked in the cold bathroom. I could feel the chill passing through the ill-fitting storms of the dormer windows. It was as if the chill were passing right through me, as if I had been opened up wide.

And I knew that Nathan was in trouble. The thought came to me like a shock of cold water. But I could *feel* Nathan's presence, and I suddenly felt pain shoot through my chest, concentrated in the tattoo, and then I felt a great sadness, an oceanic grief.

I dressed quickly and drove back to Trout Creek. The fairgrounds were well-lit, but deserted. It had stopped snowing. The lights were on in Nathan's trailer. I knocked on the door, but there was no answer. The door was unlocked, as I had left it, and I walked in.

Nathan was dead on the floor. His shirt was open and his chest was bleeding — he had the same tattoo I did. But his face was calm, his demons finally exorcised. I picked him up, carried him to the couch, and kissed him goodbye.

As I left, I could feel his strength and sadness and love pumping inside me. The wind blew against my face, drying my tears... it was the cold fluttering of angel's wings.

CAMPS

. . . .

As Stephen lies in bed, he can think only of pain.

He imagines it as sharp and blue. After receiving an injection of Demerol, he enters pain's cold regions as an explorer, an objective visitor. It is a country of ice and glass, monochromatic plains and valleys filled with wash blue shards of ice, crystal pyramids and pinnacles, squares, oblongs, and all manner of polyhedron — block upon block of painted blue pain.

Although it is mid-afternoon, Stephen pretends it is dark. His eyes are tightly closed, but the daylight pouring into the room from two large windows intrudes as a dull red field extending infinitely behind his eyelids.

"Josie," he asks through cotton mouth, "aren't I due for another shot?" Josie is crisp and fresh and large in her starched white uniform. Her peaked nurse's cap is pinned to her mouse brown hair.

"I've just given you an injection, it will take effect soon." Josie strokes his hand, and he dreams of ice.

"Bring me some ice," he whispers.

"If I bring you a bowl of ice, you'll only spill it again."

"Bring me some ice . . ." By touching the ice cubes, by turning them in his hand like a gambler favouring his dice, he can transport himself into the beautiful blue country. Later, the ice will melt, and he will spill the bowl. The shock of cold and pain will awaken him.

Stephen believes that he is dying, and he has resolved to die properly. Each visit to the cold country brings him closer to death; and death, he has learned, is only a slow walk through icefields. He has come to appreciate the complete lack of warmth and the beautifully etched face of his magical country.

But he is connected to the bright, flat world of the hospital by plastic tubes — one breathes cold oxygen into his left nostril; another passes into his right nostril and down his throat to his stomach; one feeds him intravenously, another draws his urine.

"Here's your ice," Josie says. "But mind you, don't spill it." She places the small bowl on his tray table and wheels the table close to him. She has a musky odor of perspiration and perfume; Stephen is reminded of old women and college girls.

"Sleep now, sweet boy."

Without opening his eyes, Stephen reaches out and places his hand on the ice.

"Come now, Stephen, wake up. Dr Volk is here to see you."

Stephen feels the cool touch of Josie's hand, and he opens his eyes to see the doctor standing beside him. The doctor has a gaunt long face and thinning brown hair; he is dressed in a wrinkled green suit.

"Now we'll check the dressing, Stephen," he says as he tears away a gauze bandage on Stephen's abdomen.

Stephen feels the pain, but he is removed from it. His only wish is to return to the blue dreamlands. He watches the doctor peel off the neat crosshatchings of gauze. A terrible stink fills the room.

Josie stands well away from the bed.

"Now we'll check your drains." The doctor pulls a long drainage tube out of Sephen's abdomen, irrigates and disinfects the wound, inserts a new drain, and repeats the process by pulling out another tube just below the rib cage.

Stephen imagines that he is swimming out of the room. He tries to cross the hazy border into cooler regions, but it is difficult to concentrate. He has only a half-hour at most before the Demerol will wear off. Already, the pain is coming closer, and he will not be due for another injection until the night nurse comes on duty. But the night nurse will not give him an injection without an argument. She will tell him to fight the pain.

But he cannot fight without a shot.

"Tomorrow we'll take that oxygen tube out of your nose," the doctor says, but his voice seems far away, and Stephen wonders what he is talking about.

He reaches for the bowl of ice, but cannot find it.

"Josie, you've taken my ice."

"I took the ice away when the doctor came. Why don't you try to watch a bit of television with me; Soupy Sales is on."

"Just bring me some ice," Stephen says. "I want to rest a bit." He can feel the sharp edges of pain breaking through the gauzy wraps of Demerol.

"I love you, Josie," he says sleepily as she places a fresh bowl of ice on his tray.

As Stephen wanders through his ice blue dreamworld, he sees a rectangle of blinding white light. It looks like a doorway into an adjoining world of brightness. He has glimpsed it before on previous Demerol highs. A coal-dark doorway stands beside the bright one.

He walks toward the portals, passes through white-blue cornfields.

Time is growing short. The drug cannot stretch it much longer. Stephen knows that he has to choose either the bright doorway or the dark, one or the other. He does not even consider turning around, for he has dreamed that the ice and glass and cold blue gem-stones have melted behind him.

It makes no difference to Stephen which doorway he chooses. On impulse he steps into blazing, searing whiteness.

Suddenly he is in a cramped world of people and sound.

The boxcar's doors were flung open. Stephen was being pushed out of the cramped boxcar that stank of sweat, faeces and urine. Several people had died in the car, and added their stink of death to the already fetid air.

"Carla, stay close to me," shouted a man beside Stephen. He had been separated from his wife by a young woman who pushed between them, as she tried to return to the dark safety of the boxcar.

SS men in black, dirty uniforms were everywhere. They kicked and pummeled everyone within reach. Alsatian guard dogs snapped and barked. Stephen was bitten by one of the snarling dogs. A woman beside him was being kicked by soldiers. And they were all being methodically herded past a high barbed-wire fence. Beside the fence was a wall.

Stephen looked around for an escape route, but he was surrounded by other prisoners, who were pressing against him. Soldiers were shooting indiscriminately into the crowd, shooting women and children alike.

The man who had shouted to his wife was shot.

"Sholom, help me, help me," screamed a scrawny young woman whose skin was as yellow and pimpled as chicken flesh.

And Stephen understood that *he* was Sholom. He was a Jew in this burning, stinking world, and this woman, somehow, meant something to him. He felt the yellow star sewn on the breast of his filthy jacket. He grimaced uncontrollably. The strangest thoughts were passing through his mind, remembrances of another childhood: morning prayers with his father and rich uncle, large breakfasts on Saturdays, the sounds of his mother and father quietly making love in the next room, *yortzeit* candles burning in the living room, his brother reciting the "four questions" at the Passover table.

He touched the star again and remembered the Nazi's facetious euphemism for it: *Pour le Semite.*

He wanted to strike out, to kill the Nazis, to fight and die. But he found himself marching with the others, as if he had no will of his own. He felt that he was cut in half. He had two selves now; one watched the other. One self wanted to fight. The other was numbed; it cared only for itself. It was determined to survive.

Stephen looked around for the woman who had called out to him. She was nowhere to be seen.

Behind him were railroad tracks, electrified wire, and the conical tower and main gate of the camp. Ahead was a pitted road littered with corpses and their belongings. Rifles were being fired and a heavy, sickly sweet odor was everywhere. Stephen gagged, others vomited. It was the overwhelming stench of death, of rotting and burning flesh. Black clouds hung above the camp, and flames spurted from the tall chimneys of ugly buildings, as if from infernal machines.

Stephen walked onward; he was numb, unable to fight or even talk. Everything that happened around him was impossible, the stuff of dreams.

The prisoners were ordered to halt, and the soldiers began to separate those who would be burned from those who would be worked to death. Old men and women and young children were pulled out of the crowd. Some were beaten and killed immediately while the others looked on in disbelief.

Stephen looked on, as if it was of no concern to him. Everything was unreal, dreamlike. He did not belong here.

The new prisoners looked like *Musselmänner*, the walking dead. Those who became ill, or were beaten or starved before they could "wake up" to the reality of the camps became *Musselmänner*. *Musselmänner* could not think or feel. They shuffled around, already dead in spirit, until a guard or disease or cold or starvation killed them.

"Keep marching," shouted a guard, as Stephen stopped before an emaciated old man crawling on the ground. "You'll look like him soon enough."

Suddenly, as if waking from one dream and finding himself in another, Stephen remembered that the chicken-skinned girl was his wife. He remembered their life together, their children and crowded flat. He remembered the birthmark on her leg, her scent, her hungry love-making. He had once fought another boy over her.

His glands opened up with fear and shame; he had ignored her screams for help.

He stopped and turned, faced the other group. "Fruma," he shouted, then started to run.

A guard struck him in the chest with the butt of his rifle, and Stephen fell into darkness.

He spills the icewater again and awakens with a scream.

"It's my fault," Josie says, as she peels back the sheets. "I should have taken the bowl away from you. But you fight me."

Stephen lives with the pain again. He imagines that a tiny fire is burning in his abdomen, slowly consuming him. He stares at the television high on the wall and watches "Soupy Sales".

As Josie changes the plastic sac containing his intravenous saline solution, an orderly pushes a cart into the room and asks Stephen if he wants a print for his wall.

"Would you like me to choose something for you?" Josie asks.

Stephen shakes his head and asks the orderly to show him all the prints. Most of them are familiar still-lifes and pastorals, but one catches his attention. It is a painting of a wheat field. Although the sky looks ominously dark, the wheat is brightly rendered in great broad strokes. A path cuts through the field and crows fly overhead.

"That one," Stephen says. "Put that one up."

After the orderly hangs the print and leaves, Josie asks Stephen why he chose that particular painting.

"I like Van Gogh," he says dreamily, as he tries to detect a rhythm in the surges of abdominal pain. But he is not nauseated, just gaseous.

"Any particular reason why you like Van Gogh?" asks Josie. "He's my favourite artist, too."

"I didn't say he was my favourite," Stephen says, and Josie pouts, an expression which does not fit her prematurely lined face. Stephen closes his eyes, glimpses the cold country, and says, "I like the painting because it's so bright that it's almost frightening. And the road going through the field" — he opens his eyes — "doesn't go anywhere. It just ends in the field. And the crows are flying around like vultures."

"Most people see it as just a pretty picture," Josie says.

"What's it called?"

"*Wheatfields with Blackbirds.*"

"Sensible. My stomach hurts, Josie. Help me turn over on my side." Josie helps him onto his left side, plumps up his pillows, and inserts a short tube into his rectum to relieve the gas. "I also like the painting with the large stars that all look out of focus," Stephen says. "What's it called?"

"*Starry Night.*"

"That's scary, too," Stephen says. Josie takes his blood pressure, makes a notation on his chart, then sits down beside him and holds his hand. "I remember something," he says. "Something just —" He jumps as he remembers, and pain shoots through his distended stomach. Josie shushes him, checks the intravenous needle, and asks him what he remembers.

But the memory of the dream recedes as the pain grows sharper. "I hurt all the fucking time, Josie," he says, changing position. Josie removes the rectal tube before he is on his back.

"Don't use such language, I don't like to hear it. I know you have a lot of pain," she says, her voice softening.

"Time for a shot."

"No, honey, not for some time. You'll just have to bear with it."

Stephen remembers his dream again. He is afraid of it. His breath is short and his heart feels as if it is beating in his throat, but he recounts the entire dream to Josie.

He does not notice that her face has lost its colour.

"It's only a dream, Stephen. Probably something you studied in history."

"But it was so real, not like a dream at all."

"That's enough!" Josie says.

"I'm sorry I upset you. Don't be angry."

"I'm *not* angry."

"I'm sorry," he says, fighting the pain, squeezing Josie's hand tightly. "Didn't you tell me that you were in the Second World War?"

Josie is composed once again. "Yes, I did, but I'm surprised you remembered. You were very sick. I was a nurse overseas, spent most of the war in England. But I was one of the first servicewomen to go into any of the concentration camps."

Stephen drifts with the pain; he appears to be asleep.

"You must have studied very hard," Josie whispers to him. Her hand is shaking just a bit.

It is twelve o'clock and his room is death quiet. The sharp shadows seem to be the hardest objects in the room. The fluorescents burn steadily in the hall outside.

Stephen looks out into the hallway, but he can see only the far white wall. He waits for his night nurse to appear: it is time for his injection. A young nurse passes by his doorway. Stephen imagines that she is a cardboard ship sailing through the corridors.

He presses the buzzer, which is attached by a clip to his pillow. The night nurse will take her time, he tells himself. He remembers arguing with her. Angrily, he presses the buzzer again.

Across the hall, a man begins to scream, and there is a shuffle of nurses into his room. The screaming turns into begging and whining. Although Stephen has never seen the man in the opposite room, he has come to hate him. Like Stephen, he has something wrong with his stomach, but he cannot suffer well. He can only beg and cry, try to make deals with the nurses, doctors, God and angels. Stephen cannot muster any pity for this man.

The night nurse finally comes into the room, says, "You have to try to get along without this," and gives him an injection of Demerol.

"Why does the man across the hall scream so?" Stephen asks, but the nurse is already edging out of the room.

"Because he's in pain."

"So am I," Stephen says in a loud voice. "But I can keep it to myself."

"Then stop buzzing me constantly for an injection. That man across the hall has had half of his stomach removed. He's got something to scream about."

So have I, Stephen thinks; but the nurse disappears before he can tell her. He tries to imagine what the man across the hall looks like. He thinks of him as being bald and small, an ancient baby. Stephen tries to feel sorry for the man, but his incessant whining disgusts him.

The drug takes effect; the screams recede as he hurtles through the dark corridors of a dream. The cold country is dark, for Stephen cannot persuade his night nurse to bring him some ice. Once again, he sees two entrances. As the world melts behind him, he steps into the coal-black doorway.

In the darkness he hears an alarm, a bone-jarring clangor.

He could smell the combined stink of men pressed closely together. They were all lying upon two badly constructed wooden shelves. The floor was dirt; the smell of urine never left the barracks.

"Wake up," said a man Stephen knew as Viktor. "If the guard finds you in bed, you'll be beaten again."

Stephen moaned, still wrapped in dreams. "Wake up, wake up," he mumbled to himself. He would have a few more minutes before the guard arrived with the dogs. At the very thought of dogs, Stephen felt revulsion. He had once been bitten in the face by a large dog.

He opened his eyes, yet he was still half-asleep, exhausted. You are in a death camp, he said to himself. You must wake up. You must fight by waking up. Or you will die in your sleep. Shaking uncontrollably, he said, "Do you want to end up in the oven; perhaps you will be lucky today and live."

As he lowered his legs to the floor; he felt the sores open on the soles of his feet. He wondered who would die today and shrugged. It was his third week in the camp. Impossibly, against all odds, he had survived. Most of those he had known in the train had either died or become *Musselmänner*. If it was not for Viktor, he, too, would have become a *Musselmänner*. He had a breakdown and wanted to die. He babbled in English. But Viktor talked him out of death, shared his portion of food with him, and taught him the new rules of life.

"Like everyone else who survives, I count myself first, second and third — then I try to do what I can for someone else," Viktor had said.

"I will survive," Stephen repeated to himself, as the guards opened the door, stepped into the room, and began to shout. Their dogs growled and snapped but heeled beside them. The guards looked sleepy; one did not wear a cap, and his red hair was tousled.

Perhaps he spent the night with one of the whores, Stephen thought. Perhaps today would not be so bad . . .

And so begins the morning ritual: Josie enters Stephen's room at quarter to eight, fusses with the chart attached to the footboard of his bed, pads about aimlessly, and finally goes to the bathroom. She returns, her stiff uniform making swishing sounds. Stephen can feel her standing over the bed and staring at him. But he does not open his eyes. He waits a beat.

She turns away, then drops the bedpan. Yesterday it was the metal ashtray; day before that, she bumped into the bedstand.

"Good morning, darling, it's a beautiful day," she says, then walks across the room to the windows. She parts the faded orange drapes and opens the blinds.

"How do you feel today?"

"Okay, I guess."

Josie takes his pulse and asks, "Did Mr Gregory stop in to say hello last night?"

"Yes," Stephen says. "He's teaching me how to play gin rummy. What's wrong with him?"

"He's very sick."

"I can see that; has he got cancer?"

"I don't know," says Josie, as she tidies up his night table.

"You're lying again," Stephen says, but she ignores him. After a time, he says, "His girl friend was in to see me last night. I bet his wife will be in today."

"Shut your mouth about that," Josie says. "Let's get you out of that bed so I can change the sheets."

Stephen sits in the chair all morning. He is getting well but is still very weak. Just before lunchtime, the orderly wheels his cart into the room and asks Stephen if he would like to replace the print hanging on the wall.

"I've seen them all," Stephen says. "I'll keep the one I have." Stephen does not grow tired of the Van Gogh painting; sometimes, the crows seem to have changed position.

"Maybe you'll like this one," the orderly says as he pulls out a cardboard print of Van Gogh's *Starry Night*. It is a study of a village nestled in the hills, dressed in shadows. But everything seems to be boiling and writhing as in a fever dream. A cypress tree in the foreground looks like a black flame, and the vertiginous sky is filled with great blurry stars. It is a drunkard's dream. The orderly smiles.

"So you did have it," Stephen says.

"No, I traded some other pictures for it. They had a copy in the West Wing."

Stephen watches him hang it, thanks him, and waits for him to leave. Then he gets up and examines the painting carefully. He touches the raised facsimile brushstrokes and turns toward Josie, feeling an odd sensation in his groin. He looks at her, as if seeing her for the first time. She has an overly full mouth which curves downward at the corners when she smiles. She is not a pretty woman — too fat, he thinks.

"Dance with me," he says, as he waves his arms and takes a step forward, conscious of the pain in his stomach.

"You're too sick to be dancing just yet," but she laughs at him and bends her knees in a mock plié.

She has small breasts for such a large woman, Stephen thinks. Feeling suddenly dizzy, he takes a step toward the bed. He feels himself slip to the floor, feels Josie's hair brushing against his face, dreams that he's all wet from her tongue, feels her arms around him, squeezing, then feels the weight of her body pressing down on him, crushing him . . .

He wakes up in bed, catheterised. He has an intravenous needle in his left wrist, and it is difficult to swallow, for he has a tube down his throat.

He groans, tries to move.

"Quiet, Stephen," Josie says, stroking his hand.

"What happened?" he mumbles. He can only remember being dizzy.

"You've had a slight setback, so just rest. The doctor had to collapse your lung; you must lie very still."

"Josie, I love you," he whispers, but he is too far away to be heard. He wonders how many hours or days have passed. He looks toward the window. It is dark, and there is no one in the room.

He presses the buzzer attached to his pillow and remembers a dream . . .

* * *

"You must fight," Viktor said.

It was dark, all the other men were asleep, and the barrack was filled with snoring and snorting. Stephen wished they could all die, choke on their own breath. It would be an act of mercy.

"Why fight?" Stephen asked, and he pointed toward the greasy window, beyond which were the ovens that smoked day and night. He made a fluttering gesture with his hand — smoke rising.

"You must fight, you must live, living is everything. It is the only thing that makes sense here."

"We're all going to die, anyway," Stephen whispered. "Just like your sister . . . and my wife."

"No, Sholom, we're going to live. The others may die, but we're going to live. You must believe that."

Stephen understood that Viktor was desperately trying to convince himself to live. He felt sorry for Viktor; there could be no sensible rationale for living in a place like this.

Stephen grinned, tasted blood from the corner of his mouth, and said, "So we'll live through the night, maybe."

And maybe tomorrow, he thought. He would play the game of survival a little longer.

He wondered if Viktor would be alive tomorrow. He smiled and thought; If Viktor dies, then I will have to take his place and convince others to live. For an instant, he hoped Viktor would die so that he could take his place.

The alarm sounded. It was three o'clock in the morning, time to begin the day.

This morning Stephen was on his feet before the guards could unlock the door.

"Wake up," Josie says, gently tapping his arm. "Come on, wake up."

Stephen hears her voice as an echo. He imagines that he has been flung into a long tunnel; he hears air whistling in his ears but cannot see anything.

"Whassimatter?" he asks. His mouth feels as if it is stuffed with cotton; his lips are dry and cracked. He is suddenly angry at Josie and the plastic tubes that hold him in his bed as if he was a latter-day Gulliver. He wants to pull out the tubes, smash the bags filled with saline, tear away his bandages.

"You were speaking German," Josie says. "Did you know that?"

"Can I have some ice?"

"No," Josie says impatiently. "You spilled again, you're all wet."

" . . . for my mouth, dry . . ."

"Do you remember speaking German, honey. I have to know."

"Don't remember, bring ice, I'll try to think about it."

As Josie leaves to get him some ice, he tries to remember his dream.

"Here, now, just suck on the ice." She gives him a little hill of crushed ice on the end of a spoon.

"Why did you wake me up, Josie?" The layers of dream are beginning to slough off. As the Demerol works out of his system, he has to concentrate on fighting the burning ache in his stomach.

"You were speaking German. Where did you learn to speak like that?"

Stephen tries to remember what he said. He cannot speak any German, only a bit of classroom French. He looks down at his legs (he has thrown off the sheet) and notices, for the first time, that his legs are as thin as his arms. "My God, Josie, how could I have lost so much weight?"

"You lost about forty pounds, but don't worry, you'll gain it all back. You're on the road to recovery now. Please, try to remember your dream."

"I can't, Josie! I just can't seem to get ahold of it."

"Try."

"Why is it so important to you?"

"You weren't speaking college German, darling. You were speaking slang. You spoke in a patois that I haven't heard since the forties."

Stephen feels a chill slowly creep up his spine. "What did I say?"

Josie waits a beat, then says, "You talked about dying."

"Josie?"

"Yes," she says, pulling at her fingernail.

"When is the pain going to stop?"

"It will be over soon." She gives him another spoonful of ice. "You kept repeating the name Viktor in your sleep. Can you remember anything about him?"

Viktor, Viktor, deep-set blue eyes, balding head and broken nose called himself a Galitzianer. Saved my life. "I remember," Stephen says. "His name is Viktor Shmone. He is in all my dreams now."

Josie exhales sharply.

"Does that mean anything to you?" Stephen asks anxiously.

"I once knew a man from one of the camps." She speaks very slowly and precisely. "His name was Viktor Shmone. I took care of him. He was one of the few people left alive in the camp after the Germans fled." She reaches for her purse, which she keeps on Stephen's night table, and fumbles an old, torn photograph out of a plastic slipcase.

As Stephen examines the photograph, he begins to sob. A thinner and much younger Josie is standing beside Viktor and two other emaciated-looking men. "Then I'm not dreaming," he says, "and I'm going to die. That's what it means." He begins to shake, just as he did in his dream, and, without thinking, he makes the gesture of rising smoke to Josie. He begins to laugh.

"Stop that," Josie says, raising her hand to slap him. Then she embraces him and says, "Don't cry, darling, it's only a dream. Somehow, you're dreaming the past."

"Why?" Stephen asks, still shaking.

"Maybe you're dreaming because of me, because we're so close. In some ways, I think you know me better than anyone else, better than any man, no doubt. You might be dreaming for a reason; maybe I can help you."

"I'm afraid, Josie."

She comforts him and says, "Now tell me everything you can remember about the dreams."

He is exhausted. As he recounts his dreams to her, he sees the bright doorway again. He feels himself being sucked into it. "Josie," he says, "I must stay awake, don't want to sleep, dream . . ."

Josie's face is pulled tight as a mask; she is crying.

Stephen reaches out to her, slips into the bright doorway, into another dream.

It was a cold cloudless morning. Hundreds of prisoners were working in the quarries; each work gang came from a different barrack. Most of the gangs were made up of *Musselmänner*, the faceless majority of the camp. They moved like automatons, lifting and carrying the great stones to the numbered carts, which would have to be pushed down the tracks.

Stephen was drenched with sweat. He had a fever and was afraid that he had contracted typhus. An epidemic had broken out in the camp last week.

Every morning several doctors arrived with the guards. Those who were too sick to stand up were taken away to be gassed or experimented upon in the hospital.

Although Stephen could barely stand, he forced himself to keep moving. He tried to focus all his attention on what he was doing. He made a ritual of bending over, choosing a stone of certain size, lifting it, carrying it to the nearest cart, and then taking the same number of steps back to his dig.

A *Musselmänn* fell to the ground, but Stephen made no effort to help him. When he could help someone in a little way, he would, but he would not stick his neck out for a *Musselmänn*. Yet something niggled at Stephen. He remembered a photograph in which Viktor and this *Musselmänn* were standing with a man and a woman he did not recognise. But Stephen could not remember where he had ever seen such a photograph.

"Hey, you," shouted a guard. "Take the one on the ground to the cart."

Stephen nodded to the guard and began to drag the *Musselmänn* away.

"Who's the new patient down the hall?" Stephen asks as he eats a bit of cereal from the breakfast tray Josie has placed before him. He is feeling much better now; his fever is down, and the tubes, catheter and intravenous needle have been removed. He can even walk around a bit.

"How did you find out about that?" Josie asks.

"You were talking to Mr Gregory's nurse. Do you think I'm dead already? I can still hear."

Josie laughs and takes a sip of Stephen's tea. "You're far from dead! In fact, today is a red-letter day; you're going to take your first shower. What do you think about that?"

"I'm not well enough yet," he says, worried that he will have to leave the hospital before he is ready.

"Well, Dr Volk thinks differently, and his word is law."

"Tell me about the new patient."

"They brought in a man last night who drank two quarts of motor oil; he's on the dialysis machine."

"Will he make it?"

"No, I don't think so; there's too much poison in his system."

We should all die, Stephen thinks. It would be an act of mercy. He glimpses the camp.

"Stephen!"

He jumps, then awakens.

"You've had a good night's sleep; you don't need to nap. Let's get you into that shower and have it done with." Josie pushes the tray table away from the bed. "Come on, I have your bathrobe right here."

Stephen puts on his bathrobe, and they walk down the hall to the showers. There are three empty shower stalls, a bench, and a whirlpool bath. As Stephen takes off his bathrobe, Josie adjusts the water pressure and temperature in the corner stall.

"What's the matter?" Stephen asks, after stepping into the shower. Josie stands in front of the shower stall and holds his towel, but she will not look at him. "Come on," he says, "you've seen me naked before."

"That was different."

"How?" He touches a hard, ugly scab that has formed over one of the wounds on his abdomen.

"When you were very sick, I washed you in bed, as if you were a baby. Now it's different." She looks down at the wet tile floor, as if she is lost in thought.

"Well, I think it's silly," he says. "Come on, it's hard to talk to someone who's looking the other way. I could break my neck in here and you'd be staring down at the fucking floor."

"I've asked you not to use that word," she says in a very low voice.

"Do my eyes still look yellowish?"

She looks directly at his face and says, "No, they look fine."

Stephen suddenly feels faint, then nauseated; he has been standing too long. As he leans against the cold shower wall, he remembers his last dream. He is back in the quarry. He can smell the perspiration of the men around him, feel the sun baking him, draining his strength. It is so bright . . .

He finds himself sitting on the bench and staring at the light on the opposite wall. I've got typhus, he thinks, then realises that he is in the hospital. Josie is beside him.

"I'm sorry," he says.

"I shouldn't have let you stand so long; it was my fault."

"I remembered another dream." He begins to shake, and Josie puts her arms around him.

"It's all right now, tell Josie about your dream."

She's an old, fat woman, Stephen thinks. As he describes the dream, his shaking subsides.

"Do you know the man's name?" Josie asks. "The one the guard ordered you to drag away."

"No," Stephen says. "He was a *Musselmänn*, yet I thought there was something familiar about him. In my dream I remembered the photograph you showed me. He was in it."

"What will happen to him?"

"The guards will give him to the doctors for experimentation. If they don't want him, he'll be gassed."

"You must not let that happen," Josie says, holding him tightly.

"Why?" asks Stephen, afraid that he will fall into the dreams again.

"If he was one of the men you saw in the photograph, you must not let him die. Your dreams must fit the past."

"I'm afraid."

"It will be all right, baby," Josie says, clinging to him. She is shaking and breathing heavily.

Stephen feels himself getting an erection. He calms her, presses his face against hers, and touches her breasts. She tells him to stop, but does not push him away.

"I love you," he says as he slips his hand under her starched skirt. He feels awkward and foolish and warm.

"This is wrong," she whispers.

As Stephen kisses her and feels her thick tongue in his mouth, he begins to dream . . .

Stephen stopped to rest for a few seconds. The *Musselmänn* was dead weight. I cannot go on, Stephen thought; but he bent down, grabbed the *Musselmänn* by his coat, and dragged him toward the cart. He glimpsed the cart, which was filled with the sick and dead and exhausted; it looked no different than a carload of corpses marked for a mass grave.

A long, grey cloud covered the sun, then passed, drawing shadows across gutted hills.

On impulse, Stephen dragged the *Musselmänn* into a gully behind several chalky rocks. Why am I doing this? he asked himself. If I'm caught, I'll be ash in the ovens, too. He remembered what Victor had told him: "You must think of yourself all the time, or you'll be no help to anyone else."

The *Musselmänn* groaned, then raised his arm. His face was grey with dust and his eyes were glazed.

"You must lie still," Stephen whispered. "Do not make a sound. I've hidden you from the guards, but if they hear you, we'll all be punished. One sound from you and you're dead. You must fight to live, you're in a death camp, you must fight so you can tell of this later."

"I have no family, they're all —"

Stephen clapped his hand over the man's mouth and whispered, "Fight, don't talk. Wake up, you cannot survive the death camp by sleeping."

The man nodded, and Stephen climbed out of the gully. He helped two men carry a large stone to a nearby cart.

"What are you doing?" shouted a guard.

"I left my place to help these men with this stone; now I'll go back where I was."

"What the hell are you trying to do?" Viktor asked.

Stephen felt as if he was burning up with fever. He wiped the sweat from his eyes, but everything was still blurry.

"You're sick, too. You'll be lucky if you last the day."

"I'll last," Stephen said, "but I want you to help me get him back to the camp."

"I won't risk it, not for a *Musselmänn*. He's already dead, leave him."

"Like you left me?"

Before the guards could take notice, they began to work. Although Viktor was older than Stephen, he was stronger. He worked hard every day and never caught the diseases that daily reduced the barrack's numbers. Stephen had a touch of death, as Viktor called it, and was often sick.

They worked until dusk, when the sun's oblique rays caught the dust from the quarries and turned it into veils and scrims. Even the guards sensed that this was a quiet time, for they would congregate together and talk in hushed voices.

"Come, now, help me," Stephen whispered to Viktor.

"I've been doing that all day," Viktor said. "I'll have enough trouble getting you back to the camp, much less carry this *Musselmänn*."

"We can't leave him."

"Why are you so preoccupied with this *Musselmänn*? Even if we can get him back to the camp, his chances are nothing. I know, I've seen enough, I know who has a chance to survive."

"You're wrong this time," Stephen said. He was dizzy and it was difficult to stand. The odds are I won't last the night, and Viktor knows it, he told himself. "I had a dream that if this man dies, I'll die, too. I just feel it."

"Here we learn to trust our dreams," Viktor said. "They make as much sense as this . . ." He made the gesture of rising smoke and gazed toward the ovens, which were spewing fire and black ash.

The western portion of the sky was yellow, but over the ovens it was red and purple and dark blue. Although it horrified Stephen to consider it, there was a macabre beauty here. If he survived, he would never forget these sense impressions, which were stronger than anything he had ever experienced before. Being so close to death, he was, perhaps for the first time, really living. In the camp, one did not even consider suicide. One grasped for every moment, sucked at life like an infant, lived as if there was no future.

The guards shouted at the prisoners to form a column; it was time to march back to the barracks.

While the others milled about, Stephen and Viktor lifted the *Musselmänn* out of the gully. Everyone nearby tried to distract the guards. When the march began, Stephen and Viktor held the *Musselmänn* between them, for he could barely stand.

"Come on, dead one, carry your weight," Viktor said. "Are you so dead that you cannot hear me? Are you as dead as the rest of your family?" The *Musselmänn* groaned and dragged his legs. Viktor kicked him. "You'll walk or we'll leave you here for the guards to find."

"Let him be," Stephen said.

"Are you dead or do you have a name?" Viktor continued.

"Berek," croaked the *Musselmänn*. "I am not dead."

"Then we have a fine bunk for you," Viktor said. "You can smell the stink of the sick for another night before the guards make a selection." Viktor made the gesture of smoke rising.

Stephen stared at the barracks ahead. They seemed to waver as the heat rose from the ground. He counted every step. He would drop soon, he could not go on, could not carry the *Musselmänn*.

He began to mumble in English.

"So you're speaking American again," Viktor said.

Stephen shook himself awake, placed one foot before the other.

"Dreaming of an American lover?"

"I don't know English and I have no American lover."

"Then who is this Josie you keep taking about in your sleep . . .?"

"Why were you screaming?" Josie asks, as she washes his face with a cold washcloth.

"I don't remember screaming," Stephen says. He discovers a fever blister on his lip. Expecting to find an intravenous needle in his wrist, he raises his arm.

"You don't need an IV," Josie says. "You just have a bit of a fever. Dr Volk has prescribed some new medication for it."

"What time is it?" Stephen stares at the whorls in the ceiling.

"Almost three p.m. I'll be going off soon."

"Then I've slept most of the day away," Stephen says, feeling something crawling inside him. He worries that his dreams still have a hold on him. "Am I having another relapse?"

"You'll do fine," Josie says.

"I should be fine now. I don't want to dream anymore."

"Did you dream again, do you remember anything?"

"I dreamed that I saved the *Musselmänn*," Stephen says.

"What was his name?" asks Josie.

"Berek, I think. Is that the man you knew?"

Josie nods and Stephen smiles at her. "Maybe that's the end of the dreams," he says, but she does not respond. He asks to see the photograph again.

"Not just now," Josie says.

"But I have to see it. I want to see if I can recognise myself . . ."

Stephen dreamed he was dead, but it was only the fever. Viktor sat beside him on the floor and watched the others. The sick were moaning and crying; they slept on the cramped platform, as if proximity to one another could insure a few more hours of life. Wan moonlight seemed to fill the barracks.

Stephen awakened, feverish. "I'm burning up," he whispered to Viktor.

"Well," Viktor said, "you've got your *Musselmänn*. If he lives, you live. That's what you said, isn't it?"

"I don't remember, I just knew that I couldn't let him die."

"You'd better go back to sleep, you'll need your strength. Or we may have to carry *you*, tomorrow."

Stephen tried to sleep, but the fever was making lights and spots before his eyes. When he finally fell asleep, he dreamed of a dark country filled with gem-stones and great quarries of ice and glass.

"What?" Stephen asked, as he sat up suddenly, awakened from damp black dreams. He looked around and saw that everyone was watching Berek, who was sitting under the window at the far end of the room.

Berek was singing the *Kol Nidre* very softly. It was the Yom Kippur prayer, which was sung on the most holy of days. He repeated the prayer three times, and then once again in a louder voice. The others responded, intoned the prayer as a recitative. Viktor was crying quietly, and Stephen imagined that the holy spirit animated Berek. Surely, he told himself, that face and those pale unseeing eyes were those of a dead man. He remembered the story of the golem, shuddered, found himself singing and pulsing with fever.

When the prayer was over, Berek fell back into his fever trance. The others became silent, then slept. But there was something new in the barracks with them tonight, a palpable exultation. Stephen looked around at the sleepers and thought: We're surviving, more dead than alive, but surviving . . .

"You were right about that *Musslemänn*," Viktor whispered. "It's good that we saved him."

"Perhaps we should sit with him," Stephen said. "He's alone." But Viktor was already asleep; and Stephen was suddenly afraid that if he sat beside Berek, he would be consumed by his holy fire.

As Stephen fell through sleep and dreams, his face burned with fever.

Again he wakes up screaming.

"Josie," he says, "I can remember the dream, but there's something else, something I can't see, something terrible . . ."

"Not to worry," Josie says, "it's the fever." But she looks worried, and Stephen is sure that she knows something he does not.

"Tell me what happened to Viktor and Berek," Stephen says. He presses his hands together to stop them from shaking.

"They lived, just as you are going to live and have a good life."

Stephen calms down and tells her his dream.

"So you see," she says, "you're even dreaming about surviving."

"I'm burning up."

"Dr Volk says you're doing very well." Josie sits beside him, and he watches the fever patterns shift behind his closed eyelids.

"Tell me what happens next, Josie."

"You're going to get well."

"There's something else . . ."

"Shush, now, there's nothing else." She pauses, then says, "Mr Gregory is supposed to visit you tonight. He's getting around a bit; he's been back and forth all day in his wheelchair. He tells me that you two have made some sort of a deal about dividing up all the nurses."

Stephen smiles, opens his eyes, and says, "It was Gregory's idea. Tell me what's wrong with him."

"All right, he has cancer, but he doesn't know it, and you must keep it a secret. They cut the nerve in his leg because the pain was so bad. He's quite comfortable now, but, remember, you can't repeat what I've told you."

"Is he going to live?" Stephen asks. "He's told me about all the new projects he's planning. So I guess he's expecting to get out of here."

"He's not going to live very long, and the doctor didn't want to break his spirit."

"I think he should be told."

"That's not your decision to make, nor mine."

"Am I going to die, Josie?"

"No!" she says, touching his arm to reassure him.

"How do I know that's the truth?"

"Because I say so, and I couldn't look you straight in the eye and tell you if it wasn't true. I should have known it would be a mistake to tell you about Mr Gregory."

"You did right," Stephen says. "I won't mention it again. Now that I know, I feel better." He feels drowsy again.

"Do you think you're up to seeing him tonight?"

Stephen nods, although he is bone-tired. As he falls asleep, the fever patterns begin to dissolve, leaving a bright field. With a start, he opens his eyes: he has touched the edge of another dream.

"What happened to the man across the hall, the one who was always screaming?"

"He's left the ward," Josie says. "Mr Gregory had better hurry, if he wants to play cards with you before dinner. They're going to bring the trays up soon."

"You mean he died, don't you."

"Yes, if you must know, he died. But *you're* going to live."

There is a crashing noise in the hallway. Someone shouts, and Josie runs to the door.

Stephen tries to stay awake, but he is being pulled back into the cold country.

"Mr Gregory fell trying to get into his wheelchair by himself," Josie says. "He should have waited for his nurse, but she was out of the room and he wanted to visit you."

But Stephen does not hear a word she says.

There were rumours that the camp was going to be liberated. It was late, but no one was asleep. The shadows in the barracks seemed larger tonight.

"It's better for us if the Allies don't come," Viktor said to Stephen.

"Why do you say that?"

"Haven't you noticed that the ovens are going day and night? The Nazis are in a hurry."

"I'm going to try to sleep," Stephen said.

"Look around you, even the *Musslemänner* are agitated," Viktor said. "Animals become nervous before the slaughter. I've worked with animals. People are not so different."

"Shut up and let me sleep," Stephen said, and he dreamed that he could hear the crackling of distant gunfire.

"Attention," shouted the guards as they stepped into the barrack. There were more guards than usual, and each one had two Alsatian dogs. "Come on, form a line. Hurry."

"They're going to kill us," Viktor said, "then they'll evacuate the camp and save themselves."

The guards marched the prisoners toward the north section of the camp. Although it was still dark, it was hot and humid, without a trace of the usual morning chill. The ovens belched fire and turned the sky aglow. Everyone was quiet, for there was nothing to be done. The guards were nervous and would cut down anyone who uttered a sound, as an example for the rest.

The booming of big guns could be heard in the distance. If I'm going to die, Stephen thought, I might as well go now and take a Nazi with me. Suddenly, all of his buried fear, aggression and revulsion surfaced; his face became hot and his heart felt as if it was pumping in his throat. But Stephen argued with himself. There was always a chance. He had once heard of some women who were waiting in line for the ovens; for no apparent reason the guards sent them back to their barracks. Anything could happen. There was always a chance. But to attack a guard would mean certain death.

The guns became louder. Stephen could not be sure, but he thought the noise was coming from the west. The thought passed through his mind that everyone would be better off dead. That would stop all the guns and screaming voices, the clenched fists and wildly beating hearts. The Nazis should kill everyone, and then themselves, as a favour to humanity.

The guards stopped the prisoners in an open field surrounded on three sides by forestland. Sunrise was moments away; purple black clouds drifted across the sky, touched by grey in the east. It promised to be a hot, gritty day.

Half-Step Walter, a Judenrat sympathiser who worked for the guards, handed out shovel heads to everyone.

"He's worse than the Nazis," Viktor said to Stephen.

"The Judenrat thinks he will live," said Berek, "but he will die like a Jew with the rest of us."

"Now, when it's too late, the *Musselmänn* regains consciousness," Viktor said.

"Hurry," shouted the guards, "or you'll die now. As long as you dig, you'll live."

Stephen hunkered down on his knees and began to dig with the shovel head.

"Do you think we might escape?" Berek whined.

"Shut up and dig," Stephen said. "There is no escape, just stay alive as long as you can. Stop whining, are you becoming a *Musselmänn* again?" Stephen noticed that other prisoners were gathering up twigs and branches. So the Nazis plan to cover us up, he thought.

"That's enough," shouted a guard. "Put your shovels down in front of you and stand in a line."

The prisoners stood shoulder to shoulder along the edge of the mass grave. Stephen stood between Viktor and Berek. Someone screamed and ran and was shot immediately.

I don't want to see trees or guards or my friends, Stephen thought as he stared into the sun. I only want to see the sun, let it burn out my eyes, fill up my head with light. He was shaking uncontrollably, quaking with fear.

Guns were booming in the background.

Maybe the guards won't kill us, Stephen thought, even as he heard the crack-crack of their rifles. Men were screaming and begging for life. Stephen turned his head, only to see someone's face blown away.

Screaming, tasting vomit in his mouth, Stephen fell backward, pulling Viktor and Berek into the grave with him.

Darkness, Stephen thought. His eyes were open, yet it was dark, I must be dead; this must be death . . .

He could barely move. Corpses can't move, he thought. Something brushed against his face; he stuck out his tongue, felt something spongy. It tasted bitter. Lifting first one arm and then the other, Stephen moved some branches away. Above, he could see a few dim stars; the clouds were lit like lanterns by a quarter moon.

He touched the body beside him; it moved. That must be Viktor, he thought. "Viktor, are you alive, say something if you're alive." Stephen whispered, as if in fear of disturbing the dead.

Viktor groaned and said, "Yes, I'm alive, and so is Berek."

"And the others?"

"All dead. Can't you smell the stink? You, at least, were unconscious all day."

"They can't *all* be dead," Stephen said, then he began to cry.

"Shut up," Viktor said, touching Stephen's face to comfort him. "We're alive, that's something. They could have fired a volley into the pit."

"I though I was dead," Berek said. He was a shadow among shadows.

"Why are we still here?" Stephen asked.

"We stayed in here because it is safe," Viktor said.

"But they're all dead," Stephen whispered, amazed that there could be speech and reason inside a grave.

"Do you think it's safe to leave now?" Berek asked Viktor.

"Perhaps. I think the killing has stopped. By now the Americans or English or whoever they are have taken over the camp. I heard gunfire and screaming. I think it's best to wait a while longer."

"Here?" asked Stephen. "Among the dead?"

"It's best to be safe."

It was late afternoon when they climbed out of the grave. The air was thick with flies. Stephen could see bodies sprawled in awkward positions beneath the covering of twigs and branches. "How can I live when all the others are dead?" he asked himself aloud.

"You live, that's all," answered Viktor.

They kept close to the forest and worked their way back toward the camp.

"Look there," Viktor said, motioning Stephen and Berek to take cover. Stephen could see trucks moving toward the camp compound.

"Americans," whispered Berek.

"No need to whisper now," Stephen said, "We're safe."

"Guards could be hiding anywhere," Viktor said. "I haven't slept in the grave to be shot now."

They walked into the camp through a large break in the barbed-wire fence, which had been hit by an artillery shell. When they reached the compound, they found nurses, doctors, and army personnel bustling about.

"You speak English," Viktor said to Stephen, as they walked past several quonsets. "Maybe you can speak for us."

"I told you, I can't speak English."

"But I've heard you!"

"Wait," shouted an American army nurse. "You fellows are going the wrong way." She was stocky and spoke perfect German. "You must check in at the hospital; it's back that way."

"No," said Berek, shaking his head. "I won't go in there."

"There's no need to be afraid now," she said. "You're free. Come along, I'll take you to the hospital."

Something familiar about her, Stephen thought. He felt dizzy and everything turned grey.

"Josie," he murmured, as he fell to the ground.

* * *

"What is it?" Josie asks. "Everything is all right, Josie is here."

"Josie," Stephen mumbles.

"You're all right."

"How can I live when they're all dead?" he asks.

"It was a dream," she says as she wipes the sweat from his forehead. "You see, your fever has broken, you're getting well."

"Did you know about the grave?"

"It's all over now, forget the dream."

"Did you know?"

"Yes," Josie says. "Viktor told me how he survived the grave, but that was so long ago, before you were even born. Dr Volk tells me you'll be going home soon."

"I don't want to leave, I want to stay with you."

"Stop that talk, you've got a whole life ahead of you. Soon, you'll forget all about this, and you'll forget me, too."

"Josie," Stephen asks, "let me see that old photograph again. Just one last time."

"Remember, this is the last time," she says as she hands him the faded photograph.

He recognises Viktor and Berek, but the young man standing between them is not Stephen. "That's not me," he says, certain that he will never return to the camp.

Yet the shots still echo in his mind.

DA VINCI RISING

ONE

Dressed as if he were on fire — in a doublet of heliotrope and crimson over a blood-red shirt — Leonardo da Vinci entered the workshop of his master, Andrea Verrochio.

Verrochio had invited a robust and august company of men to what had become one of the most important salons in Florence. The many conversations were loud and the floor was stained with wine. Leonardo's fellow apprentices stood near the walls, discreetly listening and interjecting a word here and there. Normally, Master Andrea cajoled the apprentices to work — he had long given up on Leonardo, the best of them all, who worked when he would — but tonight he had closed the shop. The aged Paolo del Pozzo Toscanelli, who had taught Leonardo mathematics and geography, sat near a huge earthenware jar and a model of the lavabado that would be installed in the old Sacristy of San Lorenzo. A boy with dark intense eyes and a tight accusing mouth stood behind him like a shadow. Leonardo had never seen this boy before; perhaps Toscanelli had but recently taken this waif into his home.

"I want you to meet a young man with whom you have much in common," Toscanelli said. "His father is also a notary, like yours. He has put young Niccolo in my care. Niccolo is a child of love, also like you, and extremely talented as a poet and playwright and rhetorician. He is interested in everything, and he seems unable to finish anything! But unlike you, Leonardo, he talks very little, isn't that right, Niccolo."

"I am perfectly capable of talking, Ser Toscanelli," the boy said.

"What's your name?" Leonardo asked.

"Ach, forgive me my lack of manners," Toscanelli said. "Master Leonardo, this is Niccolo Machiavelli, son of Bernardo di Niccolo and Bartolomea Nelli. You may have heard of Bartolomea, a religious poetess of great talent."

Leonardo bowed and said with a touch of sarcasm, "I am honoured to meet you, young sir."

"I would like you to help this young man with his education," Toscanelli said.

"But I —"

"You are too much of a lone wolf, Leonardo. You must learn to give generously of your talents. Teach him to see as you do, to play the lyre, to paint. Teach him magic and perspective, teach him about the streets, and women, and the nature of light. Show him your flying machine and your sketches of birds. And I guarantee, he will repay you."

"But he's only a boy!"

Niccolo Machiavelli stood before Leonardo, staring at him expectantly, as if concerned. He was a handsome boy, tall and gangly, but his face was unnaturally severe for one so young. Yet he seemed comfortable alone here in this strange place. Merely curious, Leonardo thought.

"What are you called," Leonardo asked, taking interest.

"Niccolo," the boy said.

"And you have no nickname?"

"I am called Niccolo Machiavelli, that is my name."

"Well, I shall call you Nicco, young sir. Do you have any objections."

After a pause, he said, "No, Maestro," but the glimmer of a smile compressed his thin lips.

"So your new name pleases you somewhat," Leonardo said.

"I find it amusing that you feel it necessary to make my name smaller. Does that make you feel larger?"

Leonardo laughed. "And what is your age?"

"I am almost fifteen."

"But you are really fourteen, is that not so?"

"And you are still but an apprentice to Master Andrea, yet you are truly a master, or so Master Toscanelli has told me. Since you are closer to being a master, wouldn't you prefer men to think of you as such? Or would you rather be treated as an apprentice such as the one there who is in charge of filling glasses with wine? Well, Master Leonardo . . .?"

Leonardo laughed again, taking a liking to this intelligent boy who acted as if he possessed twice his years, and said, "You may call me Leonardo."

At that moment, Andrea Verrochio walked over to Leonardo with Lorenzo de' Medici in tow. Lorenzo was magnetic, charismatic, and ugly. His face was coarse, overpowered by a large, flattened nose, and he was suffering one of his periodic outbreaks of eczema; his chin and cheeks were covered with a flesh-coloured paste. He had a bull-neck and long, straight brown hair, yet he held himself with such grace that he appeared taller than the men around him. His eyes were perhaps his most arresting feature, for they looked at everything with such friendly intensity, as if to see through things and people alike.

"We have in our midst Leonardo da Vinci, the consummate conjurer and prestidigitator," Verrochio said, bowing to Lorenzo de Medici as he presented Leonardo to him; he spoke loud enough for all to hear. "Leonardo has fashioned a machine that can carry a man in the air like a bird . . ."

"My sweet friend Andrea has often told me about your inventiveness, Leonardo da Vinci," Lorenzo said, a slight sarcasm in his voice; ironically, he spoke to Leonardo in much the same good-humoured yet condescending tone that Leonardo had used when addressing young Machiavelli. "But how do you presume to affect this miracle of flight? Surely not be means of your cranks and pulleys. Will you conjure up the flying beast Geryon, as we read Dante did and so descend upon its neck into the infernal regions? Or will you merely paint yourself into the sky?"

Everyone laughed at that, and Leonardo, who would not dare to try to seize the stage from Lorenzo, explained, "My most illustrious Lord, you may see that the beating of its wings against the air supports a heavy eagle in the highest and rarest atmosphere, close to the sphere of elemental fire. Again, you may see the air in motion over the sea fill the swelling sails and drive heavily laden ships. Just so could a man with wings large enough and properly connected learn to overcome the resistance of the air and, by conquering it, succeed in subjugating it and rising above it.

"After all," Leonardo continued, "a bird is nothing more than an instrument that works according to mathematical laws, and it is within the capacity of man to reproduce it with all its movements."

"But a man is not a bird," Lorenzo said. "A bird has sinews and muscles that are incomparably more powerful than a man's. If we were constructed so as to have wings, we would have been provided with them by the Almighty."

"Then you think we are too weak to fly?"

"Indeed, I think the evidence would lead reasonable men to that conclusion," Lorenzo said.

"But surely," Leonardo said, "you have seen falcons carrying ducks and eagles carrying hares; and there are times when these birds of prey must double their rate of speed to follow their prey. But they only need a little force to sustain themselves, and to balance themselves on their wings, and flap them in the pathway of the wind and so direct the course of their journeying. A slight movement of the wings is sufficient, and the greater the size of the bird, the slower the movement. It's the same with men, for we possess a greater amount of strength in our legs than our weight requires. In fact, we have twice the amount of strength we need to support ourselves. You can prove this by observing how far the marks of one of your men's feet will sink into the sand of the seashore. If you then order another man to climb upon his back, you can observe how much deeper the foot marks will be. But remove the man from the other's back and order the first man to jump as high as he can, and you will find that the marks of his feet will now make a deeper impression where he has jumped than in the place where he had the other man on his back. That's double proof that a man has more than twice the strength he needs to support himself . . . more than enough to fly like a bird."

Lorenzo laughed. "Very good, Leonardo. But I would have to see with my own eyes your machine that turns men into birds. Is *that* what you've been spending your precious time doing, instead of working on the statues I commissioned you to repair?"

Leonardo let his gaze drop to the floor.

"Not at all," Verrochio interrupted, "Leonardo has indeed been with me in your gardens applying his talent to the repair of —"

"Show me this machine, painter," Lorenzo said to Leonardo. "I could use such a device to confound my enemies, especially those wearing the colours of the south" — the veiled reference was to Pope Sixtus IV and the Florentine Pazzi family. "Is it ready to be used?"

"Not just yet, Magnificence," Leonardo said. "I'm still experimenting."

Everyone laughed, including Lorenzo. "Ah, experimenting is it . . . well, then I'll pledge you to communicate with me when it's finished. But from your past performance, I think that none of us need worry."

Humiliated, Leonardo could only avert his eyes.

"Tell me, how long do you anticipate that your . . . experiments will take?"

"I think I could safely estimate that my 'contraption' would be ready for flight in two weeks," Leonardo said, taking the advantage, to everyone's surprise. "I plan to launch my great bird from Swan Mountain in Fiesole."

The studio became a roar of surprised conversation.

Leonardo had no choice except to meet Lorenzo's challenge; if he did not, Lorenzo might ruin his career. As it was, his Magnificence obviously considered Leonardo to be a dilettante, a polymath genius who could not be trusted to bring his commissions to fruition.

"Forgive my caustic remarks, Leonardo, for everyone in this room respects your pretty work," Lorenzo said. "But I will take you up on your promise: in two weeks we travel to Fiesole!"

TWO

One could almost imagine that the great bird was already in flight, hovering in the gauzy morning light like a great, impossible hummingbird. It was a chimerical thing that hung from the high attic ceiling of Leonardo's workshop in Verrocchio's *bottega*: a tapered plank fitted with hand operated cranks, hoops of well-tanned leather, pedals, windlass, oars, and saddle. Great ribbed batlike wings made of cane and fustian and starched taffeta were connected to the broader end of the plank. They were dyed bright red and gold, the colours of the Medici, for it was the Medici who would attend its first flight.

As Leonardo had written in his notebook: *Remember that your bird must imitate only the bat because its webbing forms a framework that gives strength to the wings. If you imitate the birds' wings, you will discover the feathers to be disunited and permeable to the air. But the bat is aided by the membrane which binds the whole and is not pervious.* This was written backwards from right to left in Leonardo's idiosyncratic "mirror" script that was all but impossible to decipher. Leonardo lived in paranoid fear that his best ideas and inventions would be stolen.

Although he sat before a canvas he was painting, his eyes smarting from the miasmas of varnish and linseed oil and first grade turpentine, Leonardo nervously gazed up at his invention. It filled the upper area of the large room, for its wingspan was over fifteen ells — more than twenty-five feet.

For the past few days Leonardo had been certain that something was not quite right with his great bird, yet he could not divine what it might be. Nor could he sleep well, for he had been having nightmares; no doubt they were a consequence of his apprehensions over his flying machine, which was due to be flown from the top of a mountain in just ten days. His dream was always the same: he would be falling from a great height . . . without wings, without harness . . . into a barely luminescent void, while above him the familiar sunlit hills and mountains that overlooked Vinci would be turning vertiginously. And he would awaken in a cold sweat, tearing at his covers, his heart beating in his throat as if to choke him.

Leonardo was afraid of heights. While exploring the craggy and dangerous slopes of Monte Albano as a child, he had fallen from an overhang and almost broken his back. But Leonardo was determined to conquer this and every other fear. He would become as familiar with the airy realms as the birds that soared and rested on the winds. He would make the very air his ally, his support and security.

There was a characteristic knock on the door: two light taps followed by a loud thump.

"Enter, Andrea, lest the dead wake," Leonardo said without getting up.

Verrocchio stormed in with his foreman Francesco di Simone, a burly, full-faced, middle-aged man whose muscular body was just beginning to go to seed. Francesco carried a silver tray, upon which were placed cold meats, fruit, and two cruses of milk; he laid it on the table beside Leonardo. Both Verrocchio and Francesco had been at work for hours, as was attested by the lime and marble dust that streaked their faces and shook from their clothes. They were unshaven and wore work gowns, although Verrocchio's was more a frock, as if, indeed, he envisioned himself as a priest to art — the unblest "tenth muse".

Most likely they had been in one of the outer workshops, for Andrea was having trouble with a terra cotta *risurrezione* relief destined for Lorenzo's villa in Careggi. But this bottega was so busy that Andrea's attention was constantly in demand. "Well, at least *you're* awake," Andrea said to Leonardo as he looked appreciatively at the painting-in-progress. Then he clapped his hands, making such a loud noise that Niccolo, who was fast asleep on his pallet beside Leonardo's, awakened with a cry, as if from a particularly nasty nightmare. Andrea chuckled and said, "Well, good morning, young ser. Perhaps I could have one of the other apprentices find enough work for you to keep you busy during the spine of the morning."

"I apologise, Maestro Andrea, but Maestro Leonardo and I worked late into the night." Niccolo removed his red, woollen sleeping cap and hurriedly put on a gown that lay on the floor beside his pallet, for like most Florentines, he slept naked.

"Ah, so now it's Maestro Leonardo, is it?" Andrea said good-naturedly. "Well, eat your breakfast, both of you. Today I'm a happy man; I have news."

Niccolo did as he was told, and, in fact, ate like a trencherman, spilling milk on his lap.

"One would never guess that he came from a good family," Andrea said, watching Niccolo stuff his mouth.

"Now tell me your news," Leonardo said.

"It's not all that much to tell." Nevertheless Andrea could not repress a grin. "*Il Magnifico* has informed me that my 'David' will stand prominently in the Palazzo Vecchio over the great staircase."

Leonardo nodded. "But, certainly, you knew Lorenzo would find a place of special honour for such a work of genius."

"I don't know if you compliment me or yourself, Leonardo," Andrea said. "After all, you are the model."

"You took great liberties," Leonardo said. "You may have begun with my features, but you have created something sublime out of the ordinary. You deserve the compliment."

"I fear this pleasing talk will cost me either money or time," Andrea said.

Leonardo laughed. "Indeed, today I must be out of the city."

Andrea gazed up at Leonardo's flying machine and said, "No one would blame you if you backed out of this project, or, at least, allowed someone else to fly your contraption. You need not prove yourself to Lorenzo."

"I would volunteer to fly your mechanical bird, Leonardo," Niccolo said earnestly.

"No, it must be me."

"Was it not to gain experience that Master Toscanelli sent me to you?"

"To gain experience, yes; but not to jeopardise your life," Leonardo said.

"You are not satisfied it will work?" Andrea asked.

"Of course I am, Andrea. If I were not, I would bow before Lorenzo and give him the satisfaction of publicly putting me to the blush."

"Leonardo, be truthful with me," Verrocchio said. "It is to Andrea you speak, not a rich patron."

"Yes, my friend, I am worried," Leonardo confessed. "Something is indeed wrong with my Great Bird, yet I cannot quite put my finger on it. It is most frustrating."

"Then you must not fly it!"

"It will fly, Andrea. I promise you that."

"You have my blessing to take the day off," Verrocchio said.

"I am most grateful," Leonardo said; and they both laughed, knowing that Leonardo would have left for the country with or without Andrea's permission.

"Well, we must be off," Leonardo said to Andrea, who nodded and took his leave.

"Come on, Nicco," Leonardo said, suddenly full of energy. "Get yourself dressed"; and as Niccolo did so, Leonardo put a few finishing touches on his painting, then quickly cleaned his brushes, hooked his sketchbook onto his belt, and once again craned his neck to stare at his invention that hung from the ceiling. He needed an answer, yet he had not yet formulated the question.

When they were out the door, Leonardo felt that he had forgotten something. "Nicco, fetch me the book Maestro Toscanelli loaned to me . . . the one he purchased from the Chinese trader. I might wish to read in the country."

"The country?" Niccolo asked, carefully putting the book into a sack, which he carried under his arm.

"Do you object to nature?" Leonardo asked sarcastically. "*Usus est optimum magister* . . . and in that I agree wholeheartedly with the ancients. Nature herself is the mother of all experience; and experience must be your teacher, for I have discovered that even Aristotle can be mistaken on certain subjects." As they left the bottega, he continued: "But those of Maestro Ficino's Academy, they go about all puffed and pompous, mouthing the eternal aphorisms of Plato and Aristotle like parrots. They might think that because I have not had a literary education, I am uncultured; but they are the fools. They despise me because I am an inventor, but how much more are they to blame for *not* being inventors, these trumpeters and reciters of the works of others. They considered my glass to study the skies and make the moon large a conjuring trick, and do you know why?" Before Niccolo could respond, Leonardo said, "Because they consider sight to be the most untrustworthy of senses, when, in fact, it is the supreme organ. Yet that does not prevent them from wearing spectacles in secret. Hypocrites!"

"You seem very angry, Maestro," Niccolo said to Leonardo.

Embarrassed at having launched into this diatribe, Leonardo laughed at himself and said, "Perhaps I am, but do not worry about it, my young friend."

"Maestro Toscanelli seems to respect the learned men of the Academy," Niccolo said.

"He respects Plato and Aristotle, as well he should. But he does not teach at the Academy, does he? No, instead, he lectures at the school at Santo Spirito for the Augustinian brothers. That should tell you something."

"I think it tells me that you have an axe to grind, Master . . . and that's also what Maestro Toscanelli told me."

"What else did he tell you, Nicco?" Leonardo asked.

"That I should learn from your strengths and weaknesses, and that you are smarter than everyone in the Academy."

Leonardo laughed at that and said, "You lie very convincingly."

"That, Maestro, comes naturally."

The streets were busy and noisy and the sky, which seemed pierced by the tiled mass of the Duomo and the Palace of the Signoria, was cloudless and sapphire-blue. There was the sweet smell of sausage in the air, and young merchants — practically children — stood behind stalls and shouted at every passerby. This market was called *Il Baccano*, the place of uproar. Leonardo bought some cooked meat, beans, fruit, and a bottle of cheap local wine for Niccolo and himself. They continued on into different neighbourhoods and markets. They passed Spanish Moors with their slave retinues from the Ivory Coast; Mamluks in swathed robes and flat turbans; Muscovy Tartars and Mongols from Cathay; and merchants from England and Flanders, who had sold their woollen cloth and were on their way to the Ponte Vecchio to purchase trinkets and baubles. Niccolo was all eye and motion as they passed elegant and beautiful "butterflies of the night" standing beside their merchant masters under the shade of guild awnings; these whores and mistresses modelled jewelled garlands, and expensive garments of violet, crimson, and peach. Leonardo and Niccolo passed stall after stall — brushing off young hawkers and old, disease-ravaged beggars — and flowed with the crowds of peddlers, citizens, and visitors as if they were flotsam in the sea. Young men of means, dressed in short doublets, wiggled and swayed like young girls through the streets; they roistered and swashbuckled, laughed and sang and bullied, these favoured ones. Niccolo could not help but laugh at the scholars and student wanderers from England and Scotland and Bohemia, for although their *lingua franca* was Latin, their accents were extravagant and overwrought.

"Ho, Leonardo," cried one vendor, then another, as Leonardo and Niccolo turned a corner. Then the screes and cries of birds sounded, for the bird-sellers were shaking the small wooden cages packed with wood pigeons, owls, mousebirds, bee-eaters, hummingbirds, crows, blue rockthrushes, warblers, flycatchers, wagtails, hawks, falcons, eagles, and all manner of swans, ducks, chickens, and geese. As Leonardo approached, the birds were making more commotion than the vendors and buyers on the street. "Come here, Master," shouted a red-haired man wearing a stained brown doublet with torn sleeves. His right eye appeared infected, for it was bloodshot, crusted, and tearing. He shook two cages, each containing hawks; one bird was brown with a forked chestnut tail, and the other was smaller and black with a notched tail. They banged against the wooden bars and snapped dangerously. "Buy these, Maestro Artista, please . . . they are just what you need, are they not? And look how many doves I have, do they not interest you, good Master?"

"Indeed, the hawks are fine specimens," Leonardo said, drawing closer, while the other vendors called and shouted to him, as if he were carrying the grail itself. "How much?"

"Ten denari."

"Three."

"Eight."

"Four, and if that is not satisfactory, I can easily talk to your neighbour, who is flapping his arms as if he, himself, could fly."

"Agreed," said the vendor, resigned.

"And the doves?"

"For how many, Maestro?"

"For the lot."

While Leonardo dickered with the bird vendor, Niccolo wandered about. He looked at the multicoloured birds and listened, as he often did. With ear and eye he would learn the ways of the world. Leonardo, it appeared, was known in this market; and a small crowd of hecklers and the merely curious began to form around him. The hucksters made much of it, trying to sell to whomever they could.

"He's as mad as Ajax," said an old man who had just sold a few chickens and doves and was as animated as the street thugs and young beggars standing around him. "He'll let them all go, watch, you'll see."

"I've heard tell he won't eat meat," said one matronly woman to another. "He lets the birds go free because he feels sorry for the poor creatures."

"Well, to be safe, don't look straight at him," said the other woman as she made the sign of the cross. He might be a sorcerer. He could put evil in your eye, and enter right into your soul!"

Her companion shivered and followed suit by crossing herself.

"Nicco," Leonardo shouted, making himself heard above the din. "Come here and help me." When Niccolo appeared, Leonardo said, "If you could raise your thoughts from those of butterflies" — and by that he meant whores — "you might learn something of observation and the ways of science." He thrust his hand into the cage filled with doves and grasped one. The tiny bird made a frightened noise; as Leonardo took it from its cage, he could feel its heart beating in his palm. Then he opened his hand and watched the dove fly away. The crowd laughed and jeered and applauded and shouted for more. He took another bird out of its cage and released it. His eyes squinted almost shut; and as he gazed at the dove beating its wings so hard that, but for the crowd, one could have heard them clap, he seemed lost in thought. "Now, Nicco, I want you to let the birds free, one by one."

"Why me?" Niccolo asked, somehow loath to seize the birds.

"Because I wish to draw," Leonardo said. "Is this chore too difficult for you?"

"I beg your pardon, Maestro," Niccolo said, as he reached into the cage. He had a difficult time catching a bird. Leonardo seemed impatient and completely oblivious to the shouts and taunts of the crowd around him. Niccolo let go of one bird, and then another, while Leonardo sketched. Leonardo stood very still, entranced; only his hand moved like a ferret over the bleached folio, as if it had a life and will of its own.

As Niccolo let fly another bird, Leonardo said, "Do you see, Nicco, the bird in its haste to climb strikes its outstretched wings together above its body. "Now look how it uses its wings and tail in the same way that a swimmer uses his arms and legs in the water; it's the very same principle. It seeks the air currents, which, invisible, roil around the buildings of our city. And there, its speed is checked by the opening and spreading out of the tail . . . Let fly another one. Can you see how the wing separates to let the air pass?" and he wrote a note in his mirror script below one of his sketches: *Make device so that when the wing rises up it remains pierced through, and when it falls it is all united.* "Another," he called to Niccolo. And after the bird disappeared, he made another note: *The speed is checked by the opening and spreading out of the tail. Also, the opening and lowering of the tail, and the simultaneous spreading of the wings to their full extent, arrests their swift movement.*

"That's the end of it," Niccolo said, indicating the empty cages. "Do you wish to free the hawks?"

"No," Leonardo said, distracted. "We will take them with us," and Leonardo and Niccolo made their way through the crowd, which now began to disperse. As if a reflection of Leonardo's change of mood, clouds darkened the sky; and the bleak, refuse-strewn streets took on a more dangerous aspect. The other bird vendors called to Leonardo, but he ignored them, as he did Niccolo. He stared intently into his notebook as he walked, as if he were trying to decipher ancient runes.

They passed the wheel of the bankrupts. Defeated men sat around a marble inlay that was worked into the piazza in the design of a cartwheel. A crowd had formed, momentarily, to watch a debtor, who had been stripped naked, being pulled to the roof of the market by a rope. Then there was a great shout as he was dropped headfirst onto the smooth, cold, marble floor.

A sign attached to one of the market posts read:

> Give good heed to the small sums thou spendest out of the house,
> for it is they which empty the purse and consume wealth; and they
> go on continually. And do not buy all the good victuals which thou
> seest, for the house is like a wolf: the more thou givest it, the more
> doth it devour.

The man dropped by the rope was dead.

Leonardo put his arm around Niccolo's shoulders, as if to shield him from death. But he was suddenly afraid . . . afraid that his own "inevitable hour" might not be far away; and he remembered his recurring dream of falling into the abyss. He shivered, his breath came quick, and his skin felt clammy, as if he had just been jolted awake. Just now, on some deep level, he believed that the poisonous phantasms of dreams were real. If they took hold of the soul of the dreamer, they could effect his entire world.

Leonardo saw his Great Bird falling and breaking apart. And he was falling through cold depths that were as deep as the reflections of lanterns in dark water.

"Leonardo? *Leonardo!*"

"Do not worry. I am fine, my young friend," Leonardo said.

They talked very little until they were in the country, in the high, hilly land north of Florence. Here were meadows and grassy fields, valleys and secret grottos, small roads traversed by ox carts and pack trains, vineyards and cane thickets, dark copses of pine and chestnut and cypress, and olive trees that shimmered like silver hangings each time the wind breathed past their leaves. The deep red tiles of farmstead roofs and the brownish-pink colonnaded villas seemed to be part of the line and tone of the natural countryside. The clouds that had darkened the streets of Florence had disappeared; and the sun was high, bathing the countryside in that golden light particular to Tuscany, a light that purified and clarified as if it were itself the manifestation of desire and spirit.

And before them, in the distance, was Swan Mountain. It rose 1300 feet to its crest, and looked to be pale grey-blue in the distance.

Leonardo and Niccolo stopped in a meadow perfumed with flowers and gazed at the mountain. Leonardo felt his worries weaken, as they always did when he was in the country. He took a deep breath of the heady air and felt his soul awaken and quicken to the world of nature and the *oculus spiritalis*: the world of angels.

"That would be a good mountain from which to test your Great Bird," Niccolo said.

"I thought that, too, for it's very close to Florence. But I've since changed my mind. Vinci is not so far away; and there are good mountains there, too." Then after a pause, Leonardo said, "And I do not wish to die here. If death should be my fate, I wish it to be in familiar surroundings."

Niccolo nodded, and he looked as severe and serious as he had when Leonardo had first met him, like an old man inhabiting a boy's body.

"Come now, Nicco," Leonardo said, resting the cage on the ground and sitting down beside it, "let's enjoy this time, for who knows what awaits us later. Let's eat." With that, Leonardo spread out a cloth and set the food upon it as if it were a table. The hawks flapped their wings and slammed against the wooden bars of the cages. Leonardo tossed them each a small piece of sausage.

"I heard gossip in the piazza of the bird vendors that you refuse to eat meat," Niccolo said.

"Ah, did you, now. And what do you think of that?"

Niccolo shrugged. "Well, I have never seen you eat meat."

Leonardo ate a piece of bread and sausage, which he washed down with wine. "Now you have."

"But then why would people say that —"

"Because I don't usually eat meat. They're correct, for I believe that eating too much meat causes to collect what Aristotle defined as cold black bile. That, in turn, afflicts the soul with melancholia. Maestro Toscanelli's friend Ficino believes the same, but for all the wrong reasons. For him magic and astrology take precedence over reason and experience. But be that as it may, I must be very careful that people do not think of me as a follower of the Cathars, lest I be branded a heretic."

"I have not heard of them."

"They follow the teaching of the pope Bogomil, who believed that our entire visible world was created by the Adversary rather than by God. Thus to avoid imbibing the essence of Satan, they forfeit meat. Yet they eat vegetables and fish." Leonardo laughed and pulled a face to indicate they were crazy. "They could at least be consistent."

Leonardo ate quickly, which was his habit, for he could never seem to enjoy savouring food as others did. He felt that eating, like sleeping, was simply a necessity that took him away from whatever interested him at the moment.

And there was a whole world pulsing in the sunlight around him; like a child, he wanted to investigate its secrets.

"Now . . . watch," he said to Niccolo, who was still eating; and he let loose one of the hawks. As it flew away, Leonardo made notes, scribbling with his left hand, and said, "You see, Nicco, it searches now for a current of the wind." He loosed the other one. "These birds beat their wings only until they reach the wind, which must be blowing at a great elevation, for look how high they soar. Then they are almost motionless."

Leonardo watched the birds circle overhead, then glide toward the mountains. He felt transported, as if he too were gliding in the Empyrean heights. "They're hardly moving their wings now. They repose in the air as we do on a pallet."

"Perhaps you should follow their example."

"What do you mean?" Leonardo asked.

"Fix your wings on the Great Bird. Instead of beating the air, they would remain stationary."

"And by what mode would the machine be propelled?" Leonardo asked; but he answered his own question, for immediately the idea of the Archimedian Screw came to mind. He remembered seeing children playing with toy whirlybirds: by pulling a string, a propeller would be made to rise freely into the air. His hand sketched, as if thinking on its own. He drew a series of sketches of leaves gliding back and forth, falling to the ground. He drew various screws and propellers. There might be something useful . . .

"Perhaps if you could just catch the current, then you would not have need of human power," Niccolo said. "You could fix your bird to soar . . . somehow."

Leonardo patted Niccolo on the shoulder, for, indeed, the child was bright. But it was all wrong; it *felt* wrong. "No, my young friend," he said doggedly, as if he had come upon a wall that blocked his thought, "the wings must be able to row through the air like a bird's. That is nature's method, the most efficient way."

Restlessly, Leonardo wandered the hills. Niccolo finally complained of being tired and stayed behind, comfortably situated in a shady copse of mossy-smelling cypresses.

Leonardo walked on alone.

Everything was perfect: the air, the warmth, the smells and sounds of the country. He could almost apprehend the pure forms of everything around him, the phantasms reflected in the *proton organon*: the mirrors of his soul. But not quite . . .

Indeed, something was wrong, for instead of the bliss, which Leonardo had so often experienced in the country, he felt thwarted . . . lost.

Thinking of the falling leaf, which he had sketched in his notebook, he wrote: *If a man has a tent roof of caulked linen twelve ells broad and twelve ells high, he will be able to let himself fall from any great height without danger to himself.*" He imagined a pyramidal parachute, yet considered it too large and bulky and heavy to carry on the Great Bird. He wrote another hasty note: *Use leather bags, so a man falling from a height of six brachia will not injure himself, falling either into water or upon land.*

He continued walking, aimlessly. He sketched constantly, as if without conscious thought: grotesque figures and caricatured faces, animals, impossible mechanisms, studies of various madonnas with children, imaginary landscapes, and all manner of actual flora and fauna. He drew a three-dimensional diagram of a toothed gearing and pulley system and an apparatus for making lead. He made a note to locate Albertus Magnus' *On Heaven and Earth* — perhaps Toscanelli had a copy. His thoughts seemed to flow like the Arno, from one subject to another, and yet he could not position himself in that psychic place of languor and bliss, which he imagined to be the perfect realm of Platonic forms.

As birds flew overhead, he studied them and sketched feverishly. Leonardo had an extraordinarily quick eye, and he could discern movements that others could not see. He wrote in tiny letters beside his sketches: *Just as we may see a small imperceptible movement of the rudder turn a ship of marvellous size loaded with very heavy cargo — and also amid such weight of water pressing upon its every beam and in the teeth of impetuous winds that envelop its mighty sails — so, too, do birds support themselves above the course of the winds without beating their wings. Just a slight movement of wing or tail, serving them to enter either below or above the wind, suffices to prevent their fall.* Then he added, *When, without the assistance of the wind and without*

beating its wings, the bird remains in the air in the position of equilibrium, this
shows that the centre of gravity is coincident with the centre of resistance.

"Ho, Leonardo," shouted Niccolo, who was running after him. The boy
was out of breath; he carried the brown sack, which contained some leftover
food, most likely, and Maestro Toscanelli's book. "You've been gone over
three hours!"

"And is that such a long time?" Leonardo asked.

"It is for me. What are you doing?"

"Just walking . . . and thinking." After a beat, Leonardo said, "But you
have a book, why didn't you read it?"

Niccolo smiled and said, " I tried, but then I fell asleep."

"So now we have the truth," Leonardo said. "Nicco, why don't you return
to the bottega? I must remain here . . . to think. And you are obviously bored."

"That's all right, Maestro," Niccolo said anxiously. "If I can stay with you,
I won't be bored. I promise."

Leonardo smiled, in spite of himself, and said, "Tell me what you've
gleaned from the little yellow book."

"I can't make it out . . . yet. It seems to be all about light."

"So Maestro Toscanelli told me. Its writings are very old and concern
memory and the circulation of light." Leonardo could not resist teasing his
apprentice. "Do you find your memory much improved after reading it?"

Niccolo shrugged, as if it was of no interest to him, and Leonardo settled
down in a grove of olive trees to read *The Secret of the Golden Flower*; it took
him less than an hour, for the book was short. Niccolo ate some fruit and
then fell asleep again, seemingly without any trouble.

Most of the text seemed to be magical gibberish, yet suddenly these words
seemed to open him up:

> There are a thousand spaces, and the light-flower of heaven and
> earth fills them all. Just so does the light-flower of the individual
> pass through heaven and cover the earth. And when the light
> begins to circulate, all of heaven and the earth, all the mountains
> and rivers — everything — begins to circulate with light. The key is
> to concentrate your own seed-flower in the eyes. But be careful,
> children, for if one day you do not practice meditation, this light
> will stream out, to be lost who knows where . . . ?

Perhaps he fell asleep, for he imagined himself staring at the walls of his great and perfect mnemonic construct: the memory cathedral. It was pure white and smooth as dressed stone . . . it was a church for all his experience and knowledge, whether holy or profane. Maestro Toscanelli had taught him long ago how to construct a church in his imagination, a storage place of images — hundreds of thousands of them — which would represent everything Leonardo wished to remember. Leonardo caught all the evanescent and ephemeral stuff of time and trapped it in this place . . . all the happenings of his life, everything he had seen and read and heard; all the pain and frustration and love and joy were neatly shelved and ordered inside the colonnaded courts, chapels, vestries, porches, towers, and crossings of his memory cathedral.

He longed to be inside, to return to sweet, comforting memory; he would dismiss the ghosts of fear that haunted its dark catacombs. But now he was seeing the cathedral from a distant height, from the summit of Swan Mountain, and it was as if his cathedral had somehow become a small part of what his memory held and his eyes saw. It was as if his soul could expand to fill heaven and earth, the past and the future. Leonardo experienced a sudden, vertiginous sensation of freedom; indeed, heaven and earth seemed to be filled with a thousand spaces. It was just as he had read in the ancient book: everything was circulating with pure light . . . blinding, cleansing light that coruscated down the hills and mountains like rainwater, that floated in the air like mist, that heated the grass and meadows to radiance.

He felt bliss.

Everything was preternaturally clear; it was as if he was seeing into the essence of things.

And then with a shock he felt himself slipping, falling from the mountain.

This was his recurring dream, his nightmare: to fall without wings and harness into the void. Yet every detail registered: the face of the mountain, the mossy crevasses, the smells of wood and stone and decomposition, the screeing of a hawk, the glint of a stream below, the roofs of farmhouses, the geometrical demarcations of fields, and the spiraling wisps of cloud that seemed to be woven into the sky. But then he tumbled and descended into palpable darkness, into a frightful abyss that showed no feature and no bottom.

Leonardo screamed to awaken back into daylight, for he knew this blind place, which the immortal Dante had explored and described. But now he felt the horrid bulk of the flying monster Geryon beneath him, supporting him . . . this, the same beast that had carried Dante into *Malebolge*: the Eighth Circle of Hell. The monster was slippery with filth and smelled of death and putrefaction; the air itself was foul, and Leonardo could hear behind him the thrashing of the creature's scorpion tail. Yet it also seemed that he could hear Dante's divine voice whispering to him, drawing him through the very walls of Hades into blinding light.

But now he was held aloft by the Great Bird, his own invention. He soared over the trees and hills and meadows of Fiesole, and then south, to fly over the roofs and balconies and spires of Florence herself.

Leonardo flew without fear, as if the wings were his own flesh. He moved his arms easily, working the great wings that beat against the calm, spring air that was as warm as his own breath. But rather than resting upon his apparatus, he now hung below it. He operated a windlass with his hands to raise one set of wings and kicked a pedal with his heels to lower the other set of wings. Around his neck was a collar, which controlled a rudder that was effectively the tail of this bird.

This was certainly not the machine that hung in Verrocchio's bottega. Yet with its double set of wings, it seemed more like a great insect than a bird, and —

Leonardo awakened with a jolt, to find himself staring at a horsefly feeding upon his hand.

Could he have been sleeping with his eyes open, or had this been a waking dream? He shivered, for his sweat was cold on his arms and chest.

He shouted, awakening Niccolo, and immediately began sketching and writing in his notebook. "I have it!" he said to Niccolo. "Double wings like a fly will provide the power I need. You see, it is just as I told you: nature provides. Art and invention are merely imitation." He drew a man hanging beneath an apparatus with hand-operated cranks and pedals to work the wings. Then he studied the fly, which still buzzed around him, and wrote: *The lower wings are more slanting than those above, both as to length and as to breadth. The fly when it hovers in the air upon its wings beats its wings with great speed and din, raising them from the horizontal position up as high as the wing is long. And as it raises them, it brings them forward in a slanting position in such a way as almost to strike the air edgewise.* Then he drew a design for the rudder assembly. "How could I not have seen that just as a ship needs a rudder, so, too, would my machine?" he said. "It will act as the tail of a bird. And by hanging the operator below the wings, equilibrium will be more easily maintained. There," he said, standing up and pulling Niccolo to his feet. "Perfection!"

He sang one of Lorenzo de Medici's bawdy inventions and danced around Niccolo, who seemed confused by his master's strange behaviour. He grabbed the boy's arms and swung him around in a circle.

"Perhaps the women watching you free the birds were right," Niccolo said. "Perhaps you *are* as mad as Ajax."

"Perhaps I am," Leonardo said, "but I have a lot of work to do, for the Great Bird must be changed if it is to fly for *Il Magnifico* next week." He placed the book of the Golden Flower in the sack, handed it to Niccolo, and began walking in the direction of the city.

It was already late afternoon.

"I'll help you with your machine," Niccolo said.

"Thank you, I'll need you for many errands."

That seemed to satisfy the boy. "Why did you shout and then dance as you did, Maestro?" Niccolo asked, concerned. He followed a step behind Leonardo, who seemed to be in a hurry.

Leonardo laughed and slowed his stride until Niccolo was beside him. "It's difficult to explain. Suffice it to say that solving the riddle of my Great Bird made me happy."

"But how did you do it? I thought you had fallen asleep."

"I had a dream," Leonardo said. "It was a gift from the poet Dante Alighieri."

"*He* gave you the answer?" Niccolo asked, incredulous.

"That he did, Nicco."

"Then you *do* believe in spirits."

"No, Nicco, just in dreams."

THREE

In the streets and markets, people gossiped of a certain hermit — a champion — who had come from Volterra, where he had been ministering to the lepers in a hospital. He had come here to preach and harangue and save the city. He was a young man, and some had claimed to have seen him walking barefoot past the Church of Salvatore. They said he was dressed in the poorest of clothes with only a wallet on his back. His face was bearded and sweet, and his eyes were blue; certainly he was a manifestation of the Christ himself, stepping on the very paving stones that modern Florentines walked. He had declared that the days to follow would bring harrowings, replete with holy signs, for so he had been told by both the Angel Raphael and Saint John, who had appeared to him in their flesh, as men do to other men, and not in a dream.

It was said that he preached to the Jews in their poor quarter and also to the whores and beggars; and he was also seen standing upon the *ringheiera* of the *Signore* demanding an audience with the "Eight". But they sent him away. So now there could be no intercession for what was about to break upon Florence.

The next day, a Thursday, one of the small bells of Santa Maria delle Fiore broke loose and fell, breaking the skull of a stonemason passing below. By a miracle, he lived, although a bone had to be removed from his skull.

But it was seen as a sign, nevertheless.

And on Friday, a boy of twelve fell from the large bell of the Palagio and landed on the gallery. He died several hours later.

By week's end, four families in the city and eight in the *Borgo di Ricorboli* were stricken with fever and *buboes*, the characteristic swellings of what had come to be called "the honest plague". There were more reports of fever and death every day thereafter, for the Black Reaper was back upon the streets, wending his way through homes and hospitals, cathedrals and taverns, and whorehouses and nunneries alike. It was said that he had a companion, the hag Lachesis, who followed after him while she wove an ever-lengthening tapestry of death; hers was an accounting of "the debt we must all pay", created from her never-ending skein of black thread.

One hundred and twenty people had died in the churches and hospitals by *nella quidtadecima*: the full moon. There were twenty-five deaths alone at *Santa Maria Nuova*. The "Eight" of the Signoria duly issued a notice of health procedures to be followed by all Florentines; the price of foodstuffs rose drastically; and although Lorenzo's police combed the streets for the spectral hermit, he was nowhere to be found within the precincts of the city.

Lorenzo and his retinue fled to his villa at Careggi. But rather than follow suit and leave the city for the safety of the country, Verrocchio elected to remain in his bottega. He gave permission to his apprentices to quit the city until the plague abated, if they had the resources; but most, in fact, stayed with him.

The bottega seemed to be in a fervor.

One would think that the deadline for every commission was tomorrow. Verrocchio's foreman Francesco kept a tight and sure rein on the apprentices, pressing them into a twelve to fourteen hour schedule; and they worked as they had when they constructed the bronze palla that topped the dome of Santa Maria delle Fiore, as if quick hands and minds were the only weapons against the ennui upon which the Black Fever might feed. Francesco had become invaluable to Leonardo, for he was quicker with things mechanical than Verrocchio himself; and Francesco helped him design an ingenious plan by which the flying machine could be collapsed and dismantled and camouflaged for easy transportation to Vinci. The flying machine, at least, was complete; again, thanks to Francesco who made certain that Leonardo had a constant supply of strong-backed apprentices and material.

Leonardo's studio was a mess, a labyrinth of footpaths that wound past bolts of cloth, machinery, stacks of wood and leather, jars of paint, sawhorses, and various gearing devices; the actual flying machine took up the centre of the great room. Surrounding it were drawings, insects mounted on boards, a table covered with birds and bats in various stages of vivisection, and constructions of the various parts of the redesigned flying machine — artificial wings, rudders, and flap valves.

The noxious odors of turpentine mixed with the various perfumes of decay; these smells disturbed Leonardo not at all, for they reminded him of his childhood when he kept all manner of dead animals in his room to study and paint. All other work — the paintings and terra cotta sculptures — were piled in one corner. Leonardo and Niccolo could no longer sleep in the crowded, foul-smelling studio; they had laid their pallets down in the young apprentice Tista's room.

Tista was a tall, gangly boy with a shock of blond hair. Although he was about the same age as Niccolo, it was as if he had become Niccolo's apprentice. The boys had become virtually inseparable. Niccolo seemed to relish teaching Tista about life, art, and politics; but then Niccolo had a sure sense of how people behaved, even if he lacked experience. He was a natural teacher, more so than Leonardo. For Leonardo's part, he didn't mind having the other boy underfoot and had, in fact, become quite fond of him. But Leonardo was preoccupied with his work. The Black Death had given him a reprieve — just enough time to complete and test his machine — for not only did *Il Magnifico* agree to rendezvous in Vinci rather than Pistoia, he himself set the date forward another fortnight.

It was unbearably warm in the studio as Niccolo helped Leonardo remove the windlass mechanism and twin "oars" from the machine, which were to be packed into a numbered, wooden container. "It's getting close," Niccolo said, after the parts were fitted securely into the box. "Tista tells me that he heard a family living near the Porta alla Croce caught fever."

"Well, we shall be on our way at dawn," Leonardo said. "You shall have the responsibility of making certain that everything is properly loaded and in its proper place."

Niccolo seemed very pleased with that; he had, in fact, proven himself to be a capable worker and organiser. "But I still believe we should wait until the dark effluviums have evaporated from the air. At least until after the *becchini* have carried the corpses to their graves."

"Then we will leave after first light," Leonardo said.

"Good."

"You might be right about the possible contagion of corpses and *becchini*. But as to your effluviums . . ."

"Best not to take chances," Verrocchio said; he had been standing in the doorway and peering into the room like a boy who had not yet been caught sneaking through the house. He held the door partially closed so that it framed him, as if he were posing for his own portrait; and the particular glow of the late afternoon sun seemed to transform and subdue his rather heavy features.

"I think it is as the astrologers say: a conjunction of planets," Verrocchio continued. "It was so during the great blight of 1345. But that was a conjunction of *three* planets. Very unusual. It will not be like that now, for the conjunction is not nearly so perfect."

"You'd be better to come to the country with us than listen to astrologers," Leonardo said.

"I cannot leave my family. I've told you."

"Then bring them along. My father is already in Vinci preparing the main house for Lorenzo and his retinue. You could think of it as a business holiday; think of the commissions that might fall your way."

"I think I have enough of those for the present," Andrea said.

"That does not sound like Andrea del Verrocchio," Leonardo said, teasing.

"My sisters and cousins refuse to leave," Andrea said. "And who would feed the cats?" he said, smiling, then sighing. He seemed resigned and almost relieved. "My fate is in the lap of the gods . . . as it has always been. And so is yours, my young friend."

The two-day journey was uneventful, and they soon arrived in Vinci.

The town of Leonardo's youth was a fortified keep dominated by a medieval castle and its campanile, surrounded by fifty brownish-pink brick houses. Their red tiled roofs were covered with a foliage of chestnut and pine and cypress, and vines of grape and cane thickets brought the delights of earth and shade to the very walls and windows. The town with its crumbling walls and single arcaded alley was situated on the elevated spur of a mountain; it overlooked a valley blanketed with olive trees that turned silver when stirred by the wind. Beyond was the valley of Lucca, green and purple-shadowed and ribboned with mountain streams; and Leonardo remembered that when the rain had cleansed the air, the crags and peaks of the Apuan Alps near Massa and Cozzile could be clearly seen.

Now that Leonardo was here, he realised how homesick he had been. The sky was clear and the air pellucid; but the poignancy of his memories clouded his vision, as he imagined himself being swept back to his childhood days, once again riding with his Uncle Francesco, whom they called "*lazzarone*" because he did not choose to restrict his zealous enjoyment of life with a profession. But Leonardo and the much older Francesco had been like two privileged boys — princes, riding from farmstead to mill and all around the valley collecting rents for Leonardo's grandfather, the patriarch of the family: the gentle and punctilious Antonio da Vinci.

Leonardo led his apprentices down a cobbled road and past a rotating dovecote on a long pole to a cluster of houses surrounded by gardens, barns, peasant huts, tilled acreage, and the uniform copses of Mulberry trees, which his Uncle Francesco had planted. Francesco, "the lazy one", had been experimenting with sericulture, which could prove to be very lucrative indeed, for the richest and most powerful guild in Florence was the *Arte della Seta*: the silk weavers.

"Leonardo, ho!" shouted Francesco from the courtyard of the large, neatly kept, main house, which had belonged to Ser Antonio. It was stone and roofed with red tile, and looked like the ancient long-houses of the French; but certainly no animals would be kept in the home of Piero da Vinci: Leonardo's father.

Like his brother, Francesco had dark curly hair that was greying at the temples and thinning at the crown. Francesco embraced Leonardo, nearly knocking the wind out of him, and said, "You have caused substantial havoc in this house, my good nephew! Your father is quite anxious."

"I'm sure of that," Leonardo said as he walked into the hall. "It's wonderful to see you, Uncle."

Beyond this expansive, lofted room were several sleeping chambers, two fireplaces, a kitchen and pantry, and workrooms, which sometimes housed the peasants who worked the various da Vinci farmholds; there was a level above with three more rooms and a fireplace; and ten steps below was the cellar where Leonardo used to hide the dead animals he had found. The house was immaculate: how Leonardo's father must have oppressed the less than tidy Francesco and Alessandra to make it ready for Lorenzo and his guests.

His third wife, Margherita di Guglielmo, was nursing his first legitimate son; no doubt that accorded her privileges.

This room was newly fitted-out with covered beds, chests, benches, and a closet cabinet to accommodate several of the lesser luminaries in *Il Magnifico*'s entourage. Without a doubt, Leonardo's father would give the First Citizen his own bedroom.

Leonardo sighed. He craved his father's love, but their relationship had always been awkward and rather formal, as if Leonardo were his apprentice rather than his son.

Piero came down the stairs from his chamber above to meet Leonardo. He wore his magisterial robes and a brimless, silk *berretta* cap, as if he were expecting Lorenzo and his entourage at any moment. "Greetings, my son."

"Greetings to you, father," Leonardo said, bowing.

Leonardo and his father embraced. Then tightly grasping Leonardo's elbow, Piero asked, "May I take you away from your company for a few moments?"

"Of course, Father," Leonardo said politely, allowing himself to be led upstairs.

They entered a writing room, which contained a long, narrow clerical desk, a master's chair, and a sitting bench decorated with two octagonally-shaped pillows; the floor was tiled like a chessboard. A clerk sat upon a stool behind the desk and made a great show of writing in a large, leather-bound ledger. Austere though the room appeared, it revealed a parvenu's taste for comfort; for Piero was eager to be addressed as *messer*, rather than *ser*, and to carry a sword, which was the prerogative of a knight. "Will you excuse us, Vittore?" Piero said to the clerk. The young man rose, bowed, and left the room.

"Yes, father?" Leonardo asked, expecting the worst.

"I don't know whether to scold you or congratulate you."

"The latter would be preferable."

Piero smiled and said, "Andrea has apprised me that *Il Magnifico* has asked for you to work in his gardens."

"Yes."

"I am very proud."

"Thank you, father."

"So you see, I was correct in keeping you to the grindstone."

Leonardo felt his neck and face grow warm. "You mean by taking everything I earned so I could not save enough to pay for my master's matriculation fee in the Painters' Guild?"

"That money went to support the family . . . your family."

"And now you — or rather the family — will lose that income."

"My concern is not, nor was it ever, the money," Piero said. "It was properly forming your character, of which I am still in some doubt."

"Thank you."

"I'm sorry, but as your father, it is my duty —" He paused. Then, as if trying to be more conciliatory, he said, "You could hardly do better than to have Lorenzo for a patron. But he would have never noticed you, if I had not made it possible for you to remain with Andrea."

"You left neither Andrea nor I any choice."

"Be that as it may, Master Andrea made certain that you produced and completed the projects he assigned to you. At least he tried to prevent you from running off and cavorting with your limp-wristed, degenerate friends."

"Ah, you mean those who are not in *Il Magnifico*'s retinue."

"Don't you dare to be insolent."

"I apologise, father," Leonardo said, but he had become sullen.

"You're making that face again."

"I'm sorry if I offend you."

"You don't offend me, you —" He paused, then said, "You've put our family in an impossible position."

"What do you mean?"

"Your business here with the Medici."

"It does not please you to host the First Citizen?" Leonardo asked.

"You have made a foolish bet with him, and will certainly become the monkey. Our name —"

"Ah, yes, that is, of course, all that worries you. But I shall not fail, father. You can then take full credit for any honour I might bring to our good name."

"Only birds and insects can fly."

"And those who bear the name da Vinci." But Piero would not be mollified. Leonardo sighed and said, "Father, I shall try not to disappoint you." He bowed respectfully and turned toward the door.

"Leonardo!" his father said, as if he were speaking to a child. "I have not excused you."

"May I be excused, then, father?"

"Yes, you may." But then Piero called him back.

"Yes, father?" Leonardo asked, pausing at the door.

"I forbid you to attempt this . . . experiment."

"I am sorry, father; but I cannot turn tail now."

"I will explain to *Il Magnifico* that you are my first-born."

"Thank you, but —"

"Your safety is my responsibility," Piero said, and then he said, "I worry for you!" Obviously, these words were difficult for him. If their relationship had been structured differently, Leonardo would have crossed the room to embrace his father; and they would have spoken directly. But as robust and lusty as Piero was, he could not accept any physical display of emotion.

After a pause, Leonardo asked, "Will you do me the honour of watching me fly upon the wind?" He ventured a smile. "It will be a da Vinci, not a Medici or a Pazzi, who will be soaring in the heavens closest to God."

"I suppose I shall have to keep up appearances," Piero said; then he raised an eyebrow, as if questioning his place in the scheme of these events. He looked at his son and smiled sadly.

Though once again Leonardo experienced the unbridgeable distance between himself and his father, the tension between them dissolved.

"You are welcome to remain here," Piero said.

"You will have little enough room when Lorenzo and his congregation arrive," Leonardo said. "And I shall need quiet in which to work and prepare; it's been fixed for us to lodge with Achattabrigha di Piero del Vacca."

"When are you expected?"

"We should leave now. Uncle Francesco said he would accompany us."

Piero nodded. "Please give my warmest regards to your mother."

"I shall be happy to do so."

"Are you at all curious to see your new brother?" Piero asked, as if it were an afterthought.

"Of course I am, father."

Piero took his son's arm, and they walked to Margherita's bedroom.

Leonardo could feel his father trembling.

And for those few seconds, he actually felt that he was his father's son.

FOUR

The Great Bird was perched on the edge of a ridge at the summit of a hill near Vinci that Leonardo had selected. It looked like a gigantic dragonfly, its fabric of fustian and silk sighing, as the expansive double wings shifted slightly in the wind. Niccolo, Tista, and Leonardo's stepfather Achattabrigha kneeled under the wings and held fast to the pilot's harness. Zoroastro da Peretola and Lorenzo de Credi, apprentices of Andrea Verrochio, stood twenty-five feet apart and steadied the wing tips; it almost seemed that their arms were filled with outsized jousting pennons of blue and gold. These two could be taken as caricatures of *Il Magnifico* and his brother Giuliano, for Zoroastro was swarthy, rough-skinned, and ugly-looking beside the sweetly handsome Lorenzo de Credi. Such was the contrast between Lorenzo and Giuliano di Medici, who stood with Leonardo a few feet away from the Great Bird. Giuliano looked radiant in the morning sun while Lorenzo seemed to be glowering, although he was most probably simply concerned for Leonardo.

Zoroastro, ever impatient, looked toward Leonardo and shouted, "We're ready for you, Maestro."

Leonardo nodded, but Lorenzo caught him and said, "Leonardo, there is no need for this. I will love you as I do Giuliano, no matter whether you choose to fly . . . or let wisdom win out."

Leonardo smiled and said, "I will fly *fide et amore.*"

By faith and love.

"You shall have both," Lorenzo said; and he walked beside Leonardo to the edge of the ridge and waved to the crowd standing far below on the edge of a natural clearing where Leonardo was to land triumphant. But the clearing was surrounded by a forest of pine and cypress, which from his vantage looked like a multitude of rough-hewn lances and halberds. A great shout went up, honouring the First Citizen: the entire village was there — from peasant to squire, invited for the occasion by *Il Magnifico*, who had erected a great, multi-coloured tent; his attendants and footmen had been cooking and preparing for a feast since dawn. His sister Bianca, Angelo Poliziano, Pico Della Mirandola, Bartolomeo Scala, and Leonardo's friend Sandro Botticelli were down there, too, hosting the festivities.

They were all on tenterhooks, eager for the Great Bird to fly.

Leonardo waited until Lorenzo had received his due; but then not to be outdone, he, too, bowed and waved his arms theatrically. The crowd below cheered their favourite son, and Leonardo turned away to position himself in the harness of his flying machine. He had seen his mother Caterina, a tiny figure nervously looking upward, whispering devotions, her hand cupped above her eyes to cut the glare of the sun. His father Piero stood beside Giuliano de Medici; both men were dressed as if for a hunt. Piero did not speak to Leonardo. His already formidable face was drawn and tight, just as if he were standing before a magistrate awaiting a decision on a case.

Lying down in a prone position on the fore-shortened plank pallet below the wings and windlass mechanism, Leonardo adjusted the loop around his head, which controlled the rudder section of the Great Bird, and he tested the hand cranks and foot stirrups, which raised and lowered the wings.

"Be careful," shouted Zoroastro, who had stepped back from the moving wings. "Are you trying to kill us?"

There was nervous laughter; but Leonardo was quiet. Achattabrigha tied the straps that would hold Leonardo fast to his machine and said, "I shall pray for your success, Leonardo, my son. I love you."

Leonardo turned to his step-father, smelled the good odors of Caterina's herbs — garlic and sweet onion — on his breath and clothes, and looked into the old man's squinting, pale blue eyes; and it came to him then, with the force of buried emotion, that he loved this man who had spent his life sweating by kiln fires and thinking with his great, yellow-nailed hands. "I love you, too . . . father. And I feel safe in your prayers."

That seemed to please Achattabrigha, for he checked the straps one last time, kissed Leonardo and patted his shoulder; then he stepped away, as reverently as if he were backing away from an icon in a cathedral.

"Good luck, Leonardo," Lorenzo said.

The others wished him luck. His father nodded, and smiled; and Leonardo, taking the weight of the Great Bird upon his back, lifted himself. Niccolo, Zoroastro, and Lorenzo de Credi helped him to the very edge of the ridge.

A cheer went up from below.

"Maestro, I wish it were me," Niccolo said. Tista stood beside him, looking longingly at Leonardo's flying mechanism.

"Just watch this time, Nicco," Leonardo said, and he nodded to Tista. "Pretend it is you who is flying in the heavens, for this machine is also yours. And you will be with me."

"Thank you, Leonardo."

"Now step away . . . for we must fly," Leonardo said; and he looked down, as if for the first time, as if every tree and upturned face were magnified; every smell, every sound and motion were clear and distinct. In some way the world had separated into its component elements, all in an instant; and in the distance, the swells and juttings of land were like that of a green sea with long, trailing shadows of brown; and upon those motionless waters were all the various constructions of human habitations: church and campanile, and shacks and barns and cottages and furrowed fields.

Leonardo felt sudden vertigo as his heart pounded in his chest. A breeze blew out of the northwest, and Leonardo felt it flow around him like a breath. The treetops rustled, whispering, as warm air drifted skyward. Thermal updrafts flowing invisibly to heaven. Pulling at him. His wings shuddered in the gusts; and Leonardo knew that it must be now, lest he be carried off the cliff unprepared.

He launched himself, pushing off the precipice as if he were diving from a cliff into the sea. For an instant, as he swooped downward, he felt euphoria. He was flying, carried by the wind, which embraced him in its cold grip. Then came heart-pounding, nauseating fear. Although he strained at the windlass and foot stirrups, which caused his great, fustian wings to flap, he could not keep himself aloft. His pushings and kickings had become almost reflexive from hours of practice: one leg thrust backward to lower one pair of wings while he furiously worked the windlass with his hands to raise the other, turning his hands first to the left, then to the right. He worked the mechanism with every bit of his calculated two hundred pound force, and his muscles ached from the strain. Although the Great Bird might function as a glider, there was too much friction in the gears to effect enough propulsive power; and the wind resistance was too strong. He could barely raise the wings.

He fell.

The chilling, cutting wind became a constant sighing in his ears. His clothes flapped against his skin like the fabric of his failing wings, while hills, sky, forest, and cliffs spiraled around him, then fell away; and he felt the damp shock of his recurring dream, his nightmare of falling into the void.

But he was falling through soft light, itself as tangible as butter. Below him was the familiar land of his youth, rising against all logic, rushing skyward to claim him. He could see his father's house and there in the distance the Apuan Alps and the ancient cobbled road built before Rome was an empire. His sensations took on the textures of dream; and he prayed, surprising himself, even then as he looked into the purple shadows of the impaling trees below. Still, he doggedly pedaled and turned the windlass mechanism.

All was calmness and quiet, but for the wind wheezing in his ears like the sea heard in a conch shell. His fear left him, carried away by the same breathing wind.

Then he felt a subtle bursting of warm air around him.

And suddenly, impossibly, vertiginously, he was ascending.

His wings were locked straight out. They were not flapping. Yet still he rose. It was as if God's hand were lifting Leonardo to heaven; and he,

Leonardo, remembered loosing his hawks into the air and watching them search for the currents of wind, which they used to soar into the highest of elevations, their wings motionless.

Thus did Leonardo rise in the warm air current — his mouth open to relieve the pressure constantly building in his ears — until he could see the top of the mountain ... it was about a thousand feet below him. The country of hills and streams and farmland and forest had diminished, had become a neatly patterned board of swirls and rectangles: proof of man's work on earth. The sun seemed brighter at this elevation, as if the air itself was less dense in these attenuated regions. Leonardo feared now that he might be drawing too close to the region where air turned to fire.

He turned his head, pulling the loop that connected to the rudder; and found that he could, within bounds, control his direction. But then he stopped soaring; it was as if the warm bubble of air that had contained him had suddenly burst. He felt a chill.

The air became cold ... and still.

He worked furiously at the windlass, thinking that he would beat his wings as birds do until they reach the wind; but he could not gain enough forward motion.

Once again, he fell like an arcing arrow.

Although the wind resistance was so great that he couldn't pull the wings below a horizontal position, he had developed enough speed to attain lift. He rose for a few beats, but, again, could not push his mechanism hard enough to maintain it, and another gust struck him, pummeling the Great Bird with phantomic fists.

Leonardo's only hope was to gain another warm thermal.

Instead, he became caught in a riptide of air that was like a blast, pushing the flying machine backward. He had all he could do to keep the wings locked in a horizontal position. He feared they might be torn away by the wind; and, indeed, the erratic gusts seemed to be conspiring to press him back down upon the stone face of the mountain.

Time seemed to slow for Leonardo; and in one long second he glimpsed the clearing surrounded by forest, as if forming a bull's-eye. He saw the tents and the townspeople who craned their necks to goggle up at him; and in this wind-wheezing moment, he suddenly gained a new, unfettered perspective. As if it were not he who was falling to his death.

Were his neighbours cheering? he wondered. Or were they horrified and dumbfounded at the sight of one of their own falling from the sky? More likely they were secretly wishing him to fall, their deepest desires not unlike the crowd that had recently cajoled a poor, lovesick peasant boy to jump from a rooftop onto the stone pavement of the Via Calimala.

The ground was now only three hundred feet below.

To his right, Leonardo caught sight of a hawk. The hawk was caught in the same trap of wind as Leonardo; and as he watched, the bird veered away, banking, and flew downwind. Leonardo shifted his weight, manipulated the rudder, and changed the angle of the wings. Thus he managed to follow the bird. His arms and legs felt like leaden weights, but he held on to his small measure of control.

Still he fell.

Two hundred feet.

He could hear the crowd shouting below him as clearly as if he were among them. People scattered, running to get out of Leonardo's way. He thought of his mother Caterina, for most men call upon their mothers at the moment of death.

And he followed the hawk, as if it were his inspiration, his own Beatrice.

And the ground swelled upward.

Then Leonardo felt as if he was suspended over the deep, green canopy of forest, but only for an instant. He felt a warm swell of wind; and the Great Bird rose, riding the thermal. Leonardo looked for the hawk, but it had disappeared as if it had been a spirit, rising without weight through the various spheres toward the *Primum Mobile*. He tried to control his flight, his thoughts toward landing in one of the fields beyond the trees.

The thermal carried him up; then, just as quickly, as if teasing him, burst. Leonardo tried to keep his wings fixed, and glided upwind for a few seconds. But a gust caught him, once again pushing him backward, and he fell —

Slapped back to earth.

Hubris.

I have come home to die.

His father's face scowled at him.

Leonardo had failed.

FIVE

Even after three weeks, the headaches remained.

Leonardo had suffered several broken ribs and a concussion when he fell into the forest, swooping between the thick, purple cypress trees, tearing like tissue the wood and fustaneum of the Great Bird's wings. His face was already turning black when Lorenzo's footmen found him. He recuperated at his father's home; but Lorenzo insisted on taking him to Villa Careggi, where he could have his physicians attend to him. With the exception of Lorenzo's personal dentator, who soaked a sponge in opium, morel juice, and hyoscyamus and extracted his broken tooth as Leonardo slept and dreamed of falling, they did little more than change his bandages, bleed him with leeches, and cast his horoscope.

Leonardo was more than relieved when the plague finally abated enough so that he could return to Florence. He was hailed as a hero, for Lorenzo had made a public announcement from the *ringhiera* of the Palazzo Vecchio that the artist from Vinci had, indeed, flown in the air like a bird. But the gossip among the educated was that, instead, Leonardo had fallen like Icarus, whom it was said he resembled in *hubris*. He received an anonymous note that seemed to say it all: *victus honour*.

Honour to the vanquished.

Leonardo would accept none of the countless invitations to attend various masques and dinners and parties. He was caught up in a frenzy of work. He could not sleep; and when he would lose consciousness from sheer exhaustion, he would dream he was falling through the sky. He would see trees wheeling below him, twisting as if they were machines in an impossible torture chamber.

Leonardo was certain that the dreams would cease only when he conquered the air; and although he did not believe in ghosts or superstition, he was pursued by demons every bit as real as those conjured by the clergy he despised and mocked. So he worked, as if in a frenzy. He constructed new models and filled up three folios with his sketches and mirror-script notes. Niccolo and Tista would not leave him, except to bring him food, and Andrea Verrocchio came upstairs a few times a day to look in at his now famous apprentice.

"Haven't you yet had your bellyful of flying machines?" Andrea impatiently asked Leonardo. It was dusk, and dinner had already been served to the apprentices downstairs. Niccolo hurried to clear a place on the table so Andrea could put down the two bowls of boiled meat he had brought. Leonardo's studio was in its usual state of disarray, but the old flying machine, the insects mounted on boards, the vivisected birds and bats, the variously designed wings, rudders, and valves for the Great Bird were gone, replaced by new drawings, new mechanisms for testing wing designs (for now the wings would remain fixed), and various large-scale models of free-flying whirlybird toys, which had been in use since the 1300s. He was experimenting with inverted cones — Archimedian Screws — to cheat gravity, and he studied the geometry of children's tops to calculate the principle of the fly-wheel. Just as a ruler whirled rapidly in the air will guide the arm by the line of the edge of the flat surface, so did Leonardo envision a machine powered by a flying propeller. Yet he could not help but think that such mechanisms were against nature, for air was a fluid, like water. And nature, the protoplast of all man's creation, had not invented rotary motion.

Leonardo pulled the string of a toy whirlybird, and the tiny four-bladed propeller spun into the air, as if in defiance of all natural laws. "No, Andrea, I have not lost my interest in this most sublime of inventions. *Il Magnifico* has listened to my ideas, and he is enthusiastic that my next machine will remain aloft."

Verrocchio watched the red propeller glide sideways into a stack of books: *De Onesta Volutta* by Il Platina, the *Letters of Filefo*, Pliny's *Historia naturale*, Dati's *Trattato della sfera*, and Ugo Benzo's *On the Preservation of the Health*. "And Lorenzo has offered to recompense you for these . . . experiments?"

"Such an invention would revolutionise the very nature of warfare," Leonardo insisted. "I've developed an exploding missile that looks like a dart and could be dropped from my Great Bird. I've also been experimenting with improvements on the arquebus, and I have a design for a giant *ballista*, a cross-bow of a kind never before imagined. I've designed a cannon with many racks of barrels that —"

"Indeed," Verrocchio said. "But I have advised you that it is unwise to put your trust in Lorenzo's momentary enthusiasms."

"Certainly the First Citizen has more than a passing interest in armaments."

"Is that why he ignored your previous memorandum wherein you proposed the very same ideas?"

"That was before, and this is now."

"Ah, certainly," Andrea said, nodding his head. Then after a pause, he said, "Stop this foolishness, Leonardo. You're a painter, and a painter should paint. Why have you been unwilling to work on any of the commissions I have offered you? And you've refused many other good offers. You have no money, and you've gained yourself a bad reputation."

"I will have more than enough money after the world watches my flying machine soar into the heavens."

"You are lucky to be alive, Leonardo. Have you not looked at yourself in a mirror? And you nearly broke your spine. Are you so intent upon doing so again? Or will killing yourself suffice?" He shook his head, as if angry at himself. " You've become skinny as a rail and sallow as an old man. Do you eat what we bring you? Do you sleep?" Do you *paint*? No, nothing but invention, nothing but . . . this." He waved his arm at the models and mechanisms that lay everywhere. Then in a soft voice, he said, "I blame myself. I should have never allowed you to proceed with all this in the first place. You need a strong hand."

"When Lorenzo sees what I have —"

Andrea made a tssing sound by tapping the roof of his mouth with his tongue. "I bid thee goodnight. Leonardo, eat your food before it gets cold. Niccolo, see that he eats."

"Andrea?" Leonardo said.

"Yes?"

"What has turned you against me?

"My love for you . . . Forget invention and munitions and flying toys. You are a painter. Paint."

"I cannot," Leonardo answered, but in a voice so low that no one else could hear.

SIX

"Stop it, that hurts!" Tista said to Niccolo, who had pulled him away from Leonardo's newest flying machine and held his arm behind him, as if to break it.

"Do you promise to stay away from the Maestro's machine?" Niccolo asked.

"Yes, I promise."

Niccolo let go of the boy, who backed nervously away from him. Leonardo stood a few paces away, oblivious to them, and stared down the mountain side to the valley below. Mist flowed dreamlike down its grassy slopes; in the distance, surrounded by greyish-green hills, was Florence, its Duomo and the high tower of the Palazzo Vecchio golden in the early sunlight. It was a brisk morning in early March, but it would be a warm day. The vapor from Leonardo's exhalations was faint. He had come here to test his glider, which now lay nearby, its large, arched wings lashed to the ground. Leonardo had taken Niccolo's advice. This flying machine had fixed wings and no motor. It was a glider. His plan was to master flight; when he developed a suitable engine to power his craft, he would then know how to control it. And this machine was more in keeping with Leonardo's ideas of nature, for he would wear the wings, as if he were, indeed, a bird; he would hang from the wings, legs below, head and shoulders above, and control them by swinging his legs and shifting his weight. He would be like a bird soaring, sailing, gliding.

But he had put off flying the contraption for the last two days that they had camped here. Even though he was certain that its design was correct, he had lost his nerve. He was afraid. He just could not do it.

But he had to . . .

He could feel Niccolo and Tista watching him.

He kicked at some loamy dirt and decided: he would do it now. He would not think about it. If he was to die . . . then so be it. Could being a coward be worse than falling out of the sky?

But he was too late, too late by a breath.

Niccolo shouted.

Startled, Leonardo turned to see that Tista had torn loose the rope that anchored the glider to the ground and had pulled himself through the opening between the wings. Leonardo shouted "stop" and rushed toward him, but Tista threw himself over the crest before either Leonardo or Niccolo could stop him. In fact, Leonardo had to grab Niccolo, who almost fell from the mountain in pursuit of his friend.

Tista's cry carried through the chill, thin air, but it was a cry of joy as the boy soared through the empty sky. He circled the mountain, catching the warmer columns of air, and then descended.

"Come back," Leonardo shouted through cupped hands, yet he could not help but feel an exhilaration, a thrill. The machine worked! But it was he, Leonardo, who needed to be in the air.

"Maestro, I tried to stop him," Niccolo cried.

But Leonardo ignored him, for the weather suddenly changed, and buffeting wind began to whip around the mountain. "Stay away from the slope," Leonardo called. But he could not be heard; and he watched helplessly as the glider pitched upwards, caught by a gust. It stalled in the chilly air, and then fell like a leaf. "Swing your hips forward," Leonardo shouted. The glider could be brought under control. If the boy was practiced, it would not be difficult at all. But he wasn't, and the glider slid sideways, crashing into the mountain.

Niccolo screamed, and Leonardo discovered that he, too, was screaming.

Tista was tossed out of the harness. Grabbing at brush and rocks, he fell about fifty feet.

By the time Leonardo reached him, the boy was almost unconscious. He lay between two jagged rocks, his head thrown back, his back twisted, arms and legs akimbo.

"Where do you feel pain?" Leonardo asked as he tried to make the boy as comfortable as he could. There was not much that could be done, for Tista's back was broken, and a rib had pierced the skin. Niccolo kneeled beside Tista; his face was white, as if drained of blood.

"I feel no pain, Maestro. Please do not be angry with me." Niccolo took his hand.

"I am not angry, Tista. But why did you do it?"

"I dreamed every night that I was flying. In your contraption, Leonardo. The very one. I could not help myself. I planned how I would do it." He smiled wanly. "And I did it."

"That you did," whispered Leonardo, remembering his own dream of falling. Could one dreamer effect another?

"Niccolo . . .?" Tista called in barely a whisper.

"I am here."

"I cannot see very well. I see the sky, I think."

Niccolo looked to Leonardo, who could only shake his head.

When Tista shuddered and died, Niccolo began to cry and beat his hands against the sharp rocks, bloodying them. Leonardo embraced him, holding his arms tightly and rocking him back and forth as if he were a baby. All the while he did so, he felt revulsion; for he could not help himself, he could not control his thoughts, which were as hard and cold as reason itself.

Although his flying machine had worked — or would have worked successfully, if he, Leonardo, had taken it into the air — he had another idea for a great bird.

One that would be safe.

As young Tista's inchoate soul rose to the heavens like a kite in the wind, Leonardo imagined just such a machine.

A child's kite . . .

"So it is true, you are painting," Andrea Verrochio said, as he stood in Leonardo's studio. Behind him stood Niccolo and Sandro Botticelli.

Although the room was still cluttered with his various instruments and machines and models, the tables had been cleared, and the desiccated corpses of birds and animals and insects were gone. The ripe odors of rot were replaced with the raw, pungent fumes of linseed oil and varnish and paint. Oil lamps inside globes filled with water — another of Leonardo's inventions — cast cones of light in the cavernous room; he had surrounded himself and his easel with the brightest of these watery lamps, which created a room of light within the larger room that seemed to be but mere appearance.

"But what kind of painting is this?" Andrea asked. "Did the Anti-Christ need to decorate the dark walls of his church? I could believe that only he could commission such work"

Leonardo grimaced and cast an angry look at Niccolo for bringing company into his room when he was working. Since Tista had died, he had taken to sleeping during the day and painting all night. He turned to Verrochio. "I'm only following your advice, Maestro. You said that a painter paints."

"Indeed, I did. But a painter does not paint for himself, in the darkness, as you are doing"; yet even as he spoke, he leaned toward the large canvas Leonardo was working on, casting his shadow over a third of it. He seemed fascinated with the central figure of a struggling man being carried into hell by the monster Geryon; man and beast were painted with such depth and precision that they looked like tiny live figures trapped in amber. The perspective of the painting was dizzying, for it was a glimpse into the endless shafts and catacombs of hell; indeed, Paolo Ucello, may he rest in peace, would have been proud of such work, for he had lived for the beauties of perspective.

"Leonardo, I have called upon you twice . . . why did you turn me away?" Sandro asked. "And why have you not responded to any of my letters?" He looked like a younger version of Master Andrea, for he had the same kind of wide, fleshy face, but Botticelli's jaw was stronger; and while Verrocchio's lips were thin and tight, Sandro's were heavy and sensuous.

"I have not received anyone," Leonardo said, stepping out of the circle of light. Since Tista was buried, his only company was Niccolo, who would not leave his master.

"And neither have you responded to the invitations of the First Citizen," Verrocchio said, meaning Lorenzo de Medici.

"Is that why you're here?" Leonardo asked Sandro. Even in the lamplight, he could see a blush in his friend's cheeks, for he was part of the Medici family; Lorenzo loved him as he did his own brother, Giuliano.

"I'm here because I'm worried about *you*, as is Lorenzo. You have done the same for me, or have you forgotten?"

No, Leonardo had not forgotten. He remembered when Sandro had almost died of love for Lorenzo's mistress, Simonetta Vespucci. He remembered how Sandro had lost weight and dreamed even when he was awake; how Pico Della Mirandola had exorcised him in the presence of Simonetta and Lorenzo; and how he, Leonardo, had taken care of him until he regained his health.

"So you think I am in need of Messer Mirandola's services?" Leonardo asked. "Is that it?"

"I think you need to see your friends. I think you need to come awake in the light and sleep in the night. I think you must stop grieving for the child Tista."

Leonardo was about to respond, but caught himself. He wasn't grieving for Tista. Niccolo was, certainly. He, Leonardo, was simply working.

Working through his fear and guilt and . . .

Grief.

For it was, somehow, as if *he* had fallen and broken his spine, as, perhaps, he should have when he fell from the mountain ledge as a child.

"Leonardo, why are you afraid?" Niccolo asked. "The machine . . . worked. It *will* fly."

"And so you wish to fly it, too? Leonardo asked, but it was more a statement than a question; he was embarrassed and vexed that Niccolo would demean him in front of Verrochio.

But, indeed, the machine had worked.

"I am going back to bed," Verrochio said, bowing to Sandro. "I will leave you to try to talk sense into my apprentice." He looked at Leonardo and smiled, for both knew that he was an apprentice in name only. But Leonardo would soon have to earn his keep; for Verrochio's patience was coming to an end. He gazed at Leonardo's painting. "You know, the good monks of Saint Bernard might just be interested in such work as this. Perhaps I might suggest that they take your painting instead of the altarpiece you owe them."

Leonardo could not help but laugh, for he knew that his master was serious.

After Verrochio left, Leonardo and Sandro sat down on a cassone together under one of the dirty high windows of the studio; Niccolo sat before them on the floor; he was all eyes and ears and attention.

"Nicco, bring us some wine," Leonardo said.

"I want to be *here*."

Leonardo did not argue with the boy. It was unimportant, and once the words were spoken, forgotten. Leonardo gazed upward. He could see the sky through the window; the stars were brilliant, for Florence was asleep and its lanterns did not compete with the stars. "I thought I could get so close to them," he said, as if talking to himself. He imagined the stars as tiny pricks in the heavenly fabric; he could even now feel the heat from the region of fire held at bay by the darkness; and as if he could truly see through imagination, he watched himself soaring in his flying machine, climbing into the black heavens, soaring, reaching to burn like paper for one glorious instant into those hot, airy regions above the clouds and night.

But this flying machine he imagined was like no other device he had ever sketched or built. He had reached beyond nature to conceive a child's kite with flat surfaces to support it in the still air. Like his dragonfly contraption, it would have double wings, cellular open-ended boxes that would be as stable as kites of like construction.

Stable . . . and safe.

The pilot would not need to shift his balance to keep control. He would float on the air like a raft. Tista would not have lost his balance and fallen out of the sky in this contraption.

"Leonardo . . . *Leonardo*! Have you been listening to anything I've said?"

"Yes, Little Bottle, I hear you." Leonardo was one of a very small circle of friends who was permitted to call Sandro by his childhood nickname.

"Then I can tell Lorenzo that you will demonstrate your new flying machine? It would not be wise to refuse him, Leonardo. He has finally taken notice of you. He needs you now; his enemies are everywhere."

Leonardo nodded.

Indeed, the First Citizen's relationship with the ambitious Pope Sixtus IV was at a breaking-point, and all of Florence lived in fear of excommunication and war.

"Florence must show its enemies that it is invincible," Sandro continued. "A device that can rain fire from the sky would deter even the Pope."

"I knew that Lorenzo could not long ignore my inventions," Leonardo said, although he was surprised.

"He plans to elevate you to the position of master of engines and captain of engineers."

"Should I thank you for this, Little Bottle?" Leonardo asked. "Lorenzo would have no reason to think that my device would work. Rather the opposite, as it killed my young apprentice."

"God rest his soul," Sandro said.

Leonardo continued. "Unless someone whispered in Lorenzo's ear. I fear you have gone from being artist to courtier, Little Bottle."

"The honours go to Niccolo," Sandro said. "It is he who convinced Lorenzo."

"This is what you've been waiting for, Maestro," Niccolo said. "I will find Francesco at first light and tell him to help you build another Great Bird. And I'll get the wine right now."

"Wait a moment," Leonardo said, then directed himself to Sandro. "How did Nicco convince Lorenzo?"

"You sent me with a note for the First Citizen, Maestro, when you couldn't accept his invitation to attend Simonetta's ball," Niccolo said. "I told him of our grief over Tista, and then I also had to explain what had happened. Although I loved Tista, he was at fault. Not our machine . . . Lorenzo understood."

"Ah, did he now."

"I only did as you asked," Niccolo insisted.

"And did you speak to him about my bombs?" Leonardo asked.

"Yes, Maestro."

"And did he ask you, or did you volunteer that information?

Niccolo glanced nervously at Sandro, as if he would supply him with the answer. "I thought you would be pleased . . ."

"I think you may get the wine now," Sandro said to Niccolo, who did not miss the opportunity to flee. Then he directed himself to Leonardo. "You should have congratulated Niccolo, not berated him. Why were you so hard on the boy?"

Leonardo gazed across the room at his painting in the circle of lamps. He desired only to paint, not construct machines to kill children; he would paint his dreams, which had fouled his waking life with their strength and startling detail. By painting them, by exposing them, he might free himself. Yet ideas for his great Kite seemed to appear like chiaroscuro on the painting of his dream of falling, as if it were a notebook.

Leonardo shivered, for his dreams had spilled out of his sleep and would not let him go. Tonight they demanded to be painted.

Tomorrow they would demand to be built.

He yearned to step into the cold, perfect spaces of his memory cathedral, which had become his haven. There he could imagine each painting, each dream, and lock it in its own dark, private room. As if every experience, every pain, could be so isolated.

"Well . . .?" Sandro asked.

"I will apologise to Niccolo when he returns," Leonardo said.

"Leonardo, was Niccolo right? Are you afraid? I'm your best friend, certainly you can —"

Just then Niccolo appeared with a bottle of wine.

"I am very tired, Little Bottle," Leonardo said. "Perhaps we can celebrate another day. I will take your advice and sleep . . . to come awake in the light."

That was, of course, a lie, for Leonardo painted all night and the next day. It was as if he had to complete a month's worth of ideas in a few hours. Ideas seemed to explode in his mind's eye, paintings complete; all that Leonardo had to do was trace them onto canvas and mix his colours. It was as if he had somehow managed to unlock doors in his memory cathedral and glimpse what St Augustine had called the present of things future; it was as if he were glimpsing ideas he *would* have, paintings he *would* paint; and he knew that if he didn't capture these gifts now, he would lose them forever. Indeed, it was as if he were dreaming whilst awake, and during these hours, whether awake or slumped over before the canvas in a catnap or a trance, he had no control over the images that glowed in his mind like the lanterns placed on the floor, cassones, desks, and tables around him, rings of light, as if everything was but different aspects of Leonardo's dream ... Leonardo's conception. He worked in a frenzy, which was always how he worked when his ideas caught fire; but this time he had no conscious focus or goal. Rather than a frenzy of discovery, this was a kind of remembering.

By morning he had six paintings under way; one was a Madonna, transcendantly radiant, as if Leonardo had lifted the veil of human sight to reveal the divine substance. The others seemed to be grotesque visions of hell that would only be matched by a young Dutch contemporary of Leonardo's: Hieronymous Bosch. There was a savage cruelty in these pictures of fabulous monsters with gnashing snouts, bat's wings, crocodile's jaws, and scaly pincered tails, yet every creature, every caricature and grotesquerie had a single haunting human feature: chimeras with soft, sad human eyes or womanly limbs or the angelic faces of children taunting and torturing the fallen in the steep, dark mountainous wastes of hell.

As promised, Niccolo fetched Verrocchio's foreman Francesco to supervise the rebuilding of Leonardo's flying machine; but not at first light, as he had promised, for the exhausted Niccolo had slept until noon. Leonardo had thought that Niccolo was cured of acting independently on his master's behalf; but obviously the boy was not contrite, for he had told Leonardo that he was going downstairs to bring back some meat and fruit for lunch.

But Leonardo surprised both of them by producing a folio of sketches, diagrams, plans, and design measurements for kites and two and three winged soaring machines. Some had curved surfaces, some had flat surfaces; but all these drawings and diagrams were based on the idea of open ended boxes ... groups of them placed at the ends of timber spars. There were detailed diagrams of triplane and biplane gliders with wing span and supporting surface measurements; even on paper these machines looked awkward and heavy and bulky, for they did not imitate nature. He had tried imitation, but nature was capricious, unmanageable. Now he would conquer it. *Vince la natura.* Not even Tista could fall from these rectangular rafts. Leonardo had scribbled notes below two sketches of cellular kites, but not in his backward script; this was obviously meant to be readable to others: *Determine whether kite with cambered wings will travel farther. Fire from crossbow to ensure accuracy.* And on another page, a sketch of three kites flying in tandem, one above the other, and below a figure on a sling seat: *Total area of surface sails 476 ells. Add kites with sails of 66 ells to compensate for body weight over 198 pounds. Shelter from wind during assembly, open kites one at a time, then pull away supports to allow the wind to get under the sails. Tether the last kite, lest you be carried away.*

"Can you produce these kites for me by tomorrow?" Leonardo asked Francesco, as he pointed to the sketch. "I've provided all the dimensions."

"Impossible," Francesco said. "Perhaps when your flying machine for the First Citizen is finished —"

"This *will* be for the First Citizen," Leonardo insisted.

"I was instructed to rebuild the flying machine in which young Tista was . . . in which he suffered his accident."

"By whom? Niccolo?

"Leonardo, Maestro Andrea has interrupted work on the altarpiece for the Chapel of Saint Bernard to build your contraption for the First Citizen. When that's completed, I'll help you build these . . . kites."

Leonardo knew Francesco well; he wouldn't get anywhere by cajoling him. He nodded and sat down before the painting of a Madonna holding the Child, who, in turn, was holding a cat. The painting seemed to be movement itself.

"Don't you wish to supervise the work, Maestro?" asked the foreman.

"No, I'll begin constructing the kites, with Niccolo."

"Maestro, Lorenzo expects us — you — to demonstrate your Great Bird in a fortnight. You and Sandro agreed."

"Sandro is not the First Citizen." Then after a pause, "I have better ideas for soaring machines."

"But they cannot be built in time, Maestro," Niccolo insisted.

"Then no machine will be built."

And with that, Leonardo went back to his painting of the Madonna, which bore a sensual resemblance to Lorenzo's mistress Simonetta.

Which would be a gift for Lorenzo.

SEVEN

After a short burst of pelting rain, steady winds seemed to cleanse the sky of the grey storm clouds that had suffocated the city for several days in an atmospheric inversion. It had also been humid, and the air, which tasted dirty, had made breathing difficult. Florentine citizens closed their shutters against the poisonous miasmas, which were currently thought to be the cause of the deadly buboes, and were, at the very least, ill omens. But Leonardo, who had finally completed building his tandem kites after testing design after design, did not even know that a disaster had befallen Verrochio's bottega when rotten timbers in the roof gave way during the storm. He and Niccolo had left to test the kites in a farmer's field nestled in a windy valley that also afforded privacy. As Leonardo did not want Zoroastro or Lorenzo de Credi, or anyone else along, he designed a sled so he could haul his lightweight materials himself.

"Maestro, are you going to make your peace with Master Andrea?" Niccolo asked as they waited for the mid-morning winds, which were the strongest. The sky was clear and soft and gauzy blue, a peculiar atmospheric effect seen only in Tuscany; Leonardo had been told that in other places, especially to the north, the sky was sharper, harder.

"I will soon start a bottega of my own," Leonardo said, "and be the ruler of my own house."

"But we need money, Maestro."

"We'll have it."

"Not if you keep the First Citizen waiting for his Great Bird," Niccolo said; and Leonardo noticed that the boy's eyes narrowed, as if he were calculating a mathematical problem. "Maestro Andrea will certainly have to tell Lorenzo that your Great Bird is completed."

"Has he done so?" Leonardo asked.

Niccolo shrugged.

"He will be even more impressed with my new invention. I will show him before he becomes too impatient. But I think it is Andrea, not Lorenzo, who is impatient."

"You're going to show the First Citizen *this*?" Niccolo asked, meaning the tandem kites, which were protected from any gusts of wind by a secured canvas; the kites were assembled, and when Leonardo was ready, would be opened one at a time.

"If this works, then we will build the Great Bird as I promised. That will buy us our bottega and Lorenzo's love."

"He loves you already, Maestro, as does Maestro Andrea."

"Then they'll be patient with me."

Niccolo was certainly not above arguing with his master; he had, indeed, become Leonardo's confidant. But Leonardo didn't give him a chance. He had been checking the wind, which would soon be high. "Come help me, Nicco, and try not to be a philosopher. The wind is strong enough. If we wait it will become too gusty and tear the kites." This had already happened to several of Leonardo's large scale models.

Leonardo let the wind take the first and smallest of the kites, but the wind was rather puffy, and it took a few moments before it pulled its thirty pounds on the guy rope. Then, as the wind freshened, he let go another. Satisfied, he anchored the assembly, making doubly sure that it was secure, and opened the third and largest kite. "Hold the line tight," he said to Niccolo as he climbed onto the sling seat and held tightly to a restraining rope that ran through a block and tackle to a makeshift anchor of rocks.

Leonardo reassured himself that he was safely tethered and reminded himself that the cellular box was the most stable of constructions. Its flat surfaces would support it in the air. Nevertheless, his heart seemed to be pulsing in his throat, he had difficulty taking a breath, and he could feel the chill of his sweat on his chest and arms.

The winds were strong, but erratic, and Leonardo waited until he could feel the wind pulling steady; he leaned backward, sliding leeward on the seat to help the wind get under the supporting surface of the largest kite. Then suddenly, as if some great heavenly hand had grabbed hold of the guy ropes and the kites and snapped them, Leonardo shot upward about twenty feet. But the kites held steady at the end of their tether, floating on the wind like rafts on water.

How different this was from the Great Bird, which was so sensitive — and susceptible — to every movement of the body. Leonardo shifted his weight, and even as he did so, he prayed; but the kites held in the air. Indeed, they were rafts. The answer was ample supporting surfaces.

Vince la natura.

The wind lightened, and he came down. The kites dragged him forward; he danced along the ground on his toes before he was swept upwards again.

Niccolo was shouting, screaming, and hanging from the restraining rope, as if to add his weight, lest it pull away from the rock anchor or pull the rocks heavenward.

When the kites came down for the third time, Leonardo jumped from the sling seat, falling to the ground. Seconds later, as if slapped by the same hand that had pulled them into the sky, the kites crashed, splintering, as their sails snapped and fluttered, as if still yearning for the airy heights.

"Are you all right, Maestro," Niccolo shouted, running toward Leonardo.

"Yes," Leonardo said, although his back was throbbing in pain and his right arm, which he had already broken once before, was numb. But he could move it, as well as all his fingers. "I'm fine." He surveyed the damage. "Let's salvage what we can."

They fastened the broken kites onto the sled and walked through wildflower dotted fields and pastures back to the bottega. "Perhaps now, Maestro, you'll trust your original Great Bird," Niccolo said. "You mustn't bury it with Tista."

"What are you talking about?" Leonardo asked.

"These kites are too . . . dangerous. They're completely at the mercy of the wind; they dragged you along the ground; and you almost broke your arm. Isn't that right, Maestro?"

Leonardo detected a touch of irony in Niccolo's voice. So the boy was having it up on his master. "Yes," Leonardo said. "And what does that prove?"

"That you should give this up."

"On the contrary, Nicco. This experiment has only proved how safe my new Great Bird will be."

"But you —"

Leonardo showed Niccolo his latest drawing of a biplane based on his idea of open ended boxes placed at the ends of timber spars.

"How could such a thing fly?" Niccolo asked.

"That's a soaring machine safe enough for Lorenzo himself. If I could show the First Citizen that he could command the very air, do you think he would regret the few days it will take to build and test the new machine?"

"I think it looks very dangerous . . . and I think the kites are very dangerous, Maestro."

Leonardo smiled at Niccolo. "Then at least after today you no longer think I am a coward."

"Maestro, I *never* thought that."

But even as they approached the city, Leonardo could feel the edges of his dream, the dark edges of nightmare lingering; and he knew that tonight it would return.

The dream of falling. The dream of flight.

Tista . . .

He would stay up and work. He would not sleep. He would not dream. But the dream spoke to him even as he walked, told him *it* was nature and would not be conquered. And Leonardo could feel himself

Falling.

If Leonardo were superstitious, he would have believed it was a sign.

When the roof of Verrochio's bottega gave way, falling timber and debris destroyed almost everything in Leonardo's studio; and the pelting rain ruined most of what might have been salvaged. Leonardo could rewrite his notes, for they were safe in the altar of his memory cathedral; he could rebuild models and replenish supplies, but his painting of the Madonna — his gift for Lorenzo — was destroyed. The canvas torn, the oils smeared, and the still-sticky varnish surface spackled with grit and filth. Most everything but the three paintings of his nightmare-descent into hell was destroyed. They were placed against the inner wall of the studio, a triptych of dark canvases, exposed, the varnish still sticky, protected by a roll of fabric that had fallen over them. And in every one of them Leonardo could see himself as a falling or fallen figure.

The present of the future.

"Don't you think this is a sign from the gods?" Niccolo asked after he and Leonardo had salvaged what they could and moved into another studio in Verrochio's bottega.

"Do you now believe in the Greek's pantheon?" Leonardo asked.

Looking flustered, Niccolo said, "I only meant —"

"I know what you meant." Leonardo smiled tightly. "Maestro Andrea might get his wish . . . he might sell those paintings to the good monks. In the meantime, we've got work to do, which we'll start at first light."

"We can't build your Great Bird alone," Niccolo insisted.

"Of course we can. And Francesco will allocate some of his apprentices to help us."

"Maestro Andrea won't allow it."

"We'll see," Leonardo said.

"Maestro, your Great Bird is *already* built. It is ready, and Lorenzo expects you to fly it."

"Would that the roof fell upon it." Leonardo gazed out the window into the streets. The full moon illuminated the houses and bottegas and shops and palazzos in weak grey light that seemed to be made brighter by the yellow lamplight trembling behind vellum covered windows. He would make Lorenzo a model of his new soaring machine, his new Great Bird; but he would not see the First Citizen until it was built and tested. Indeed, he stayed up the night redrawing his designs, reworking his ideas, as if the destruction of his studio had been a blessing. He sketched cellular box kite designs that he combined into new forms for gliding machines, finally settling on a design based almost entirely on the rectangular box kite forms. He had broken away from the natural bird-like forms, yet this device was not unnatural in its simplicity. He detailed crosshatch timber braces, which would keep his cellular wing surfaces tight. He made drawings and diagrams of the cordage. The pilot would sit in a sling below the double wings, which were webbed as the masts of a sailing vessel; and the rudder would be attached to long spars that stretched behind him at shoulder height. A ship to sail into the heavens.

Tomorrow he would build models to test his design. To his mind, the ship was already built, for it was as tangible as the notebook he was staring into.

Notebook in hand, he fell asleep, for he had been little removed from dreams; and dream he did, dreams as textured and deep and tinted as memory. He rode his Great Bird through the moonlit night, sailed around the peaks of mountains as if they were islands in a calm, warm sea; and the winds carried him, carried him away into darkness, into the surfaces of his paintings that had survived the rain and roof, into the brushstroked chiaroscuro of his imagined hell.

EIGHT

"Tell Lorenzo that I'll have a soaring machine ready to impress the archbishop when he arrives," Leonardo said. "But he's not due for a fortnight."

"You've taken too long already." Sandro Botticelli stood in Leonardo's new studio, which was small and in disarray; although the roof had been repaired, Leonardo did not want to waste time moving back into his old room. Sandro was dressed as a dandy, in red and green, with dags and a peaked cap pulled over his thick brown hair. It was a festival day, and the Medici and their retinue would take to the streets for the Palio, the great annual horse race. "Lorenzo sent me to drag you to the Palio, if need be."

"If Andrea had allowed Francesco to help me — or at least lent me a few apprentices — I would have it finished by now."

"That's not the point."

"That's exactly the point."

"Get out of your smock; you must have something that's not covered with paint and dirt."

"Come, I'll show you what I've done," Leonardo said. "I've put up canvas outside to work on my soaring machine. It's like nothing you've ever seen, I promise you that. I'll call Niccolo, he'll be happy to see you."

"You can show it to me on our way, Leonardo. Now get dressed. Niccolo has left long ago."

"What?"

"Have you lost touch with everyone and everything?" Sandro asked. "Niccolo is at the Palio with Andrea ... who is with Lorenzo. Only you remain behind."

"But Niccolo was just here."

Sandro shook his head. "He's been there for most of the day. He said he begged you to accompany him."

"Did he tell that to Lorenzo, too?"

"I think you can trust your young apprentice to be discreet."

Dizzy with fatigue, Leonardo sat down by a table covered with books and models of kites and various incarnations of his soaring machine. "Yes, of course, you're right, Little Bottle."

"You look like you've been on a binge. You've got to start taking care of yourself, you've got to start sleeping and eating properly. If you don't, you'll lose everything, including Lorenzo's love and attention. You can't treat him as you do the rest of your friends. I thought you wanted to be his master of engineers."

"What else has Niccolo been telling you?"

Sandro shook his head in a gesture of exasperation, and said, "Change your clothes, dear friend. We haven't more than an hour before the race begins."

"I'm not going," Leonardo said, his voice flat. "Lorenzo will have to wait until my soaring machine is ready."

"He will not wait."

"He has no choice."

"He has your Great Bird, Leonardo."

"Then Lorenzo can fly it. Perhaps he will suffer the same fate as Tista. Better yet, he should order Andrea to fly it. After all, Andrea had it built for him."

"Leonardo . . ."

"It killed Tista . . . It's not safe."

"I'll tell Lorenzo you're ill," Sandro said.

"Send Niccolo back to me. I forbid him to —"

But Sandro had already left the studio, closing the large inlaid door behind him.

Exhausted, Leonardo leaned upon the table and imagined that he had followed Sandro to the door, down the stairs, and outside. There he surveyed his canvas-covered makeshift workshop. The air was hot and stale in the enclosed space. It would take weeks working alone to complete the new soaring machine. Niccolo should be here. Then Leonardo began working at the cordage to tighten the supporting wing surfaces. *This* machine will be safe, he thought; and he worked, even in the dark exhaustion of his dreams, for he had lost the ability to rest.

Indeed he was lost.

In the distance he could hear Tista. Could hear the boy's triumphant cry before he fell and snapped his spine. And he heard thunder. Was it the shouting of the crowd as he, Leonardo, fell from the mountain near Vinci? Was it the crowd cheering the Palio riders racing through the city? Or was it the sound of his own dream-choked breathing?

"Leonardo, they're going to fly your machine."

"What?" Leonardo asked, surfacing from deep sleep; his head ached and his limbs felt weak and light, as if he had been carrying heavy weights.

Francesco stood over him, and Leonardo could smell the man's sweat and the faint odor of garlic. "One of my boys came back to tell me . . . as if I'd be rushing into crowds of cutpurses to see some child die in your flying contraption." He took a breath, catching himself. "I'm sorry, Maestro. Don't take offence, but you know what I think of your machines."

"Lorenzo is going to demonstrate my Great Bird *now*?"

Francesco shrugged. "After his brother won the Palio, *Il Magnifico* announced to the crowds that an angel would fly above them and drop hell's own fire from the sky. And my apprentice tells me that *inquisitore* are all over the streets and are keeping everyone away from the gardens near *Santi Apostoli*."

That would certainly send a message to the Pope; the church of *Santi Apostoli* was under the protection of the powerful Pazzi family, who were allies of Pope Sixtus and enemies of the Medici.

"When is this supposed to happen?" Leonardo asked the foreman as he hurriedly put on a new shirt; a doublet; and *calze* hose, which were little more than pieces of leather to protect his feet.

Francesco shrugged. "I came to tell you as soon as I heard."

"And did you hear who is to fly my machine?"

"I've told you all I know, Maestro." Then after a pause, he said, "But I fear for Niccolo. I fear he has told *Il Magnifico* that he knows how to fly your inventions."

Leonardo prayed he could find Niccolo before he came to harm. He too feared that the boy had betrayed him, had insinuated himself into Lorenzo's confidence, and was at this moment soaring over Florence in the Great Bird. Soaring over the Duomo, the Baptistry, and the Piazza della Signoria, which rose from the streets like minarets around a heavenly dome.

But the air currents over Florence were too dangerous. He would fall like Tista, for what was the city but a mass of jagged peaks and precipitous cliffs.

"Thank you, Francesco," Leonardo said, and, losing no time, he made his way through the crowds toward the church of *Santi Apostoli*. A myriad of smells delicious and noxious permeated the air: roasting meats, honeysuckle, the odor of candle wax heavy as if with childhood memories, offal and piss, cattle and horses, the tang of wine and cider, and everywhere sweat and the sour ripe scent of perfumes applied to unclean bodies. The shouting and laughter and stepping-rushing-soughing of the crowds were deafening, as if a human tidal wave was making itself felt across the city. The whores were out in full regalia, having left their district which lay between Santa Giovanni and

Santa Maria Maggiore; they worked their way through the crowds, as did the cutpurses and pickpockets, the children of Firenze's streets. Beggars grasped onto visiting country villeins and minor guildesmen for a denari and saluted when the red *carroccios* with their long scarlet banners and red, dressed horses passed. Merchants and bankers and wealthy guildesmen rode on great horses or were comfortable in their carriages, while their servants walked ahead to clear the way for them with threats and brutal proddings.

The frantic, noisy streets mirrored Leonardo's frenetic inner state, for he feared for Niccolo; and he walked quickly, his hand openly resting on the hilt of his razor-sharp dagger to deter thieves and those who would slice open the belly of a passer-by for amusement.

He kept looking for likely places from which his Great Bird might be launched: the dome of the Duomo, high brick towers, the roof of the Baptistry . . . and he looked up at the darkening sky, looking for his Great Bird as he pushed his way through the crowds to the gardens near the *Santi Apostoli*, which was near the Ponte Vecchio. In these last few moments, Leonardo became hopeful. Perhaps there was a chance to stop Niccolo . . . if, indeed, Niccolo was to fly the Great Bird for Lorenzo.

Blocking entry to the gardens were both Medici and Pazzi supporters, two armies, dangerous and armed, facing each other. Lances and swords flashed in the dusty twilight. Leonardo could see the patriarch of the Pazzi family, the shrewd and haughty Jacopo de' Pazzi, an old, full-bodied man sitting erect on a huge, richly carapaced charger. His sons Giovanni, Francesco, and Guglielmo were beside him, surrounded by their troops dressed in the Pazzi colours of blue and gold. And there, to Leonardo's surprise and frustration, was his great Eminence the Archbishop, protected by the scions of the Pazzi family and their liveried guards. So this was why Lorenzo had made his proclamation that he would conjure an angel of death and fire to demonstrate the power of the Medici . . . and Florence. It was as if the Pope himself were here to watch.

Beside the Archbishop, in dangerous proximity to the Pazzi, Lorenzo and Giuliano sat atop their horses. Giuliano, the winner of the Palio, the ever handsome hero, was wrapped entirely in silver, his silk stomacher embroidered with pearls and silver, a giant ruby in his cap; while his brother Lorenzo, perhaps not handsome but certainly an overwhelming presence, wore light armour over simple clothes. But Lorenzo carried his shield, which contained "Il Libro", the huge Medici diamond reputed to be worth 2,500 ducats.

Leonardo could see Sandro behind Giuliano, and he shouted his name; but Leonardo's voice was lost in the din of twenty thousand other voices. He looked for Niccolo, but he could not see him with Sandro or the Medici. He pushed his way forward, but he had to pass through an army of the feared Medici-supported Companions of the Night, the darkly-dressed Dominican friars who held the informal but hated title of *inquisitore*. And they were backed up by Medici sympathisers sumptuously outfitted by Lorenzo in armour and livery of red velvet and gold.

Finally, one of the guards recognised him, and he escorted Leonardo through the sweaty, nervous troops toward Lorenzo and his entourage by the edge of the garden.

But Leonardo was not to reach them.

The air seemed heavy and fouled, as if the crowd's perspiration was rising like heat, distorting shape and perspective. Then the crowds became quiet, as Lorenzo addressed them and pointed to the sky.

Everyone looked heavenward.

And like some gauzy fantastical winged creature that Dante might have contemplated for his *Paradisio*, the Great Bird soared over Florence, circling high above the church and gardens, riding the updrafts and the currents that swirled invisibly above the towers and domes and spires of the city. Leonardo caught his breath, for the pilot certainly looked like Niccolo; surely a boy rather than a full-bodied man. He looked like an awkward angel with translucent gauze wings held in place with struts of wood and cords of twine. Indeed, the glider was as white as heaven, and Niccolo — if it was Niccolo — was dressed in a sheer white robe.

The boy sailed over the Pazzi troops like a bird swooping above a chimney, and seasoned soldiers fell to the ground in fright, or awe, and prayed; only Jacopo Pazzi, his sons, and the Archbishop remained steady on their horses. As did, of course, Lorenzo and his retinue.

And Leonardo could hear a kind of buzzing, as if he were in the midst of an army of cicadas, as twenty thousand citizens prayed to the soaring angel for their lives as they clutched and clicked black rosaries.

The heavens had opened to give them a sign, just as they had for the Hebrews at Sinai.

The boy made a tight circle around the gardens and dropped a single fragile shell that exploded on impact, throwing off great streams of fire and shards of shrapnel that cut down and burned trees and grass and shrub. Then he dropped another, which was off mark, and dangerously close to Lorenzo's entourage. A group of people were cut down by the shrapnel, and lay choking and bleeding in the streets. Fire danced across the piazza. Horses stampeded. Soldiers and citizens alike ran in panic. The Medici and Pazzi distanced themselves from the garden, their frightened troops closing around them like Roman phalanxes. Leonardo would certainly not be able to get close to the First Citizen now. He shouted at Niccolo in anger and frustration, for surely these people would die; and Leonardo would be their murderer. He had just killed them with his dreams and drawings. Here was truth. Here was revelation. He had murdered these unfortunate strangers as surely as he had killed Tista. It was as if his invention now had a life of its own, independent of its creator.

As the terrified mob raged around him, Leonardo found refuge in an alcove between two buildings and watched his Great Bird soar in great circles over the city. The sun was setting, and the high, thin cirrus clouds were stained deep red and purple. Leonardo prayed that Niccolo would have sense enough to fly westward, away from the city, where he could hope to land safely on open ground; but the boy was showing off and underestimated the capriciousness of the winds. He suddenly fell, as if dropped, toward the brick and stone below him. He shifted weight and swung his hips, trying desperately to recover. An updraft picked him up like a dust devil, and he soared skyward on heavenly breaths of warm air.

God's grace.

He seemed to be more cautious now, for he flew toward safer grounds to the west . . . but then he suddenly descended, falling, dropping behind the backshadowed buildings; and Leonardo could well imagine that the warm updraft that had lifted Niccolo had popped like a water bubble.

So did the boy fall through cool air, probably to his death.

Leonardo waited a beat, watching and waiting for the Great Bird to reappear. His heart was itself like a bird beating violently in his throat. Niccolo . . . Prayers of supplication formed in his mind, as if of their own volition, as if Leonardo's thoughts were not his own, but belonged to some peasant from Vinci grasping at a rosary for truth and hope and redemption.

Those crowded around Leonardo could not guess that the angel had fallen . . . just that he had descended from the Empyrean heights to the man-made spires of Florence where the sun was blazing rainbows as it set; and Lorenzo emerged triumphantly. He stood alone on a porch so he could be seen by all and distracted the crowds with a haranguing speech that was certainly directed to the Archbishop.

Florence is invincible.

The greatest and most perfect city in the world.

Florence would conquer all its enemies.

As Lorenzo spoke, Leonardo saw, as if in a lucid dream, dark skies filled with his flying machines. He saw his hempen bombs falling through the air, setting the world below on fire. Indeed, with these machines Lorenzo could conquer the Papal States and Rome itself; could burn the Pope out of the Vatican and become more powerful than any of the Caesars.

An instant later Leonardo was running, navigating the maze of alleys and streets to reach Niccolo. Niccolo was all that mattered. If the boy was dead, certainly Lorenzo would not care. But Sandro . . . surely Sandro . . .

There was no time to worry about Sandro's loyalties.

The crowds thinned, and only once was Leonardo waylaid by street arabs who blocked his way. But when they saw that Leonardo was armed and wild and ready to draw blood, they let him pass; and he ran, blade in hand, as if he were being chased by wild beasts.

Empty streets, empty buildings, the distant thunder of the crowds constant as the roaring of the sea. All of Florence was behind Leonardo, who searched for Niccolo in what might have been ancient ruins but for the myriad telltale signs that life still flowed all about here, and soon would again. Alleyways became shadows, and there was a blue tinge to the air. Soon it would be dark. A few windows already glowed tallow yellow in the balconied apartments above him.

He would not easily find Niccolo here. The boy could have fallen anywhere; and in grief and desperation, Leonardo shouted his name. His voice echoed against the high building walls; someone answered in falsetto *voce*, followed by laughter. But then Leonardo heard horses galloping through the streets, heard men's voices calling to each other. Lorenzo's men? Pazzi? There was a shout, and Leonardo knew they had found what they were looking for. Frantic, he hurried toward the soldiers, but what would he do when he found Niccolo wrapped in the wreckage of the Great Bird? Tell a dying boy that he, Leonardo, couldn't fly his own invention because he was afraid?

I was trying to make it safe, Niccolo.

He found Lorenzo's Companions of the Night in a piazza surrounded by tenements. They carried torches, and at least twenty of the well-armed priests were on horseback. Their horses were fitted out in black, as if both horses and riders had come directly from hell; one of the horses pulled a cart covered with canvas.

Leonardo could see torn fustian and taffeta and part of the Great Bird's rudder section hanging over the red and blue striped awning of a balcony. And there, on the ground below was the upper wing assembly, intact. Other bits of cloth slid along the ground like foolscap.

Several *inquisitore* huddled over an unconscious figure.

Niccolo.

Beside himself with grief, Leonardo rushed headlong into the piazza; but before he could get halfway across the court, he was intercepted by a dozen Dominican soldiers. "I am Leonardo da Vinci," he shouted, but that seemed to mean nothing to them. These young Wolves of the Church were ready to hack him to pieces for the sheer pleasure of feeling the heft of their swords.

"Do not harm him," shouted a familiar voice.

Sandro Botticelli.

He was dressed in the thick, black garb of the *inquisitore*. "What are you doing here, Leonardo? You're a bit late." Anger and sarcasm was evident in his voice.

But Leonardo was concerned only with Niccolo, for two brawny *inquisitore* were lifting him into the cart. He pushed past Sandro and mindless of consequences pulled one of the soldiers out of the way to see the boy. Leonardo winced as he looked at the boy's smashed skull and bruised body — arms and legs broken, extended at wrong angles — and turned away in relief.

This was not Niccolo; he had never seen this boy before.

"Niccolo is with Lorenzo," Sandro said, standing beside Leonardo. "Lorenzo considered allowing Niccolo to fly your machine, for the boy knows almost as much about it as you."

"Has he flown the Great Bird?"

After a pause, Sandro said, "Yes . . . but against Lorenzo's wishes. That's probably what saved his life." Sandro gazed at the boy in the cart, who was now covered with the torn wings of the Great Bird, which, in turn, was covered with canvas. "When Lorenzo discovered what Niccolo had done, he would not allow him near any of your flying machines, except to help train this boy, Giorgio, who was in his service. A nice boy, may God take his soul."

"Then Niccolo is safe?" Leonardo asked.

"Yes, the holy fathers are watching over him."

"You mean these cutthroats?"

"Watch how you speak, Leonardo. Lorenzo kept Niccolo safe for you, out of love for you. And how have you repaid him . . . by being a traitor?"

"Don't ever say that to me, even in jest."

"I'm not jesting, Leonardo. You've failed Lorenzo . . . and your country, failed them out of fear. Even a child such as Niccolo could see that."

"Is that what you think?"

Sandro didn't reply.

"Is that what Niccolo told you?"

"Yes."

Leonardo would not argue, for the stab of truth unnerved him, even now. "And you, why are you here?"

"Because Lorenzo trusts me. As far as Florence and the Archbishop is concerned, the angel flew and caused fire to rain from heaven. And is in heaven now as we speak." He shrugged and nodded to the *inquisitore*, who mounted their horses.

"So now you command the Companions of the Night instead of the divine power of the painter," Leonardo said, the bitterness evident in his voice. "Perhaps we are on different sides now, Little Bottle."

"*I'm* on the side of Florence," Sandro said. "And against her enemies. *You* care only for your inventions."

"And my friends," Leonardo said quietly, pointedly.

"Perhaps for Niccolo, perhaps a little for me; but more for yourself."

"How many of my flying machines does Lorenzo have now?" Leonardo asked, but Sandro turned away from him and rode behind the cart that carried the corpse of the angel and the broken bits of the Great Bird. Once again, Leonardo felt the numbing, rubbery sensation of great fatigue, as if he had turned into an old man, as if all his work, now finished, had come to nothing. He wished only to be rid of it all: his inventions, his pain and guilt. He could not bear even to be in Florence, the place he loved above all others.

There was no place for him now.

Leonardo could be seen as a shadow moving inside his canvas-covered makeshift workshop, which was brightly lit by several water lamps and a small fire. Other shadows passed across the vellum-covered windows of the surrounding buildings like mirages in the Florentine night. Much of the city was dark, for few could afford tallow and oil.

But Leonardo's tented workshop was brighter than most, for he was methodically burning his notes and papers, his diagrams and sketches of his new soaring machine. After the notebooks were curling ash and smoke rising through a single vent in the canvas, he burned his box-shaped models of wood and cloth: kites and flying machines of various design; and then, at the last, he smashed his partially completed soaring machine . . . smashed the spars and rudder, smashed the box-like wings, tore away the webbing and fustian, which burned like hemp in the crackling fire.

As if Leonardo could burn his ideas from his thoughts.

Yet he could not help but feel that the rising smoke was the very stuff of his ideas and invention. And he was spreading them for all to inhale like poisonous phantasms.

Lorenzo already had Leonardo's flying machines.

More children would die . . .

He burned his drawings and paintings, his portraits and madonnas and varnished visions of fear, then left the makeshift studio like a sleepwalker heading back to his bed; and the glue and fustian and broken spars ignited, glowing like coals, then burst, exploded, shot like fireworks or silent hempen bombs until the canvas was ablaze. Leonardo was far away by then and couldn't hear the shouts of Andrea and Francesco and the apprentices as they rushed to put out the fire.

Niccolo found Leonardo standing upon the same mountain where Tista had fallen to his death. His face and shirt streaked with soot and ash, Leonardo stared down into the misty valley below. There was the Palazzo Vecchio, and the dome of the Duomo reflecting the early morning sun . . . and beyond, created out of the white dressing of the mist itself, was his memory cathedral. Leonardo gazed at it . . . into it. He relived once again Tista's flight into death and saw the paintings he had burned; indeed, he looked into hell, into the future where he glimpsed the dark skies filled with Lorenzo's soaring machines, raining death from the skies, the winged devices that Leonardo would no longer claim as his own. He wished he had never dreamed of the Great Bird. But now it was too late for anything but regret.

What was done could not be undone.

"Maestro!" Niccolo shouted, pulling Leonardo away from the cliff edge, as if he, Leonardo, had been about to launch himself without wings or harness into the fog. As perhaps he was.

"Everyone has been frantic with worry for you," Niccolo said, as if he was out of breath.

"I should not think I would have been missed."

Niccolo snorted, which reminded Leonardo that he was still a child, no matter how grown up he behaved and had come to look. "You nearly set Maestro Verrocchio's bottega on fire."

"Surely my lamps would extinguish themselves when out of oil, and the fire was properly vented. I myself —"

"Neighbours saved the bottega," Niccolo said, as if impatient to get on to other subjects. "They alerted *everyone*."

"Then there was no damage?" Leonardo asked.

"Just black marks on the walls."

"Good," Leonardo said, and he walked away from Niccolo, who followed after him. Ahead was a thick bank of mist the colour of ash, a wall that might have been a sheer drop, but behind which in reality were fields and trees.

"I knew I would find you here," Niccolo said.

"And how did you know that, Nicco?"

The boy shrugged.

"You must go back to the bottega," Leonardo said.

"I'll go back with you, Maestro."

"I'm not going back." The morning mist was all around them; it seemed to be boiling up from the very ground. There would be rain today and heavy skies.

"Where are you going?"

Leonardo shrugged.

"But you've left everything behind." After a beat, Niccolo said, "I'm going with you."

"No, young ser."

"But what will I do?"

Leonardo smiled. "I would guess that you'll stay with Maestro Verrochio until Lorenzo invites you to be his guest. But you must promise me you'll never fly any of his machines."

Niccolo promised; of course, Leonardo knew that the boy would do as he wished. "I did not believe you were afraid, Maestro."

"Of course not, Nicco."

"I shall walk with you a little way."

"No."

Leonardo left Niccolo behind, as if he could leave the past for a new, innocent future. As if he had never invented bombs and machines that could fly. As if, but for his paintings, he had never existed at all.

Niccolo called to him . . . then his voice faded away, and was gone.

Soon the rain stopped and the fog lifted, and Leonardo looked up at the red tinged sky.

Perhaps in hope.

Perhaps in fear.

KADDISH

. . . .

What ails you, O sea, that you flee?

— Psalm of Hallel

Nathan sat with the other men in the small prayer-room of the synagogue. It was 6:40 in the morning. One of the three professors who taught Hebrew Studies at the university was at the bema, the altar, leading the prayers. His voice intoned the Hebrew and Aramaic words; it was like a cold stream running and splashing over ice. Nathan didn't understand Hebrew, although he could read a little, enough to say the Kaddish, the prayer for the dead, in a halting fashion.

But everything was rushed here in this place of prayer, everyone rocking back and forth and flipping quickly through the well-thumbed pages in the black siddur prayer books. Nathan couldn't keep up with the other men, even when he read and scanned the prayers in English. Young boys in jeans and designer tee-shirts prayed ferociously beside their middle-aged fathers, as if trying to outdo them, although it was the old men who always finished first and had time to talk football while the others caught up. Only the rabbi with his well-kept beard and embroidered yarmulke sat motionless before the congregation, his white linen prayer shawl wrapped threateningly around him like a shroud, as if to emphasise that he held the secret knowledge and faith that Nathan could not find.

Nathan stared into his siddur and prayed with the others.

He was the Saracen in the temple, an infidel wearing prayer shawl and phylacteries.

A shoe-polish black leather frontlet containing a tiny inscribed parchment pressed against Nathan's forehead, another was held tight to his biceps by a long strap that wound like a snake around his left arm to circle his middle finger three times. But the flaming words of God contained in the phylacteries did not seem to make the synaptic connection into his blood and brain and sinew. Nevertheless, he intoned the words of the prayers, stood up, bowed, said the kaddish, and then another kaddish, and he remembered all the things he should have said to his wife and son before they died. He remembered his omissions and commissions, which could not be undone. It was too late even for tears, for he was as hollow as a winter gourd.

And Nathan realised that he was already dead.

A shade that had somehow insinuated himself into this congregation.

But then the service was over. The congregants hurriedly folded their prayer-shawls and wound the leather straps around their phylacteries, for it was 7:45, and they had to get to work. Nathan followed suit, but he felt like an automaton, a simulacrum of himself, a dead thing trying to infiltrate the routines and rituals of the living.

He left the synagogue with the other men. He had an early-morning appointment with an old client who insisted on turning over his substantial portfolio again; the old man had, in effect, been paying Nathan's mortgage for years.

But as Nathan drove his Mercedes coupe down A1A, which was the more picturesque and less direct route to his office in downtown Fort Lauderdale, he suddenly realised that he couldn't go through with it. He couldn't spend another day going through the motions of dictating to his secretary, counseling clients, staring into the electron darkness of a CRT screen, and pretending that life goes on.

He simply couldn't do it . . .

He made a U-turn, and drove back home to Lighthouse Point. The ocean was now to his right, an expanse of emerald and tourmaline. It brought to mind memories of family outings on the public Lauderdale beaches when his son Michael was a toddler and wore braces to straighten out a birth defect. He remembered first making love to his wife Helen on the beach. The immensity of the clear, star-filled sky and the dark, unfathomable ocean had frightened her, and afterward she had cried in his arms as she looked out at the sea.

But as Nathan drove past the art-deco style pink cathedral, which was a Lighthouse Point landmark, he realised that he couldn't go home either. How was he going to face the myriad memories inhering in the furniture, bric-a-brac, and framed photographs ... the memories that seemed to perspire from the very walls themselves? Helen and Michael would only whisper to him again. He would hear all the old arguments and secret conversations, barely audible but there nevertheless, over the susurration of the air conditioner ...

He parked his car in the circular driveway of his red-roofed, white stucco home and crossed the street to his neighbour's yard, which had direct frontage on the intercoastal.

He was, after all, already a shade; he had only to make a proper passage into the next world.

And with the same calm, directed purpose that had served him so well in business over the years, Nathan borrowed his neighbour's hundred thousand dollar "cigarette" speedboat and steered it out to sea to find God.

He piloted the glossy green bullet through the intercoastals, motoring slowly, for police patrolled the quiet canals in search of offenders who would dare to churn the oily, mirrored waters into foam and froth. Yachts and sailboats gently tilted and rolled in their marinas, a gas station attendant with a red scarf around his neck leaned against an Esso gas pump that abutted a wide-planked dock where petroleum drippings shivered like rainbows caught in the wood, and the waterside pools and sun decks of the pastel-painted, expensive homes were empty.

Nathan smelled the bacon and coffee and gasoline, but could hear and feel only the thrumming of the twin engines of the speedboat. The bow reminded him of the hood of an old Lincoln he had loved: expansive and curved and showroom shiny.

As Nathan turned out of the intercoastal and into the terrifying turquoise abyss of the open sea, he felt that he had escaped the bondage that had been his life.

The calm rolling surface of the sea had become time itself. Time was no longer insubstantial and ineffable; it was a surface that could be navigated. And Nathan could steer this roaring twin-engined speedboat forward toward destiny and death, or he could return to the past . . . to any or all of the events of his life that floated atop the flowing surface of his life like plankton.

Nathan was finally the engine of his soul.

He opened the throttle, and the "cigarette" seemed to lift out of the water, which slid past underneath like oil, sparkling green and blue in the brilliance of morning.

Dressed in a herringbone blue suit of continental cut, starched white shirt with rounded french cuffs, and maroon striped tie worked into a Windsor knot, he sat straight as a die before the enamel control console of tachometers, clutches, oil-pressure and fuel gauges, compass, wheel, and throttles.

He felt a quiet, almost patrician joy. He had conquered time and space and pain and fear.

He didn't care about fuel.

His only direction was the eternal horizon ahead.

It all changed when the engines gave out, coughing and sputtering into a final silence like bad lungs taking a last glottal breath. Nathan felt the constriction of the tight collar of his silk shirt; he was wet with perspiration. The sun burned into his face and eyes, blinding him with white light turned red behind closed eyelids, and wrenching him awake. It was as if he had been dreaming, sleepwalking through all the aching, guilt-ridden days since the death of his family three months ago today.

He loosened his tie, tore open his collar. He felt short of breath. It was blisteringly hot, and there was no protection from the sun in the cigarette speedboat. He pulled off his jacket. He was breathing hard, hyperventilating, thinking that he must somehow get back to shore. What have I done? he asked himself, incredulous. He felt feverish, hot then cold, and his teeth were chattering.

The waves slapped against the hull, which bobbed up and down and to the left and right; and Nathan could *feel* the sea pulling him toward death and its handmaiden of unbearable revelation.

He looked behind him, but there was not a shadow of land. Just open sea, liquid turquoise hills descending and rising. He tried to start the engines, but they wouldn't catch. The console lights dimmed from the drainage of power. He looked in the sidewells for extra fuel and oars but found only canvas, an opened package of plastic cups, and a very good brand of unblended scotch. No first-aid kit, no flares, for his neighbour was not fastidious, nor did he ever take the boat out of the intercoastal. This was probably the first time that the throttle had ever been turned to full. The boat was a status-symbol, nothing more.

The compass read East, which was impossible, for if that were so, he would see land.

But east was the direction of God.

And the sea had become a manifestation of that direction.

The swells were higher now, and the boat rose and dipped, each time being pulled farther out, and the hours passed like days, and Nathan felt hungry and thirsty and frightened.

He thought he saw something on the horizon and stood up as best he could in the boat; he held tight to the chrome pillar of the windshield, and yes, there *was* something out there. A ship, a tanker, perhaps. He shouted into the soughing silence of the sea, but it was futile. It was as if he were being hidden in the troughs of the waves.

Hours later, when he was cried out and hoarse, cowed by the infinities of sea and sky and the desiccating heat of the sun, which had transformed itself into a blinding, pounding headache, he turned around. As if he could hide in his own shadow from the sun.

And as if turned to stone, he gazed into the past.

But not far into the past.

Not far enough to savour a moment of comfort before the tsunamis of guilt and grief.

Nathan returns to the morning that burns him still. He is shaving, his face lathered with soap from his chipped shaving mug that had once belonged to his grandfather, when Helen calls him. He can hear the muffled argument that has been going on downstairs between his wife and son, but he ignores it for as long as he can.

He simply can't face any more tension.

"*Nathan!*" Helen shouts, pushing the bathroom door open. "Didn't you hear me calling you?" She is a tiny woman, slender and heart-faced, with long, thick brown hair. She does not look thirty-eight, although Nathan, who is considered good-looking, if not handsome, because of his weathered, broad-featured face and shock of grey hair, looks every one of his forty years. "Michael's late for school again," she says. "He's missed the bus. And when I told him I'd take him to school, he told me to fuck off."

"That's *not* what I said." Michael appears behind his mother; he is sixteen and dressed in baggy slacks and a carefully torn tee-shirt. His hair is swept back from his forehead and sprayed to a laquered shine. He looks like his mother, and has her temperament. Flushed with anger and frustration, he says, "I told her I'd take the next bus, which I could have taken, if she would have let me out of the house to catch it. Now it's too late."

"Your mother said she'd take you to school."

"I don't want her taking me to school. I can't stand her."

"Well, I am taking you," Helen said, "and as a consequence for what you said to me, you're grounded this weekend."

"I didn't say *anything* to you!"

"Nathan," she said, turning to him, "he's lying again. He told me to fuck myself."

"I am not lying," Michael shouts. "And I didn't say 'fuck yourself,' I said 'fuck it' because nobody can talk sense to you. All you can do is scream and ground me every five minutes. I already bought tickets to The Flack concert," he says to Nathan, "and I'm going, whether she likes it or not. I've tried to be nice to her all week, but it's impossible."

Nathan wipes the soap from his face and, trying to remain calm, says, "We've talked about using that kind of language to your mother. It's got to stop . . ."

But there can be no quiet and rational resolve, for the family dynamics inevitably overpower him.

The argument gains momentum.

Michael is swearing and crying in frustration. Helen finally grabs him by his tee-shirt and pushes him against the hallway wall. "I've got to get to work, and you *are* coming with me. Damn you!"

Michael tries to pull away from her, but she won't let him go. He pushes her, defensively, throwing her off balance.

Seeing that, Nathan shouts, "God damn you both," and rushes into the hallway. Everything is, out of control now; it is all visceral response.

He pushes Helen aside and slaps Michael hard on the side of his face.

Helen screams, "I've told you *never* to strike him."

But before Nathan can recover and bring himself to apologise, they are out of the house.

By sunset the sky was the colour of dull metal and filled with storm clouds. Only in the west did the sun bleed through the grey as it settled into the sea, which was pellucid and unnaturally clear. Sheet lightning shot through the massive cloud countries as the temperature dropped, and the humidity seemed to roll off the sea like mist, soon to be rain.

Nathan's fever thoughts burned like his red, broken skin. There was no food, no water to drink, just the slight smell of gasoline and the salty tang of the sea. It became dark, and still Nathan sat and stared into the transparent depths of the sea, as if he were looking for something he had lost. Sometime during the agony of afternoon, he had stopped thinking about rescue. That idea had become as distant as a childhood dream.

Now, his mind raw from the sun, he watched and waited, and as expected, something was swimming up from the depths. A vague shape rose through veils of green darkness, followed by others. Fins broke the surface of the water, and twenty foot thresher sharks circled the boat. Then other fish appeared just below the surface: marlin and seabass, dolphin and barracuda, all circling, until the sea in all directions was filled with all manner of fish, from the smallest foureye to sixty foot star-speckled whale sharks.

It grew dark, and the water was lit now by moonlight and pocked by the rain that began to fall. The rain was cold on Nathan's raw skin, and it looked as if each droplet was illuminated by its own silvery light.

And as the rain struck the water, the fish became frenzied. They began to tear at each other, as if in a feeding madness. Huge white sharks snapped and gored the smaller tiger and mako sharks, while the barracuda cut sailfish and cobia and tarpon into bloody gobbets of meat.

Nathan could feel them smashing against the hull like hammers, and the ocean began to boil with the carnage.

Then, as if in concert, the storm exploded in claps and rolls of thunder and torrents of rain; and the ocean responded with high waves that almost turned over the speedboat. Reeking fish slammed into the cigarette's cockpit, as if thrown from the sky, splashing Nathan with blood and entrails. Lightning veined the moon, magnified by the atmosphere into a lifeless sun.

Nathan huddled inside the boat, pressing his legs and back against the fibreglass to prevent himself from being flung into the sea. The rain was cold, as was the seawater spraying over him, yet each raindrop and salty, spindrift burned him. He raised his head one last time to look around, only to see that it was raining fire. The ocean was illuminated, as if by blue flame; and the sky glowed like cinders.

The sea was a bloodbath.

And as his heart stopped and his breath caught in his throat —

Nathan sits behind his desk in his three-windowed, mahogany-panelled office. He is looking at the rouged and concerned face of a wealthy dowager client as he learns of the death of his wife and son.

He listens to the voice on the phone describing the accident and feels himself freezing into shock. He can only stare at the dowager's huge emerald earrings, as if the green stones are tiny tablets: the emerald grimoires of Solomon, which contain all the answers to the mysteries of life and death and guilt and anger.

Dawn revealed the bloated bodies and remains of thousands of fish that floated like grey driftwood on the calm swells of the ocean. A few cumulus clouds drifted across the sky, as if to separate the chilly perfection of heaven from the ruin below. Nathan awakened with a jolt, as if from a nightmare, only to find that all was as it had been. Repelled, he threw an eel and an ugly, spiny sargassum fish back into the sea.

He felt nauseated, but he had had the dry heaves during the night; there was nothing left in his stomach to expel. He had even tried to eat the fish that had landed in the cockpit of the speedboat, but the reek was so great that he couldn't manage to bite into the putrescent flesh. He was thirsty, but the sea was salt. Here was food and water all around him; yet he was starving and dehydrated. And naked. His clothes were not anywhere to be seen. Perhaps he had torn them off to relieve his burning skin. Nathan's flesh seemed to be pulling away from his bones. It was so scorched that his shoulders and face and arms were bleeding.

The empty bottle of scotch rolled on the fibreglass floor of the speedboat, catching the sun.

The hours passed. Nathan tried not to look at the sea, filled with the miles of decaying flesh and stink, but he could not stare into the sky forever. He surveyed the countries of flesh and sea around him, a sargasso mire that seemed endless, and he noticed something shiny bobbing in the water. It was the silver breastplate of a satin Torah covering. He scanned the ocean and found a Torah parchment floating, its Hebrew letters black mirrors reflecting the sun and sky above. Bits and pieces of the ark floated in the debris. Open prayer books seemed to move beneath the surface of the water like manta rays, their black covers dull and the golden letters washed away.

But the holy objects and bloody flesh seemed to form letters, signs, and portents that Nathan could not read. Yet when he reached for a prayer book floating beside the hull, it began to sink into the dark, shadowed water, to become a distant memory. As Nathan looked into the water that was as clear and still as the past, he remembered: His son, dressed in a new black suit, leading the Shacharis service at his bar mitzvah; his own wedding in a rundown, glot-kosher hotel in Miami Beach, Helen nervous around his eighty-year-old aunts, who insisted that she step on Nathan's foot for luck when he ceremoniously crushed the wineglass wrapped in a napkin; Helen taking him in her arms to tell him that his father had died; and the arguments and lovemaking and Sabbath candles; Michael stealing the family car, introducing him to his first "serious" girlfriend, who seemed afraid to look up from her plate, at the dinner table . . .

All the tiny realizations of changes and transitions seemed to be floating, objects on the sea.

But like the prayer book, the fish and carrion and scrolls and salt-stained pieces of the holy Ark began to sink; and Nathan was left staring into the empty green-hazed depths, as if he were looking once again into the green stone of Solomon.

The sea was like a mirror, so still and perfect that it seemed to harden into emerald. It *was* time itself, and in it he could see his own reflection.

If only Nathan could pass through its face.

He could see himself.

He could see . . .

* * *

Nathan sat with the other men in the small prayer-room of the synagogue and felt the divine presence. The ancient kabbalists called it the *Shekhinah*, the bride of God.

It was 6:40 in the morning, and Nathan couldn't discern what was different, but he felt *something*. The morning light was like blue smoke diffusing through the high, narrow stained-glass windows. Dust motes danced in the air, shivering in the air-conditioned morning. Nathan put on his tallit and phylacteries and recited the blessing and the *Akeidah* and the *Shema* and other supplications. The other men sat beside him and behind him and prayed as they did every morning. Their smells and clothes were the same, and the prayers were almost hypnotic in their monotonous intonation. A young man hummed nasally, as was his habit, throughout the prayers. One of the three professors who taught Hebrew Studies at the university was at the bema, leading the prayers. His voice intoned the Hebrew and Aramaic words.

And Nathan felt the presence of his dead son and wife sitting beside him.

He couldn't *see* them, not with the same eyes that stared straight ahead at the red satin curtains of the holy ark; but he sensed their presence nevertheless. As he prayed, he could hear Michael's voice . . . his own voice.

Young men of Michael's age paced nervously around the room; they were wrapped protectively in their prayer-shawls, and the light seemed to cling to them.

Perhaps they sensed the *Shekhinah*, too.

Helen leaned against him. She was a shadow, barely palpable, but Nathan *knew* it was his wife.

Her body was the silk of his prayer shawl, her breath was Sabbath spices, and her fingers were as cool as the leather frontlets on his arm and forehead. As she whispered to him, his past became as concentrated as old liquors.

His life became an instant of unbearable fire, blinding him. But she released him, freed him from his immolating guilt, as the prayers for the dead drifted and curled through the morning light like smoke, then fell to rest like ashes.

Then the service was over and the *Shekhinah* evaporated, its holy presence melting like snow in the furnace of another Florida morning. The congregants, seemingly deaf and blind to the miracle that had swept past them, hurriedly folded their prayer-shawls and wound the leather straps around their phylacteries, for it was 7:45, and they had to get to work.

Nathan left the synagogue with the other men. He had an early-morning appointment with an old client. As he drove his Mercedes coupe down A1A, which was the more picturesque and less direct route to his office in downtown Fort Lauderdale, he passed the resorts and grand hotels, the restaurants and seedy diners, and the endless lots of kitsch motels with neon signs in their plate glass windows and hosts of plastic pink flamingos on their lawns.

He gazed out at the ocean. It was an expanse of emerald and tourmaline. Except for the whitecaps, which were long fingers gently pulling at the sand, the sea was quiet. Nathan turned off the air-conditioner and pressed the toggles on his armrest to open all the windows.

The humidity rushed in with the pungent smell of brine, and Nathan felt his face grow wet with perspiration and tears.

Then he detoured back to the highway.

The electric windows glided up, shutting out the world; the hum of the air-conditioner muffled the honking of the early morning rush hour combatants; and the news announcer on the radio reported on the rescue of a businessman naked and adrift on a speedboat near Miami.

But even now, Nathan could sense the *Shekhinah.*

He could hear his son's voice and feel the cool, gentle touch of Helen's fingers upon his arms and perspiring forehead.

Yet in the reflection of the curving, tinted windshield, he could still see himself burning on the sea.

THE EXTRA

....

The smoke-machine was blowing noxious vapors that smelled like automobile exhaust toward the tables of the makeshift 50's diner; and although it was a cloudy day, kleig lights poured midafternoon sunlight through the plate glass window. Michael Nye had been sitting in a booth for what seemed like hours while a scene was being shot at the table beside him. The actor and actress were being paid three thousand dollars a day.

He was being paid fifty dollars a day to be an extra.

But he was only doing this to see what it was like. He was an advertising executive who specialised in political campaigns. He was very well paid, and a family man.

Of course, he had once wanted to be an actor.

And this movie was about an actor coming back to his home town. The director was German. Now what the hell would a German director know about coming home to a small town in upstate New York?

Michael stared fixedly ahead, past the old man sitting directly in front of him: another extra. The old man looked like the sort of lean, determined character Grant Wood would have painted, which was probably why he had been picked for the scene. Michael was dressed as a construction worker. His tee-shirt was stained, and he was sweating, which was in character. It must have been ninety degrees in this room.

As Michael fingered his red hardhat on the table, he glimpsed something familiar out of the corner of his eye. He turned, ever so slightly.

And saw his dead father watching him from the sidewalk.

The man was standing outside the window of the diner, between two spotlights. He wore a grey suit and a wide, striped tie. He carried his worn briefcase and looked very young.

Michael pulled himself awkwardly out of the booth and rushed outside.

It was drizzling: typical Binghamton weather. A small crowd of spectators stood under and around the doorway of the Security Mutual Building, which was across the street from the diner that had been constructed for the film. Two policemen stood beside sawhorses that formed a police line, and a few businessmen looked in Michael's direction as they walked beneath some scaffolds. It seemed that the movie company was doing construction work on every building in the town.

Of course, Michael could not find his father.

Michael was called back to work the next day, for the scene was not finished. Ordinarily, he would have turned them down flat; but now he felt compelled to be on the set. He had not told anyone of his "hallucination".

He had simply seen a man who looked like his father.

As they shot the scene over and over, Michael kept glancing out the window. The man across from him just stared down at his bowl of soup and would mechanically begin to eat whenever the assistant director ordered him to do so. And Michael would do his part by sipping coffee and smoking unfiltered Chesterfields.

It was noon when Michael saw his best friend Greg Chambers stop on the sidewalk in front of the plate glass window. But it couldn't be Greg.

Greg was forty-five and overweight.

This young man could not have been older than twenty-two or twenty-three, and he was thin as a reed. His beard was reddish, and his wispy blond hair was long, held in place with a headband.

Nevertheless, it *was* Greg.

There was a woman with him, who looked about nineteen. She wore an embroidered cotton dress and was very pretty: freckled, with unkempt curly hair. Yet there was a certain poise about her, as if she were used to having things her own way. Framing her face with her hands, she looked directly at Michael through the window. But she didn't appear to see him. After a beat, she stepped back and grimaced at Greg. Then they both laughed and walked on.

And Michael remembered. How could he have ever forgotten? She was Sandra Delaney. He had been in love with her twenty years ago.

Michael ran outside after them. "Greg, Sandra, wait," he shouted.

The afternoon shower had passed . . . vanished; it was a hot August day with only a few cirrus streamers in the clear sky. Somehow the air smelled different.

"We were wondering where the hell you went off to," Greg said, stopping and smoothing his beard back toward his throat. Sandra linked her arm through Michael's and kissed him. She smelled earthy and slightly sweaty; he remembered that she never wore perfume, nor did she shave her legs.

Michael wanted to ask questions, but couldn't form the words. He stopped, looked around, and imagined that he was in some sort of shock because it took all his strength of will to pull away from Sandra and Greg and walk back to the diner.

"Where are you going?" Sandra asked.

"I've got to check out something," he heard himself say; yet, somehow, his voice was not his own. "I'll be back in a second."

The diner, of course, wasn't there.

He peered through the tinted window into a large, unfinished room: the new addition to the First City Bank. And in the dark glass, he could see the reflection of himself. A gangly boy with thick brown hair, aviator glasses, and pimples. He was wearing jeans, a black tee-shirt, and a faded, jean jacket. The middle-aged man with the shock of grey hair had melted into the darkness behind the glass. He was trapped, yet free; and he knew, he knew, that it was 1972 and he was twenty-two years old.

He was in love with Sandra, and so was Greg. She was in love with both of them, which suited everyone fine.

He had somehow walked into a distant summer.

Just like that.

Gone were wife and family.

Gone were the stale, dreamless years.

He had left them all behind, walked out, as it were. He looked around, feeling a dead weight slide away from him; yet out of habit he felt in his pocket for money. A few crisp bills collapsed reassuringly inside his fist.

Across the street was the Security Mutual Building. Unchanged. Cars passed, all twenty years out of date. The *Strand* and *Riviera* theatres were still in business; in fact, two matinees were playing: *The Godfather* and *The Poseidon Adventure*. And there ahead of him were Greg and Sandra, waiting.

He caught up with them; and they took his car, which was parked nearby in the lot of the Treadway Inn, and drove into the country. It was a new '72 Toyota Corona, with a four-speed stick shift, and black bucket seats. Sandra sat beside him and Greg sat in the back seat behind her. She rested her hand between the seats, and Greg leaned forward to hold it. She turned around, smiled at him, kissed him, then turned to Michael. "Let's go fast," she said. All the windows were open, and the breeze blew through her hair.

"It's only a four cylinder," Michael heard himself say. Even now, he had begun to understand it. He was, quite literally, only along for the ride. Although he could exert his will — the will of the mature man from a faraway present — he could not remove his young self, his host, from the deeply set runnels that were his life.

"Well, gun it, anyway," Sandra said, turning up the volume of the radio to a roar of static, then twisting the station knob, resting on a song here or there, then moving along the band: "Where Is the Love", "Rock Me On the Water", "Summer Breeze". She finally settled on "Doctor My Eyes".

Michael brought the needle up to eighty, and ninety on the downhill. There wasn't another car on the road, which dipped and curved. He decelerated to seventy-five. The wind smelled like new-mown hay. The world suddenly seemed larger, tastier, filled with clarity and colour. He embraced it even as he drove, as if he were awash with it, as if his best friend in the back seat and their mutual girlfriend in the front seat were simply manifestations of the leafy world in which he was the hunter supreme. He was Adam and Paul Bunyan; he wanted to eat the trees and squeeze the Catskill mountains together; he wanted to press the rocks of palisade road walls against his face and swim in the heat mirages that looked like pale pools of water in the highway pavement.

And he could not help but confess his love for Sandra, right there with Greg in the back seat.

It was an exercise in humiliation, this eavesdropping on the past, which could not quite merge into the present.

Michael heard himself go on about wishing to make babies together, getting married, the strength she gave to him; but he could not stop himself. Greg interrupted, tried to change the subject, but nothing could stop Michael.

Michael could feel the power of these emotions; but the man, the visitor who was old and tired and heavy with it all, could not stop the boy.

There seemed to be a change in the atmosphere. Sandra leaned against the door, putting distance between them. When they stopped for ice cream, she left them alone for a few moments, and Greg said, "Man, was *that* fucking embarrassing."

Michael smiled and said, "I couldn't help it."

They laughed until Sandra returned; then they mooned all the customers at the Carvel's ice cream stand.

That Toyota might be only a four-cylinder, but it could certainly lay rubber.

They spent the rest of the day driving in the country, walking through Recreation Park and the zoo, talking about writing and the politics of liberation, and shopping in the antique stores and pawnshops on Clinton Street. Sandra bought some old postcards and a silk blouse. She held hands with Greg and Michael, and played to every passer-by.

Here was a real ménage à trois.

Here was a living example of the sexual and political revolution, of men's and women's liberation.

But Michael, the older Michael who was little more than a ghost in this palpable world of radiant colour and emotion, began to experience an odd fatigue, a forgetfulness. The joys and powerful endocrinological pleasures of youth were slowly and subtly overwhelming him.

While Greg discussed *new criticism* with Sandra, Michael desperately tried to remember everything he could about his wife, Helen. He had to remember, lest he lose himself in this bright but empty place.

Helen came sharply and suddenly into focus, resolving in his mind, as if she were standing before him; and Michael memorised every feature of her face, which was almost oriental in its delicacy: almond eyes; small upturned nose; fair, smooth skin; full mouth; and even teeth. Her hair was auburn, straight and long. And in his mind's eye, she was young, as young as Sandra.

If she could see him now . . .

She would laugh at him. She would think that he was affected and silly. Now that she was lost to him, he missed her. He was free of her, yet he desired her. He wanted to press himself into her familiar and comfortable body . . .

And he realised that he did, indeed, love her.

But even now it was becoming difficult to visualise her.

Sandra smiled at him and put her arm around his waist. "I want you," she whispered.

Michael became himself once again.

"I want you, too," he said, feeling suddenly empty, as if he had forgotten something very important.

When they returned to Michael's apartment, Greg became quiet, sullen. He talked of returning home to New York to "take care of business". But the only business he had there was a notice of eviction that had been nailed to his door. Sandra flitted about the small, shabby apartment and talked about her work. She was an art major, and Michael had framed one of her charcoal drawings: a nude. It was a self-portrait.

They made a stirfry and watched teevee until Greg said, "I'm going to bed."

For the last few days he had been sleeping on the couch in the living room.

Michael and Sandra had become a couple.

Although Greg had lost Sandra to Michael, he pretended that nothing had changed. But he could not stand being alone on the couch at night while Michael and Sandra made love in the bedroom. Neither could he leave, for Sandra teased him with the hope that she would soon be ready to bestow her sexual favours upon him.

"Are you sure you don't want to come to bed with us?" Sandra asked.

"You know you're more than welcome," Michael said, although he didn't mean it.

"Nah, it's all right," Greg said, and then he turned away.

Michael quickly closed the door, and Sandra undressed.

Overcome with emotion and desire, he watched her. She was attractive, but certainly not beautiful. Her face was wide, tan, and freckled; and her body was soft and fleshy, although certainly not voluptuous. Her breasts were small, her hips wide.

He was lost in a frothing ocean of adrenaline, lost in all the juices and chemical connections of passion. It was as if he needed to wear her flesh, to get so close to her that they would become each other. And Michael, the Michael who had slipped through time to find his youth, was as overwhelmed as his host.

Sandra allowed Michael to mount her; and as they made love, she watched him. She did not try to feign passion, nor was she cold. Her face expressed only curiosity. He looked down at her, staring into her steady, green eyes, trembling as he moved inside her. Michael worshipped her.

And she rewarded him.

She studied him and answered his questions. "Yes, I love you, yes, I can feel you."

But she would not give herself to him, for she was a god, an icon; and he was . . .

Spent.

He could not catch his breath for a moment. He let her take his weight, but she subtly shifted beneath him. He took her cue and lay down beside her. She took his hand and guided his fingers to the place that gave her pleasure. She moaned and thrashed about, her eyes closed tight, thinking thoughts that Michael would never know. Then she slept, her chest moving slightly as she breathed, her curly hair damp upon her forehead, her mouth open to reveal widely-spaced teeth, her arms outstretched, as if she were dreaming of flying.

As Michael watched her, in the lull of fatigue and satisfaction, he remembered. He remembered all the years that had not yet passed, he remembered his wife and children, he remembered his work, his friends, his associates; and he remembered the boy sleeping in the next room as a man. Greg would become a New York publisher. He would gain weight and cut his hair. He would wear suits and carry a briefcase and ride the train and go to conventions. He would laugh at himself and pine for the good old days. He would wish to be back here, in love, in pain, alive again.

Michael carefully got out of bed, pulling the sheet over Sandra, who was a distant stranger now. He dressed and slipped quietly out of the apartment, but Greg called to him before he could close the door. "Where are you going?" Greg's voice was hoarse, thick from sleep.

"Just out for a walk." Michael looked at his friend, as if this would be the last time he would see him.

Greg switched on the light. He had covered himself with an army blanket. His long, blond hair was tangled and his frizzly beard was flattened along the right side of his face where it had pressed against his arm. His eyes were blue and piercing; the years might change everything else, but not those eyes. They would burn with the same excited interest in the world, and reflect the same sad soul of the outsider, the observer. "You want company?"

"No, I just need to take a walk."

"Everything okay with you and Sandra?"

"Yeah, everything's fine. And you? Are you okay in here?"

"I'll survive," Greg said. "But I do think I'll go back to New York tomorrow."

"Give things a chance," Michael said, feeling guilty even as he spoke, for he could read the future, which was nothing more than recent memory.

"Yeah, maybe. You sure you don't want company?"

"I'm sure," Michael said; and he closed the door behind him. Down three flights of stairs, the banister worn and the walls stained and greasy. Everything familiar, yet ghostly. The night was clear and warm. The street empty. The branches of evenly spaced trees shifted slightly in the wind, eclipsing stars. He walked past the neighbourhood grocery store and cemetery, until he found himself on the well-lit streets of the prosperous West Side. The lawns and leaves seemed almost phosphorescent in the artificial light. His young host daydreamed as he walked; he dreamed of living with Sandra. He would marry her, and she would bear his children.

And he dreamed of writing.

Intricate plots for short stories waved and tangled in his mind like brightly coloured pennons. He would become famous. He would be another Salinger, another Fowles, another Hemingway . . .

Michael found himself on Ackley Avenue, the street where his parents lived. He stopped before the square, white, stucco house. Its windows glowed with buttery light. Upstairs a television flickered, and Michael knew he must not go inside. His father was there. He could visualise him lying on the bed and watching television. His mother would be in the bed beside him.

As he stood there, Michael yearned to see his father once again. And he remembered the funeral ceremony, remembered looking into his father's deep, open grave . . . remembered shovelling dirt over the top of the plain pine casket. He could hear the sounds of stones and dirt hitting its surface, smell the loamy soil as he mechanically dug and pitched the darkness over the remains of his father. Then he passed the shovel to his brother. Their white-haired mother stood beside them and stared into the grave in disbelief.

Michael remembered; indeed, he remembered.

Family and friends stood in line behind the dumpster load of soil, which would soon cover his father. Everyone would have a chance to drop a few stones and clots of earth over Michael's father.

But in *this* here and now, his father was alive. He was right inside that house; and all Michael had to do was take a few steps and knock on the door.

Instead, he turned and walked away.

It would be too dangerous to knock on that door. If he did, he would certainly be lost. He would disappear into this loop of time and cheat the future.

He would forget.

Helen . . .

The beautiful Colonial and Victorian homes along the river seemed faded now. The air was sweet and heavy. Michael hurried, racing against the amnesia that was overtaking him. He walked back to the business district.

Back to Chenango Street, which was deserted, except for a bag lady who pushed her grocery cart as if it were a pram.

Back to the *Strand* and *Riviera.*

The movie houses were dark, as were the office buildings. A cab slowed down, but Michael waved him on. He stopped before the new addition to the First City Bank, where in a different time he had sat in a film set. He peered into the window, but it showed him only his own reflection: a young man wearing a tee-shirt. He leaned his forehead against the thick pane, pressing his weight against it, as if it was the only thing holding him back from his future. The glass felt cold and lifeless against his forehead. But he was determined to pass through it, to fling himself back into his life.

He stepped back from the building, and then threw himself into the glass.

Mercifully, it accepted him.

He passed through it.

Into blinding light.

Into sunlight.

Into kleig lights.

A QUIET REVOLUTION
FOR DEATH

* *

No other epoch has laid so much stress as the
expiring Middle Ages on the thought of death.

— J. Huizinga

It is a lovely day for a drive and a picnic. There is not a hint of rain in the cerulean sky, and the superhighway snakes out ahead like a cement canal. The cars are moving in slow motion like gondolas skiffing through God's magical city.

"What a day," says Roger as he leans back in his cushioned seat. Although the car is on automatic, he holds the steering stick lightly between his thumb and forefinger. His green Chevrolet shifts lanes and accelerates to a hundred and thirty miles an hour. "This is what God intended when he made Sunday," Roger says as he lets go of the steering stick to wave his arms in a stylised way. He dreams that he is an angel of God guiding the eyeless through His realms.

The children are in the back seat, where they can fight and squeal and spill their makeup until Sandra becomes frustrated enough to give them some *Easy-Sleep* to make the trip go faster. But the monotony of the beautiful countryside and the hiss of air pushing past rubber and glass must have lulled Sandra to sleep. She is sitting beside Roger. Her head lolls, beautiful blond hair hiding her beautiful face.

"I'm practising to be an angel," shouts Bennie, Roger's eldest, and favourite son. The other children giggle and make muffled shushing noises.

Roger turns around and sees that his son has painted his face and smeared it with ashes. He's done a fair job, Roger thinks. Blue and grey rings of makeup circle Bennie's wide brown eyes. "That's very good indeed," Roger says. "Your face is even more impressive than your costume."

"I could do better if I wanted to," says Rose Marie, who is seven and dressed in a mock crinoline gown with great cloth roses sewn across the bodice.

But Bennie is unimpressed. He beams at his father and says: "You said that everyone, even kids, must have their own special vision of death. Well, my vision is just like yours." Bennie is twelve. He's the little man of the family, and next year with God's help he will be bar mitzvahed, since Sandra is half Jewish and believes that children need even more ceremony than adults.

Rose Marie primps herself and says, "Ha," over and over. Samson and Lilly, ages five and six respectively, are quietly playing "feelie" together. But Samson — who will be the spitting image of his father, same cleft in his chin, same nose — is naked and shivering. Roger raises the car's temperature to seventy-nine degrees and then turns back to Bennie.

"How do you know what my vision is?" Roger asks, trying to find a comfortable position. His cheek touches the headrest and his knee touches Sandra's bristly leg. Sandra moves closer to the door.

"You're nuts over Guyot Marchant and Holbein," says Bennie. "I've read your library fiche. Don't you think I'm acquainted intellectually with the painted dances of death? Well, ha, I know the poetry of Jean Le Fèvre, and I've seen the holos of the mural paintings in the church of La Chaise-Dieu. I've read Gédéon Huet in fiche and I've even looked at your books — I'm reading *Totentanz*, and I'm almost finished."

"You must ask permission," says Roger, but he is proud of his son. He certainly is the little man of the family, Roger tells himself. The other children only want to nag and cry and eat and play "feelie".

Sandra wakes up, pulls her hair away from her face, and asks: "How much longer?" Her neck and face are glossy with perspiration. She lowers the temperature, makes a choking noise, and insists that this trip is too long and she's hungry.

"I'm hungry too," says Rose Marie. "And it's hot in here and everything's sticky."

"We'll be there soon," Roger says to his family as he gazes out the large windshield at the steaming highway ahead. The air seems to shimmer from the exhaust of other cars, and God has created little mirages of blue water.

"See the mirages on the highway," Roger says to his family. What a day to be alive! What a day to be with your family. He watches a red convertible zoom right through a blue mirage and come out unscathed. "What a day," he shouts. He grins and squeezes Sandra's knee.

But Sandra swats his hand as if it were a gnat.

Still, it *is* a beautiful day.

"Well, here we are," says an excited Roger as the dashboard lights flash green, indicating that everyone can now get out of the car.

What a view! The car is parked on the sixteenth tier of a grand parking lot that overlooks the grandest cemetery in the East. From this vantage ground (it is certainly worth the forty-dollar parking fee) Roger can view beautiful Chastellain Cemetery and its environs. There, to the north, are rolling hills and a green swath that must be pine forest. To the west are great mountains that have been worn down by God's hand. The world is a pastel palette: it is the first blush of autumn.

The cemetery is a festival of living movement. Roger imagines that he has slipped back in time to fifteenth-century Paris. He is the noble Bouciquaut and the duke of Berry combined. He looks down at the common folk strolling under the cloisters. The peasants are lounging amid the burials and exhumations and sniffing the stink of death.

"I'm hungry," whines Rose Marie, "and it's windy up here."

"We came up here for the view," Roger says. "So enjoy it."

"Let's go eat and put this day behind us," Sandra says.

"Mommy lives in her left brain, huh, Dad?" says Bennie. "She suffers from the conditioning and brainwashing of the olden days."

"You shouldn't talk about your mother that way," Roger says as he opens the trunk of the car and hands everyone a picnic basket.

"But Mother is old-fashioned," Bennie says as they walk toward the elevators. "She thinks everyone must conform to society to tame the world. But she is only committed to appearances, she cares nothing for substance."

"You think your father's so modern?" Sandra says to Bennie, who is walking behind her like a good son.

"You're an antique," Bennie says. "You don't understand right-brain living. You can't accept death as an ally."

"Then, what am I doing here?"

"You came because of Dad. You hate cemeteries."

"I certainly do not."

But the argument dies as the silvery elevator doors slide open to take them all away from left-brain thinking.

"Let's take a stroll around the cemetery," Roger says as they pass under a portiere that is the cemetery's flag and insignia. Roger pays the gateman, who wears the cemetery's "colours" on the sleeves and epaulets of his somber blue uniform.

"That's fifty-*three* dollars, sir," says the gateman. He points at Bennie and says, "I must count him as an adult, it's the rules."

Roger cheerfully pays and leads his noisy family through the open wrought-iron gates. Before him is Chastellain Cemetery, the "real thing", he tells himself — there it is, full of movement and life, neighbour beside neighbour, everyone eating, drinking, loving, selling, buying, and a few are even dying. It is a world cut off from the world.

"This is the famous Avenue d'Auvergne," Roger says, for he has carefully studied Hodel's *Guidebook to Old and Modern Cemeteries*. "Here are some of the finest restaurants to be found in any cemetery," he says as they pass under brightly coloured restaurant awnings.

"I want to go in here," Rose Marie says as she takes a menu card from a doorman and holds it to her nose. "I can smell Aubergine Fritters and Pig's Fry and Paupiette de Veau and I'm sick of Mommy's cooking. I want to go in here."

The doorman grins (probably thinking of his commission) and hands Roger a menu card.

"We have a fine picnic lunch of our own," Roger says, and he reminds himself that he's sick of French food anyway.

As they stroll north on the beautiful Avenue d'Auvergne, which is shaded by old wych elms, restaurants give way to tiny shops. Farther north, the

Avenue becomes a dirty cobblestone street filled with beggars and hawkers pushing wooden handcarts.

"I don't like it here," says Rose Marie as she stares at the Jettatura charms and lodestone ashtrays arrayed behind a dirty shop window.

"You can find all manner of occult items in these little shops," Roger says. "This cemetery is a sanctuary for necromancy. Some of the finest astrologers and mediums work right here." Roger pauses before a shop that specialises in candles and oils and incense made of odoriferous woods and herbs. "What a wonderful place," Roger says, as he takes Sandra's hand in his own. "Perhaps we should buy a little something for the children."

A hunchbacked beggar pulls at Roger's sleeve and says, "Alms for the poor," but Roger ignores his entreaties.

"The children are getting restless," Sandra says, her hand resting limply in Roger's. "Let's find a nice spot where they can play and we can have our picnic."

"This is a nice spot," Bennie says as he winks at a little girl standing in an alleyway.

"Hello, big boy," says the girl, who cannot be more than twelve or thirteen. "Fifty dollars will plant you some life in this body." She wiggles stylishly, leans against a shop window, and wrinkles her nose. "Well?" She turns to Roger and asks, "Does Daddy want to buy his son some life?" Then she smiles like an angel.

Roger smiles at Bennie, who resembles one of the death dancers painted on the walls of the Church of the Children.

"C'mon, Dad, please," Bennie whines.

"Don't even consider it," Sandra says to Roger. "We brought the children here to acquaint them with death, not sex."

"That smacks of left-brain thinking," says the little girl as she wags her finger at Sandra. "Death is an orgasm, not a social artifact."

"She's right about that," Roger says to Sandra. Only youth can live without pretense, he thinks. Imagining death as a simple return to nature's flow, he hands Bennie a crisp fifty-dollar bill.

"Thanks, Dad," and Bennie is off, hand in hand with his five-minute friend. They disappear into a dark alley that separates two long, tumbledown buildings.

"He shouldn't be alone," Sandra says. "Who knows what kind of people might be skulking about in that alley."

"Shall we go and watch him, then?" Roger asks.

"It's love and death," Rose Marie says as she primps her dress, folding the thin material into pleats.

"I want to go *there*," says Samson, pointing at a great Ferris wheel turning in the distance.

Roger sighs as he looks out at the lovely gravestone gardens of the cemetery. "Yes," he whispers, dreaming of God and angels. "It's love and death."

Sandra prepares the picnic fixings atop a secluded knoll that overlooks spacious lawns, charnel houses, cloisters adorned with ivory gables, and even rows of soap-white monuments. Processions of mourners wind their way about like snakes crawling through a modern Eden. Priests walk about, offering consolation to the bereaved, tasting tidbits from the mourners' tables, kissing babies, touching the cold foreheads of the dead, and telling wry jokes to the visitors just out for a Sunday picnic and a stroll.

"All right," Sandra says as she tears a foil cover from a food cylinder and waits for the steam to rise. "Soup's on. Let's eat everything while it's hot." She opens container after container. There is a rush for plates and plasticware and the children argue and fill their dishes with the sundry goodies. Then, except for the smacking of lips, a few moments of silence: a burial is taking place nearby and everyone is caught up in profound emotion.

"It's a small casket," Roger says after a proper length of time has passed. He watches two young men clad in red lay the casket down on the grass beside the burial trench. "It must be a child," Roger says. A middle-aged man and woman stand over the tiny casket; the man rocks back and forth and rends his garments while the woman sobs.

"You see," Bennie says after he has cleaned his plate. "That kind of crying and tearing clothes is for the old, left-brain thinkers. *I* wouldn't mind dying right now. Death is wasted on the old. Look at Mommy, she's haunted by silly dreams of immortality. Old people are too perverse to joyously give themselves back to nature." Bennie stands up, looking ghoulish and filthy in his death costume.

"And where are you going?" Sandra asks.

"To dance on the fresh grave."

"Let him go," Roger says. "It is only proper to continue great traditions."

* * *

The sun is working its way toward three o'clock. There is not a cloud in the sky, only the gauzy cross-hatching of jet trails. A few birds wing overhead like little blue angels. Roger sits beside his lovely Sandra, and they watch Bennie as he dances stylishly with the two young mourners clad in red. Roger is proud and his eyes are moist. Bennie has stolen the show. He has even attracted a small crowd of passersby.

This is a sight that would have made Jean Le Fèvre turn his head! Roger says to himself as he watches Bennie work his way through a perfect *danse macabre*. The mourners are already clapping. Bennie has their hearts. He has presented a perfect vision of death to his spectators.

"Wave to Benjamin," Roger says to his family. "See, he's waving at us." Roger imagines that he can hear the sounds of distant machinery. He dreams that God has sent angels to man the machinery of His cemetery.

And with the passing of each heavenly moment, the noise of God's machinery becomes louder.

But God's machines turn out to be only children, hundreds of noisy boys and girls come to join in the Sunday processions. They're here to burn or bury innocents and bums and prostitutes, to learn right thinking and body-knowing, and share in the pleasures and exquisite agonies of death's community. The children seem to be everywhere. They're turning the cemetery into a playground.

As Roger watches children playing bury-me-not and hide-and-seek between the tombstone teeth of the cemetery, he thinks that surely his son Bennie must be in their midst. Bennie might be anywhere: taking a tour through the ossuarium, lighting fires on the lawns, screwing little girls, or dancing for another dinner.

"We should not have permitted Bennie to leave in the first place," Sandra says to Roger. "He's probably in some kind of trouble." She pauses, then says, "Well, *I'm* going to go and look for him." Another pause. "What are you going to do?"

"Someone has to remain with the children," Roger says. "I'm sure Bennie is fine. He'll probably be back."

Sandra, of course, rushes off in a huff. But that's to be expected; Roger tells himself. Bennie was right: she is perverse. After a few deep breaths, Roger forgets her. He stretches out on the cool grass, looks up at the old maple trees that appear to touch the robin's-egg sky, and he feels the touch of God's thoughts. He yawns. This bounty of food, fresh air, and inspiration has worn him out. He listens to the children, and dreams of tractors.

A fusillade echoes through the cemetery.

"Daddy, what's that noise?" asks Rose Marie.

"The children are probably shooting guns," Roger says. He opens his eyes; then closes them.

"Why are they shooting guns?"

"To show everyone that death must be joyous," Roger says. But he can't quite climb out of his well of sleep. He falls through thermoclines of sleep, and dreams of tractors rolling over tombstones and children and trees.

"When is Mommy coming back?" asks Rose Marie.

"When she finds Bennie," Roger says, and he buttons the collar of his shirt. There is a slight chill to the air.

"When will that be?"

"I don't know," Roger says. "Soon, I hope." He watches the rosy sunset. The western mountains are purple, and Roger imagines that rainbows are leaking into the liquid blue sky.

Another fusillade echoes through the cemetery.

"Maybe Mommy was shot," Rose Marie says in a hushed tone.

"Maybe," Roger replies.

"Maybe she's dead," says Rose Marie, smoothing out her dress, then making cabbage folds.

"Is that so bad?" Roger asks. "You must learn to accept death as an ally. If Mommy doesn't come back, it will teach you a lesson."

"I want to ride on the Ferris wheel," Samson says. "You promised."

"If Mommy doesn't return soon, we'll go for a ride," Roger says, admiring the cemetery. Even at dusk, in this shadow time, Chastellain Cemetery is still beautiful, he tells himself. It is a proud old virgin, but soon it will become a midnight whore. It will become a carnival. It will be Ferris wheels and rides and lights and candlelight processions.

Lying back in the grass, Roger searches for the first evening stars. There, he sees two straight above him. They blink like Sandra's eyes. He makes a wish and imagines that Sandra is staring at him with those cold, lovely eyes.

In the evening haze below, the candlelight processions begin.

JUMPING THE ROAD

• •

It really isn't right that I should give you my name. True enough that this is history; and history, if it is to be kept alive, must be recorded for posterity. But the name of Isaac ibn Chabib of Philadelphia need not be mentioned.

However, does not the *Pirkei Avos*, the *Ethics of the Fathers*, demand that we repeat a saying in the name of the one who said it?

I will admit to being Isaac ibn Chabib, fool, hypocrite, rabbi, and unregenerate disbeliever in miracles.

So for posterity, for all those who will listen, here is my story.

First of all, I should tell you that I didn't want to go to Tobias.

Tobias is not even the real name of the planet. The Jews who live there call it *Bharees*, or Covenant, because the remnants of one of its moons form a ring of dust and stones that appear as a gauzy rainbow in the night sky. It is, I will admit, a beautiful sight; and as if that's not enough, the comets rain across the heavens and sheets of aurorae shimmer like tinted crystal.

Everyone else calls the place *Ulim*, which means world. We named it Tobias, after Martin Tobias, President of the United States of Canada. But I'm getting away from the point. The point is that all Jews — *any* Jews on any planet — must trace their cultural heritage back to Earth. There can be only one Sinai, one Torah, one Adonoi.

If Jews have scaly skin like alligators and yellow eyes and seven fingers on each hand, that's fine. Good for them; they're converts. The Torah doesn't discriminate. At some time, some adventurous Jews colonised Covenant and converted the natives. Or the natives listened in on our radio transmissions — not that Jews have so many programs on the air — and decided to become Jewish. (Which just goes to prove that you don't need to be human to be a masochist.) That's the only logical explanation why the Good Will Traders discovered Jews on Covenant.

That was my argument, but the xeno-historians and cultural anthropologists had written an *Encyclopedia Galactica* detailing that the "*Ulim* Jews" were as indigenous to the planet as the electric cats and the flimflams that soared in the sky like birds and burrowed into the earth like worms. It seemed that Judaism had actually, impossibly, evolved *independently* on a different planet. Oh, there were plenty of theories about how such a thing could happen, but they were as wild and esoteric as anything Leibniz or the Lurianic Kabbalists could have imagined: ghostly quantum worlds splitting into imperfect copies of themselves (not so different from the mystic's worlds of angels and demons), the Copenhagen collapse, mirror universes, splitting universes, the Everett Wheeler Graham metatheorem, the turbulent effects of chaos, the great fractal chain, and who knows what else.

So now we are to believe in two Sinai's, two Torahs, and four Talmuds, for like us, the *Ulim* Jews had two versions of Talmud, which, in case you might not know, are chronicles of Jewish culture, law, and myth. They even spoke Hebrew . . . well, they spoke something like Hebrew.

Why didn't I want to go to Tobias — to Covenant, to *Ulim*, if you like? Why wouldn't I want to verify a miracle and renew my faith?

The truth?

I was afraid. I had come to terms with history. Faith could not supplant reason. The evidence was incontrovertible.

Had been incontrovertible . . .

The shuttle landed in the country of *Chakk*, which had once been the Mesopotamia of this planet. Although it was in a northern latitude, it was quite temperate. The landing field was huge, for this was a major spaceport;

but it was, in effect, a crater in the centre of a coral green city of bole and root and leaf the size of New Boston. I waited in the airlock, alone, staring out the bolted plastocene door, as if I was a pariah; the crew and other passengers had debouched earlier. As this was my first visit, I had to wait in isolation. It seemed like days, but it was only hours. By exposing me to enough radiation to make me glow like a tropical fish, they would certainly make me kosher. I guess they didn't trust anyone's infection control procedures but their own. So what could be lost but a little time? I'm ninety-seven years old. I've got a slow metabolism. A little radiation won't kill me, and if it does, that wouldn't be such a loss.

The *Tzaddik* — the "Good Jew who makes miracles and talks with God," the grand rabbi, my boss — would just have to send someone younger and less cynical to discover the nature of God.

So I stood before the lock and stared out into the landing field. It would soon be time, for an alien stood on the field below and waited for me. He didn't wave, nor did he move around or shift his weight from foot to foot. He stood still as stone, his yellowish eyes fixed on me. He wore a blue yarmulke that fitted tightly to his bald, blue-grey head — the kind of yarmulkes handed out at bar mitzvahs on Long Island, and a black-striped prayer-shawl was draped over his shoulders. Suddenly a crowd of Ulimites gathered before the shuttle, but they stayed well away from the one dressed as a Jew. Those that came too close to him, moved away quickly with nervous grins on their faces. Except for the Jew, they all seemed agitated. The Ulimites were dressed in fine linens that billowed and ballooned, multi-hued gowns and coats and breeches that were meant to create new shapes rather than accentuate or improve nature. It reminded me of sixteenth century English fashion, the kind of clothes worn during the reign of Henry VIII.

A human delegation arrived, all in evening clothes; so I was to be formally received.

I would have preferred to go off quietly with the alien in the *tallis.*

Then the ship wished me farewell, the lock sighed open, and I walked down the enclosed gangway. The mossy smells of forest and grass, which were carried on gentle breezes, were overwhelming. I shook hands with the ambassador from the Canadian States and his officers from the foreign office, and was introduced to the alien ambassador and other dignitaries who extended their seven-fingered hands to greet me. Their skin was surprisingly hot, and leathery as the case of an old book. It took a moment to get used to looking at the aliens and listening to the translator, who was a young woman with a hard, shiny face and a deep voice.

Two men clutched my elbows as if I were a fugitive and gently propelled me toward what looked to be a slidewalk the size of a thoroughfare. They were going to ghost me away before the alien in the *tallis* could introduce himself. "Excuse me," I said to the man on my right (after all, I'm right-handed), "but what about my friend there?" I waved to the alien in the yarmulke, who stood alone away from the crowd. He frowned, which for an Ulimite is the same thing as a smile. (I had had the whole voyage in the starship to study, so I knew a *few* things.)

"*Shalom,*" he said in a voice that carried over the noise of the others. The intonation was odd: he pronounced the word as if it were divided into three distinct syllables, and he glottalised the "al" and "om".

I asked him who he was: "*Mee Ahtaw?*"

He spoke quickly, as if the group surrounding me would stop him any second, but it was as if he didn't exist: his brethren either didn't notice him or were purposely ignoring him. Although he used words I had never heard, I understood most of what he said. His name was Tahlmeade, which meant student, at least in Terran Hebrew.

A member of the Ulimite delegation stepped right in front of me, even as I was speaking to Tahlmeade. I though it very rude, and odd; but Tahlmeade simply moved around the periphery of the nervous crowd and re-established eye-contact with me. As he moved about, like a child playing peekaboo, I could not help but smile. All the Ulimites were short — about four and a half feet tall — and their flattened features, serious expressions, and roundish heads made them seem . . . cute. But even to think about them that way was condescending. No, more than that. Was it not just another form of prejudice? Of racism? Indeed, the human dignitaries might well think that an old man with a long beard and earlocks was *cute,* especially one wearing a fur-brimmed hat, and a black caftan with a silk cord knotted around his waist to separate the Godly parts — the mind, the soul, and the heart — from the lower parts.

And who knows what the Ulimites thought of *humans?* Most likely, they didn't perceive us as cute. Perhaps they considered us smelly, sweaty, brutelike, fleshy as mushrooms, and most likely crazy: *meshuggener.*

The uniformed young man beside me motioned to Tahlmeade. He was with the consulate mission and held onto my elbow as if I was on my last leg and about to fall face-flat on the ground. "Don't worry, Rabbi, he knows his way around. He'll catch up with us later."

"I should *hope* he knows his way around, but where are we going?"

"To the consulate. A party has been prepared in your honour." The young bureaucrat was quite handsome: dark hair, a good sharp nose that you could see, a strong chin, and dark eyes that would make women talk.

"Please, let's bring the alien in the prayer-shawl along with us. It's obvious that —"

"I'm afraid that would not do, Rabbi."

"Would not *do*?"

The young men pulled me along, and I, of course, did not resist; I just walked slowly — after all, I'm an old man.

"After the briefing, you'll understand."

"Ah, now it's a briefing!" and after a step or two, I asked, "So if Jews are not allowed at this party, what am *I* going to do there?"

"With all due respect, Rabbi, you're jumping to conclusions," said the ambassador, who walked beside us; he was tall and grey, and wore a thin moustache that was black as a pencil mark. Then he frowned at the aliens and smiled at me. The Ulimites frowned happily back at us, indicating that all was well with their world.

As I was whisked across the spaceport, I looked over my shoulder. But Tahlmeade and the ship had disappeared, replaced by an architectural chaos of brown and green. The city of Khârig, the largest and most fabulous city on Ulim, was a sculpted garden, and I was passing through it at a hundred miles an hour. Arches, stadiums, peristyle courts, statues as large as skyscrapers, castles, rotundas, pavilions, halls, lodges, offices, governmental complexes vaulted over razor-cut avenues; they grew out of the ground complete with flying buttresses, towers, domes, and cupolas; their architectural styles were as exotic as the Hagia Sophia or the Cetian monoliths. I imagined that I could see the façades of San Carlo, the Doric porticos of Hagley Park, the Romanesque and gothic pinnacles of the Milan Cathedral, and the glass skyscraper needles of Van der Rohe. The Ulim had planted a city, had shaped trees and shrub and mirrored leaves into habitation: into civilization. I felt dizzy, overwhelmed, enraptured. I felt swallowed by the silvery green *alienness* of it all.

So this was culture shock.

If such a thing could turn an old man with earlocks into a poet, imagine what it might do to someone who still had some *juice* left inside him?

The cocktail party was endless, the talk small, and although the ambassador took special pains to provide me with some ninety-proof Slivovitz whiskey (which he thought all Jews drank), I left all the *schnapps* alone; neither did I take any narcodrines or enhancers; neither did I attend any of the Virtual parties that were also being held in my honour. I am a simple man. I drink in private. I am too old for sex. (I could still perform, I suppose; but, I've courted peace and privacy for far too long to give them up for a wife.) I like to read, go to bed early, eat like a glutton at the Tzaddik's court, argue pilpul and philosophy with the other rabbis, smoke the flat, foul-smelling cigarettes from Turkey, and wake up with the cock (not what you think!) to begin another — and perhaps final — day.

Yet I felt like the alien here, and not because I was carrying on conversations with creatures with yellow eyes and blue-grey skin the texture of alligators (albeit through my interpreter, who indicated that she would be willing to warm me up during the night, and then gave me a blank look when I told her that I was no Ghandi — she probably thought "Ghandi" was a Jewish perversion); no, I felt just now like the hypocrite I was. You see, Jewish guilt is indeed a fact. I was a fraud, and these people, both alien and human, thought they were talking to a real Chassid master rebbeh, a living anachronism, a mystic who believed in kabbalah and amulets, who had his own *derekh*, his own special channel to communicate with God, and who knew His secret name: the Tetragrammaton. Indeed, they thought they had found a human who would understand and could explain the mystery of the Jews of this planet. The "Jewish Mystery" seemed to be a major philosophical problem for the intelligentsia of Ulim, both human and alien. It was as if they had to go to secondary sources to find out about these Jews . . . as if it never occurred to anyone just to go and ask a blue-skinned Jew.

So they asked *me*, a human hypocrite who remained a Chassid and a rabbi only because that was all I knew. I was too old and frightened, too corrupt, to leave the *Tzaddik's* court and die alone among strangers. I needed respect, and wasn't willing to give up my few servants and my small congregation. I could tell you that I lost my faith because of Auschwitz, but who remembers Auschwitz? Not my Tzaddik who believed himself to be the *melits yoysher*, the one who pleads for the Jews who violate any one of the six hundred and thirteen positive and negative commandments, who believes that all *tsores*, all the troubles visited upon the Jews, are punishment for collective and individual sin. So six million Jews die because they sinned . . .

Oh, I argued with the Tzaddik. I told him that only a madman could believe in prayer after the Holocaust. If there was a God, He was no longer in the world; He was not the God of history. He could not be propitiated. After all, what terrible crime had we committed? The Torah says, "for our sins we are punished," but who was punished, who was murdered? The poorest, the faithful, the most pious. This, then, was the revelation, the holocaust was the modern Sinai — if one could call an event that happened two hundred years ago *modern*.

So what did my Tzaddik do? He told his three thousand followers that *I* had had a revelation, that God had revealed himself to me alone, that *I* was now a Tzaddik.

And *that's* why he sent me to Tobias instead of going himself.

I told the story of my Tzaddik to my hosts, and everyone frowned and shook my hands; until I actually almost began to feel like a Tzaddik who could do no wrong. I told them funny stories, and they especially liked Rabbi Nachman of Bratslav's story of the wise but sceptical man who had been sent a message from his king, but refused to open it because the messenger couldn't prove to the wise man that the king existed; nor could anyone else.

"'Now do you see?' the sceptical wise man said to the messenger. 'People are foolish and naïve and believe what they wish. They live a lie because they fear the truth.'"

Everyone agreed with Rabbi Nachman, who probably would have gotten a kick out of knowing his story was being told by a poor Jew to goyim who lived in the heavens.

Against all my good judgement, I began to enjoy myself a little; and just when I was about to indulge in a finger of Slivovitz (even if it tastes like rubbing alcohol, why break tradition?), the ambassador's aide relieved me of my newfound admirers and took me down narrow, labyrinthine corridors to an inner sanctum for the threatened briefing. I have to say, though, that these people were poets; they knew a good metaphor when they saw one. Although the striated walls of this grand salon seemed to be made of wood, they looked like meat. Whether it was sap or water, I don't know; but the very walls seemed to be sweating.

And there were no windows in here. A perfect place for an interrogation.

"Well?" I asked the ambassador, who was sitting opposite me with his staff beside him. We sat at a conference table made of the same stuff as the walls, but I didn't touch the table or anything on it. There was a setting before me: blue monochrome Delft china, heavy silverware and crystal; and within easy reach were sandwiches on painted porcelain plates, and liquor, juice, and wine in clear Bristol goblets. A pear-shaped silver coffee pot took up an entire corner of the table, which seemed to be sweating profusely under the feet of the pot. The slightly acrid aroma of coffee was delicious.

"It's all kosher," he said, gesturing at the food and drink. "I noticed you neither ate nor drank at the party. Surely you must be hungry . . ."

"Why all this fuss over a rabbi from Brooklyn who's not even published?"

"Because it seems that you're the key to the mystery."

"Ah, yes, the mystery of the Jews," I said. "Why are these blue people asking *me* to tell them about their own Jews."

"Ulimites," the ambassador said, correcting me; yet there was no condescension in his voice.

"Ulimites." Then after a beat, I said, "They had a Jew right at the shuttle port. Why didn't they ask *him*? And why wasn't he allowed to come along?"

"That's just the problem. They can't even *see* him. They have some kind of proprioceptive sense that he's there, but that's all."

"That's crazy!"

The ambassador shrugged. "The Ulimites can't see Jews. Why? We don't know. Yet they're absolutely obsessed with finding out all they can about the Jews."

"Well, they certainly seem to be able to see *me*," I said. "So either I'm not a Jew or —"

"They have no trouble seeing humans whether they're Jewish or not," the ambassador said, humouring me. After all, what else could he do?

"So before you came to colonise —"

"Not to colonise, Rabbi. We do not colonise planets that —"

"Excuse me for my ignorance, Ambassador, but before you came here to visit —"

"— To establish diplomatic relations."

"— How could they be obsessed with finding out about Jews *before* you arrived, if they couldn't *see* Jews or ask anyone else who *could*?"

"It was like an itch they couldn't scratch," one of the aides said; the one with the handsome face and good nose.

The ambassador glanced at the aide, who reddened slightly, and then said to me, "They discovered various Jewish texts that had not been destroyed."

"Destroyed?"

Again he shrugged. "We know very little about what happened. We expect, or hope, that you can answer those questions for us. But the Ulimite Jews here seem to be the only religious group on the planet. None of the other Ulimites have any sense of the spiritual at all. It's as if part of their psyche has been entirely wiped away, lost."

"They lost their ability to hear their God, or gods," said the aide who had spoken before. "That's what they've told us, anyway."

"And what about the . . . encyclopedia your historians and anthropologists wrote about the Jews?"

"All correct, as far as we know."

"Then they interviewed the Jews?"

"No," the ambassador said. "All the information is gleaned from secondhand sources. Although we know where the Jews live — or think we do — we have not been able to initiate any direct contact, except with their intermediaries."

"Ah, the *shtadlans*," I said. "The fixers. So Tahlmeade is a fixer . . . But why *should* he help you? You treated him as if he were *dreck*. A nothing."

"He had planned to see you, Rabbi. He understood that it would be impossible for him to join us."

"Why? If no one can see him, what's the difference?"

"They sense him and become very nervous. Believe me, it would be a mistake; but you'll see for yourself soon enough."

I waited for him to tell me what I would see soon enough, and when he didn't, I let it alone; I would find out due time. "How can one believe anything when it's all secondhand and censored, when nothing is mentioned about your claim that the Jews are . . . invisible?" I asked. "Why wasn't that in your reports?"

"This is a very sensitive and . . . explosive issue," the ambassador said. "We considered what to do very carefully, and finally decided to keep the mystery confidential until we've resolved it. All the reports and monographs, although true, are smoke-screens." He paused, as if to study my expression, but I have what's called a poker-face, which I understand has something to do with an ancient game of chance. "There are too many implications for Jews at home," he continued.

"Implications?"

"Something terrible has happened here. We do not wish to give extremists an excuse to kill any more Jews, not after what happened in Savannah."

I didn't retreat from his stare. History repeats itself in different guises. What had once been America was now like ancient Poland.

"You know," I said, "I'm going to ask you something every Jew asks himself: Why *me*?"

The ambassador pushed his chair back, and an aide stood up to help him, although I saw no reason why he needed help. The ambassador was a relatively young man. "Because the Jewish government here, if indeed there *is* a government, *asked* for you."

"Asked for *me*?"

"Over a month ago, Earth time. The one you call Tahlmeade made the request."

"He asked for *me*?" I was sounding like an echo, but I couldn't help it.

"Yes. He specifically asked for you, by name."

"How could he have known my name?" I asked.

The ambassador stood up and looked at me until I felt uncomfortable. "That's exactly what *we'd* like to know, Rabbi."

Tahlmeade came to the consulate to pick me up. He had come right into the suite where the party was being held in my honour, and was standing in the doorway waiting for me. His prayer shawl was wrapped around himself as if for protection, but it didn't seem to be Tahlmeade who needed protection. The other aliens in the room seemed somehow dislocated, lost; they moved aimlessly about the room, every one in a sudden state of agitation. I could not help but imagine that they were in some kind of psychic pain, yet — if I didn't know better — I would have thought them happy. They were all grinning at each other, at me, at the tables and walls and ceiling.

But their grins were frozen.

And I knew that on Ulim, a smile was not a smile.

Tahlmeade and I left quickly. We rode an elevator though the centre of the building, which was a tree, or a forest that had grown into one solid mass. We stepped outside; and for a few moments we were in the streets, streets that smelled like thyme and roses, that were as clean as my wife's (may she rest in peace) table. But the street crowds were agitated, too; people dashed past us and eddied around us, giving us a wide berth.

We were the quiet eye of the storm.

Then Tahlmeade led me below ground, into what seemed to be another city. We waited on a transparent platform that seemed to be situated on the edge of an abyss. Above and below were contrasts of light and dark; but below were huge organic stalactites and stalagmites worked with glastex and metal: trees as large and high as skyscrapers, their flesh smooth and irised. People lived in these illuminated boles, which were connected by communication grids and transportation tubes. I looked down into the descending levels of habitation. I might have been looking at jewels, at strings of light set upon velvet; I might as well have been looking into the eternity of space.

Just looking down made me dizzy, made me a little *meshuggener.*

Made me, God forbid, want to leap into the darkness. But such things I ignore; even when I was young, I had a fear of heights.

A transpod rushed into the station and hushed to a stop. The pod cracked open and we climbed in. Tahlmeade punched in the coordinates, and it suddenly seemed as if we were falling. Yet there was no definite sense of motion, just the buildings rushing past us as we sped forward through tubes that choked through the city like transparent vines.

"If you would close the windows," I said in Hebrew, forgetting that that was slang for "opaque the walls". "I'm getting dizzy." But Tahlmeade seemed to comprehend what I meant immediately, for in an instant, grey walls surrounded us. Graffitoed images glowed redly over the grey: some smart youngster must have figured out how to change the light patterns.

My dizziness passed and I asked, "Why can't they see you?" Only after I spoke the words did I realise how blunt I had been.

Tahlmeade frowned at me and said, "Perhaps for the same reason that they are able to see *you.*"

I was going to ask him what he meant, yet somehow I knew . . . I *knew* what he meant.

They could not see Tahlmeade because he was a Jew.

But they *could* see me.

And what did they see?

A fraud, a fool, a counterfeit. A phony.

We hurtled forward at three hundred miles an hour, a slight rhythmic vibration and the digital read-outs on the control console the only indications of movement. I tried to communicate with Tahlmeade, but he was preoccupied. One thing was certain: to him I was not a Tzaddik. He stared at the control console intently as if the apocalyptic words of the Torah were flaming across the screen, and tented his fingers. I interrupted his thoughts a few times, but he simply frowned and then turned back to the console. He was, of course, shutting me out. My questions would have to wait . . . at least, until he awakened.

For he gave himself away when he began to snore.

So our species were not so different, after all.

It took five hours to reach out destination: *Michborah.*

Which meant graveyard.

This was mountain country: cold, rugged, inhospitable, and beautiful. The mountains — white and bald and worn, except for foothill sheathing of bright green scrub — seemed to reach into the hazy expanse of red sky like the towers of a completed Babel, and huge cumulous cloud formations scudded past above, carried on storm-winds. The sky was in constant movement: continents formed and reformed, arms and ships and towers swirled into being, and then dissolved; phantoms and spirits roiled and sailed in pursuit, one after another, chasing themselves into the ominous blackness of a storm, which suddenly erupted, dropping torrents and covering the world in a caftan of fog. The sun was smeary, and low; and night, which came fast on this planet, was but footsteps away.

But night would be like twilight, and the sky like the inside of a dance hall.

I pulled my threadbare coat tightly around me for protection from the rain, which splashed from the wide brim of my hat, and I followed Tahlmeade down the winding road that cut into the side of a mountain; the road was paved with sharp, jagged, and slippery stones. As would be our luck, we were walking along the side of the mountain that offered us no protection from the pounding rain.

Lightning snaked across the sky ahead of us, lighting up cliffs, gorges, and the grotesque rock cones in the valley ahead. I shivered and remembered the blessings: the blessing upon seeing lighting and — I waited a few seconds for the crashing boom of thunder — the blessing upon hearing thunder. A Jew must pronounce a minimum of a hundred blessings every day: a blessing when he gets up, when he eats, prays, goes to bed, puts on clothes, eliminates, sees a rainbow, a scholar, a beautiful or strange-looking person, or hears bad news, or good news. Breathing itself is a prayer, yet breathe as I might, I had been silent for years. Only in public would prayers pass through my mouth as naturally as greetings and commands. Yet just now I remembered my *Tata*, my father, teaching me the prayer over lightning as we both stood in just such a rain as this one.

"*Borouch ahtaw Hashem Eloheinu melech ha'olam . . .*"

"Well?" Tahlmeade asked. "Are you going to say the blessings, or not?"

Startled, I glanced to the side, as if I would see my father standing there, my father who had been dead for over thirty years: Tahlmeade had asked the question exactly as my father used to, with the same intonation, the same voice, the same accent. In fact, it was as if my father had just spoken to me from heaven, where there is no distance.

Of course, I didn't believe that for a moment, but nevertheless . . .

"Did you read my thoughts?" I asked him.

"The blessing . . .?"

I said it: "Blessed are You, Hashem, our God, King of the Universe, who makes the work of Creation."

Together, we said the blessing for thunder: "Blessed are You, Hashem, our God, King of the Universe, for His strength and His power fill the universe."

" . . . *v-g'vuraso mahlay olam . . .*"

The rain became drizzle as day gave way to twilight.

"Well," I asked again as we walked. "*Did* you read my thoughts?"

"Yes, but not the way you think."

"Then how?"

"You'll see, I assure you, Reb Isaac." It was kind of Tahlmeade to address me by the title of teacher, but perhaps that was an Ulimite form of sarcasm. Who could know?

"Nevertheless, I *don't see*."

"You will," Tahlmeade insisted, yet I had the very strong feeling that he was speaking by rote, as a good salesman often does when making a sale, although his thoughts might be entirely elsewhere.

I suddenly smelled something acrid, like smoke, and tar, and as I looked around to discover the source, Tahlmeade said, "Do you smell the volcano, Rebbe? It's old and quiet now, but it was quite an artist in its day, and still wakes up to cough and fart." The road turned and then abruptly ended in a sheer drop. Ahead was a chasm, and below and beyond were canyons within canyons, ravines, and a huge dry lake. Steps cut into the rock led down to a high plateau that was filled with conical fairy chimneys, which were over fifty feet high and capped with hard stone: natural sculptures created by millennia of wind, rain, and snow. But the chimneys were dwarfed by stone chimeras that stood hundreds of feet high and were evenly spaced along terraced cliff walls that had been carved and sculpted and hollowed into a city. The chimeras had heads like cats, or tigers, and the bodies of eagles — that's what they looked like to me anyway. Yet as I looked down at them, I felt a terrible emptiness, as if somehow gravity itself was leaching away the stuff of my soul, as if I were falling, falling into a grave; and I could only think of Auschwitz, of death and the choking, second-by-second eternity of gasping pain that ended in the chest-still darkness of the ovens.

I felt as if I was looking straight into hell, and I felt soiled and frightened, for it was horrifyingly, terrifyingly beautiful, in the same way that a cat must appear to the bird caught in its claws.

"Thought is like an atmosphere, like clouds," Tahlmeade said, although I must admit I was still caught by this place, by its dead immensities, and I heard Tahlmeade's voice as if it was my own thoughts, my own internal voice. "Usually you can make out vague shapes, and sometimes you can see with absolute clarity, but not as often as we'd like. So you're making out shapes now, am I correct? And what do you see, Rebbe? What do you see?"

I was fixed on the chimeras and the city carved out of the cliff behind them; the city was like a bas-relief of rust-red arches, columns, cupolas, pavilions, spires, and balustrades, all fluted, the arches and horizontal planes covered with chimeras, smaller versions of those that stood guard, blindly waiting through the centuries. The storm had blown itself away, leaving the sky pink and still; spirals of clouds seemed to cling to *Me'al'lim*, one of Ulim's two moons, which was now a pale crescent.

"I don't know," I said, replying to his question.

"Yes, you do, Rebbe. Reveal yourself."

"I fear I am already revealed."

Tahlmeade was silent.

"I feel empty in this place, as if something terrible has happened here. It reminds me of death, of what Jews on Earth refer to as the Holocaust."

"It reminds you of Auschwitz."

"So you know of our history," I said.

"Yes, Rebbe. We know each other's histories."

"What do you mean?" I asked, but Tahlmeade led the way down the steps into the valley, and I followed him.

Into hell.

The emptiness seemed to take everything from me, especially my questions; it was as if I could feel gravity pulling harder on me with every step. I clung to the side of this stairwell chipped out of the mountainside, afraid that I would become too heavy and fall. Water pooled in the hollows of the steps, and I was careful, for the stone was slippery. I was soaked, and my clothes smelled musty. Once at the bottom, we walked toward the chimeras. The sandy ground was muddy from the rain. As we walked, the sun set, shadows deepened and lengthened, and the shattered remains of Ulim's third moon appeared as pale fire overhead: a celestial rainbow. Now there were two moons in the sky, one vague, the other as sharp and distinct as Earth's; and the stationary fireworks above provided enough light to read by.

I saw movement ahead of me in the distance, and at first imagined that smaller versions of the chimeras were alive and prowling about. They glowed like ocean algae and fluoresced with every movement.

"*N'már.*"

I turned to Tahlmeade, happy to hear a sound in this desolation . . . and then I realised that he had not *said* anything. I thought he had said "tigers".

"This is their mating season," Tahlmeade said; and this time he *was* speaking. "They come here to mate, and to die. Ancient peoples worshipped them, for they believed the animals had souls, which were what they saw glowing." Tahlmeade's skin, which was scored, as if made up of thousands of shale pebbles, glistened, and his wet tallis clung to his shoulders like a mantle. "But don't worry, Rebbe, voracious as they can be, they can't see us . . . or smell us. We are like ghosts, even here — *especially* here."

I felt suddenly weary, exhausted; every step was a trial. I could only concentrate on getting out of here, of putting the great stylised, stone chimeras behind us, souls or no souls, ghosts or no ghosts.

"Now you have no questions," Tahlmeade said. Or perhaps it was a question; I could not be sure. After a beat, he said, "You see, Rebbe, you *are* a Tzaddik."

"What do you mean?"

"Because you can see, and feel, and hear."

"So can all men."

"No, not all men . . . nor all of us."

Although we had turned away from the chimeras and the glowing tigers and had cut across to the southern edge of the field, which was close to us, I felt the place pulling at me, pulling me back as if into a vortex, pulling me to its centre, which I imagined was as deep and lifeless as the pits in Poland. Mass graves . . .

"It is," Tahlmeade said.

"What?" I asked, still shocked at the soft explosion of his thoughts touching my mind.

"It *is* a mass grave, all of it a cemetery. As are the cliffs, the cities in the cliffs: a necropolis. On Earth you have nothing like this, Rebbe. You ask where the Jews are." He swept his hand in the air, as if he were throwing sand. "They are *here*, all twelve million of them. We walk on bones, on lives, on ashes."

"How did this happen?" I asked, but for an instant I could see engines of death working in the labyrinths behind the carved façades in the cliffs. I could smell the charnel house. Here was where Ulimite technology had reached its perfection.

"It happened as it happened on your world. Those who killed us, if they were alive to talk, would say their gods told them to do it. *Those* Gods, the N'már that guard the ground."

"But you are alive," I said, and there was desperation in my voice. "*We* are alive."

"Do you feel alive . . . here?" Tahlmeade asked, and I felt rooted to the ground, as if their gods had buried me where I stood. For an instant I panicked; but I could indeed still move my arms, my legs.

"Is it because of what happened here that your brethren can't see you?" I asked.

Tahlmeade did not answer my question, but said, "The statues are almost as old as the cliffs. This place is known as the Valley of Creation." He frowned, as if savouring the irony, and then led the way to a corner of the cliff wall and into an arched entrance flanked by fluted columns, all carved into the stone.

I followed him through pitch-dark catacombs.

I was blind, but I could feel the weight of the dead all around me, as heavy as the crushing darkness itself.

I was breathing it, dissolving in it.

I could hear Tahlmeade's voice. Or his thoughts.

And then I saw light, a dim flicker at the end of a long tunnel. I felt relief, as if I had escaped the death that permeated the very air of the Valley of Creation; death was like a thought, and thought like a vapor, or perhaps an odor, a perfume that could be breathed, inhaled and exhaled, passing from one person to another. Thus could I feel the heaviness of the martyrs buried in the valley . . . thus could I hear Tahlmeade even when he didn't speak.

We walked out of the catacomb into the bright night, and my mood suddenly lightened, as if the mass of the mountain we had passed through was acting like a psychic shield.

"Good *Shabbos*," Tahlmeade said. He frowned at me and nodded his head; his mood, too, had changed.

So on Ulim it was Friday, *Erev Shabbos*: Sabbath eve.

"I apologise that we had to pass through *Gehennà* to greet the Queen Bride of the Sabbath, but I assure you, she is here."

The Sabbath was a Queen to be made welcome, for she was the foretaste of heaven, God's great gift to those who obeyed his Torah. But for me, for years, *Shabbos* was not a gift, not a freedom, but a prison of rules and regulations. It was, of course, not enough merely to *obey* the Law. You had to *believe* in it, take joy from it, give yourself up to it.

I was bursting with questions, but *Shabbos* would not allow sadness or bitterness: I would have to wait.

A *Shabbos* calmness came over me, such as I hadn't felt in years.

"Good *Shabbos*," I whispered.

* * *

We came to a sheer cliff that looked unscalable. Tahlmeade guided me through a concealed opening in the rock, and we took a lifter deep inside the mountain.

It was cold and bitter atop the mountain plateau, yet this place was verdant: trees were thick, if stunted, and we took a winding road through forest. Past the edge of the forest with its sharp tang of wood and sap, we came to fields covered with flowers that appeared translucent in the night light; and the ring glittered above, a metallic rainbow of colour that appeared and reappeared as cloud masses scudded across it. The haze of aurorae was purple and pink, sheets of gauze that seemed to shimmer in the sky like illuminated silk curtains.

"It's beautiful," I said. "But how can anything grow in this cold?" I pulled my coat around me.

"The ground is warm, Rebbe. You see, your feet aren't cold. The mountain is alive, it breathes, and one day, it will explode." He frowned. I was beginning to understand his humour.

Children were shouting ahead; they stood on the edge of the field and were bundled in shiny black caftans and caps. Behind him was the village, which seemed ethereal in the coloured veils of night. The town seemed to be cut out of the mountain itself, but it was an incongruous, yet charming marriage of wood and stone: elongated domes sat upon thick towers, buildings were tent shaped, and had galleries with open sides to give shelter; and everything was glimmerous and multi-hued, as if the village was mimicking the heavens.

"Rebbe Tahlmeade," they shouted and waved their arms. "Good *Shabbos*."

Tahlmeade motioned to them, and then stopped walking. He looked up at the sky, at the ring — at Ulim's night rainbow — and made a prayer. He gazed at me steadily and said, "The rainbow is our covenant, just as it is yours."

He continued to stare at me, making me uncomfortable. I was beginning to realise that Tahlmeade was not merely a fixer, an intermediary, as the ambassador mistakenly thought, but that he must be the Tzaddik himself.

"Have you nothing to say to that?" he asked.

"The children, if they are children, are waiting for you."

"Waiting will not hurt them. And, yes, Rebbe, of course they are children."

"What do you wish me to say, Rebbe." I had to smile, for I had not called him a rabbi before. Then I caught myself, for I remembered that a smile did not signal pleasure to a Ulimite.

"I wish you to say the truth. That you believe the Covenant has been broken."

"Can it be otherwise?" I asked. "You have been nearly destroyed. Did God hear your prayers? And do *nothing*?" I recited the words of the Prophets, one of the Thirteen Articles of Faith, "'I believe with perfect faith that the Creator, blessed be His name, rewards those who keep His commandments and punishes those who transgress them.' Is that not the pact between God and the Jewish people? But if Jews are to remain Jews, they must suspend that; they must suspend all traditional doctrine and remove God from history, for it would be sacrilege even to *contemplate* that God would allow millions of innocent children to die as punishment for the sins of other Jews!" After I said that, I asked, out of respect, "But do you wish to speak of such things on the Sabbath?"

"One can always question, Rebbe, especially on the Sabbath, for that is the time when God is most visible."

"Let me ask you then, if you *knew* that the Holocaust would come to the next generation, would you raise your children Jewish? If Jews are responsible to each other, you to me, me to you, and both of us to all of them" — I motioned toward the children, who were waiting impatiently — "then those who died in the Holocaust did *not* die because they failed to keep the Covenant. They died because their grandparents and parents kept it. So, Rebbe, I suppose I answered my own question. They did die because of the sins of others . . . the sin of their parents for remaining faithful to the Covenant!"

"So God has abandoned us?" Tahlmeade said.

"Unless you wish to believe our respective Holocausts were the means by which God tested his people, as he did Job. But I cannot imagine such a cruel conclusion."

"Then what *do* you imagine, Rebbe?"

"Emptiness," I said. The cold worked itself over my face until I felt I was wearing a mask.

"Better Job." Tahlmeade frowned and then made a coughing noise, which I understood as a laugh — but I could not tell if it was good-natured or derisive. He opened his arms and walked toward the children, who ran to meet us. Their small, pebbled faces seemed very grey; perhaps it was the light of the night, or the cold. "Perhaps you'll feel differently when you jump the road."

"What?" I asked, surprised. "Jumping the Road" was an old superstition, like the "evil eye".

"We'll talk tomorrow, Rebbe, after you've —" The children distracted him with questions.

But I learned what he meant that night.

In the middle of the night, as light poured like mercury though the small high windows of my little room in the highest part of Tahlmeade's house, I listened to the voices downstairs and dreamed.

I felt myself being hurled into the darkness. Yet who could imagine speed without the reference of light or the pressure of gravity? Perhaps I flew. Perhaps I fell.

To Earth. Into the heart of Philadelphia. Into the Tzaddik's court.

Into the Tzaddik's dream.

"So, have you renewed your faith?" he asked. "We sat on stone steps in the ruins of a synagogue; after all, it was my Tzaddik's dream.

"I'm asleep," I said.

"As am I, but certainly you'll remember this when you wake up."

"Remember what?"

"That you jumped the road and spoke with your Tzaddik." He smiled at me, and then looked down at his age-freckled hands, which rested on his lap. He was several years younger than me, yet I always thought of him as much older. (Of course, how much older than me could anyone *be* and still be alive?) His beard was mottled white and grey, which gave it a yellowish cast.

"I told Tahlmeade that you were a Tzaddik," he continued. "I told him that you had the '*kuk*', that you could 'see'. But I told him you didn't know any of these things." When I didn't reply, he said, "Of course, Tahlmeade helped you jump, just to get you started."

To "jump the road" was to see into other places without being there. It was the miraculous means by which Tzaddiks could help and protect other Jews who were in trouble.

It was pure, unadulterated, medieval, Jewish superstition.

"If it's superstition, then what are you doing here?" the Tzaddik asked. "You came to *me.*"

"I am *not* here," I said.

"Well, as long as you aren't here, do you wish to ask me a question?"

"Ah, so you'll give me proof that I've jumped the road."

"Tahlmeade told you that you would do so. Doesn't that tell you anything?

"It tells me that I'm suggestible."

"Ask him how Jews came to be on two planets," the Tzaddik said. "And tell Ruchel that I send my felicitations."

Ruchel was Tahlmeade's wife. But *I* knew that, and it was *my* dream.

I awakened with a start and stared up at the ceiling, which, like the walls, seemed to be constructed out of one solid piece of wood the colour of mahogany. I wiped my eyes, for the ceiling seemed to be moving, undulating ever so slightly, but that had to be an effect of the light drifting in.

I heard something, whisperings that seemed to be right here in the room. A voice that could not be denied, for I could not help but think that God was speaking directly to me.

Giving me a history lesson.

The children woke me up with an aromatic glass of sweetened tea. It was barely dawn, and the light made everything in the room seem soft and gauzy. My back ached from sleeping on the mattress on the floor, for I was too large to fit on the bed, sumptuous as it might be. I sat up and thanked these two tiny versions of Tahlmeade, dressed in their Sabbath best. They fell over each other to get out of the room and made loud chirping noises as they ran down the hallway; I assumed they were feigning terror, for I understood their chirps to be laughter. Last night at *Shabbos* dinner, they stared at me throughout the meal, except when Tahlmeade made them sing the *z'miros,* the traditional songs of praise.

As I dressed, I remembered that I had dreamed of my Tzaddik, and that he had told me — no, a voice whispered to me, whispered the answer to my questions ... but I couldn't remember. It frustrated me for a moment, and then I shrugged it off and went downstairs. Dreams were always like that. They make sense only to the sleeper.

By the time I came downstairs, the house was already filled with people, male Ulimites wearing shiny hats and large black-and-white prayer shawls the size of blankets. Like Tahlmeade, they dressed in black caftans that were tied around the waist with cords to separate the lofty parts from the profane. There must have been sixty Ulimites in the living room and more crowded in doorways, all here for the privilege of accompanying Tahlmeade to synagogue. Tahlmeade's home, I should mention, was huge, more an inn than a house for a single family. It was all rather plainly furnished, except for the dining room, where the candelabra and kiddish cups were kept. Tahlmeade's table could comfortably seat twenty-five, and at the head was his golden chair: a throne. The table was filled for every meal, for many of his followers had sacrificed to come to his court; in return, he gave advice and relief and expounded the word of God — who better to do so, for was he not a direct conduit to the Creator?

We went to the *shul*, to the synagogue, like a conquering army returning home. It was a parade, and everyone was in uniform, as I was. I was dressed no differently than the Ulimites — in black caftan and prayer shawl — and as I entered the *shul* with the crowd, as I was seated near the eastern wall — a place of honour — I remembered that I had jumped the road last night. I remembered my dream, talking to my Tzaddik. There was more to the dream, though, but I could not recall what it might have been.

Tahlmeade sat in a plushly upholstered high-backed chair beside the red curtained Ark where the Holy Scrolls reposed; he looked out upon his congregation, as if each person was a book that he could read in a trice. The *shul* was packed, every seat accounted for, both upstairs and downstairs (for the women, dressed in their drab finery, sat together in the balcony, separated from the men by tradition, if not choice); and in the rear, around a study table, stood the *prosteh yidden*, those without learning.

"Better an educated bastard than an ignorant rabbi."

That's from the Talmud, which has something to say about everything.

A cantor led the morning *Shacharis* service, and I *davened*, which is how Jews pray — we rock back and forth, as if shaking out the prayers from a saltshaker. Like shaking oneself into a trance. Well, that's how the Ulimites in the *shul* prayed, every one of them; their yarmulkes were pulled over their hairless heads, their pebbly faces expressionless. I must confess to becoming caught up in the mood, caught up in the familiarity of the surroundings, the chanting, the prayers and blessings, the readings from the Torah that was resplendent upon the *bimah* platform, which was itself crowded with honoured "guests of the Holy Scrolls". It was true: a Jew can go anywhere among Jews and be at home. So did I feel at home on this faraway world, with aliens whose faces were like blue leather with bumps. I felt sleepy, as I always did in *shul* on *Shabbos*, for it was a day to rest. One could not light a fire or switch on a light, for today God was in control. He was the maker and shaker. Not us.

But could I *believe*, as I sat and rested with strangers who looked like nothing I had ever seen?

Let's just say that I was comfortable. That was enough; and I could lose myself in the moment, in the prayers that were said standing up with feet together, as if at attention. I was called up to the *bimah* to read from the Scrolls. I bowed and shook everyone's hand when I was finished. I returned to my seat. It was *pro forma*, familiar. Like sleeping in your own bed. As I prayed, I thought about my dream, and remembered. "Ask him how Jews came to be on two planets," my Tzaddik had said. And what would Tahlmeade tell me? That Jews have been jumping the road for centuries, for millennia?

That would explain how these Jews came to be.

Or perhaps it would explain how Jews on *Earth* came to be . . .

But it was superstition. I could more easily believe that worlds and universes were splitting into 10^{100+} imperfect copies of themselves: the Isaac ibn Chabib quantum theory of creating Jews.

"He who pays attention to dreams should have his head examined."

That's from Isaac ibn Chabib, not the Talmud.

Thus the service went on, from the morning into the afternoon, sleeping hours dissolving into an aromatic Jewish stew of routine and memory. As we prayed, I suddenly realised that, indeed, the world around me was dissolving. Praying was a dream, and the congregation dreamed.

They dreamed Tahlmeade's dream . . .

And I found myself alone. In the Valley of Creation.

The Jews who had died, their twelve million souls massing like clouds in the sky, whispered to me, telling me their myriad stories. They were safe, beyond pain and chance and care.

But the *other* Jews — those who were alive and singing and chanting and praying with me in the synagogue — had disappeared.

For their dream was death and oblivion. It was protection. It was a river: Lethe, the drowning river of forgetfulness.

A river that covered the world.

So this was a dream . . . and it wasn't a dream. If I were religious in the sense that I had set out to be when I entered the rabbinate, I would call it a revelation. I had entered what the sages called *Pardes*, which means orchard, or Paradise. Ah, irony of ironies, that revelation would come to me on the mountain of graves. The Talmud tells the story of the four rabbis who entered Pardes: Ben Azzai, Ben Zoma, Ben Abuyah, and the great Rabbi Akiba. (Of course, it's not the Talmud that tells the story. But for Jews the Talmud is like a person; when we read the sages in this tractate or that, it is as if the Talmud itself is talking.) They all entered Pardes through their dreams, which took the form of fiery chariots. Akiba said to the other travellers, "Don't be distracted, lest you lose yourselves," but Ben Azzai looked about and lost his soul, Ben Zoma lost his way, and Ben Abuyah became an apostate. Only Rabbi Akiba entered in peace and departed with his life.

I'm certainly no Akiba, or Ben Zoma — perhaps a Ben Abuyah, God forbid — but here I was in the dream that was not a dream. Like them I had, indeed, jumped the road; and this time without Tahlmeade's help. If Tahlmeade was worth his robes, he would be searching for me frantically right now. But I had learned a few more things, and I wouldn't let him in.

Here I sat in the Valley of Creation beside a fairy chimney the colour of chalk, facing the stone chimeras and the city of death hollowed out of the cliffs. The chimeras rose above me like Incan cenotaphs, huge and stylised and not yet worn smooth by the turbulent elements. The sky was clear, washed of clouds, and the cliffs stood sharply against it. It was cold, but I felt nothing of the physical senses: wind was an idea, sight a shadow, voice an abstraction.

And as I sat facing death, listening to the instructions of dead martyrs, the collective unconscious of the Ulimite Jewish race, I watched the glowing tigers, the *N'már*, padding around me, sniffing the air. They were frustrated, for although they could see me, they couldn't detect my essence.

You see, Tahlmeade hadn't told me that the tigers could not be seen by *most* people. That was their defence mechanism. But through the eons there were those who had learned to see them . . . who saw them as souls glowing in the light. Who worshipped them and learned to use them as familiars.

Just so had Tahlmeade, who had inherited the second sight and the mantle of the Tzaddik, learned to use them to protect those in his charge: all the Jews. He had learned from his father, who had learned from *his* father.

Thus, Jews had become like the *N'már*.

Invisible.

Invulnerable . . . for how can you kill what you can't see?

A tiger stood before me, gazing at me, as I gazed at him. The creature seemed to draw my essence through its burning eyes, and I had to anchor myself to my own reality — to my past and present, or I would become another Rabbi Ben Azzai, who lost his soul in Pardes.

But as I stared into those numinous eyes, I drew the creature to *me*. I took its habits and its tricks of evolution.

And I knew then what I had to do.

I met Tahlmeade in the *bais medrash* after sunset: the conclusion of the Sabbath. The *bais medrash*, which means "House of Study", was a small room in the Synagogue, It had a high ceiling and long narrow windows, which let in the hazy starglow. I could see comets raining like fire through the narrow slats.

We both sat across from each other at a study table piled with ancient books and interactives that rested inches above the tables like rectangular clouds.

"I looked for you during the afternoon," Tahlmeade said, touching an interactive, which spoke and shivered into being, becoming its subject: another touch and it would transform the entire room into a mnemonic of the twentieth century mystical text *Sh'ar Hayichud* by Rabbi Dov Ber of Lubavitch. Tahlmeade withdrew his finger and the interactive dissolved into its former state. "It seems that you have become quite efficient at Jumping the Road, Rebbe."

"You are a good teacher."

"Ah, so your Tzaddik told you that I gave you an initial push to get you started."

"He did," I said.

"Then you believe?"

"Only after you pulled the entire congregation into your dream this afternoon."

"But *you* were not pulled into our dream," Tahlmeade said. "Why?"

"Do you think that I have some great strength that I was not sucked into your dream?" I asked. "I could see into your dream, and it frightened me. But then I am not a courageous man. No, Rebbe, I simply dreamed my *own* dream. The Valley of Creation drew me to itself, the souls of your martyrs — of our martyrs — drew me to them. It was the power of the dead. They snatched me into their dream before you could carry me into yours."

"So you chose death."

"It wasn't a matter of choice, Rebbe." I paused, and then said, "But I know what you have done."

Tahlmeade looked at me intently and nodded his head slightly as he read my thoughts, my memories. "So you know the *N'már*. You have seen the tigers."

I nodded

"And you have spoken to the dead."

"I heard voices," I said. "Perhaps I heard the tigers, perhaps they've absorbed —"

"You are a strange creature, Rebbe," Tahlmeade said. "You disbelieve your own senses because they conflict with your preconceptions. You spoke to the dead. You spoke to the tigers. Now you know."

"And you know what I must do."

"You wish to give us up, to reveal us to the world."

"You have not only hidden yourselves," I said. "You have taken the Gentiles' souls from them; you have taken their religion, their spirit."

"We simply concealed ourselves," Tahlmeade said.

"No, you did *more* than that. You stole from them. You took revenge. You've —" I paused, searching for words. "It's very much like murder."

"No, Rebbe, it was *they* who murdered us. We have blinded them, perhaps, but no more than that."

"And would you blind them unto the fourth generation?" I asked "Until they became machines? When would you stop? When would you stop being afraid? When there were no more Gentiles left alive . . .?" Tahlmeade did not answer, so I continued; after all, I have a reputation for stuffing my feet into my mouth, for speaking when listening would be a *mitzvah*, a judicious act of kindness. "You have robbed them," I said, quoting *Tosefta Baba Kamma*: "It's a more heinous crime for a Jew to rob a Gentile than a Jew, for such a crime involves the desecration of the Name. And does not the *Sefer Hasidim* say, 'If a Jew attempts to kill a Gentile, help the Gentile'? You must stop dreaming their souls away, Tahlmeade. You must return to the world."

"You, who believes that the Holocaust has rendered all traditional doctrine absurd ... *you* are quoting *Tosefta Baba Kamma* and *Sefer Hasidim* to me? You, who cannot even find his *own* faith, you would preach to *me* in the words of the sages?" Tahlmeade smiled at me, showing small, even teeth: an expression of pure hatred. "The Gentiles will only kill us again," he said in a soft voice, as if he were teaching a child.

"You are killing *yourselves* by robbing *them*. My hypocrisy or lack of faith will not change that."

"We will not submit to them," Tahlmeade said. "We will not allow another Holocaust, another Valley of Creation."

I pushed myself away from the table and stood up.

"I cannot let you leave, Rebbe."

"You cannot stop me," I said; and I allowed myself to dream the beast, the tiger, the *N'már*. I would jump the road. I would leave this place in the time it takes a hummingbird to flap its wings. And Tahlmeade would not find me, just as he had not been able to find me when I was in the Valley of Creation. I had learned from the beasts ... just as Tahlmeade had, and as his father before him.

I could be as invisible as the Jews of Ulim.

I slipped into a dream, a dream of glowing tigers, and I imagined myself ... away. But I was lead. I was all mass, as heavy as any body without its root, without its soul.

And Tahlmeade could see me, as I could see him. We could not disappear from each other's sight. We could not escape each other's grasp. Tahlmeade stared into me like fire, for he was fire. He was the tiger, the beast.

And the *bais medrash* began to burn with a cold light.

As stars fell by outside the windows.

* * *

Tahlmeade and I were locked claw to claw, eye to eye, in mortal combat.

Whosoever would let go — let down his guard — would suffer. We two were tigers fighting in a dream — *N'már* — each caught in the grip of the other. Our eyes were our weapons, for they are the mirrors of the soul. Tahlmeade and I fought and burned. I tried to pull away, to disappear, to jump the road, to escape. But Tahlmeade was like my own thought, my own volition, myself.

It was a stalemate.

I remembered being in the Valley of Creation and staring at the tiger. As he gazed at me, so had I gazed at *him*; and he tried to draw my essence into his burning eyes. Eyes of fire, of sleep, of dream, of loss, of perdition. So it was now, except Tahlmeade was no *N'már*. He was much, much stronger.

He drew me into his eyes, into his dream . . .

As I drew him into mine.

And yet, for all this wrestling of souls and minds, we were sitting quietly at the study table in the *bais medrash*: two Jews staring each other down. Two Jews trying to jump the road, trying to escape each other by any means possible.

But we found ourselves jumping the road *together*, as if we had but one will . . . as if our two dreams had suddenly merged into one, and the one became a chariot, the same chariot that Ezekiel had seen in a vision. In just such a chariot had the four sages — Ben Azzai, Ben Zoma, Ben Abuyah, and Akiba — entered Paradise.

We were hurled like a meteor into the darkness.

And a voice said, "How dare you disgrace yourselves before this court! Stop fighting! Immediately!"

It sounded like my Tzaddik.

I was not surprised to find that it *was*.

Tahlmeade stood beside me; before us were the Tzaddik and two other men.

I had been here before when I jumped the road and met the Tzaddik. We were in the courtyard of a ruined temple, a synagogue. The air was warm and full of moisture, and the sun was high in the sky. I thought I was back in the Tzaddik's dream, in Philadelphia, but he corrected my thoughts and revealed that we were not in our own time, or place. We were in Judea, in a place called *Benei Berak*, and we were standing before the judges of a *Bais Din*: a Rabbinical Court. The Tzaddik and two other men who were as old as me — as old as the sand itself — sat upon cushions, which faced east, the direction of prayer. They sat, and we stood, upon cracked and crumbling stone. Although I did not know the other two men, I knew the seating arrangements for a *Bais Din*: the one who sat in the centre — who leaned forward — as if to hear every word, even when nothing was being said, was the *Nasi*, the big shot: the president of the Court. The Tzaddik and the other rabbi were his deputies.

They were certainly all Tzaddiks, all saints. They all clucked their tongues and shook their heads as we stood before them.

"You should be ashamed," the *Nasi* said to us. "You are learned men, not brawlers."

"To be one is to be the other," I said, but the Tzaddiks were not receptive to my wit.

Tahlmeade began to speak, but the *Nasi* interrupted him and said, "All has been decided. You will do as Rebbe Isaac ibn Chabib asks. We sent him to you. You received him. Now let him liberate you."

"*Avol* —" Tahlmeade began to say, which was "but" in Hebrew.

"There is no argument, Rebbe," the *Nasi* said to Tahlmeade.

Tahlmeade stood rigid as a bar mitzvah boy saying the blessings in front of an entire congregation. He smiled, but would not go against the decision of a *Bais Din*.

Perhaps the Tzaddiks misunderstood his expression of hatred and frustration and anger, for they smiled back at him.

On second thought, perhaps they did understand.

So even if Jumping the Road wasn't a dream but a form of revelation, we would dream ourselves back to *Ulim* in a fiery chariot. (After all, rabbis are naturally a grandiloquent and flamboyant lot.)

But before I departed, I asked the *Nasi* one question: "Who are you Rebbe?"

"Elazar ben Azaryah Akiba," he said, leaning toward me.

Rabbi Akiba . . .?

"But don't worry, Isaac," he said. "You're not in Paradise."

So now . . . we shall see what we shall see.

The Ulimite Gentiles will soon be able to remember . . . to hear the voices of their Gods and consciences again. What will their voices tell them to do?

Who can know? (Well, perhaps Rabbi Akiba knows, but the rest of us *potzers* — those of us who barely manage to get by — we'll just have to take our chances.) Even if we are to be slaughtered in the next generation, even if we will have to become invisible again, even if we have to fight like animals, we will live *today*. We *will* endure.

And as for myself —

I decided to stay right here and see this thing through.

So do I believe in miracles?

Do I believe in God?

Perhaps it is enough to say that I believe in *Shabbos*. I believe in its bready tastes, its music and spicy smells. When the candles flicker and gutter like life itself, when the kiddish cups glisten and the stars fall into the night like fireworks, I can feel *something*... the Queen Bride of the Sabbath... the *Shekhinah*, which is the holy presence, the second soul we are given for but one day a week. And then I, too, can taste *Pardes*... Paradise.

And after all, if *I* can be a Tzaddik, then who am I to doubt the Creator?

BLIND SHEMMY

● ●

After covering the burning and sacking of the Via Roma in Naples, Carl Pfeiffer, a famous newsfax reporter, could not resist his compulsion to gamble. He telephoned Joan Otur, one of his few friends, and insisted that she accompany him to Paris.

Organ-gambling was legal in France.

They dropped from the sky in a transparent Plasticine egg, and Paris opened up below them, Paris and the glittering chip of diamond that was the Casino Bellecour.

Except for the dymaxion dome of the Right Bank, Joan would not have been able to distinguish Paris from the suburbs beyond. A city had grown over the city: The grid of the ever-expanding slung city had its own constellations of light and hid Haussmann's ruler-straight boulevards, the ancient architectural wonders, even the black, sour-stenched Seine, which was an hourglass curve dividing the old city.

Their transpod settled to the ground like a dirty snowflake and split silently open, letting in the chill night air with its acrid smells of mudflats and cinders and clogged drains. Joan and Pfeiffer hurried across the transpad toward the high oaken doors of the casino. All around them stretched the bleak, brick-and-concrete wastelands of the city's ruined districts, the fetid warrens on the dome's peripheries, which were inhabited by skinheads and

Screamers who existed outside the tightly controlled structure of Uptown life. Now, as Pfeiffer touched his hand to a palm-plate sensor, the door opened and admitted them into the casino itself. The precarious outside world was closed out and left behind.

A young man, who reminded Joan of an upright (if possible) Bedlington terrier, led them through the courtyard. He spoke with a clipped English accent and had tufts of woolly, bluish-white hair inplanted all over his head, face, and body. Only his hands and genitals were hairless.

"He *has* to be working off an indenture," Pfeiffer said sharply as he repressed a sexual urge.

"Shush," Joan said, as the boy gave Pfeiffer a brief, contemptuous look — in Parisian culture, you paid for the service, not for the smile.

They were led into a simple, but formal, entry lounge, which was crowded, but not uncomfortable. The floor was marbled; a few pornographic icons were discreetly situated around the carefully laid-out comfort niches. The room reminded Joan of a chapel with arcades, figures, and stone courts. Above was a dome, from which radiated a reddish, suffusing light, lending the room an expansiveness of height rather than breadth.

But it was mostly holographic illusion.

They were directed to wait a moment and then presented to the purser, an overweight, balding man who sat behind a small desk. He was dressed in a blue camise shirt and matching caftan, which was buttoned across his wide chest and closed with a red scarf. He was obviously, and uncomfortably, dressed in the colours of the establishment.

"And good evening, Monsieur Pfeiffer and Mademoiselle Otur. We are honoured to have such an important guest, or guests, I should say." The purser slipped two cards into a small console. "Your identification cards will be returned to you when you leave." After a pause he asked, "Ah, does Monsieur Pfeiffer wish the lady to be credited on his card?" The purser lowered his eyes, indicating embarrassment. Quite simply, Joan did not have enough credit to be received into the more sophisticated games.

"Yes, of course," Pfeiffer said absently. He felt guilty and anxious about feeling a thrill of desire for that grotesque boy.

"Well, then," said the purser, folding his hands on the desk, "we are at your disposal for as long as you wish to stay with us." He gestured toward the terrier and said, "Johnny will give you the tour," but Pfeiffer politely declined.

Johnny ushered them into a central room, which was anything but quiet, and — after a wink at Pfeiffer — discreetly disappeared.

The room was as crowded as the city ways. It was filled with what looked to be the ragtag, the bums and the street people, the captains of the ways. Here was a perfect replica of a street casino, but perfectly safe. This *was* a street casino, at least to Pfeiffer, who was swept up in the noise and bustle, as he whetted his appetite for the dangerous pleasures of the top level.

Ancient iron bandits whispered "chink-chinka" and rolled their picture-frame eyes in promise of a jackpot, which was immediately transferred to the winner's account by magnetic sleight of hand. The amplified, high-pitched voices of pinball computers on the walls called out winning hands of poker and blackjack. A simulated stabbing drew nothing more than a few glances. Tombstone booths were filled with figures working through their own Stations of the Cross. Hooked-in winners were rewarded with bursts of electrically induced ecstacy; losers writhed in pain and suffered through the brain-crushing aftershock of week-long migraines.

And, of course, battered robots clattered around with the traditional complement of drugs, drink, and food. The only incongruity was a perfectly dressed geisha, who quickly disappeared into one of the iris doors on the far wall.

"Do you want to play the one-armed bandits?" Joan asked, fighting her growing claustrophobia, wishing only to escape into quiet; but she was determined to try to keep Pfeiffer from going upstairs. Yet ironically — all her emotions seemed to be simultaneously yin and yang — she also wanted him to gamble away his organs. She knew that she would feel a guilty thrill if he lost his heart. Then she pulled down the lever of the one-armed bandit; it would read her finger- and odor-prints and transfer or deduct the proper amount to or from Pfeiffer's account. The eyes rolled and clicked and one hundred international credit dollars was lost. "Easy come, easy go. At least, this is a safe way to go. But you didn't come here to be safe, right?" Joan said mockingly.

"You can remain down here, if you like," Pfeiffer said, looking about the room for an exit, noticing that iris doors were spaced every few meters on the nearest wall to his left. *The casino must take up the whole bloody block,* he thought. "How the hell do I get out of here?"

Before Joan could respond, Johnny appeared, as if out of nowhere, and said, "Monsieur Pfeiffer may take any one of the ascenseurs, or, if he would care for the view of our palace, he could take the staircase to heaven." He smiled, baring even teeth, and curtsied to Pfeiffer, who was blushing. The boy certainly knows his man, Joan thought sourly.

Am I jealous? She asked herself. She cared for Pfeiffer, but didn't *love* him — at least she didn't think she did.

"Shall I attend you?" Johnny asked Pfeiffer, ignoring Joan.

"No," said Pfeiffer. "Now please leave us alone."

"Well, which is it?" asked Joan. "The elevator would be quickest, zoom you right to the organ room."

"We can take the stairs," Pfeiffer said, a touch of blush still in his cheeks. But he would say nothing about the furry boy. "Jesus, it seems that every time I blink my eye, the stairway disappears."

"I'll show you the way," Joan said, taking his arm.

"Just what I need," Pfeiffer said, smiling, eliminating one small barrier between them.

"I think your rush is over, isn't it? You don't really want to gamble out your guts."

"I came to do something, and I'll follow it through."

The stairwell was empty and, like an object conceived in Alice's Wonderland, it appeared to disappear behind them. "Cheap tricks," Pfeiffer said.

"Why are you so intent on this?" Joan asked. "If you lose, which you most probably will, you'll never have a day's peace. They can call in your heart, or liver, or —"

"I can buy out, if that should happen." Pfeiffer reddened, but it had nothing to do with his conversation with Joan, to which he was hardly paying attention; he was still thinking about the furry boy.

"You wouldn't gamble them, if you thought you could buy out. That's bunk."

"Then I'd get artificials."

"You'd be taking another chance, with the quotas — thanks to your right-wing friends in power."

Pfeiffer didn't take the bait. "I admit defeat," he said. Again he thought of the furry boy's naked, hairless genitals. And with that came the thought of death.

The next level was less crowded and more subdued. There were few electronic games to be seen on the floor. A man passed dressed in medical white, which indicated that deformation games were being played. On each floor the stakes became increasingly higher; fortunes were lost, people were disfigured or ruined but — with the exception of the top floor, which had dangerous games other than organ-gambling — at least no one died. They might need a face and body job after too many deformations, but those were easily obtained, although one had to have very good credit to ensure a proper job.

On each ascending level, the house whores, both male and female, became more exotic, erotic, grotesque, and abundant. There were birdmen with feathers like peacocks and flamingos, children with dyed skin and overly large, implanted male and female genitalia, machines that spoke the language of love and exposed soft, fleshy organs, amputees and cripples, various drag queens and kings, natural androgynes and mutants, cyborgs, and an interesting, titillating array of genetically engineered mooncalves.

But none disturbed Pfeiffer as had that silly furry boy. He wondered if, indeed, the boy was still following him.

"Come on, Joan" Pfeiffer said impatiently. "I really don't want to waste any more time down here."

"I thought it was the expectation that's so exciting to seasoned gamblers," Joan said.

"Not to me," Pfeiffer said, ignoring the sarcasm. "I want to get it over with." With that, he left the room.

Then why bother at all? Joan asked herself, wondering why she had let Pfeiffer talk her into coming here. *He doesn't need me. Damn him,* she thought, ignoring a skinny, white-haired man and a piebald, doggie mooncalf coupling beside her in an upright position.

She took a lift to the top level to be with Pfeiffer.

It was like walking into the foyer of a well-appointed home. The high walls were stucco and the floor was inlaid parquet. A small Dehaj rug was placed neatly before a desk, behind which beamed a man of about fifty dressed in camise and caftan.

He had a flat face, a large nose that was wide, but had narrow nostrils, and close-set eyes roofed with bushy, brown eyebrows, the colour his hair would have been, had he had any.

Actually, the room was quite small, which made the rug look larger and gave the man a commanding position.

"Do you wish to watch or participate, Monsieur Pfeiffer?" he asked, seeming to rise an inch from the chair as he spoke.

"I wish to play," Pfeiffer said, standing upon the rug as if he had to be positioned just right to make it fly.

"And does your friend wish to watch?" the man asked, as Joan crossed the room to stand beside Pfeiffer. "Or will you give your permission for Miz Otur to become telepathically connected to you." His voice didn't rise as he asked the question.

"I beg your pardon?"

"A psyconnection, sir. With a psyconductor" — a note of condescension crept into his voice.

"I *know* what it is, and I don't want it," Pfeiffer snapped and then moved away from Joan. But a cerebral hook-in was, in fact, just what Joan had hoped for.

"Oh, come on," Joan said. "Let me in."

"Are you serious?" he asked, turning toward her. Caught by the intensity of his stare, she could only nod. "Then I'm sorry. I'm not a window for you to stare through."

That stung her, and she retorted, "Have you ever done it with your wife?" She immediately regretted her words.

The man at the desk cleared his throat politely. "Excuse me, monsieur, but are you aware that *only* games *organe* are played in these rooms?"

"Yes, that's why I've come to your house."

"Then, you are perhaps not aware that all our games are conducted with psyconductors on this floor."

Pfeiffer, looking perplexed, said, "Perhaps you had better explain it to me."

"Of course, of course," the man said, beaming, as if he had just won the battle and a fortune. "There are, of course, many ways to play, and, if you like, I can give you the address of a very nice house nearby where you can play a fair, safe game without hook-ins. Shall I make a reservation for you there?"

"Not just yet," Pfeiffer said, resting his hands, knuckles down, upon the flat-top Louise XVI desk.

His feet seemed to be swallowed by the floral patterns of the rug, and Joan thought it an optical illusion, this effect of being caught before the desk of the casino captain. She felt the urge to grab Pfeiffer and take him out of this suffocating place.

Instead, she walked over to him. Perhaps he would relent just a little and let her slide into his mind.

"It is one of our house rules, however," said the man at the desk, "that you and your opponent, or opponents, must be physically in the same room."

"Why is that?" Joan asked, feeling Pfeiffer scowling at her for intruding.

"Well," he said, "it has never happened to us, of course, but cheating has occurred on a few long-distance transactions. Organs have been wrongly lost. So we don't take any chances. None at all." He looked at Pfeiffer as he spoke, obviously sizing him up, watching for reactions. But Pfeiffer had composed himself, and Joan knew that he had made up his mind.

"Why must the game be played with psyconductors?" Pfeiffer asked.

"That is the way we do it," said the captain. Then, after an embarrassing pause, he said, "We have our own games and rules. And our games, we think, are the *most* interesting. And we make the games as safe as we can for all parties involved."

"What do you mean?"

"We — the house — will be observing you. Our gamesmaster will be telepathically hooked in, but, I assure you, you will not sense his presence in the least. If anything should go wrong, or look as if it might go wrong, then *pfft*, we intercede. Of course, we make no promises, and there have been cases where —"

"But anything that could go wrong would be because of the cerebral hook-in."

"Perhaps this *isn't* the game for you, sir."

"You must have enough privileged information on everyone who has ever played here to make book," Pfeiffer said.

"The hook-in doesn't work that way at all. And besides, we are contract-bound to protect our clients."

"And yourselves."

"Most certainly." The casino captain looked impatient.

"If both players can read each other's mind," Pfeiffer said to the captain, "then there can be no blind cards."

"Aha, now you have it, monsieur." At that, the tension between Pfeiffer and the desk captain seemed to dissolve. "And, indeed," the captain continued, "we have a modified version of chemin de fer, which we call blind shemmy. All the cards are played facedown. It is a game of control (and, of course, chance), for you must block out certain thoughts from your mind, while, at the same time, tricking your opponent into revealing his cards. And that is why it would be advantageous for you to let your friend here connect with you."

Pfeiffer glanced toward Joan and said, "Please clarify that."

"Quite simply, while you are playing, your friend could help block your thoughts from your opponent with her own," said the captain. "But it does take some practice. Perhaps, it would be better if you tried a hook-in in one of our other rooms, where the stakes are not quite so high." Then the captain lowered his eyes, as if in deference, but 'in actuality he was looking at the CeeR screen of the terminal set into the antique desk.

Joan could see Pfeiffer's nostrils flare slightly. *The poor sonofabitch is caught,* she thought. "Come on, Carl, let's get out of here now."

"Perhaps you should listen to Miss Otur," the captain said, but the man must have known that he had Pfeiffer.

"I wish to play blind shemmy," Pfeiffer said, turning toward Joan, glaring at her. She caught her breath: If he lost, then she knew he would make certain that Joan lost something, too.

"I have a game of nine in progress," the captain said. "There are nine people playing and nine others playing interference. But you'll have to wait for a space. It will be quite expensive, as the players are tired and will demand some of your points for themselves above the casino charge for the play."

"How long will I have to wait."

The captain shrugged, then said, "I have another man waiting, who is ahead of you. He would be willing to play a game of doubles. I would recommend you play him rather than wait. Like you, he is an amateur, but his wife, who will be connected with him, is not. Of course, if you wish to wait for the other . . ."

Pfeiffer accepted, and while he and Joan gave their prints to the various forms, the captain explained that there was no statute of limitations on the contract signed by all parties, and that it would be honoured even by those governments that disapprove of this particular form of gambling.

Then the furry boy appeared like an apparition to take them to their room where they would be given time to practice and become acquainted.

The boy's member was slightly engorged, and Pfeiffer now became frightened. He suddenly thought of his mother and the obligatory hook-in service at her funeral. His skin crawled as he remembered her last filthy thoughts . . .

The furry boy led Joan and Pfeiffer into the game room, which smelled of oiled wood, spices, traditional tobacco, and perfume. There were no holos or decoration on the walls. Everything, with the exception of the felt top of the gaming table, cards, thick natural carpet, computer consoles, and cowls, was made of precious woods: oak, elm, cedar, teak, walnut, mahogany, redwood, ebony. The long, half-oval gaming table, which met the sliding partition wall, was made of satinwood, as were the two delicate, but uncomfortable, high-backed chairs placed side by side. On the table before each chair was a psyconductor cowl, each one sheathed in a light, silvery mask.

"We call them poker-faces," the boy said to Pfeiffer, as he placed the cowl over Joan's head. He explained how the psyconductor mechanism worked, then asked Pfeiffer if he wished him to stay.

"Why should I want you to stay?" Pfeiffer asked, but the sexual tension between them was unmistakable.

"I'm adept at games of chance. I can redirect your thoughts — without a psyconductor." He looked at Joan and smiled.

"Put the mechanism on my head and then please leave us," Pfeiffer said.

"Do you wish me to return when you're finished?"

"If you wish," Pfeiffer replied stiffly, and Joan watched his discomfort. Without saying a word, she had won a small victory.

The boy lowered the cowl over Pfeiffer's head, made some unnecessary adjustments, and left reluctantly.

"I'm not at all sure that I want to do this," Pfeiffer mumbled, faltering.

"Well," Joan said, "we can easily call off the game. Our first connection is just practice —"

"I don't mean the game. I mean the psyconnection."

Joan remained silent. Dammit, she told herself. I should have looked away when Pfeiffer's furry pet made a pass at him.

"I was crazy to agree to such a thing in the first place."

"Shall I leave?" Joan asked. "It was *you* who insisted that I come along, remember?" She stood up, but did not judge the distance of the cowl/console connections accurately, and the cowl was pulled forward, bending the silvery mask.

"I think you're as nervous as I am," Pfeiffer said appeasingly.

"Make the connection, right now. Or let's get out of here." Joan was suddenly angry and frustrated. *Do it,* she thought to herself, and for once she was not passive. Certainly not passive. *Damn him and his furry boy!* She snapped the wooden toggle switch, activating both psyconductors, and was thrust into vertiginous light. It surrounded her, as if she could see in all directions at once. But she was simply seeing through Pfeiffer's eyes. Seeing herself, small, even in his eyes, small.

After the initial shock, she realised that the light was not brilliant; on the contrary, it was soft and diffused.

But this was no connection at all: Pfeiffer was trying to close his mind to her. He appeared before her as a smooth, perfect, huge, sphere. It slowly rotated, a grim, grey planet, closed to her, forever closed . . .

"*Are you happy now?*" asked Pfeiffer, as if from somewhere deep inside the sphere. It was so smooth, seamless. *He really doesn't need me,* she thought, and she felt as if she were flying above the surface of his closed mind, a winged thing looking for any discontinuity, any fault in his defenses. "*So you see,*" Pfeiffer said, exulting in imagined victory, "*I don't need you.*" The words came wreathed in an image of a storm rolling angrily over the planet.

She flew, in sudden panic, around his thoughts, like an insect circling a source of light. She was looking for any blister or crack, any anomaly in the smooth surface. He would gamble his body away without her, that she knew, unless she could break through his defenses, prove to him how vulnerable he really was.

"*So you couldn't resist the furry boy, could you?*" Joan asked, her thoughts like smooth sharks swimming through icy water. "*Does he, then, remind you of yourself, or do I remind you of your mother?*"

His anger and exposed misery were like flares on the surface of the sun. In their place remained an eruption on Pfeiffer's smooth protective surface. A crack in the cerebral egg.

Joan dove towards the fissure, and then she was inside Pfeiffer — not the outside of his senses where he could verbalise a thought, see a face, but in the dark, prehistoric places where he dreamed, conceptualised, where he floated in and out of memory, where the eyeless creatures of his soul dwelled.

It was a sliding, a slipping in, as if one had turned over inside oneself; and Joan was sliding, slipping on ice. She found herself in a dark world of grotesque and geometric shapes, an arctic world of huge icebergs floating on a fathomless sea.

And for an instant, Joan sensed Pfeiffer's terrible fear of the world.

"*Mindfucker!*" Pfeiffer screamed, projecting the word in a hundred filthy, sickening images; and then he smashed through Joan's defenses and rushed into the deep recesses of her mind. He found her soft places and took what he could.

All that before the psyconnection was broken. Before the real game began. As if nothing had happened.

A man and woman, wearing identical cowled masks, sat across from Joan and Pfeiffer. The partition wall had been slid back, revealing the oval shape of the gaming table and doubling the size of the woodpanelled room. The dealer and the gamesmaster sat on each side of the long table between the opponents. The dealer was a young man with an intense, roundish face and straight black hair cut at the shoulders; he was most likely in training to become a gamesmaster.

The gamesmaster's face was hidden by a black cowl; he would be hooked in to the game. He explained the rules, activated the psyconductors, and the game began. Joan and Pfeiffer were once again hooked in, but there was no contact, as yet, with the man and woman across the table.

Pfeiffer cleared his mind, just as if he were before lasers or giving an interview. He had learned to cover his thoughts, for, somehow, he had always felt they could be seen, especially by those who wanted to hurt him politically and on the job.

White thought, he called it, because it was similar to white noise.

Pfeiffer could feel Joan circling around him like the wind. Although he couldn't conceal everything, he could hide from her. He could use her, just as she could use him . . . had used him. They had reached an accord via mutual blackmail. Somehow, during their practice hook-in, Joan had forced herself into Pfeiffer's mind; shocked, he attacked her.

So now they knew each other better.

They built a simply symbol structure: He was in the world, a perfect sphere without blemish, made by God's own hands, a world as strong and divine as thought; and she was his atmosphere. She contained all the elements that could not exist on his featureless surface. She was the protective cloak of his world.

They built a mnemonic in which to hide, yet they were still vulnerable to each other. But Pfeiffer guessed that Joan would remain passive — after all, she always had. She also had the well-developed conscience of a mystical liberal, and she was in love with him. He had seen that — or thought he had.

She would not expose him to danger.

Pfeiffer congratulated himself for being calm, which reinforced his calmness. Perhaps it was Joan's presence. Perhaps it was the mnemonic. But perhaps not. He had the willpower; this was just another test. He had managed to survive all the others, he told himself.

Joan rained on him, indicating her presence, and they practised talking within geometric shapes as a protective device — it was literally raining geodesic cats and dogs.

When the gamesmaster opened the psyconductor to all involved, Joan and Pfeiffer were ready.

But they were not ready to find exact duplicates of themselves facing them across the table. The doppelgängers, of course, were not wearing cowls.

"First, mesdames and messieurs, we draw the wager," said the dealer, who was not hooked in. The gamesmaster's thoughts were a neutral presence. "For each organ pledged, there will be three games consisting of three hands to a game," continued the dealer. "In the event that a player wins twice in succession, the third hand or game will not be played." His voice was an intrusion; it was harsh and cold and came from the outside where everything was hard and intractable.

"*How do they know what we look like?*" Pfeiffer asked, shaken by the hallucination induced by his opponents.

But before Joan could reply, he answered his own question. "*They must be picking up subliminal stuff.*"

"*The way we perceive ourselves,*" Joan said. The doppelgängers became hard and ugly, as if they were being eroded by time. And Joan's double was becoming smaller, insignificant.

"*If we can't cover up, we won't have a chance.*"

"*You can't cover everything, but neither can they.*" Joan said. "*It cuts both ways.*" She noticed a fissure in the otherwise perfect sphere below, and she became black fog, miasma, protective covering. Pfeiffer was afraid and vulnerable. But she had to give him credit: He was not hiding it from her, at least. That was a beginning . . .

"*Did you pick up anything from them, an image, anything?*" Pfeiffer asked.

"*We've been too busy with ourselves. We'll just wait and be ready when they let something slip out.*"

"*Which they will,*" Pfeiffer said, suddenly confident again.

From deep inside their interior, symbolised world, Joan and Pfeiffer could look into the external world of croupier, felt-top table, cards, wood-covered walls, and masked creatures. This room was simply a stage for the play of thought and image.

Pfeiffer was well acquainted with this sensation of perceiving two worlds, two levels: inside and outside. He often awakened from a nightmare and found himself in his living room or library. He knew that he was wide awake, and yet he could still see the dream unfurl before him, watch the creatures of his nightmare stalk about the room — the interior beasts let loose into the familiar, comforting confines of his waking world. Those were always moments of terror, for surely he was near the edge then . . . and could fall.

The dealer combined two decks of cards and placed them in a shoe, a box from which the cards could be slid out one by one. He discarded three cards: the traditional burning of the deck.

Then he dealt a card to Pfeiffer and one to his opponent. Both cards landed face up. A queen of hearts for Pfeiffer. A nine of hearts for his opponent.

So Pfeiffer lost the right to call the wager.

Just as the object of blackjack was to draw cards that add up to twenty-one, or as near to that figure as possible, the object of blind shemmy was to draw cards that add up to nine. Thus, face cards, which would normally be counted as ten, were counted as zero. Aces, normally counted as eleven, became one; and all other cards had their normal pip (or face) value, with the exception of tens, which, like aces, were counted as one.

"Monsieur Deux wins, nine over zero," said the dealer, looking now at Pfeiffer's opponent. Pfeiffer was Monsieur Un and his opponent Monsieur Deux only because of their positions at the table.

"*A hell of a way to start,*" Pfeiffer said.

"*Keep yourself closed,*" Joan said, turning into mist, then dark rain, pure sunlight and rainbows, a perceptual kaleidoscope to conceal Pfeiffer from his enemies. "*Look now, he'll be more vulnerable when he speaks. I'll cover you.*"

"*Your choice,*" said the gamesmaster. The thought was directed to Pfeiffer's opponent, who was staring intently at Pfeiffer.

"*Look now,*" Joan said to Pfeiffer.

"Since we both turned up hearts, perhaps that is where we should begin." Pfeiffer's opponent said, speaking for the benefit of the dealer. His words felt like shards of glass to Pfeiffer. "They're the seats of our emotions: so we'd best dispose of them quickly." Pfeiffer felt the man smile. "Do you assent?"

"It's your choice." Pfeiffer said to the dealer tonelessly.

"*Don't let anything out,*" Joan said.

Pfeiffer couldn't pick up anything from his opponent and the woman with him; they were both empty doppelgängers of himself and Joan, "*Pretend that nothing matters,*" she said. "*If you expect to see his cards and look inside of him for weakness, you must be removed.*"

She's right. Pfeiffer thought. He tried to relax, smooth himself down: he thought innocuous white thoughts and ignored the knot of anxiety that seemed to be pulling at his groin.

"*Cartes,*" said the dealer, dealing two cards from the shoe, face down, one for Pfeiffer, the other for his opponent. Another two cards, and then a palpable silence; not even thoughts seemed to cut the air. It was an unnatural waiting . . .

Pfeiffer had a natural nine, a winning hand (a queen and a nine of diamonds), and he looked up, about to turn over his cards, when he saw the furry boy sitting across the table from him.

"What the hell —"

"*Call your hand,*" Joan said, feeling his glands open up, a warm waterfall of fear. But before Pfeiffer could speak, his opponent said, "My friend across the table has a natural nine. A queen and a nine, both diamonds. Since I called his hand — and I believe I am correct, then . . ."

The dealer turned Pfeiffer's cards over and said, "Monsieur Deux is correct, and wins by call." If Pfeiffer's opponent had been mistaken about the hand, Pfeiffer would have won automatically, even if his opponent had better cards.

The dealer then dealt two more cards from the shoe.

"*You're supposed to be covering my thoughts,*" Pfeiffer said, but he was composed, thinking white thoughts again.

"*I'm trying,*" Joan said. "*But you won't trust me: you're trying to cover yourself from me as well as your opponent. What the hell am I supposed to do?*"

"*I'm sorry,*" Pfeiffer thought.

"*Are you really so afraid that I'll see your true feelings?*"

"*This is neither the time nor the place.*" His rhythm of white thought was broken; Joan became a snowstorm, aiding him, lulling him back to white blindness. "*I think the gamesmaster is making me nervous, having him hooked in, privy to all our thoughts . . .*"

"*Forget the gamesmaster . . . and for God's sake, stop worrying about what I'll see. I'm on your side.*"

"Monsieur Un, will you *please* claim your cards," said the dealer. The gamesmaster nodded at Pfeiffer and thought neutral, papery thoughts.

Pfeiffer turned up the edges of his cards. He had a jack of diamonds — which counted as zero — and a two of spades. He would need another card.

"*Don't think about your cards,*" Joan exclaimed. "*Are you picking up anything from the other side of the table?*"

Pfeiffer listened, as if to his own thoughts. He didn't raise his head to look at his opponent, for seeing his own face — or that of the furry boy's — staring back at him from across the table was disconcerting, and fascinating. An image of an empty, hollow woman without any organs formed in his mind. He imagined her as a bag somehow formed into human shape.

"*Keep that,*" Joan said. "*It might be usable.*"

"*But I can't see his cards.*"

"*Just wait awhile. Keep calm.*"

"Does Monsieur wish another card?" the dealer asked Pfeiffer. Pfeiffer took another card and so did his opponent.

Pfeiffer had no idea what cards his opponent was holding; it promised to be a blind play. When the cards were turned over, the dealer announced, "Monsieur Deux wins, six over five." Pfeiffer had lost again.

"*I'm playing blind,*" Pfeiffer said anxiously to Joan.

"*He couldn't see your cards, either,*" she replied.

But that gave him little satisfaction, for by losing the first two hands, he had lost the first game.

And if he lost the next game, he would lose his heart, which, white thought or not, seemed to Pfeiffer to be beating in his throat.

"Try to calm yourself," Joan said, *"or you'll let everything out. If you trust me, and stop throwing up your defenses, maybe I can help you. But you've got to let me in; as it is, you're giving our friends quite the edge. Let's make a merger . . . a marriage."* But Pfeiffer was in no mood for irony. His fear was building, steadily, slowly.

"You can fold the game," Joan said. *"That is an alternative."*

"And give up organs I haven't yet played for!" The smooth surface of Pfeiffer's sphere cracked, and Joan let herself be swallowed into it. The surface of the sphere changed, grew mountain chains, lush vegetation, flowers, deserts, all the mingled moods of Joan and Pfeiffer.

Pfeiffer was no longer isolated; he was protected, yet dangerously exposed. Inside him, in the human, moist dark, Joan promised not to take advantage of him. She caught a fleeting thought of Pfeiffer's dead mother, who had been a fleshy, big-boned, flat-faced woman. She also saw that Pfeiffer hated his mother, as much now as when she was alive.

In the next hand — the opening hand of the second game — Pfeiffer held a five of clubs and a two of spades, a total of seven points. He would not take another card unless he could see his opponent's. But when he looked up, Pfeiffer saw the furry boy, who blew him a kiss.

"You're exposed again," Joan said, and they thought themselves inside their world, thought protective darkness around themselves, except for one tiny opening through which to see into their enemies.

"Concentrate on that image of the empty woman," Joan said to Pfeiffer. *"She has to be Monsieur Deux's wife or woman. I can't quite visualise it as you did."* But Pfeiffer was trying to smooth down his emotions and the dark, dangerous demon that was his memory. The image of the furry boy sparked memories, fears, guilts. Pfeiffer remembered his father, who had been a doctor. There was always enough money, but his father extracted emotional dues for every dollar he gave his son. And, as a result, the young Pfeiffer had recurrent nightmares that he was sucking off his father. Those nightmares began again after his mother died: she had seen that homosexual fantasy when Pfeiffer hooked in to her on her deathbed.

Pfeiffer still had those nightmares.

And now, against his will, the image of his sucking off the furry boy passed through his mind, drawing its train of guilt and revulsion. The boy and his father, somehow one and the same.

"You're leaking," Joan said, her thoughts an icestorm. She could see her way into Pfeiffer now, into those rooms of buried memories. Rather than rooms, she thought of them as subterranean caverns; everything inside them was intact, perfect, hidden from the harmful light and atmosphere of consciousness. Now she knew him . . .

Pfeiffer collected himself and peered into his opponent's mind. He thrust the image of the organless woman at the man.

It was like tearing a spiderweb.

Pfeiffer felt the man's pain as a feather touching flesh: The organless woman was Monsieur Deux's permanent wife. Pfeiffer had broken through and into his thoughts; he could feel his opponent's name, something like Gayah, Gahai, Gayet, that was it, and his wife was used up. Gayet saw her, in the darkness of his unconscious, as an empty bag. She was a compulsive gambler, who had spent her organs; and Gayet hated gambling, but she possessed him, and he hated her and loved her, and was just beginning his self-destructive slide.

Now she was using him up. She was gambling his organs.

"She's used up." Pfeiffer thought at Gayet. But Pfeiffer could only glimpse Gayet's thoughts. His wife was not exposed.

Nor was she defenseless.

She thrust the image of the furry boy at Pfeiffer, and Pfeiffer felt his head being forced down upon the furry boy's lap. But it suddenly wasn't the furry boy anymore. It was Pfeiffer's father!

There was no distance now. Pfeiffer was caught, tiny and vulnerable.

Gayet and his wife were swallowing him, thoughts and all.

It was Joan who saved him. She pulled him away, and he became the world again, wrapped in snow, in whiteness. He was safe again, as if inside Joan's cold womb.

"Look now," Joan said an instant later, and like a revelation, Pfeiffer saw Gayet's cards, saw them buried in Gayet's eyes with the image of his aging wife. In that instant, Pfeiffer saw into Gayet and forgot himself. Gayet's wife was named Grace, and she had been eroded from too many surgeries, too

many deformation games. She was his Blue Angel (yes, he had seen the ancient film) and Gayet the fool.

The fool held an ace of hearts and a five of diamonds.

Now Pfeiffer felt that the odds were with him; it was a familiar sensation for gamblers, a sense of harmony, of being a benevolent extension of the cards. No anger, no fear, no hate, just victory. Pfeiffer called Gayet's hand, thereby preventing Gayet from drawing another card, such as a lucky three, which would have given him a count of nine.

Pfeiffer won the hand, and he thanked Joan. His thoughts were of love, but his repertoire of images was limited. Joan was now part of his rhythm and harmony, a constant presence; and she dreamed of the victorious cats that padded so gracefully through the lush vegetation of Pfeiffer's sphere.

The cats that rutted, then devoured one another.

Pfeiffer won the next hand to take the second game. Pfeiffer and his opponent were now even. The next game would determine the outcome. Pfeiffer felt that calm, cold certainty that he would take Gayet's heart. The obsession to expose and ruin his opponent became more important than winning or losing organs; it was bright and fast flowing, refreshing as water.

He was in a better world now, a more complete, fulfilling plane of reality. All gamblers dreamed of this: losing or winning everything, but being inside the game. Even Joan was carried away by the game. She, too, wanted to rend — to whittle away at the couple across the table, take their privacies, turn over their humiliations like worry beads. They were Pfeiffer's enemies . . . and his enemies were her own.

Everyone was exposed now, battleweary, mentally and physically exhausted, yet lost in play, lost in perfect, concentrated time. Pfeiffer could see Gayet's face, both as Gayet saw himself and as Grace saw him. A wide nose, dark complexion, low forehead, large ears; yet it was a strong face, and handsome in a feral, almost frightening way — or so Grace thought. Gayet saw himself as weak; the flesh on his face was too loose.

Gayet was a failure, although he had made his career and fortune in the Exchange. He had wanted to be a mathematician, but he was lazy and lost the "knack" by twenty-five.

Gayet would have made a brilliant mathematician, and he knew it.

And Grace was a whore, using herself and everyone else. Here was a woman with great religious yearnings, who had wanted to join a religious order, but was blackballed by the cults because of her obsession for gambling and psyconductors. But Pfeiffer could see into her only a little. She was a cold bitch and, more than any of the others, had reserves of strength.

This last game would be psychological surgery. Tearing with the knife, pulping with the bludgeon. Pfeiffer won the first hand. This was joy; so many organs to win or lose, so little time.

Pfeiffer lost the next hand, Gayet exposed Joan, who revealed Pfeiffer's cards without realizing it. Gayet had opened her up, penetrated all that efficiency and order to expose anger and lust and uncontrolled oceanic pity. Joan's emotions writhed and crawled over her like beautifully coloured, slippery snakes.

Pfeiffer had been too preoccupied to protect her.

Joan's first uncontrolled thought was to revenge herself on Pfeiffer, expose him; but he opened up to her, buried her in white thought, which was as cold and numbing as ice, and apologised without words, but with the soft, rounded, comforting thoughts he equated with love. She couldn't trust him, nor could she expose him. Right now, she could only accept him.

The dealer gave Pfeiffer a three of diamonds and an ace of clubs. That gave him only four points; he would have to draw again. He kept his thoughts from Joan, for she was covering him. She could attack Gayet and his whore, expose them for their cards. Gayet's heart was not simply his organ — not now, not to Pfeiffer. It was his whole life, life itself. To rip it away from him would be to conquer life, if only for a moment. It was life affirming. It was being alive. Suddenly he thought of his father.

"*Close yourself up*," Joan said. "*You're bleeding.*" She did not try to penetrate his thoughts; that would have exposed Pfeiffer even more dangerously.

"*Help me*," Pfeiffer asked Joan. This hand would determine whether he would win or lose the game . . . and his heart.

Once again she became his cloak, his atmosphere, and she weaved her icy threads of white thought into his.

This was love, she thought.

Pfeiffer couldn't see Gayet's cards and nervously asked Joan to do something. Gayet was playing calmly, well covered by Grace, who simply hid him. No extravagance there.

Joan emptied her mind, became neutral; yet she was a needle of cold, coherent thought. She prodded, probed, touched her opponents' thoughts. It was like swimming through an ever-changing world of dots and bars, tangible as iron, fluid as water. It was as if Gayet's and Grace's thoughts were luminous points on a fluorescent screen.

And still she went unnoticed.

Gayet was like Pfeiffer, Joan thought. Seemingly placid, controlled, but that was all gingerbread to hide a weak house. He was so much weaker than Grace, who was supporting and cloaking him. But Grace was concentrating all her energies on Gayet; and she had the fever, as if she were gambling her own organs once again.

Undoubtedly, Grace expected Joan and Pfeiffer to go straight for Gayet, who had read the cards.

So Joan went for Grace, who was in the gambler's frenzy as the hand was being played. Joan slipped past Grace's thoughts, worked her way into the woman's mind, through the dark labyrinths and channels of her memory, and into the dangerous country of the unconscious. Invisible as air, she listened to Grace, read her, discovered: A sexual miasma. Being brutally raped as a child. After a riot in Manosque. Raped in a closet, for God's sake. The man tore her open with a rifle barrel, then inserted himself. Taking her, piece by bloody piece, just as she was taking Gayet. Just as others had taken her in rooms like this, in this casino, in this closet.

And Gayet, now Joan could see him through Grace, unperturbable Gayet, who had so much money and so little life, who was so afraid of his wife's past, of her lovers and liberations he called perversions. But he called *everything* a perversion.

How she hated him beneath what she called love.

But he looked just like the man who had raped her in that closet so long ago. She could not remember the man's face — so effectively had she blocked it out of her mind — yet she was stunned when she first met Gayet. She felt attracted to him, but also repelled; she was in love.

Through Joan, Pfeiffer saw Gayet's cards; a deuce and a six of clubs. He could call his hand, but he wasn't sure of the deuce. It looked like a heart, but it could just as easily be a diamond. If he called it wrong, he would lose the hand, and his heart.

"*I can't be sure*," Pfeiffer said to Joan, expecting help.

But Joan was in trouble. Grace had discovered her, and she was stronger than Joan had ever imagined. Joan was trapped inside Grace's mind; and Grace, who could not face what Joan had found, denied it.

And snapped.

In that instant, Joan felt that *she* was Grace. She felt all of Grace's pain and the choking weight of memory, as souls and selves incandescently merged. But before Joan and Grace could fuse inescapably, Joan recoiled, realizing that she was fighting for her life. She screamed for the gamesmaster to deactivate the game. But her screams were lost as Grace instantly slipped into the gamesmaster's mind and caught him, too. She had the psychotic's strength of desperation, and Joan realised that Grace would kill them all rather than face the truth about herself and Gayet.

Furiously Grace went after Pfeiffer. To kill him. She blamed him for Joan's presence, and Joan felt crushing pain, as if she were being buried alive in the dirt of Grace's mind. She tried to wrench herself away from Grace's thoughts, lest they intertwine with and become her own.

She felt Grace's bloodlust . . . her need to kill Pfeiffer.

Grace grasped Pfeiffer with a thought, wound dark filaments around him that could not be turned away by white thought or anything else.

And like a spider, she wrapped her prey in darkness and looked for physiological weakness, any flaw, perhaps a blood vessel that might rupture in his head . . .

Joan tried to pull herself away from the pain, from the concrete weight crushing her. Ironically, she wondered if thought had mass. What a stupid thought to die with, she told herself, and she suddenly remembered a story her father had told her about a dying rabbi who was annoyed at the minyan praying around him because he was trying to listen to two washerwomen gossiping outside. Many years later, her father confessed to her that it wasn't really a Jewish story at all; it was Buddhist.

She held on to that thought, remembered how her father had laughed after his confession. The pain eased as she followed her thoughts.

. . . If thought had mass.

She was thinking herself free, escaping Grace by finding the proper angle, as if thought and emotion and pain were purely mathematical.

That done in an instant.

But if she were to save Pfeiffer's life, and her own, she would have to do something immediately. She showed Grace her past. Showed her that she had married Gayet because he had the face of the man who had raped her as a child.

Gayet, seeing this too, screamed. How he loathed Grace, but not nearly as much as she loathed herself. He had tried to stop Grace, but he was too weak. He, too, had been caught.

As if cornered, as if she were back in the closet with her rapist, she attacked Gayet. Only now she had a weapon. She thought him dead, trapped him in a scream, and, as if he were being squeezed from the insides, his blood pressure rose. She had found a weakened blood vessel in his head, and it ruptured.

The effort weakened Grace, and a few seconds later the gamesmaster was able to regain control and disconnected everyone. Gayet was immediately hooked in to a life-support unit which applied CPR techniques to keep his heart beating.

But he was dead . . .

There would be some rather sticky legal complications, but by surviving, Pfeiffer had won the game, had indeed beaten Grace and won all of Gayet's organs.

As Pfeiffer gazed through the transparent walls of the transpod that whisked him and Joan out of Paris, away from its dangers and sordid delights, he felt something new and delicate toward Joan.

It was newfound intimacy and gratitude . . . and love.

Joan, however, still carried the echoes of Grace's thoughts, as if a part of her had irreversibly fused with Grace. She too felt something new for Pfeiffer. Perhaps it was renewal, an evolution of her love.

They were in love . . . yet even now Joan felt the compulsion to gamble again.

TEA

. . . .

Lorelei met Mr Fleitman the same day that she had covered all the windows in her apartment with aluminum foil.

It had been a pure day; completely clear and lambent, and Lorelei sat on her tiny side-porch, taking in the morning sun, and gazing out at a strip of ocean that was visible from the porch. She was sitting beside the corner where the rather rickety railings met, and by leaning over ever-so-much, she could see the play of light on the now-turquoise ribbon of water. It was still as a mirror, more like lake-water than the smashing waves that sprayed the rocks and stones of what she considered the "primitive" part of the beach. Most of the beach in Sea-Gate, a tiny walled city on the eastmost tip of Brooklyn, was combed white sand; although in the last few years dead black fish and spots of tar had begun to appear on the shore like a sin.

But for now, as far as Lorelei was concerned, it was all fresh and white and beautiful. She could hear the waves and the screeing of the gulls that wheeled overhead like soft-shaped white angels. And for this luminous moment, as she sipped her sweetened tea, she forgot who she was now and felt like a young girl. If she didn't touch her face, which was wrinkled and dry as parchment, even though she used oils and creams and balms, she could imagine that she was once again thirty. Her fingers ached slightly — arthritis — but then she had had those pains when she was a girl. The important thing was that she not look at her hands, which were further reminders of how time had ravaged her, but at the universe outside; that she keep her focus on the stone perron steps and the sidewalk and the chockablock two-family houses that were made of stone and bleached like bones from angry howling winters and summer days like this. There was a high mesh fence on the other side of the wide street below her, which was Atlantic Avenue, and sand and sea behind it; but her own building cut off most of the view to the left, and a large, ugly, transient hotel cut off the view to the right.

Which left only the ribbon of sand and sea.

But she had the sky and the gulls and this perfect translucent day. Still, she couldn't remain too long in the sun, for it was dangerous. It would wreck and wrinkle her skin, and at her age could cause cancer. So she went back inside, going immediately to her little bathroom off the kitchen to freshen her face and comb and spray her hair. She had had a permanent just last week, and it was still tight and wiry. Nevertheless, the wind had blown a few golden strands out of place.

The mirror had become an enemy these past forty years, as was to be expected, but she had become accustomed to the face that looked back at her, had become so used to it that she had long ago stopped seeing it for what it was. She had made the proper corrections in her mind so that what she really saw was a more mature version of the pretty, youthful face men used to admire. She saw the thick make-up she used as her skin, smooth as oiled wood, and her eyes were still clear, although she needed her contact lenses in place in order to see them.

But this morning, as she gazed into the mirror affixed to the rather cheap medicine cabinet, the glass tricked her.

It happened so suddenly, as if she had somehow caught a false reflection with her peripheral vision; and in that horrifying, petrifying instant she saw her mother-in-law, whom she had taken care of like a baby after Sam died, until her mother-in-law, too, had died of cancer. Lorelei glimpsed what she knew with dead certainty was her true self: an old woman painted up in clownish imitation of a young girl.

She had had glimpses such as this before, but somehow this one was so terribly strong that it would not be denied.

And she could do nothing but accept and grieve for that face in the mirror.

Afraid of looking into the mirror again, Lorelei went into the kitchen and washed the make-up and lipstick from her face. Then she took out a roll of aluminum foil from the drawer and neatly and methodically covered every mirror and window in her apartment, for every window could also become a mirror. Layer by layer, she applied the foil to the glass panes, as if she were a mason bricking up a tomb, a final refuge, secure and dark.

It was an inspired act of creation and desperation.

She used transparent tape to secure the foil, pressing it into the relief and grooves of the sashes and stiles to insure permanence. Although the foil was reflective, its surface was too wrinkled and distorted to harm her. It was what every mirror should be: opaque and dull as silver paint.

When she was finished, she felt better.

She sat down to tea in her newly-darkened, postage stamp living room and felt safe once again, as she had when she was first married to Sam, God rest his soul, or when she was a little girl and living at home in her parents' fifth floor walk-up in Brighton. She had made a pact with shadow and darkness, for there, in pools of grey and silver and velvet, she could be — if not forever young — at least hidden from the harridan that had gazed back at her in the bathroom mirror.

And then there was a light, tentative tapping at her door.

Lorelei considered not answering it, but she was superstitious, and it seemed to her odd and propitious that someone should knock at her door just now. "Who is it?" she asked, after a considered amount of time.

"Viktor Fleitman, your neighbour from downstairs. I'm a bit embarrassed to be asking, but might I impose upon you to borrow some tea, and perhaps a little sugar? It seems I've managed to run out of both at the same time. I shall be going to the grocery tomorrow and can repay you then."

Lorelei had seen the old man who lived downstairs. He was always polite and actually rather nice looking. Like her, he kept mostly to himself and was, in fact, somewhat of a mystery. She hadn't intended to let him into her apartment, but, when she finally opened the door to give him his sugar and teabags, which she had individually wrapped in plastic sandwich bags for him, he stood in the doorway and looked around the room. His gaze rested for an instant on the aluminum-foiled windows, and he nodded. She didn't know why he did that, yet somehow she couldn't help feeling that he alone understood and comprehended something deep and precious and profound about her that was hidden to the rest of the world.

The miracle of it all for Lorelei was that she knew Mr Fleitman to be almost blind.

Yet he had looked around the room.

Perhaps he was able to make out vague shapes. But could he have recognised the foil covering the windows? Perhaps he had nodded only in appreciation of the darkness of the room. But it meant much more to Lorelei, who could recognise deep and symbolic truths in the most mundane gesture or odd happenstance, as if she were reading Tarot cards or tea leaves or the very entrails of things. When she had had a family, they were always asking her to read their tea leaves, as did her friends; and she was very good. She had seen Uncle Harry's death, hadn't she, and Lorraine's wedding in the tarry black shapes that stuck to the sides and bottoms of their cups.

"Would you care for a cup of tea while you're here?" Lorelei asked Mr Fleitman, surprising even herself with her boldness; but he seemed especially eager for the company, and for a time she forgot about herself and her revelation in the mirror. The world was now reduced to the comfortable rustling of napkins and the awkward yet reassuring whisper of small talk.

It wasn't just coincidence that Mr Fleitman had come to her door on that very day; it was providence.

Lorelei was certain of that.

Every Wednesday Mr Fleitman came upstairs from his first floor apartment for afternoon tea.

It had become a formal ritual for both of them, the high point of each of Lorelei's uneventful weeks. Not much of a life, but what else was she to do? On Friday nights she lit Sabbath candles and waved her hands over them in circles as her mother and her grandmother before her had done, and she would sit in the living room and watch them quickly evaporate into the glass candleholders. Lorelei was not a devout woman, though she believed in God and was a Jew. But just about everything else had slipped past her: the years, her life, her husband, her looks . . . and her daughter, may she live and be well, who had her own children now, and her own life to lead.

But this Wednesday Mr Fleitman was late, which was most unusual. He apologised, and Lorelei was overly solicitous, which was her way. However, she felt she had reason to be because of Mr Fleitman's blindness, or poor sight, as he insisted. She had once been to his apartment, and had felt very uncomfortable, as she would have in any man's apartment. It was very cluttered and messy, and there were records everywhere — it was a wonder he could ever find them to return to the library — for he played the "talking books". But there had been paintings on all the walls, covering every inch, it seemed, as if they themselves were reminders of sight; most likely, they had been hung when he could still see and appreciate them.

"I was a bit worried about you," Lorelei said, "but then I thought that something important must have come up and —"

"No, no, Mrs Lanzman, I'm fine, I assure you," Mr Fleitman said as they sat down to tea at the little folding table she had prepared in the living room. She had covered it with linen, of course, and her silver tea set on its filigreed tray almost glowed in the dim light from a lamp in the corner. "I took a short nap and didn't hear the alarm. Or else I turned it off in my sleep." He made a soft clucking noise, as if he were admonishing himself.

"Well, you must have needed to rest," Lorelei said. She could detect the trace of a foreign accent in his voice, but that was mostly because he spoke very precisely, although she remembered that he had once told her that he had been born in Villach, Poland. He had emigrated here when he was very young. He had been a tailor, and had made custom shirts and suits for personages such as Prince Oblensky, who was residing in America, and would have been in line to be the crown prince of Russia, but for the revolution.

But that was all before Mr Fleitman's eyes had clouded. Before he was forced to retire.

Lorelei loved his stories . . . and, of course, believed them.

This was going to be a good afternoon; she could feel it. Mr Fleitman sat stiffly at the table, as he always did, gazing right at her, although not focussing on anything in particular, and smiled. He wore a black double-breasted suit and a wide vermilion tie; his clothes were pressed and fit perfectly, even though they were years out of fashion. But perhaps in these times that didn't matter, Lorelei told herself, because now practically everything is back in fashion. Still, it was much too hot for such clothes, although it pleased her that he always dressed when he came upstairs for tea.

"Tell me about your name," Mr Fleitman asked. "We are always so formal, you and I."

"Well, I know that it comes from the German, and means countryman —"

"No, no, I mean Lorelei, which is such a beautiful and uncommon name."

Lorelei brushed her hand through her stiff, bleached hair, a self-conscious gesture; nevertheless, she was pleased. "It comes from a German legend, I think. My mother insisted on the name, although my father hated it. And when I was growing up here in Brooklyn, I did too. There weren't a lot of children named Lorelei." The boys used to refer to her as Lori-lie-down, although, contrary to their opinions, she was a virgin until she got married.

"But you came to like it."

"Well, it was different, certainly." But what she couldn't express was that the name had somehow formed her, had once given her the appearance of beauty, even though she certainly had not been a beauty. But she *had* been a siren; indeed, that was once how she thought of herself: as wild, smoking cigarettes, not averse to having a drink in a speakeasy.

"So you spent your youth combing your hair with a golden comb by the river, while sailors and fishermen crashed on the rocks for love of you." Lorelei blushed and giggled, as if she were nineteen once again and out on a first date in a terribly sophisticated club.

"Do you mind if I call you Lorelei?" Mr Fleitman asked.

Lorelei was pleased with the new intimate turning their relationship had suddenly taken, although she enjoyed the formality of last names; it was somehow romantic and mysterious . . . and safe. But she said, "Of course we should use our first names. We are, after all, old friends."

"Good, then so be it . . . Lorelei." He used the word that first time hesitatingly, but immediately went on in his cool, sure manner. "And you should call me Viktor. I do have one other request, though. Would you be kind enough to read my tea leaves?" Mr Fleitman asked.

That took her aback. Mr Fleitman was certainly full of the unexpected today. "Yes, of course," she said, "but how on earth did you know about that?"

"Mrs Simpson told me you were very good. She raved about you." Mrs Simpson was Lorelei's next-door neighbour — and Lorelei would also have to admit that she was her friend — a flabby-armed woman who always wore flowered sun dresses in the summer; they seemed to exaggerate, rather than hide, her considerable weight. "Yes, my daughter met her in the hallway once and told her about that, so she came to my door and asked for a reading the very next day. But she didn't seem very happy with what I had to tell her, which is why I'm always a little nervous about giving readings. I never used to do them for my family, but they insisted. I didn't mind doing it for cousins, but with immediate family I was always afraid I would see something terrible in their cup, and when you love somebody —"

"Well, you'll have no worries such as that with me," Mr Fleitman said. "But if it's going to make you uncomfortable in any way . . ."

Lorelei went back to the kitchen for more tea; she had used a very good tea to steep in her teapot, but it was a bag. She had given readings using teabags — she would just break the teabag with her spoon — but she didn't feel right about doing it that way, somehow. Everything always looked wrong. So when he was finished with his cup, she gave him loose tea, a wonderfully pungent black oolong that she had bought directly from the owner of a Vietnamese restaurant in Coney Island.

"Just let it settle for a bit before you drink," she said, and they sat in the shadowy darkness for a moment without speaking. Mr Fleitman would often lapse into silence and Lorelei had learned that she didn't have to try desperately to fill in those awkward moments with small talk. Lorelei relaxed; it seemed that when Mr Fleitman was here, she enjoyed and appreciated the odd juxtaposition of day-noise and cool interior shadow as if it were all her creation and idea. She had often considered tearing the foil from the windows. She had lived in the dark long enough, but she couldn't bring herself to destroy one of her few acts that she felt had any meaning.

The darkness was her security. Only here could she be safe. Here she could shut off the world like a lamp. If she wished, she could be as blind as Mr Fleitman within these dim autumnal confines: too often light and sight brought remembrance, which for Lorelei could only be a euphemism for sorrow. The clearest, cleanest, most beautiful day could always turn on her, bringing back the fickle, mundane, heartbreaking memories of Lorelei's youth and the stabbing, aching loneliness. Then she would remember swimming at Brighton Beach with boys in striped wool swim-suits that covered their chests and legs. She would return to the days of shingled hair and cloche hats and family picnics and week-long vacations in Atlantic City, and her young husband's quiet, gentle lovemaking "so as not to wake up the children": all the transparent, lingering moments that were the essence of joy and promise. Even now, in the dimness of her living room, she could almost smell popcorn and hear the boardwalk barkers on a neon-frosted Saturday night, could almost see her husband's handsome, youthful face superimposed upon Mr Fleitman's.

Lorelei could easily make out Mr Fleitman's features, for it wasn't dark in her living room, just dim, a twilight of sorts. She had turned the art deco floor lamp on, but the three-way bulb was on its lowest setting, and the scalloped rose-tinted glass cover gave little illumination; it just glowed, as if light were passing through a stained-glass window. But light streamed in from the kitchen, where she kept the overhead light on, and through the cracks around the front door.

Lorelei had always thought Mr Fleitman was a handsome man, with his high cheekbones, his shock of white hair that was receding just a bit at the temples (and was also just a bit thin in the back), his intense blue eyes that seemed too small for his wide face, and the deep cleft in his chin. Lorelei liked that, the cleft, for, to her mind, it signified strength and character.

When he finished his second cup of tea, Lorelei snapped the glass-bowled art deco lamp that stood in the corner of the room to its highest illumination and looked at Mr Fleitman's tea leaves. She swished the tea and the small amount of liquid in the cup to distribute the leaves and then turned the cup over the saucer to drain away the liquid. Then she looked for pictures and symbols and signs and portents in the almost crystalline patterns of the tea leaves. Most of them were on the bottom of the cup, and the sides were unusually clean. It was like looking down upon a microscopic land cut with streams and valleys; but almost in the centre was a cross; exposed hairlines of porcelain.

"Well, tell me what you see, my dear Lorelei."

But she saw more than just a cross, and it was an oddly shaped cross at that. She had a sense that she was looking down into a strange, wild country; she imagined that she was seeing a specific place, a town, perhaps, for there were houses and roads, and surrounding the town were hills. The black lumps and scatterings of tea looked like deep forest, and she imagined that she could see people, masses of people in . . . but only dormitories came to mind. Then, as she stared into the cup, a symbol began to form. That's how it always happened, but usually she saw only the symbols which she had once read on a teacup that she had bought at a five-and-dime, a cup and saucer specifically made for tea readings. She remembered the thirteen symbols and their very short interpretations that were painted on the bone-white cup and saucer.

Lorelei had expected, had looked for, hearts, clover leaves, birds' eggs, keys, boots, grapes, ships, triangles, lilies, and the like, but instead she imagined that she was seeing this town, and drawn over it was a blotch of tea that looked like a bird's wing. But she knew it was a cloak. From the configuration of the tea leaves, she thought she could make out the figure of a man wearing the cloak, but the figure was so misshapen and ill-defined that it could be anything one imagined; the cloak, however, was perfect. She looked intently into the teacup, for she had seen that same cloak in Uncle Harry's cup before he died, and this one looked exactly like it. Of course, it didn't necessarily have to mean death, she supposed, rationalizing.

But a chill feathered up her spine, nevertheless. Lorelei was shaken; and had it not been dim in the room, and had not Mr Fleitman been near-blind, he would have seen the colour drain from her face.

"I am getting quite anxious," Mr Fleitman said, a touch of humour in his voice. "Here I am, totally at your mercy."

"According to the cup you're a religious man," Lorelei said, not wanting to tell him just yet of the cape. "I see a cross, but everything else —" she shrugged, feeling awkward and somehow embarrassed. Mr Fleitman didn't respond; he just waited for her to continue. "I can't quite make out what it all means. I see what looks like a village, and people, and maybe forest." She paused and then said, "And I also see a figure that looks like it's wearing a cloak."

"Ah," Mr Fleitman said. "And is that good or bad?"

"It means you should take care of yourself, and be careful."

"And what should I be careful of?" he asked.

Lorelei wasn't sure if he was teasing. "You should just be careful."

"What exactly does the cloak mean?"

"Just what I told you."

"Does it mean death, Lorelei?" Mr Fleitman asked.

"It could . . . in some cases," she said. "But I would interpret it as some kind of danger, which could be financial, or anything. If you're careful, you'll be just fine." Lorelei smiled at him, although she knew well enough what the cape meant. But she didn't want to alarm him. Maybe it did just mean danger or risk.

That was entirely possible, too.

But Mr Fleitman didn't look upset about the reading, Lorelei thought. More than likely, he just doesn't believe it, which is probably all to the good.

Yet she thought it strange that he looked somehow relieved. As if she had told him that she had seen the happy symbols of lilies, acorns, grapes, or the sun in the glistening configurations of his tea leaves.

As if she had given him good news.

It was already dark; Lorelei was going out the door to buy groceries for the week at the Pathmark, when she saw Mrs Simpson waiting for her. Mrs Simpson's door was wide open, always a sure sign she wanted to talk; all her lights were blazing, and she was dusting furniture in her living room. Her husband Milton was nowhere to be seen, which meant that he was asleep in the bedroom. The only air conditioner in their apartment was in the bedroom.

"Hello, Lorelei, how are you? You've had me a bit worried."

"Why on earth would you be worried about me, Mavis, I'm just fine," Lorelei said, expecting trouble. Mrs Simpson was a busybody, although Lorelei had to admit to herself that she loved to hear all the neighbourhood gossip. But Lorelei wanted to get on her way; it felt like the temperature was a hundred degrees in this hallway. Outside the night air would be cool, but it was dangerous to be on the streets. She had wanted to be back by ten.

"Well, you haven't been out of your apartment for a week."

"I didn't need to be."

"And then when you do go out, it's at night, which isn't safe at all. Who ever heard of shopping in the middle of the night?"

"It's not the middle of the night," Lorelei said. "And many people shop when I do. The supermarkets are very busy now."

Mavis averted her eyes, and then, as if her mind had once again slipped into a familiar groove, she looked back at Lorelei and said, "It's still not right to just sit in the dark all the time."

"I don't just sit in the dark, I also sit on my balcony," Lorelei said, lying, a touch of sarcasm in her voice, for Mrs Simpson didn't have a balcony, although her apartment was much larger than Lorelei's.

"Well, I've told you how I feel about all of that . . ."

"Yes, you've told me a hundred times, Mavis, but you know, it's —"

"I know, it's none of my business."

"I don't mean to sound so nasty," Lorelei said, "but, really, I'm just fine."

"I'm sorry," Mavis said. "I shouldn't make judgements; after all, we all live in glass houses. I did want to talk with you, though, about Mr Fleitman. But if you think I'm just prying into your affairs, I'll keep my mouth shut and my door closed."

"Mavis, we've been neighbours over fifteen years. You're my friend. What about Mr Fleitman?"

"I can't talk about it in the hallway, for heaven's sake. Put your shopping cart in here," she said, meaning the living room, "and I'll make you a cup of tea."

Lorelei rested her folding shopping cart against Mrs Simpson's living room wall and followed her into the kitchen. "You know, Mr Fleitman is really a very nice man. I can't imagine why you dislike him so."

"Now I never said I dislike him, and you know that, but he's so . . . shadowy. And now I know why. My intuitions are always sound."

"What are you talking about?" Lorelei asked.

They sat down at the kitchen table. The kitchen was very large, with a tiled bathroom adjacent to it. A window beside the table overlooked other buildings, brownstones. On another wall, which was papered in a confusing floral pattern, was a black cat clock, which had glowing red eyes that moved back and forth and a fake pendulum in the shape of a tail. And on the remaining wall, which was not papered, hung an ornate cross that always made Lorelei uncomfortable. Mrs Simpson was a devout Catholic, and Lorelei could understand and respect that, but she still thought it somehow inappropriate to sip tea and gossip while Christ hung in his agony from the wall.

"Maybe I shouldn't tell you this, it's just going to make trouble."

"Now stop fencing around, Mavis, and get on with it. You certainly can't leave it at this . . . you're having too much fun."

"That's a terrible thing to say," Mavis said as she gave Lorelei a cup with a fresh teabag on the saucer; then she poured herself some coffee. There was an envelope on the table; she opened it and removed a yellowed scrap of newsprint.

"What's that?" Lorelei asked. She was too distracted even to put her teabag into the water.

But Mavis hid it in her folded hands. "I've been trying to think how to tell you. Milton's known for years and never told me, until I found this." She waved the paper. "You know how Milton is, like a clam. He said it would only make trouble. But I still think you should know, here —" and she handed Lorelei the newspaper clipping.

It had to be thirty years old. When she opened it, the paper cracked like ceiling plaster on the edges and where it had been folded. She read: NAZI WAR CRIMINAL RESIDES IN BROOKLYN. The small print described an Austrian doctor who was accused of performing selections, of sending Jews and gypsies and political prisoners to the gas chambers in the Polish concentration camp Birkenau. Lorelei felt the blood drain from her face. She felt dizzy and the print seemed to waver before her.

"This can't be," she whispered, thinking of Mr Fleitman as being so courteous, gallant, and soft-spoken. She gasped, remembering. It had all been in the tea leaves. She felt herself tremble and through sheer will controlled it. His life and deeds and sins and passions were represented in microcosm in the cup. The leaves had settled into his patterns and had formed a delicate, literal representation of hell. Lorelei had seen it, but hadn't been able to interpret what she saw. The cross was a swastika, and what she had thought was a village was, in fact, a concentration camp. Those townspeople modelled in the bottom of the cup were internees.

And death . . . the cape.

Mr Fleitman wasn't going to die, she should have seen that. *He* was the cape.

But that was just impossible.

"I'm afraid it is," Mavis said. "It gives his name, which was an alias, right there in the article."

Lorelei saw his name, but it didn't register, for she was reading the words as she would tea leaves. The words and letters had suddenly lost all their original meanings; they became runes, inkings and smudgings on old paper that might just as well have been written in some swirling Persian script or Egyptian hieroglyphs. She laid the scrap of newsprint down on the formica tabletop.

"Well, I see you've landed your prey," said a man's voice. It was Milton, who wore Bermuda shorts and a bleached white vee-neck undershirt that exposed his curly grey chest hair. He was pot-bellied and spindle-legged, but he had a full head of hair and, except for a double-chin, was not really bad-looking. His hair was disheveled and one side of his face was blotched red from the pressure of his pillow or his arm. "Good evening, Lorelei. My wife was bound and determined to get that information to you." He nodded toward the scrap of newspaper. "But it all happened a long, long time ago, and nothing more was ever heard about it."

"Was he acquitted?" Lorelei heard herself say.

Milton shrugged, then sat down. "That's all I know. Nobody's ever said a word about it, and I can promise you that Mavis will abide by the same rule from now on." He glanced sharply at his wife, who returned his gaze matter of factly. They had lived together for fifty years, had worn each other smooth; Lorelei had never heard them argue, and walls were thin.

"Well, I had better get to my shopping," Lorelei said.

"Are you angry with me for telling you? After all, he was a Nazi, and you being a Jew, I thought . . ."

"No, you were absolutely right to tell me," Lorelei said.

"I think the whole thing would have been better left alone," Milton said. "What the hell difference does it make? If he was a criminal, he would've been put in jail. Isn't that right, Mavis?" he said pointedly.

Mavis shrugged and would not meet his eyes.

Lorelei calmly got up, thanked them for the tea and information, took her grocery cart, and left.

She went shopping as planned, so as not to let her neighbours know anything was wrong. But when she returned to her apartment, and after she unpacked her three double-bagged sacks of groceries, she methodically tore down the aluminum foil from every window in her apartment. It took her over an hour, for she stripped away every piece of tape, every crinkle of foil. She felt exhausted when she had finished, as if she had been running or lifting, and she sat down in the cushioned chair in the living room and fell asleep. Now she was vulnerable even in the humid, unprotecting darkness.

When she woke up, after what seemed only a nodding instant, the morning sun poured in, as golden and artificial-looking as margarine, but its warmth was not life-giving, for, like the tea leaves, it was just another representation. It enervated her; and she could feel it drying her out like a dead thing left on cement. There could be no safety now. Somehow she had always known that. But in the cool aluminum-foiled darkness, she had been able to forget.

She sat there in her chair and looked at her hands, runneled with blue veins, as if she were examining old photographs found in an attic. She could feel the air becoming hotter with every moment, and there was a cloying smell in the room. It was a familiar odor, one that she remembered as a little girl: the close, sweet smell of old people that pervaded their bodies and their rooms.

The days passed by, white and blue and golden yellow, invading her rooms, streaming through her windows, and she went about her business as if nothing was wrong, except she wouldn't go out of the house. Only at night did she feel a little better, but still not protected, for the windows that had allowed the sunlight to pass could now become opaque, soul-shattering mirrors ... unless she sat in darkness, which she did. She adapted. She fixed herself quick meals in the microwave that her daughter had bought her and waited.

During the days she waited and remembered, for the sun was her enemy, bringing her no revelation, just clarity: memory: all the times, the lulling family regularities, which promised to go on for eternity, until children grew up, or died, as did her first child, Katherine, hit by a car when she was eight. She remembered, even with her eyes squinted shut to give her the solace of darkness, but there she was again at the kitchen sink, washing dishes with Ivory Soap when she heard a noise outside, and then the shouting of children, as they came to the door to tell her that it was her child. Her child. Running out of the apartment in her pink and blue housedress, down four flights of worn stairs covered with broken rubber, and there was her daughter, lying on the sidewalk beside scraggly bushes, her hair clean and shiny, her white dress merely smudged with everyday dirt. She was perfectly fine. Asleep.

Dead.

And Sam begging her forgiveness for having had a fling with that secretary who worked on Mott Street. Oh, she remembered, remembered when the woman came to her home to tell her that she was pregnant and that she, Lorelei, should give Sam a divorce. Lorelei remembered her name, Fran Kempton, and she was thick-featured and full-bodied, and her hair was long and luxurious and she wore a pillbox hat and black patent shoes. Her dress was silk gauze with black trim, and the harlot carried a fox fur in the middle of the afternoon. She sat herself right down, big as life, at Lorelei's kitchen table, as if she had come in for an ordinary visit. All she had wanted was Sam. "Let her have him," she had told her mother, but Sam wanted Lorelei, who had left him, and he pestered and soft-talked her mother, the whole family, until they convinced Lorelei to take him back because she was pregnant with Litta, and a child needed a father. And then regular days, white with snow and white with sun, and weddings and parties and meals, and then Lorelei's mother died and Sam's mother moved in with them, and more regular days, merging, becoming one long day, and Sam died and his mother lived and called for tea every hour, even on her deathbed, each eternal day leaving a tiny mark, until she found herself here, in her living room, her face the map of her experiences, and yet . . . it was a lie. It couldn't be almost over.

It had hardly begun.

And yet she was alone and achingly lonely. How could that be? she asked herself as the sun heated her apartment like tin on a roof.

Where were Sam and Katherine? How could it be that only Litta, her second daughter, was alive? How could it be . . .?

But Litta had her own life to lead; she had always been very independent.

Lorelei made tea for her dead mother-in-law and drank it herself.

Lorelei didn't answer the phone, which didn't ring that often, but when it did she would count the rings. Most likely, it was her daughter, Litta . . . who else could it be? And there were knockings at the door: that, she thought, must be Mavis, for she didn't hear the squeak and groan of the stairs, as she would if anyone came up or down. She began to listen, to lose herself in every sound: birds screeing, cars passing, the muffled conversations of Mavis and Milton next door, the comings and goings of those in the house, but the ache of being alone never left her. It was only magnified now, as if Mr Fleitman's past revealed in the tea leaves had sensitised her.

The second knocking at the door was not Mavis, for she heard someone coming up the stairs. It had to be Litta because after a while there was a knock on Mavis's door, and the door opened and shut, and then the phone rang, sixteen rings, and there were more knockings. Her surmise was correct because Litta called to her from the other side of the door. She sounded terribly upset, and, inexplicably, angry, but Lorelei simply couldn't respond. She was frozen in her folding chair by the table where she had been playing solitaire. She wanted to see her daughter, but she was punishing herself, for growing old, for being a fool, for misreading Mr Fleitman and his cards. And, anyway, her daughter never came to see her unless she was worried and feeling guilty.

I shouldn't let her worry, Lorelei thought, yet still she sat there, thumbing the cards, as if imprisoned in this empty, roasting tomb of an apartment. After a half-hour or so, there was more stomping up the stairs, talking in the hall, and a firm, hard knocking.

It was announced that the police were here.

Lorelei opened the door and, feigning her most innocent and coquettish manner, asked what on earth all the commotion was about. "I'm fine," she told the policeman standing before her. Litta stood beside him, and Mavis, ever nosy and interested, stood behind them in her doorway. "I must have been asleep," she lied to Litta.

"How could you not have heard me knocking," Litta said. "And I let the phone ring off the hook." She looked like her mother had at her age: the same thick brown hair, full of highlights; an angular, intense face that could subtly change from openness to slyness; her changeable facial expressions produced an aura of mystery that men found attractive — that and her deeply-set blue eyes (which gave her the appearance of distance and aloofness) and her full peasant mouth. Litta also had her mother's trim figure and slightly oversized bust. Even now, after having three children, she looked like a child-woman, exuberant, constantly animated.

But for Lorelei, she was another mirror.

"I dreamed I heard knocking," Lorelei said, "but I haven't been able to sleep lately, and so I took two of those pills Dr Ashman gave me. I guess I needed the sleep." She smiled at Litta and at the policeman, who, satisfied that all was in order, politely excused himself.

Lorelei thanked Mavis for her concern and invited her daughter in for coffee — Litta didn't drink tea — and after Lorelei opened the windows to "air the place out" (orders from her daughter), they spent the afternoon talking about the grandchildren and Litta's husband, who was in advertising, and they reminisced about the old days, and Litta, of course, was "thrilled and relieved" that her mother had finally taken down the foil from the windows.

"I never understood why you did that," she said. "I always felt it was partly my fault, I know I don't get to see you often enough —"

"You're busy, you've got a life to lead."

"That's no excuse," Litta said. "If you were only closer to us. It takes almost two hours to get here from the Island." But she didn't offer to give up her guest room.

"I wouldn't live anywhere else but here, anyway," Lorelei said, lying. But could she have stood to live in her daughter's house? To observe life pulsing all around her, to sit and watch this younger version of herself taking up the whole present, constantly reminding Lorelei that all she had was a past?

"I would have put up the aluminum foil, with or without you," Lorelei said. That was probably a lie too.

And then again, maybe it wasn't.

Lorelei waited. Her daughter called once, and that was that. The days seemed to lengthen, and she felt like a child again, living through a succession of endlessly boring days.

She thought about Mr Fleitman. Although he had knocked on her door this past Wednesday (at least Lorelei assumed it was him), she had refused to answer. She was determined never to see him. But he deserved at least the courtesy of a fair trial. Had he been a Nazi? Had he really done terrible things? And why, why on earth had he come to Brooklyn? Why had he stayed here after that newspaper article? Had he been tried? What would he say if he knew I was Jewish? But he must know.

And everyone deserves a chance . . .

Those were the thoughts that collected themselves in various order through the sunlit hours. At night, her mind rested, as if the questions could somehow be the answers, and she thought no more about them. She would become sleepy, as if her clock was now the sun and the seasons, and she would sleep.

A sleep full of rooms, all of them empty save one.

Mr Fleitman knocked on Lorelei's door at one o'clock sharp. Lorelei waited for a moment, perhaps testing him, perhaps giving herself this one last chance to decide. She was his judge, although it was a thin punishment she had to mete out. Finally, she opened the door, and said, "Hello, Mr Fleitman. Come in, please."

He looked nervous and apprehensive as he stood in the doorway. But that lasted only an instant; and then he smiled and nodded and entered the apartment, pausing to look around, obviously aware of the light streaming in from the windows.

He did not correct her formal use of his name.

Perhaps he had heard what had gone on during the week. Perhaps he knew that he had been found out. Or perhaps that was all Lorelei's imagination.

"Would you care for some tea?" she asked. The table was, of course, prepared; had been prepared since this morning on the chance that he would come to the door . . . and that she would invite him in.

"Yes, that would be very nice," Mr Fleitman said, and was about to seat himself in his usual place at the folding table when Lorelei impulsively asked him if he would rather take tea on the balcony, it would only take a moment to fix everything up.

And Lorelei knew then that she would never question him about his past. Other men could be his judge, but not her. Whatever he had been, whatever terrible things he might have done, were part of the dead, desolate country that was the past. And the past was like the cruel photographs of Auschwitz Lorelei had once seen in a book: ash and bones and hollow emptiness. She grieved for what she remembered about the holocaust, for its victims; and she also grieved for Mr Fleitman, who had smiled at the thought of his own death, who carried the ash and bones and emptiness to her door. Who would forever have to carry all that he had done.

But there was little enough left to give and share.

It would be enough if she could just sit on the balcony and talk and laugh and sip tea . . . and share the life-giving, afternoon sun.

It was all there was left, and for these few Wednesday afternoon moments before God summoned her and Mr Fleitman to His own judgement, it would be enough.

JUBILEE

. . . .

The coming of the jubilee is usually sensed by one or another of a few people who have the gift of seeing the signs in the sea and air. When the signs appear, they go down to the shore and wait. If the feeling has been authentic, flounders and crabs begin to gather in holes in ankle-deep bottom, and eels soon turn up where no eels were before. When the eels come, word quickly spreads inland, and people begin to move down to the beach . . .

— Archie Carr, *A Celebration of Eden*

I found myself in a dilapidated hotel in Athens' ancient Turkish quarter where prices were inflated, the gawking German and American tourists were fleeced without even an obligatory smile, and the air was so polluted that I was already sniffing and coughing as if I had a cold.

I had been here before with Sandra, who loved this converted nineteenth century mansion. She loved Athens, loved its noise and food and antiquity, and imagined she could see the ghosts of ancient Greeks like Socrates and Pericles walking the streets as we ate squid and yogurt and oily *pastitsio* in an outdoor restaurant that overlooked the ruins of a Neolithic necropolis.

Now I was back. I had even requested our old room. But the room was all I had, for now I had no business, no home, no life. My books were in numbered boxes that lined the walls of a storage shed in upstate New York, as if mutely guarding the few pieces of furniture, prints, and cherished objects that I had taken from my old house.

And Sandra was now with someone else . . .

I unpacked my flight bag, took a shower, and then went out on my little balcony to look at the Saturday night tourists teeming below. The balcony was filthy, layered with dirt, and I wouldn't sit down on the white, sticky plastic chairs; below, the narrow back streets were littered with garbage. I could hear the background hum of the city, sense its jittery buzz, as if Greece was a nervous sleeper and Athens its choking, yearning, flash-flickering dream.

How I hated this garbage-strewn place; and yet here I was, drawn back, as if I could find solace in happy memories, in the twisting, vendor-infested streets; in the tavernas and hotels, or away in the hill country of factories and olive groves, and the cruel upthrusted islands overwhelmed by the sea.

But instead of happy memories, bad thoughts invaded my mind.

I could not help but think of Sandra with her new lover in our bed, and I knew that I had to get out of my room, into open streets, into crowds. I had to keep moving. The plane ride from New York to LA and then to Paris and finally Athens had been its own hell. I could not bear to be alone, yet here I was in this ancient, alien place where I knew only the hotel manager, Aristides, who liked to get drunk with the European and American guests and then make surreptitious passes at their wives.

I smiled as I passed him at the bottom of the stairs.

"*Kalispera*, Mister Blackford," he said, promising to stay past his shift if I would only have an Ouzo with him.

"Perhaps later," I replied, and he grinned, as if he knew everything, as perhaps he did, for he did not ask about Sandra. But just as I was about to step into the hot, crowded street, I turned on impulse and walked back to his little desk. I needed something — or someone — to distract me from the past.

"Ari," I said in a low voice, "could you find me a woman?"

The manager gave me a sly, condescending look, as if he had forgotten himself, and then said, "This cannot be done, Mister Blackford, not here, this is not that kind of hotel. Did you not see me have to kick that poor woman out of the bar earlier. She wanted a room for two thousand drachmas."

An English family came down the stairs, everyone saying hello to Ari, who smiled at them benevolently and waved to the children.

I felt my face become hot, for surely they had heard Ari talking.

"But you have been a good friend to me," he said before they were even through the doorway. "You have drank into the night with me." Then, in a low, conspiratorial voice, he said, "I will do what I can to help you. I know someone who might know someone. But it will be expensive . . ."

Suddenly I just wanted to get out of this narrow, dirty, panelled lobby. It was difficult to breathe. The heat and the steamy walls were pressing in on me. I had humiliated myself, and the very idea of being with a woman gave me claustrophobia.

But what was I afraid of?

Being hurt again?

And then I realised that I felt guilty, as if *I* was cheating on Sandra.

But *she* had cheated on me.

"Perhaps fifty thousand drachmas."

I turned toward the glass doors, as if Ari's whisper was a shout, exposing me. I was too embarrassed to look at him directly, but as I left, I saw his reflection in the dark, smeary glass: his merry, pudgy face and thin moustache. He looked as satisfied as a cat that had drawn blood.

And as I walked down Nikis Avenue, pushing past the tourists looking for dinner or looking in shop windows at reproductions of ancient vases and plates and pots and statues, or looking at fake icons slathered with silver and gold, I noticed that something was amiss: the streets were quiet.

Oh, the tourists were chattering and scuffing and pointing, but the shop owners weren't standing outside their stores, selling their wares; and the maitre de's weren't pushing and corralling the Americans and Germans and Japanese into their courtyards.

What was going on? It wasn't a religious holiday.

As I wandered through the bricked, narrow streets of the Plaka — the Acropolis a well-lit, floating mirage on the hill above — I realised how alien this place felt without Sandra. It was like being in a familiar wood on a summer night and wondering why the cicadas were quiet.

And as I edged out of the tourist area, out of the centre of the ancient Plaka, Athens became dead quiet.

Which was . . . impossible.

* * *

After his wife Nedra died, Peter Lindsay began to dream of water deep and green and bright, as if lit from its depths by klieg lights as bright as the noon sun. He had the same dream every night. He did not dream of Nedra, bless her sweet, gentle soul; he did not dream of his past, of his youth, or of missed opportunities; but just as Hemingway's old man dreamed every night of his lions, so did Peter Lindsay dream of the ocean. An ocean that was as alive as the lions, that breathed and sighed and whispered, whispered the answers to all the questions.

The ocean contained all the creatures.

All the creatures that had come vast distances to dream the world anew . . .

Although several months passed before Peter realised it, he had stopped painting. He still awakened at dawn, made coffee, played loud jazz on his ancient stereo, and spent the hours in the studio behind his dilapidated house, working in oils or water colours; but he worked a little less every day, and slept a little more, until he could smell the tang of the ocean, feel it buoying him, carrying him away from the lurching, frantic darkness of sleep into emerald light. Pulling him.

When he was awake, he felt tired. Drugged.

When he slept, he heard voices like static mixed with the rushing of the sea. And as he grew weaker, dying a little more as he drifted further away, he began to differentiate voices. The sea was sound and speech.

It was white and sharp as pain.

Hospital white.

There he could finally fall back into grief, into life, which was green, glaucous green, and as large and bright and purple shadowed as the creeping, encroaching rain forest. But that was just another dream, like that of the ocean, as large as the ocean: a sea of living foliated green . . .

I didn't venture out of the Plaka, nor did I stop in any of the tavernas or ouzeria. They certainly weren't empty, for I passed a courtyard full of German tourists, who seemed to be having a grand time eating and drinking; and indeed the tourists seemed somehow more real than anything or anyone else around me. Perhaps it was an effect of the light, for they seemed like characters on a stage, clear and defined, while everything else was drowned in shadow.

As I left the German tourists behind, the streets became muffled once again.

I said hello to a passerby, just to hear the sharpness of a voice, even if my own; and I anticipated the delicious, plosive retort of "*kalispera*". But there was no response, for I was as shadowy and evanescent as the grey-haired fellow who walked silently by me.

When I passed the ruins of the Agora, which had once been the hub of ancient Athens, I realised that I had gotten turned around. All the narrow, winding, crisscrossing streets in the old quarter looked alike. I was surprised to find hundreds of people pressing against a high mesh fence that enclosed the ruins of the Agora, which were barely illuminated by surrounding street lamps. Yet the crowd was unnaturally quiet. It was made up mostly of women dressed in traditional black with shawls pulled over their heads; the men were kneeling.

They were all praying.

I had, of course, been here before; it was a tourist attraction, a great, fenced-in archaeological garbage heap, with piles of stone scattered everywhere. Here was where Socrates lectured any citizen who would listen, here was where Saint Paul proselytised for a new millennium.

What could these people be looking at?

What could they be praying to?

I made my way to the chain-link fence and shouldered my way between two women, who were fingering their rosaries and praying as if their very lives depended on every word and motion. And I realised that I could hear a thousand beads clicking around me, as if a thousand roulette wheels were spinning.

I stared hard into the Agora.

All the ancient stones were still there — the alters and stoa and piles tagged for restoration — but what had been sandy ground was now covered with a gnarly carpet of grass and vine, its thick tangle was everywhere, and in the dim light it looked so dark as to be purple. Vines were curled around the piles of cut stones, connecting them like sail shrouds, and directly before me, the vines and shoots and what looked like the trunks and limbs of olive trees had taken a definite architectural shape: three columns separated by arches. And in the arches were masses that looked like bells.

A church made of trunk and vine.

* * *

Peter Lindsay was back home. Had he been gone a day, a week . . . a month? He still felt disoriented, as if he had just awakened in the wrong house; but indeed this was his house, the familiar one story 1890s Victorian gingerbread nestled between the million dollar duplexes that had just been built within the last year. He stared out his kitchen window that overlooked the street as if he were alone, while his friend Stephen, who had just brought him home from the hospital, was puttering by the sink, making tea.

How could Nedra be dead? Peter asked himself. It seemed a cruel trick, for nothing else had changed: the neighbour's yard across the street was afire with red and gold flowers; their white cement house, which was as old as his own, reminded him of a mosque; and he thought that he might have been in Tunisia or Morocco instead of Melbourne, Australia. His little street was quiet, but for the occasional car. If he listened, though, he could hear the heavy traffic on Punt Road, the street behind the house, a reminder that he lived near the centre of a city of three million people. He had lost part of his back yard ten years ago when they widened Punt Road to turn it into an avenue, and he had gotten used to the constant background noise: the dull roar of engines, the plashing of tires, and the sudden horns and sirens. He had learned to paint to the new rhythm of traffic; he thought of it as the rushing of blood in his arteries. Not even double glazed windows could keep it out.

But now, as he looked at quiet Affleck Street, with its new extrusions of townhouses, he *felt* Nedra's absence. And every knickknack on the windowsill, every lithograph and woodcut on the kitchen wall, even the old stains on the floor seemed . . . haunted. The room grew thick with the ghosts of the past; and Peter remembered, remembered living in Ithaca, New York, remembered meeting Nedra at an outdoor art show in Atlantic City where he was exhibiting his paintings and graphics. She was tall and blond and freckled and sunburnt, and she had long fingers and chewed half-moon fingernails. She had bought Peter's woodcut of a fern, a miniature, and he followed her here, to her house, 9,000 miles away from home.

That was twenty years ago.

Peter gazed at the woodcut of the fern on the kitchen wall; Nedra had insisted on hanging it in the kitchen because that was the heart of the house. He stood up and removed it from the wall. But the smooth frame slipped out of his hands, and glass and wood broke on the hardwood floor.

"I'll clean up the glass," Stephen said, gently leading Peter back to the kitchen table and a cup of tea. Stephen was in his early fifties, an accountant with a black beard, high forehead, and frizzy greying hair tied into a ponytail. He was dressed in jeans and a faded workshirt, the same clothes he would wear to his office.

"Leave it," Peter said. "I'll get it later. What you can do is take me for a drive."

Stephen looked surprised. "If you need groceries, I can pick them up while you settle back in."

Peter pulled on his beard — an old habit as obsessive as children twisting their hair when daydreaming. Nedra called it "woolgathering". His beard was white and long and considerably thicker than his hair. "I want to go out to the rain forest." He forced a grin. "The trams won't take me that far."

"You haven't even unpacked your bags. How about I take you tomorrow?"

"You've already taken time off today."

"To get you settled in," Stephen said.

"And I appreciate that, and all the other trouble you've gone to for me."

"It was no trouble," Stephen said emphatically. "I told you, I'm happy to be able to pay back a little for all the time and help and good advice you've given me over the years."

"Well, then take me for a drive."

"Peter, you just got out of the hospital."

"And I'm damned well fucking determined not to go back. So humour me. I miss Nedra so much that I can't catch my breath. I miss her especially now that I'm back . . . home. But I'm not going to curl into a ball; I'm going to paint like never before. That's what she would have wanted. I'm going to paint for her. You just fucking watch me."

"Well, you're certainly sounding like your old self."

"Come on, we'll do male-bonding, and I'll tell you what it was like in the loony bin." Peter was fond of Stephen, who had been buying his paintings for years. Stephen used to say that he had the money, but Peter had the answers. Peter had made good friends in this country; they had all given him what support they could. But Nedra had always been the strong one. Hadn't she consoled him while she fought the cancer that was metastasizing into her kidneys, liver, and lung? Hadn't she finally kicked him and the nurses out of her room so she could get on with the business of dying? "It's a job I've got to do by myself," she had told him.

"You weren't in the loony bin," Stephen insisted. "You were in the respiratory wing because your lung collapsed. You were exhausted, and after what you went through, who wouldn't be?" After a beat, he asked, "Don't you remember?"

"Yes, of course I remember," Peter said. "Now take me for a ride in your expensive Jaguar."

"Why the rain forest?"

"Because I want to paint it. I need to refresh my eyes; I haven't been in the bush for years."

He didn't tell Stephen that he had dreamed of the rain forest after his operation, when he was coming out of the anesthesia. He had also dreamed of the ocean, dreamed of alien beings swimming and gliding in the deep wastes.

Huge floating creatures that were themselves dreaming . . .

Are you the creature dreaming, as the reef spawns, as the coral discharges its egg and sperm into the watery light of the full moon? The sea is black glass, its calm surface hiding the hot agitation in its depths. Gill-dreams of new life, ancient life, breaking the surface, changing everything; as you wait in the rolling darkness.

Are you the sea or the creature? The alien or the indigene? The answer or the conundrum?

Are you the messiah at the end of time turned serene nightmare or just a great seawall of star spotted dorsal skin, a highway of lateral ridges and electromagnetic sensory pores? Are you the beast at the end of the world? Even now the sea changes, and reefs grow not by slow accretion but in whole stands. Sea change in the crystal waters of the South Pacific, in the once dead, fished-out Mediterranean now pregnant with skate and shark and ray, now aglow in red and yellow profusions of coral.

From without or within — from the stars or the watery bowels of the earth — do you dream as the great Parisian avenues of Melbourne become canals for gondoliers and Athens turns into Atlantis?

"*Pos i-ste,* Mister Blackford?" Ari asked as I stepped into the lobby, which was empty, as was the adjoining combination bar and breakfast room.

"I'm very well, thank you," I said, impatient to get back to my room; but I had to tell Ari to cancel the whore. Being with a stranger would only intensify my sense of loss. I just needed some sleep . . . just some sleep. "Ari —"

"No, no, Mister Blackford, it's all taken care of." Ari flung his hands up, and I stepped back reflexively. He laughed at that. "And everything has been done with great discretion."

"That's what I wanted to talk to you about. I've changed my mind."

"No, it's too late. It's all settled."

"Ari, I'll take care of any embarrassment this might cause you. How much to take care of it?"

He would not look at me directly and stared into his guest record book. "I will not see this person again tonight."

"Doesn't he have a phone?"

He shrugged. "It's not possible."

"All right, Ari. Goodnight."

But as I turned to leave he said, "I will tell the girl when she comes . . . if I am here. If it's too late, then —" He shrugged.

"Thanks, I'd appreciate that very much."

Perhaps my voice was surly and he thought he'd surely lose his tip of 5,000 drachs at the end of my stay, for he asked, "Would you like some Ouzo? It's on the house."

"Not tonight, Ari, perhaps tomorrow." But before I left him, I asked, "Is today some sort of religious holiday?"

"No, I don't think so. It may be some minor fast day, that I wouldn't know." He grinned at me, as if we were both involved in a conspiracy against the Greek Orthodox Church. Yet he wore a silver crucifix and a saint's medallion around his neck . . . just in case. "Did you find people going to church?"

"No, but I walked down to the Agora —"

"Aha . . ."

"What's going on there?" I asked.

"Did you look in?"

"Yes," I said, somehow feeling defensive.

"And what did you see when you looked in?" He suddenly looked quite interested.

"It was too dark to make anything out," I said, lying.

He nodded, as if confirming something to himself.

"Well?" I asked.

"It's a miracle. That's what I've been told. But only for us."

"What do you mean?"

"For Christians."

"How do you know *I'm* not a Christian?"

"Because I know you are Jewish." He smiled, but seemed distracted.

"Tell me about this miracle at the Agora?" I asked, probing, but he only shrugged. "Have you been there?"

"I think I will go tonight."

"You must have heard *something* about it," I insisted.

"It's a miracle, that's all I know."

"I didn't see anything about it on the English language channel. Is there anything in the papers?"

Ari shrugged. "It would not be in them or on the television."

"Why not?"

"Because it is a real miracle." He nodded again and said, "I will go tonight."

"Is that why the streets are so quiet?" I was humouring him, yet even as I said it, I realised I wanted to know the answer.

"I will go tonight," Ari said, ignoring my question; and as I climbed the stairs to my room, I could hear the faint clicking and clacking of his worry beads as he dropped the amber stones, one atop the other, down to the knot at the end of their silver thread.

Or perhaps it was a rosary.

They drove with the top down because it was after 3:00 p.m. and the UV radiation was in the safe zone, or so said the radio announcer on the FOX station. Peter enjoyed the warm flat feel of sunlight on his face and the wind whipping his long white hair about, enjoyed the hot smell of February's summer, and the clear sharp air that was so transparent he could see the veins in leaves fifty feet away. This was certainly not Italy, or New York State with its heavy, water vapour atmosphere that blunted the edges of things, that veiled the world. Here was clarity; and Peter inhaled it all as if he had just been given a reprieve from death. This was Nedra's gift to him, even as the poignancy of her loss clotted like thick phlegm in the back of his throat.

He would stay in the moment. For this moment and the next he would not think of what had been lost: he felt twenty-five, and he was going to paint his ass off; he was going to find the colours that were in the inside of things, not just what could be only seen with the eyes. Synaesthesia. He had felt the colours before, when he had first started painting, when he had been so swept up in the very act of putting brush and colour to canvas that he forgot all analytical skill. Then he could hear a music that was like a differentiated thunder: musical tones of the rainbow. He closed his eyes and imagined that he was flying, flying just feet away from the macadam in Stephen's waxed leather and wood scented XJ40 Daimler Jaguar, swept into a bright cone of greenness ahead; and he could see the colours shifting as if in a kaleidoscope, each shade melding into another like emotion itself: absinth, green apple, aquamarine, beryl, bice, and bottle green; chrysoidine and chrysolite and chrysoprase, corbeau and cobalt green, green exploding, evaporating, melting like metal into milori and mitis and moss, into peas and patina and terre-verte, into serpentine and shamrock and sea-water fronds reaching toward him, cool and wet and undulating jade, a rainforest of green, choking, inhaling, fertilizing everything, overwhelming everything that was.

And Peter came awake with a jolt and looked around. They had driven out of Central Melbourne on the Maroondah Highway and were now in the northern suburbs, the Dandenongs. Green dreams had dissolved into miles of grey strip malls: chockablock McDonald's, Coles, Hungry Jacks; carparks, department stores, computer stores; industrial parks and auction barns. This could easily be Hempstead, Long Island or Paramus, New Jersey. But Stephen was heavy footed, and they roared down the highway at around 140 kilometres an hour; other cars seemed to be standing still. Soon they were in the Upper Yarra Valley, driving past grey-barked gum trees and sheep and cattle grazing in dull yellow fields, and through the bush, a thick canopy of trees shading the road. In the distance were ancient mountains, blue-tinged from air heavy with eucalyptus. Nearer were yellowish hills; small copses of trees stood upon their swells like toy soldiers. Farm country. Bush. Miles without sight of habitation. Green and gold country. God's country.

The road narrowed, turned from two laned macadam to dirt. Stephen turned off the road. A sign nailed to a tree read TALL TREES, and Stephen parked the green Jag, now grey with dust, on the shoulder. This was temperate rain forest, cool and autumnal; the narrow-boled gum trees rose into the grey light above, and giant ferns shivered in the woody air like shields held by warriors waiting to march into battle.

Peter had not told Stephen of his dreams, or how it had been in the hospital; in fact, neither man had spoken very much during the trip. Each seemed to be isolated, and Peter was certain that Stephen wished himself anywhere else but here in this green and brown nowhere of mountain ash so tall that one had to bend backwards to see their tops. Yet Peter didn't care. That thought itself jolted him. Well, he'd make it up to Stephen. He would give him a painting, or perhaps one of the pastels he intended working on here.

Stephen followed him along the worn path into the forest; they had not gone more than a few hundred feet when they encountered fallen trees and brush over the path. Looking for the right place to sketch, Peter pushed through on his own.

"Is it going to bother you, me hanging around while you paint?" Stephen asked. "I could just as well go back to the car."

"It won't bother me at all," Peter said. "I'll just make some quick sketches, and then we can get out of here." But why would anyone want to leave this place? he asked himself. This was bliss. The place seemed to have a depth of colour and space Peter couldn't find in the city; and he started working, his hand moving as if of its own volition, sketching in rough outlines, then the soft, dry smearing of pastel, the cool chalky feel of it on the fingers, clean and sure; and he gazed into the distance, as if the forest were his sketchbook, and he sensed the luminous order of this place in the trees that appeared like the columns of some natural heliotropic temple. But his reverie was broken when Stephen said he was going back to the car.

"What time is it?" Peter asked.

"Well, old son, you've been painting for over two hours." Stephen smiled, as if he was pleased. "I'm going to take a whiz and sit in the air con. It's gotten fucking humid out here. Take your time. My shrink will be more than pleased that I've been forced to just hang out and enjoy nature . . . and take a piss in the forest."

"Okay, I'm done," Peter said, lying. "Give me a minute, and I'll have all this stuff put away."

"No you *won't*," Stephen insisted. "Do I really have to have company when I pee? Take your time. I really am enjoying it out here. But all this fresh air makes me feel sleepy." Then he gazed out into the forest as if Peter wasn't there. It was as if he was transfixed, or was somehow dreaming with his eyes open.

"Steve, are you okay?" Peter asked.

"I was just thinking about something. I'll see you in a while." And with that he walked away.

"Steve, what were you thinking about?"

Stephen stopped, turned around, and looked past his friend. He blinked, as if he were looking into the sun. "The trees were just playing tricks on my eyes."

"What kind of tricks?"

But Stephen disappeared, leaving Peter to look into the forest, where Stephen had been staring.

The light changed, as if clouds had passed across the sun. The trees and ferns seemed to form an arbor . . . no, not an arbor, that wasn't it. The trunks and limbs of the trees had taken a definite architectural shape: three columns separated by arches. And in the arches were masses that looked like bells. A church.

Peter looked away, relaxing his eyes, then stared again. But the illusion wouldn't be shaken.

He set his pastel kit and sketchbook on the ground and walked toward the phantom church, looking away from it, then into it, as if to shake away its substance; but the illusion of bells and arches was broken only when he was almost upon the spot. He looked past what had been woody arches and stepping through them, felt warmth. It was as if the atmosphere had suddenly changed, becoming hot and humid. Even the odors were different: pungent, overpowering, as if everything was ripe and rotting, both flesh and vegetable. And as the light shifted, this new place became tangible, palpable, and he knew what had happened. He, or this place, had slipped backwards, the past was somehow intermingling with the present, hot with cold, temperate with tropical. The forest was here, too, but this was the lush forest of tropical Queensland a thousand miles to the north. It was so thick that the sun could barely shine through its roof of leaf and branch and grasping fern. The trees were straight-stemmed, narrow boled, and encrusted with lichens and clusters of brilliant flowers and fruits. The hues and complexities were those of a Breughel painting, dark and deep and mysterious. Peter could smell the damp greenness. The pointed drip-tip leaves were huge, as were the ferns that seemed to be caught in some millennium-long motion, in mid-stride across the world; and lianas and epiphytes hung from the high tree limbs, twisted and tangled around branch and stem, winding along the forest floor like snakes, connecting the canopy, pulling the steaming, hot barked fingers into a great fist, growing, growing.

Peter was drenched with sweat.

Turn around, get out of here, he told himself, swallowing hard, as if panic could be dissolved in saliva. But where had he come in? There were no arches, no church, no path back to the safety of the familiar. He whispered to himself, a nonsensical droning, a barely audible pleading; and he was electrified with fear, for he imagined that this place was made up of eyes, eyes watching him from every direction, every angle; and then he talked out loud to himself, as he might to a frightened child, that this was a dream, that there was nothing to be afraid of.

But this was not the dream. The dream had been . . .

Of rainforest, yes, here, this.

But it was ocean, the recurring dream had been of ocean and the great dreaming creatures that would dwarf ships yet resembled them, ships of flesh, with pores for eyes . . . eyes that has seen distant worlds, Dresden blue eyes watching, dreaming, and changing the very stuff of being.

He heard something move, something snap, but it was his own foot stepping upon dead branch and vine. He froze, as if some ancient, racial memory had taken over, the response of prey, trapped, to become the background, as if what is still cannot be seen. For he could feel the weight of distant vision, not the feral, hot-eyed, mammalian glare. And as he looked at the large leaves hanging before him, leaves tipped crimson and splotched with blue, blue the colour of ancient, alien eyes, he saw them, saw them watching him, as if he were looking into mirrors; and the eyes gazed at him from years and infinities away. Peter felt caught; and he could sense the presence of the creatures from his dreams, the smooth behemoths swimming in the black alien depths of the sea; creatures dreaming and swimming, one the same as the other, dreaming him, dreaming him inside green dreams of root and vine and frond, chlorophyll dreams swimming out of the blue; and he could sense their thoughts, or some part of a vast machinery of thought, so large and so slow as to almost thicken into substance.

But he could not reach into their depths, only dream the surface: green sea turning blue. The ocean, mother mystery, pulling at him with green rainforest fingers, the world slipping back into dreamtime, pulling him back.

Leaf eyes staring, Peter crashed through them, running to hide, to escape, an aging Adam in a malevolent unblinking Eden.

Sick with fear, he fled in the direction he had come: back to the familiar. Yet even as he did, a distant voice, the tinny voice of his consciousness, said, "*You can't go back.*" Tubers caught at his feet, his legs. He pressed himself past the thin-bowled trees being strangled by parasite roots, past glistening ferns spotted with crimson and turquoise, as if all pigments had been dreamed into this green reality.

And then he was free.

He stopped, tried to catch his breath, and found himself standing on his pastels, crushing the cylindrical, coloured pieces into the soft loamy dirt. The air was dry and cool. Only he was drenched and sweating. He looked for the arching church, and, indeed, when he began to calm down, he could see its natural columns and arches once again. They seemed so much closer in the softer light of the late afternoon.

Although it was a warm night, I closed the windows and the balcony shutters. October was usually a cooler month, the last gasp of the tourist season, but the weather hadn't changed. Who knows, perhaps it wouldn't. Aristides had turned off the air conditioning on September 30 and wouldn't turn it on again if the temperature rose to 100 degrees. I didn't care. It was quiet, the world was shut out, I was safe. I thought of Sandra sleeping with her lover in our bed, but my face didn't get hot and my digestive juices didn't start eating my stomach.

Throughout the last few weeks, I had tried to locate the pain, that region of loss and loneliness, and discovered it was in the pit of my stomach. I felt as if I was constantly hungry, yet the thought of food made me queasy. Although I usually slept with my fist pressed against my chest, as if to prevent the aching and burning from expanding, tonight I lay on my back and stared at the stained ceiling.

I had been happy to move out of the house, to split all our assets, get an amicable divorce, and start life fresh. The children were grown and in college. They were old enough to understand, and I would support them and pay for their education. But the pain didn't start until I found out that Sandra had been having an affair.

For years. For fucking years.

Still, no reaction. No change in my breathing. No constriction. No claustrophobia. I reached for the fraying lamp cord that hung between the bed and night table and pushed the plastic switch. The room was so dark as to appear flat. Perhaps tonight I would sleep. I hadn't slept more than five hours at a time for the last month.

If only I could stop thinking about Sandra, about the past, I could sleep. I thought of the sea, of warm, long curlers on a shelf of virgin white sand. I visualised a place where the sea and sky were one and the same, and realised it was Lefkada, an island where Sandra and I had been happy. But the whisper of the sea soothed me, spoke to me with distinct voices, caressed me, then turned into a roaring crashing pounding and . . .

I woke up, gasping for breath.

Someone was knocking at the door.

I bumped my eyeglasses off the night table as I tried to find the light switch, and then I realised who it must be. No, I wouldn't turn on the light. I would wait until she left. But she was insistent. She would knock, then wait. I imagined I could hear her breathing outside the door, and I thought of swimming, of mermaids, of sea sounds, I remembered my dream of Lefkada; and feeling my way to the door, I let the whore in. For company, out of curiosity, I don't know. Perhaps it was loneliness. She had awakened me from a dream I wished wouldn't end, and I was . . . frightened now to be alone in the clammy darkness.

She was tiny, barely five feet tall, with very long, very thick black hair. She could have been Sandra, and for an instant I caught my breath; but in the dark, at midnight, any woman with a petite build and dark hair would have jagged my imagination. She closed the door behind her, but said nothing, nor did she reach for me in the flat darkness.

As I was reluctant to turn on a light, I said, "*Si-gno-mi*," and felt my way across the room to the windows. I pulled open the shutters, letting in moonlight and city light, but when I looked down at the street, I saw dark water streaming and rippling between the old office buildings and apartment houses. It was as if the sea had broken through a great dam to fill the dusty, dirty streets of the city with clear fast-flowing water, white water sweeping silently as oil leaking over ancient cobblestones and steps. It wasn't water, of course, simply an effect of light and mist and humidity. Yet I couldn't help but feel that I was looking into reality, into someone else's dream of the future; and as I stood there looking into Athens' watery light, I felt the prostitute's arms slide around my naked waist, felt her flesh press against my back; in that instant, I found a relief from private pain. I felt a new security, a poignant longing for the ocean, for green islands and blue sea, for what might lie in its shimmering depths.

And as we made our clutching way back to the bed, as we tore at each other, as if ecstasy was a pain that could be only momentarily endured, I imagined I could hear the voices of the sea, as if I had lifted a conch shell to my ear.

The voices whispered, and in that instant of gasping pain I felt completely alone.

As if only I could swim.

Stephen had taken the Jag.

Perhaps he had gone for help. Perhaps he thought Peter was lost or hurt. Or, perhaps, he had followed Peter into the bush, into the rainforest, and panicked.

Peter waited two hours and then walked out to the main highway, which was choked with cars, as if this was a public holiday. He walked along the road's shoulder until he came to the source of the jam: a head-on collision between a Volvo and a small Russian made car. Glass had shattered across the road, and the bodies of the cars were twisted one into the other, like shiny, chitinous burrowing beasts. Slowly, cars were making their way around the accident, over the glass-strewn road shoulder. Peter crossed the road and peered inside the Volvo and the Russian car. Although the seats and smashed windshields were stained with blood, the cars were empty. The ambulance must have already come and gone, Peter thought. Surely wreckers would have towed away the cars, and road crews would have swept away the debris. But where were the police?

On either side of the road, the bush looked thicker and darker. Peter remembered walking through the scrim of one reality into another, from bush into deep, tropical rain forest; and although he *knew* it was real, it felt like a dream. Just as he knew that Nedra was dead, that she would not be waiting for him when he returned home. The bush — the thick knot of trees and climbers that deepened into green darkness, into a greener darkness than should have been ordinarily possible — seemed somehow impersonally malevolent.

Peter could feel the bush, the forest, the dreaming weight of it. He hurried, wanting only to escape it, for he imagined that it was staring hard at him, trying to possess him. Perhaps he should have stayed in the hospital.

Perhaps . . .

No! and he stepped into the road, extending his thumb for a ride, forcing those drivers who would pass him to steer around him.

A woman driving a small, but very new and polished Japanese car picked him up. She was overweight, pretty with a ruddy, freckled complexion and brownish-red hair, which was heavily sprayed; and she looked to be in her late thirties. She seemed nervous. "I usually don't pick up hitchhikers." She brushed her fingers back and forth over the cellular phone handset cradled between the seats as if she was dusting it.

"Well, I haven't hitchhiked since I was a kid," Peter said, trying to calm her. "A friend gave me a ride out here and then left me stranded. I'm a bit worried about him. For a second, when I saw those cars wrapped around each other, I thought it might have been him. But, thank God, it wasn't." Peter waited for her to take the bait and talk about the accident.

"You have an American accent," she said, looking slightly less tense, as if being an American was credential enough.

"Well, I've lived here for twenty years." After a beat, Peter said, "My wife just died."

"I'm sorry," she said distractedly as she stopped and waited to turn onto the macadam road. Traffic was heavy.

"Where are you from?" Peter asked.

She accelerated onto the highway; the little car certainly had zip. "Melbourne."

Peter waited for her to continue, but she drove on in silence, an uncomfortable silence. "I thought that accident back where you picked me up was very odd."

Still no response.

Peter shrugged and leaned away from her, against the window. He would not try to force conversation with her. It was enough that she had given him a ride. Why had she? he asked himself.

"Why do you think the accident was odd?" she asked. She seemed tense again. "An ambulance must have taken the people in the cars to hospital. They just haven't cleaned up yet."

"I would expect police to be directing traffic," Peter said, "and cordoning the area."

"Police are too busy."

"Doing what?"

She shrugged. "There have been a lot of drownings."

"Drownings?"

"I called my sister while I was tangled up in traffic, waiting for the accident to sort itself out. She lives in Saint Kilda, a few blocks from the beach, and she told me that she had never seen so many police around there. Seems people have just been walking into the water and drowning."

"I'll bet it was a shark attack," Peter said. "We've had problems before. And people panic and think they see all sorts of things." He felt a chill even as he said it. How could he tell anyone what *he* had seen? Somehow the drownings were connected with the creatures in his dreams . . . and with the forest that was — even now — watching them.

"No," she insisted. "My sister told me just what I told you."

"But that wouldn't affect the police out here." Peter said.

"Something's going on here, just like in Saint Kilda. I tried calling the police emergency number, to make sure the accident back where I picked you up was properly reported and because traffic had completely stopped — and that wasn't exactly a four-lane freeway back there."

"What happened when you called?" Peter asked.

"I couldn't get through. The line was constantly engaged." She rubbed the corner of her mouth with her index finger, correcting her lipstick. Peter suspected it was a nervous habit.

"Did you try again?"

She handed the phone to Peter, who dialled 000.

The line was busy.

When I woke up, it was still dark; yet I could see faint greyness through the balcony door windows. I sat up on the side of the bed, completely awake. Jet lag. There was a rustling behind me; and I found myself looking at my reflection in black window glass, for the prostitute had turned on the lamp on the bed table. But I could not see her in the glass. Well, vampires have no reflection, I thought sourly. Yet I did not feel soiled. And as *she* had insisted on using a prophylactic, I thought my chances were quite good that I hadn't been infected.

"I'm sorry I woke you up," I said, not yet turning around. I really didn't know what she looked like: my only glimpse of her was in the dimly lit hallway and when she turned on the bathroom light, which was on the wall outside. For the first few breathless moments I had pretended that she was Sandra, and I felt the edges of a familiar emptiness; but she didn't feel or taste like Sandra, and I discovered that I didn't want Sandra; I just wanted to be blind in the sweat-scented darkness.

"You will tell me that I look like your wife, no?" she asked, coming around the bed to stand in front of me. I was shocked, I must admit, for there was a resemblance. But Sandra, always a girl-child, had become brittle and too polished; this woman would soften and fade with the years. I could see lines around her eyes; she was certainly in her late thirties, and her body was more voluptuous than Sandra's. She turned around and pulled her hair away from her neck. "Zip me up, please."

When I had pulled the loop of thread over a tiny hook that neatly closed the top of her dress, she turned around. "Well, do I look like her?"

"No," I said, easing away from her.

"Ari thought I did." She looked out the balcony into the grey light and smiled. "But many men think I look like women they love. I think there are many women with dark hair and faces like mine."

"How much do I owe you?"

"Whatever you agreed with Ari."

I gave her 50,000 drachmas, which she counted. She smiled and said, "You did not cheat me. Goodbye." With that she closed the door.

"Wait." I dashed to the door and opened it.

"Yes?"

"Where are you going?"

"To church."

"May I come with you?" I asked.

She studied me and said, "Yes, but only if you promise not to ask me stupid questions."

"Such as why you're going to church at dawn?"

"Or why such a nice girl would fuck you for money."

"Do you need to drive this fast?" Peter asked. They were in the suburbs, driving through the bright afternoon tunnel of strip malls and fast food chains; and Mary-Ellen — she had finally told him her name — was tailgating and weaving erratically through the traffic.

"I want to make sure my sister's all right."

"But you just talked to her."

"When I tried to call her again, she didn't answer the phone."

"Then what's the rush?" Peter asked. "We can try her again now, and if she doesn't answer, we'll try her again later. She probably just stepped out."

Mary-Ellen rubbed the corner of her mouth.

"Why are you so anxious? Peter asked.

"Just a feeling."

"Feeling?" Peter became uncomfortable. He would have preferred small-talk, for he sensed she was going to draw him to her, entangle him. He thought of Stephen. Perhaps it was time to call him; he would certainly be home by now.

"We're very close," Mary-Ellen said. "We're six years apart, but we always know when something's wrong. Would you come with me to check on her? I'll take you to your home right after."

Peter remembered a woman who had picked him up when he was hitchhiking. That was forty years ago. Once the car was in motion, she had told him that she was afraid to drive alone because something had just gone wrong with the brakes.

"Well?" asked Mary-Ellen. "Will you go with me?"

Peter agreed, then asked to make a call. Stephen wasn't home; neither was Mary-Ellen's sister; and as she drove through Melbourne's streets, between the 1970s reflecting glass monoliths and past the turn of the century iron lacework façades and ever-present gardens, he told her what he had seen in the rainforest. He glanced at her as he talked, but her face was neutral, and he was unable to tell what she thought from her expression. Yet it was easier to talk to this stranger than it would have been to tell Stephen. He could have told Nedra, may she rest in peace; surely he could have told her. She would have believed him.

Rest in peace...

So now he could admit that she was dead; her death was penetrating him slowly and deeply, like the bitter cold winter nights in Ithaca, New York. And as he talked, as he remembered what he had seen, as he visualised the rainforest, he imagined that he could look right into its arches, into its green darkness, as if he was looking into dark glass. The faint reflections were the stuff of dreams and thought, the diaphanous shapes of possibility. A thousand epiphanies, a thousand transformations.

We walked quickly along the dead labyrinthine streets, for she seemed to be in a hurry. When I asked, she told me that her name was Georgia; I didn't argue, or try to find out her real name. It was still dark, but there was a bit of grey in the sky, prefiguring dawn. All was shadow and emptiness. An occasional car sped by, dangerously fast, taking up most of the street; but the city was asleep; and all these narrow cobbled streets, the walls of windowed flats and storefronts, the paper devils and rusted cans — even the cars — seemed somehow insubstantial, dream projections of the millions of sleepers in the millions of apartments and houses and hotel rooms that formed a hive capped by the Acropolis, which was uncharacteristically dark. The klieg lights must have been turned off at the first glimpse of morning.

When we came to the church, I took a start.

"What is the matter?" she asked, breaking the silence.

"That is the shape of the trees and stones I saw in the Agora." It was a small Byzantine church, square, with a terra cotta roofed dome on pendentives; in the arches of the pendentives hung three large bells. "Have you been to the Agora?" I asked.

She looked at me quizzically. "I didn't think Americans believed in miracles."

"Do *you?*"

"I believe what I see," and Georgia headed into the church, as if she was afraid to remain outside, or simply impatient. I followed her in, past a woman dressed in black seated behind a high counter; she stared ahead, as if blind. Past the wooden offering box. The interior, from floor to ceiling, was covered with paintings, frescos, mosaics, and icons. The figures seemed to move in the flickering candle light; I felt claustrophobic, even though the main room was large and high-ceilinged, for I could feel the weight of the years in this place. A thousand years of art and devotion. The prayers of the dead filled the space like millions of invisible feathers. They were the shadows, the jittery guttering of votive candles, dim reflections on silver and gold. Every wall and ceiling was covered with painted figures: on the upper walls was the celestial hierarchy dominated by a gold haloed Christ — a shadow Pantocrantor waiting for the first strong rays of morning light to proclaim his majesty; the Virgin Mary stood in the eastern apse, half hidden in darkness, as if she were naked and shy; and as I gazed upon her, I knew where the old Greek gods were hiding, for she was Hera, and, perhaps, Aphrodite thinly disguised. I moved from room to room, and the ancient figures in the paintings and gold and silver encased icons seemed to shift, to watch me as I passed. I looked at a painting of a saint riding a chariot pulled by sea horses. The water was a flat, faded blue, yet as I looked it deepened, and St Poseidon receded, the gold scaling of his halo lightened by grey light streaming in like water from cisterns that were small, high windows. And I could smell the sea; for just that instant it swelled and rippled, as if the painted image had been elevated to hallucination. Details emerged, like figures from a fog, revealing a long shoal descending into the sea. Men and women and children were stepping naked into the water to meet finned angels and cherubim. A Hieronymous Bosch caricature of heaven.

I heard hurried footsteps behind me.

I called to Georgia, looked for her in the main chapel, and caught up with her outside. The courtyard was filling with people. Despite the size of the crowd, no one spoke.

"Why did you leave without telling me?" I asked.

"I'm going home," she said, as if that answered my question.

I reached for her arm, and she clasped my hand, pressing it hard. Then she pulled away, as if in revulsion.

"Come back to the hotel with me."

"Why?"

Because I didn't want to walk through the streets alone. Because I was anxious, uneasy, frightened by shadows . . . and miracles. Because I couldn't face going back to my room alone. Because she looked like Sandra. Because she wasn't. Or perhaps it was just humiliation. I couldn't just fuck a whore; I had to have a relationship with her, turn a trick into more than money.

I could not answer.

We walked along the edge of the Plaka, skirting the commercial section: the upscale fashion and textile stores, carpet and glitzy jewellery shops. The city had suddenly come frantically alive with people. It was as if they appeared with the light, explosions of them; and in the humid, polluted morning — the sun a wavery smear in the east — the world roared and stank. Everything was noise and touch and motion: car horns blared, children howled and laughed and chased each other while adults spoke at the top of their lungs and drove their cars and motorcycles and motorbikes as if Jesus himself was directing traffic. It was as if everyone needed to get close to everyone else, to breathe each other's flatulent air, to drive in each other's space, to push, shove, and step over and beside each other; and then we were in the market. Smells of cheese and fish and the musty tang of meat.

Athens had awakened from its night stupor.

Vendors shouted to one another in the flea market. Businessmen crowded into the central metro stop. A heavy woman with enormous arms and unkempt hair thumped the hood of a car. A motorcyclist drove along the crowded sidewalk straight at us. The roar of machines and people was transformed into a droning, continuous streamer of sound, an exhalation that promised to end but didn't; and I remembered my mother measuring the length of the cicada's buzzing to predict how hot the day would be.

She led me down a narrow street filled with huckster tables selling kitsch: blue stone evil eyes glued onto the handles of miniature brooms, decaled icons of saints, plastic worry beads. She held my hand tightly, so we would not become separated.

"Where are we going?" I asked.

"Home . . ."

Suddenly the commotion of the street was swallowed, as if we had walked a great distance from the market . . . from the city. I looked down the narrow street into the green and brown darkness of liana, into the leaves and roots and vines and acid-smelling humus of forest. Rainforest. I felt dizzy, for it was like looking down from a height into its thick green canopy. Below this layer of branch and leaf would be tomb-like silence punctuated by shafts of light; and the boles of trees distorted and disguised by parasitic tubers would create imaginary rooms and corridors, naves and chapels and altars of humus. I watched people walking down the street ahead of us, tentatively stepping over broken blocks of concrete pushed upward by brush and root and tuber to enter the green shade of forest. I felt warm, as if the trees and shoots and vines ahead were radiating heat . . . and something else: I felt myself yearning for the green shade.

I walked toward the forest, imagining that Georgia was with me; I felt numbed, intoxicated, and I could hear voices whispering. And, impossibly, as I gazed into this welcoming cave of green, I thought of the sea. I moved closer to hear better, for the rushing shushing-ticking-breathing whispers would not quite resolve into words, yet I was certain that's what they were. Green words, cool as the sea, cool as memory; and I heard my wife Sandra speaking to me, as if she were the mother and I was the child; and I remembered the luminous, night-lit green lawns of a resort in the Catskills. I was six or seven and the grass and trees seemed to glow with their own light . . . and extend forever in all directions. I could not remember seeing the klieg lights that surely illuminated the grounds.

Just so did the forest at the end of the street seem to glow, as if lit by memory. There, before me, was safe haven. And I could hear the forest and everything in it. Yet even as the tubers broke through cement before me, cracking like branches in a New England ice storm, even as the forest approached me like a green god aswirl in leaves, trunk-tall as the eucalyptus, so tall that the canopy of pale trees blocked out the sun, even then and there, in the blood warm shadows did I look into the heart of the sea.

For there I saw the creatures dreaming . . .

Home . . .

Fish creature, do you wait in the sea dreaming forests? Or do you wait in the forests dreaming the sea? Do you have moments or eons to dream the world, this one or your own, while you float in the seas, large as Dorian islands — Skorpios or Madouri or even tree carpeted Meganissi? Is this theatre or architecture? Are you here or there?

Yes, you dream.

We can hear you and see you and feel you.

But are these your dreams or our own . . .?

And where, where are you from . . .?

What sun's planet?

What watery world?

They could not get anywhere near the beach. St Kilda Road, a grand eight-laned thoroughfare lined with palms, had almost no traffic; yet once they turned west into St Kilda proper, they found the roads impassable: cars blocked every street, every alleyway. It was as if the Mercedes, Holden Jackaroo vans, Falcons, Russian Neva Four by Fours, and Lasers had been simply abandoned, some with their engines still running.

"I think we should get out of here," Peter said.

"We're almost there," Mary-Ellen insisted. "We can go up and around and take Jackson Street to the beach." She backed the car into a driveway and turned around; but she was boxed in, for a 1967 cherry red, mint-condition Chevy Impala convertible was blocking the road.

"I'll see what I can do to get it moved," Peter said. "Whoever owns the damn thing must've just parked it there this minute." Mary-Ellen nodded her head impatiently, as if she had something more important to think about.

Peter got out of the car and for a beat he stood still, like an animal testing the air for sound or smell. There was not a soul around; the street was quiet, except for the thrumming of Mary-Ellen's car . . . and the empty Chevy, idling loudly in a throaty purr. Peter felt a shiver of fear snake up his back, for something had shifted, just as it had in the rain forest; but it wasn't the eerie quiet or the lack of people on the streets. It was a pervading — and sickening — sense of . . . permanence and immanence. The atmosphere itself seemed to be different, and there was a whiff of ozone in the air, as if prefiguring a storm. The light was hard and brilliant, seemingly reflecting off every surface to hurt the eyes; yet it cast shadows sharp as compass lines; and it was humid, as humid as in the rain forest; and Peter felt as if he was falling. He hadn't felt that since he had first come to Australia to be with Nedra. He remembered how everything had seemed slightly off centre in those first few months, and how often he had felt the urge to cry. As he did now. As if everything precious had suddenly been lost to the past, or to this bright and hollow future.

He called out to the owner of the Chevy, but no one answered; there was hardly an echo in the empty street. He waited — the polished hood radiated heat like hot tarmac — then got into the convertible and parked it facing away from Mary-Ellen's car. But in that time, in the few seconds that his back was turned to Mary-Ellen, she had disappeared. Unlike the Chevy's owner, she had turned off the ignition and locked the doors — as if to keep Peter out. Peter shouted her name and ran down the street. He had a clear view ahead, but she was nowhere to be seen. Obviously she had cut across to another street; most likely she knew the area. Peter was certain that she would be heading toward the water. He stopped, out of breath and sweating. He could just go back, take the Chevy and try to drive the fuck out of here, perhaps drive through some invisible scrim back into reality; but just now, in the quiet of the streets, he remembered with the force and clarity of hallucination his days and nights in hospital. He smelled the sharp limy tang of the ocean again, the ocean that had filled his recurrent dreams. And now that human and mechanical noise was stilled, he could hear the ocean, could hear its whispers as it breathed and sighed. Could there be something in the ocean calling him against all reason?

He remembered dreaming of the creatures who were themselves dreaming, dreaming the familiar world into something as alien as themselves.

Once again, here was the dream.

He was standing in it, listening to it; and he felt himself being pulled toward the sea. "Nedra, help me," he whispered, pleading, or praying; and somehow it seemed as if he had suddenly awakened, pushing his way out of the dream; and indeed he must have jolted himself awake, for now he could hear a faint roaring in the distance. Was it a crowd by the beach? Or traffic? Or the sea itself?

He hurried through the silent, empty streets toward the sound. He passed the entrance to Luna Park, a bright yellow cement face with a gaping red-lipped mouth; he passed the Palace Theatre and the children's castle with its blue and red and green towers; he walked through terraced neighbourhoods of chockablock terra cotta roofed houses; until he came to a palm-lined esplanade where he could look down to the beach.

It was as crowded as a hot Saturday. People were milling about the narrow shelf of sand like fleas, and Peter imagined that he was watching a pitched battle, for it seemed as if those closest to the water were being pushed into it, their space on the wet sand immediately possessed by the next rank of citizen soldiers. And the crowd was screaming . . . no that's wrong, Peter thought. They're calling out to the sea.

To the creatures in the sea . . .

And Peter looked beyond the thronging crowds, out to the water, beyond, to the other side of the harbor, across to Port Phillip Bay where shipbuilding cranes were silhouetted against a flat, blue, cloudless sky. He looked into the water, scanning it like words on paper. Its inky shoals of dead vegetable matter were purple, bleeding into bands of turquoise and a region of pale blue that could have been mistaken for the sky itself. There he saw the creature, at first mistaking it for an island. He imagined he could hear it, as if it were the sea itself, imagined that what he had thought was the roaring calling shouting of the crowd was but an echo of the island creature, a public clarion, a megaphone screaming what everyone wanted and yearned to hear.

Destiny revealed.

And Peter, standing away from the massed tumult, away from the eye of the action, away from the crowding thoughts of those below, saw the death and transformation of thousands of ordinary people as peripheral, for he, too, saw and heard the creature.

Saw it through its eyes. Curved expanses of flesh smooth as glass and harder than diamonds; indeed, the creature was transparent, but that was a psychological, not a physiological state. Or perhaps both were the same. Peter saw it as a vague, distant, elliptical shape, but that was overlaid with the image he saw in his mind's eye — the image directed toward him like coherent light by the creature: its greyish pink gill slits shivered, and its vertical tail moved slowly from side to side, and Peter recognised the creature as the enemy. Sharklike, larger than even a whale shark, the largest creature on earth, it stalked him with infinite patience. It drew him down to the beach, bathing him in the radiance of its musing; and Peter could feel an ancient phylogenic urge to return to the sea, back to the watery womb from which he had been torn.

And so did he walk to the beach, to the crowds, to the sea. He yearned, like the crowds milling around him, to swim and breathe as the creature. The slow, comforting, clock-ticking thoughts of the creature turned the sea and all its dark depths into a bath. The cold water that would cleanse and transform.

The creature's sea thoughts . . .

The sea . . .

Rolling, thrusting white fingers into dark, damp sand, repeating, demanding, controlling . . .

Still Peter found it in himself to resist.

There *must* be an explanation. Maybe he was caught up in some sort of mass hysteria, or some millennial manifestation of mob behaviour, or perhaps he tried to withstand the creatures' call because he was tied to the dead past and deaf to the present. Or perhaps he was crazy, yes, that was just as plausible; and *Peter remembers a childhood dream . . . The dream is in colour; he remembers that. The overwhelming colour is deep blue, and it's night, a flat moonless night; and he is asleep in a bed beside the window of a large mountain cabin. He is on vacation, and Mom and Dad are in the next room. It's the middle of the night. In his dream he wakes up and looks out the window. He has never experienced such silence. It's as if he has suddenly gone deaf; he doesn't hear the familiar night noises: the creaking and groaning of clapboard and shingle, the distant whistle of a train, the cheechee scry of bats; but before he can try to speak and break out of the dream, he sees lights falling like petals ever so slowly out of the sky. They are beautiful, perfect, unearthly, and there are so very many of them dropping everywhere. Wherever they fall he can see explosions of soft yellow light. A fluorescence. He cannot imagine anything more beautiful, yet he's suddenly terrified because he knows that something terrible is happening, something terrible and beautiful, something that will change everything forever. But he can't scream himself awake. Instead he watches the lights falling out of the sky by the hundreds . . .*

"*No!*" he screamed, as the crowd pushed, carrying him with them to the sea that was thick with spawning krill and boiling with eels and rays and yabbies and coral reef fish that had never been seen in these waters. Peter's shout seemed deafening, even among the rustling of thousands of people, for it was as if speech had been swallowed by the sea, as if everyone was already under water, already swimming, darting forward, swirling around each other to form a roiling mass. Food for the sea. For the fishes in the sea.

He saw the faces of those around him emptied out by the beast that was an island in the sea. He smelled the bloated corpses, which were strewn all over the wet sand and stepped over without notice, as if they were stones or plastic litter. He smelled the sea, thick with organic perfumes, and then he was in it. The crowd pushed him, carried him, crawled over him, stepped on him, in their common rush to get to deep water.

He could gain no purchase on the sandbar.

He choked and gagged and inhaled water.

He would breathe or drown, dream or die, for like the others he was being pulled into the submerged eye of the shark, into the pale blue of dreams, into sky and sea and transformation. And so he dreamed, as if the cold, living water were itself the stuff of dreams, a conduit of thought that connected Peter to the great shark, the mind and motor of the sea.

But it wasn't either or, it wasn't dream or die; it was breathe or drown, but not as the creature and the sea demanded. He breathed, he inhaled, but not the sea. He pushed and kicked himself to the surface and gasped for air. He fought to stay on the surface, and he swam and treaded water and walked out of the sea onto the corpse-strewn beach. He was alone with the dead, but the shark's dream still clung to him like his sodden clothes. He resisted, yet could not quite walk away from the beach. He felt empty, as he had when Nedra died; and as if the creature and the sea held all his yearnings, he could not completely leave it. Neither would he succumb to its lure. So he made his way to the timber pier, as if the Victorian kiosk at its end was some sort of half-way house. Here he would be safe. Here he could watch and try to understand, marooned on this narrow strip that was neither earth nor sea.

Beyond the kiosk was a curving rock breakwater, usually occupied by penguins and sea birds. But not today. Peter leaned over the railing: thousands of people were now swimming underwater without coming up for air. Some still wore their clothes, but most were naked; and Peter glimpsed the new, raw slashes in their necks — gill slits. Reflexively he felt his own neck, felt the raised spots that ached and burned, but his flesh had not opened, for he had resisted. He watched the swimmers; their legs and feet had already fused together — a grotesque renunciation of earth and air and sky.

Flesh transformed by a thought, flesh evolving toward the watery womb, a miracle of flesh finned flesh gilled flesh: a gift from creatures as distant as heaven.

Peter gazed, transfixed, into the water at the finned and gilled men and women and children; he could see the vague shapes of corpses in the shallows below, those who could not or would not be transformed. Their arms waved, as they danced with eels and crabs in the undertow. Below, by the pylons of the pier, a woman rose to the surface, gasping for air, flailing her arms above the water. She looked like Mary-Ellen, but he could not be sure; and then she slid downward into the grey-green water, into the purpling depths.

He could still feel the creature's cold thoughts beating against him like curlers on a beach . . .

"It's been happening like this all day."

Startled, Peter turned to find a balding man in a black suit. He spoke with an American accent, and his shoulders were hunched, as if he found being tall an embarrassment. He wore black thick-framed plastic glasses and had uneven teeth that were so white they might have been caps. His full moustache exaggerated his thin face, which was an expanse of forehead, gaunt cheeks, and a cleft chin.

"You've been here all day?" Peter asked.

"Most of it. They come down to the beach and walk into the sea." The man turned his head slightly, indicating that he meant those who were now swimming. "But they don't stay long." He stepped beside Peter and leaned against the rail. "See?"

Peter looked down. Indeed, the swimmers were gone, as were the corpses. As if they had never been.

"They come in waves. You came in with the last of them. You were the straggler, that's why you didn't find anyone on the streets."

"How did you get here?" Peter asked, suddenly frightened, sensing something deadly and dangerous and close.

The man chuckled. "Same way you did. It's jubilee. Soon *you'll* be down there. How long can you resist the inevitable?"

"Who are you?" Peter asked, looking up quickly; but there was no one there.

Had been no one there . . .

Only the creature swimming toward him, sending its waves to beat upon the beach like tendrils of thought, sending itself like Christ to the man who would not listen.

I woke up exhausted in the darkness of my hotel room. I had been having fever dreams; and for an instant, as I hung between the borders of sleep and wakefulness, I was in the rain forest. I could smell its rich vapors — the flowering lianas, the gagging fish-rot of a river that twisted and disappeared, tree mushrooms blooming and decaying, dampness cloying, enveloping, misting my skin until I could not bear my sweat-soaked clothes. I wanted to leave them behind, throw them away . . . as Georgia did.

I bolted fully awake.

Georgia . . .

I sat up on the bed, shivering in a cold sweat, and pulled off my soaking undershirt. I turned on the light on the night table, but the room seemed to grow huge, and I quickly switched off the lamp. Blazing white afterimages receded to grey, and as my heart slowed, I remembered . . .

I remembered walking into the green mirage at the end of the narrow street in the Plaka flea market. Georgia walked with me — walked across the broken street that was being crushed, overwhelmed, by root and leaf and fern — walked with me into the rain forest. The dim rooms and rows and phantasms created by the great-boled trees were but manifestations of yearning itself, and so we were drawn, pulled, sucked into the silent, sweating shade, into the soft, life-giving sunlight of immanence radiated by fronds and boles and tubers, by the jewelled insects and scurrying beasts, by vipers slipping through grotto blue river water, by salamanders glittering along the banks. Monkeys hung shining on branches, prey for eagles that were, in turn, like reflected sunlight on the water below them. Clouds of parrots, glowing, flew overhead, tiny stars in a living, moving constellation; and Georgia beside me, sweating and pulling me along, overtaking the others, who moved slowly, as if in a trance. She led me through alleys and streets and avenues created by trees and vines that seemed to reach upward forever, along the leaf-mulched floor of the forest, toward a narrow gap ahead . . . a blue eye unblinking . . . a hole, a tear in the silent living creature that was the rain forest. It grew as we pressed toward it. There were no human tracks here, just those of jaguar, ocelot, and panther; and not a sound could be heard, except for the crunching of twigs and leaves beneath our feet. Even the cicadas were silenced. And I remember that my heart was beating quickly, not from fear but anticipation.

And the eye grew larger, revealing itself as sky, as sea the colour of sky, as if one were merely the reflection of the other. There, as rain forest ended — a living, breathing, green wall — we padded along soft sandy beach toward the sea, toward the creatures as large as islands that were waiting, willing, dreaming. Dreaming the forest and the sea, dreaming us.

Georgia let go of my hand and ran ahead toward the sea, toward the creatures. I watched her strip off her dress and fall into the sea, as if into a mirror. I could feel her joy, hear the creatures that were coaxing me to follow. They whispered like thought itself, as if they were the memories of ancient conversations. Georgia did not turn back; overcome with bliss, she left me without a glance, and I . . . I ran back through the forest, which now seemed suddenly dark and dead and dangerous. I ran back to the street, to the crowds milling in the market, back to the hotel, here . . .

I closed my eyes, trying to clear my head of memories, then got up and walked across the room to the balcony. I threw open the doors, expecting a rush of air and noise. It was quiet, silent, and the air was heavy with musk and perfume, the damp, sweet smells of rain forests, of jungle. The familiar acrid smell of Athens' pollution had disappeared. The city had stopped. Yet below me, in the street, I saw water purling once again over cobblestones and steps, lapping against cement rails, perrons, and brick walls. But this time my eyes weren't being tricked by light and mist and humidity. Water was indeed streaming through the lamp-lit streets. What I had glimpsed from the balcony earlier, as Georgia had closed her arms around me for 50,000 drachmas, had now coalesced into reality.

Were the creatures in the sea dreaming this into being? Was this my own private dream of coursing water and death? Or was it some watery manifestation of Athens' collective yearning? I could only watch and listen, expecting to hear voices in the breeze, in the water below, for, of course, I was dreaming.

I had to be dreaming.

Only in a dream could reality twist and change like this. Only in a dream could I look on, unafraid; and, as if I had given myself the suggestion, I felt a vertiginous longing and emptiness. Georgia, why hadn't I followed you? Why did I turn and run? I clung to a tiny core in myself that rejected the security, the empty warmth, the longing for transformation. I wanted the world back, the world we had made, the failed, imperfect, human world. I thought of Sandra and reached inside myself, searching for familiar pain . . . the pain I had tried to run away from, the pain that could not be undone with a wink and a nod; but it was lost, buried, hidden. Stolen. Sandra was a name, a familiar smell, a recollection; and I knew as I watched the water purling below, that even if I could wake up and find the fear that had saved me from the beast, it would, eventually, draw me back to the sea, to itself.

I listened. Silent Athens. The city lights looked hazy, haloed, blinking like stars obscured by clouds. I needed to see people, needed to hear conversation, for I could not help but feel that everything had just died, that Athens itself had died, and that I was alone, marooned. No use to pick up the phone as a test and call for Ari. The phone had never worked. And what if I went downstairs? Would the lobby be flooded? How deep the water . . .? *Wake up!* I struck the desk with my fist, hard, and felt the pain radiate up my arm.

I was awake.

I dressed, went downstairs, and found Ari. He was sitting in the lobby behind his desk, which was perched on a ledge joined to the staircase. He wore an open shirt that looked soiled and wrinkled; he had undoubtedly slept in it. His face was flushed, and his hair was dishevelled, revealing his bald spot, usually carefully covered with long strands of pomaded hair. He held a glass, probably Ouzo, in both hands.

"Greetings, Mister Blackford. *Kali-ni-hta*. Would you like a drink? On the house." He smiled hopefully. "Come, we will go into the bar. I have scotch if you do not wish Ouzo. It is only you and me left in the hotel and —" He gestured toward the door, at the water running along the street.

I nodded and walked down the few steps into the lobby foyer. The door was closed, but as it was mostly glass, I had a clear view of the street. The stream, although shallow, was filled with fish sliding under the oily water like shadows. I could see cod, bass, whitebait, mullet, and eels. There were small silvery fish in profusion, swirling, reflecting schools of them swimming below bobbing, plastic bottles and bits of paper.

"The water here is not deep," Ari said, as if the stream seething with fish was a perfectly natural phenomenon. "It has not yet come over the front steps to the hotel. However, in some streets you need a boat. I have seen it. Like Venice, is it not?"

"Like Venice," I said, glad to be following Ari into the combination bar and breakfast room.

"But we have time," Ari insisted. "This is as good a place to be as any. Did you not see the fish swimming in the street? You would not be hungry here. Would you like me to cook you a fish? I would not charge you. After all, it is from God, is it not?"

I declined his offer, and we sat down at a table. Ari brought glasses, a bottle of scotch, and a bottle of Ouzo "Where are the other guests?"

He laughed sourly, then took a large swallow of Ouzo. It was transparent in his glass, which meant he had not bothered to add the traditional splash of water, which would have turned the liquor cloudy. "They all left to swim with the fish."

"What do you mean?" I asked, although I knew . . . I knew.

"You won't see them here, of course, for the water is so, uh . . . undeep." He looked to me for the correct word.

"Shallow."

"Ah, yes, 'shallow'," Ari said. "Only good for small fishes. But go to Syntagmatos Street. You can stand on higher ground and see everyone under the water. They are now fish, no longer men. Fish . . . But here it is almost dry. You are safe here, Mister Blackford."

"Why are *you* here, Ari?" I asked.

He sighed. "I am waiting for God to take me. But perhaps he does not want me. I think that is so."

"Why don't you go to your family?"

"You cannot drive anywhere now. The streets that are not underwater are filled with cars, all empty. Or covered with jungle. There is jungle, too, Mister Blackford, here, in Athens. Remember the miracle in the Agora? That you told me you did not see? There was a church there. I, too, couldn't see it, but many did. It's big now. A cathedral." He crossed himself. "I looked, but I couldn't see it."

"What did you see?" I asked.

"Jungle, all the way up the hill to the Acropolis, too. Big trees — and birds and animals and flowers — such as have never been seen in Greece."

"Then you've seen the . . . miracle."

"No, it is not the same, Mister Blackford. For you, I could understand, you're a Jew. So — I mean no disrespect, Mister Blackford — it could be understood why you would not see the church, or the cathedral. But I am a Christian. But a bad one. So, you see. Here we are." He tried to refill my glass, but I stopped him.

"So there are others like us," I said, but it was a question.

Ari shrugged. "Probably . . . some. But everyone is in the water or in the jungle. So quickly, no?" He laughed, as if he had just thought of a joke.

Had Ari and I rejected this new world . . . or had it rejected us, leaving us to become outcasts on deserted islands?

I stood up to leave.

"Maybe it will change, Mister Blackford," he said. "Maybe it will go back to the way it was before . . . before God. Maybe everyone will come back."

"Maybe they will."

"Maybe we are here to take care of everything in the meantime." Again he laughed, sourly. Then he said, a touch of desperation in his voice, "Stay here. It's good as any place."

"I'll have a look around. Perhaps I'll come back."

As I stood up to leave, he said, "None of the others came back . . ."

* * *

Peter Lindsay retraced his steps, walked back past Luna Park, past the Palace Theatre and the pastel painted children's castle, walked down the neatly kept streets of terra cotta roofed houses, working his way through the seemingly endless traffic jam of empty cars . . . cars that had been parked on the streets and sidewalks and lawns. He walked quickly, and his footsteps echoed like shots, for he was alone here, completely and absolutely alone. It was as if the sea and sky had swallowed everything alive, yet Peter could still feel a presence.

As if the man on the pier were right behind him, stalking him. A ghost.

But Peter sensed a change as he approached St Kilda Road. The air seemed to clear, to become lighter and drier, as if humidity and its accompanying whiff of ozone were the messengers of dreams. He saw someone walking, walking ahead, threading his way through parked cars, pausing here and there, as if to decide which one to take. Here was another human being, someone who could walk and breathe and swing his arms. Peter called out to the figure. The man stopped, turned to look at him, then disappeared down another street; and for one terrible instant, Peter imagined that it was the same man he had seen on the pier: another phantasm, a creation of the sea.

But suddenly he heard traffic, the plashing of tires, a distant white noise that made him homesick for his own home just miles from here, homesick for his own familiar things. He wanted to shave and wash his face with his own towel. He wanted to make a cup of tea, listen to the traffic on Punt Road, look at his collection of prints and paintings that covered his walls, assure himself that there still was a familiar world of small comforts.

As he approached the last of the cars left in the road, he saw a green Jaguar convertible. The top was down, the keys in the ignition. He checked the glove compartment, found the registration papers. Thank God it wasn't Stephen's. He'd call when he got home. If he could get home.

Without a qualm, he drove the Jaguar down the empty street, turned onto St Kilda Road, and after a few long, palm-lined blocks, found himself in traffic . . . cars stopping at intersections, people dressed in business clothes walking by on sidewalks, business as usual. Nothing had changed here; and he drove west home. Couples jogged along elm shaded lanes, an old man fed popcorn to the pigeons, high school students in red and white uniforms played cricket.

Peter parked the car in front of his house and noticed that in his rush to leave with Stephen he had left the mesh metal gate open. He closed it, stood in his yard for a moment, taking in the familiarity of it all: his rose bushes, small compost pile, the trees that he refused to trim or cut down, although they scratched against his roof and windows in the slightest wind. He looked at Nedra's earthen pots of busy lizzie and flowering cherry. He could almost feel her presence here; and he felt the tears come, along with the curious thunder sound that he always heard inside his head when he cried. He remembered hearing that sound when he was a child, and now he was sixty-three and still hearing it. *Nedra, I miss you so.* I'll call Stephen, he told himself, opening the door, feeling better at being in surroundings he could control; but as he stepped in the house, he felt a profound exhaustion. He would sleep all of this away, as if it had never happened.

But first he would make himself a cup of tea.

You whisper to them, you embrace them. Even as they call your name, you devour them. You draw them down. Into the depths where the stars burn.
Reefs of them.
Dreaming.

I made my way down Nikkis Street through water that was well above my ankles and hoped I could get back to the Agora. The eels and schools of shiny small fish gave me wide berth, but I could feel crayfish being crushed underfoot. It was easy to get lost in this maze of narrow, winding streets, which were already turning into canals. Indeed, Athens was turning into Venice, an empty Venice. There was not another soul on the street, and I imagined that this watery city was a machine, a great neon clockwork automatically ticking away. That it was empty was but a minor detail. The lights in the shops were on. The street lamps were bright. Except for the fish swimming through the dark water that streamed down the street, everything seemed dead. I could not hear the creatures of the sea that had whispered to me in my dreams . . . or their dreams. I was deaf, isolated, as if I were being punished for not following Georgia into the sea.

The water receded as I made my way back to the Agora, which was dry. The streets had been broken by roots. Slabs of concrete had buckled, there were hills of ancient cobblestones, and, of course, the great trees. I could not tell where the high chain-link fence had stood, which had enclosed the ancient temple stones . . . which had enclosed the church I had seen, the mirage formed from the impossibilities of root and vine and leaf. Perhaps the fence still stood, buried in the tangled, humid, woody darkness ahead. Yet street lamps blazed in the humid air, as if the creatures of this new world had left them on so they could see their handiwork. A child walked out of an alley toward the rain forest, which was claiming everything west of Athinas Street. I called to him, ran after him, but he disappeared into the shadow tangle of the Agora like a cherub passing into heaven.

I stopped before the upheavals of stone and cement. I could hear them cracking and breaking, and I could hear the groaning of wood and vine as they reached upward, grasping tendrils, connecting and thickening and melding into every other leafy limb and torso. Giving birth in that connection to the silent beasts and reptiles, to the birds and insects wriggling in the soil and forming clouds in the spore infected air.

And as I stared into the rain forest, into the darkness, for it looked to me like a well, a pit, I began to make out the outlines of Ari's cathedral, and as I stared at it, so did it seem to gain substance, and the forest began to fluoresce, as if covered with the microscopic phosphorescent organisms that set beaches and water aglow on summer nights, fluoresced into the organic flowing lines of a Gothic cathedral . . . into flying buttresses supporting flowering vaults — living, growing scaffolding — into naves, defined by thin boles and fronds, into spires and pinnacles, towers and gables and galleries and arches, all reaching like a hundred towers integrated into one shifting, knotted structure. Here were Reims and Sainte-Chapelle and St Maclou combined.

If I entered, I might be lost. But what else was there to do? Wait for God with Ari and drown? Wait for the creatures to speak? Wait for dreams while getting drunk on Ouzo?

But the simple truth was that I *wanted* to go.

I wanted to feel once again the warm, green security. In fact, I yearned for the intoxicating, numbing bliss, for the whisperings and soft corridors of dream, for secret conversations profoundly sensed and heard in the susurration and ululation of leaf and sea; and I yearned to see Georgia, whom I imagined as a long, lithe mermaid, a naiad transformed, rather than one of Ari's grotesque "fish".

I entered the vined cathedral, walked through naves and chapels and transepts of glowing vines, palms, and dead spinifex. I walked along a dark trail, confined by a great vine forest on either side of me that was like two receding walls; although it was the dark of night, a suffusing glow of trees and fronds extended away from me in all directions. But I was being led along a dead path, a pavement of bones and shells and spongy dirt that was the residue of rot. I heard no voices, no whispers of comfort, and I felt the isolation and despair of the damned. I had turned away from the warmth and succouring light, and now it was being withheld, even now while I walked in the belly of the beast, as I followed the way I had taken with Georgia. Around me, everything had crystalised into silence, and I imagined that if I tapped any of the twisted tree limbs or huge veined fronds that glittered as I passed, I would send a reverberation through this tangled, twisted beast, would set this glacier of forms a-shiver. And it would shatter around me, the branches becoming spears of beryl and jade and emerald. But there was no life here as there had been before, no animals padding, no birds or insects made out of light. No sound but my feet crunching upon dead matter.

I came to a river, which was as glassy as winter ice. Mushrooms scattered along its banks looked like frosted jewels or coloured baubles. I had seen this river before, with Georgia. We had passed it. Now it glowed like the quiet water in Capri's Blue Grotto, and there led my path. To the creatures in the sea? To Georgia?

I looked for a blue parting in the forest, looked for the sea that would glow even in the night, for the sea that had accepted Georgia; and then, suddenly, I understood. I was still inside the cathedral, which now began to pulse with life, as if needing only recognition. The river was glass, part of the *ars de geometria* that curved overhead; and the translucent trees were but large mullions that separated enormous stained glass windows. As I looked through the forest turned to glass — to ice that radiated heat and light — I could see the blue of sky and sea through the branches and fronds and vines.

And I walked out of the forest into sunlight, into eternal day. Before me was a long shoal descending into a faded blue sea, and ahead were familiar figures, the same ones that I had gazed upon when Georgia had taken me to her church. Here were the images and icons I had seen on the walls come to life: the finned angels standing in the shallows, watching, and the naked supplicants — the men and women and children — waiting on the beach. Here was Georgia — her hair long and wet, her skin pale as porcelain — welcoming me, giving me another chance.

I knew this place. I had been here before.

This was the island of Lefkada, near the fabled palace of the old wanderer Odysseus. I could see the smaller islands of Madouri, Skorpios, and dark Meganisi in the hazy blue distance. But there were also other islands floating like mirages in the clear calm water, islands I had never seen before, islands as smooth as stone . . . or glass.

I called out to Georgia.

I called to her as I walked into the sea that was viscous, heavy as oil.

I called to her as the islands — glass smooth creatures — moved toward me, swallowing oceans and pumping them back through gill slits high as cathedrals.

I called to her . . .

Peter turned on the electric kettle, dropped a tea bag in his mug, and then looked out the kitchen window, expecting to see the neighbour's white cement house, red and gold flowers, cars parked on both sides of the street.

But there was no house, no street.

There was water. Ocean. Perpendicular cliffs and gorges and great waves crashing, attacking, grinding and wearing down rock walls to create huge castles and spires and towers: detached cliffs rising from the sea, from the reefs.

From his kitchen window, Peter looked out at the cliffs and rock stacks and ocean. Looked out at the creature in the sea, a creature larger than any of the rock stacks. A creature transparent as glass. A heat distortion in the water. An aberration of light curving into the smooth shape of a whale shark. Waiting.

The rocks looked purple in the sunset. The red sky filled with twisted braids of yellow clouds; and the ocean was undulating, expanding and contracting, as if it were breathing, as if it contained all the dark depths of space . . . a void without stars, the ultimate darkness.

Peter turned away from the window. The light on the electric kettle blinked on, indicating that the water was hot. He walked out of the kitchen, through the living room, where Stephen had left the suitcases, and into the studio, which smelled of oil and varnish and turpentine and the reassuring sweet musk of memory. He pulled the drawstring of the pleated linen window blinds and prayed for a view of the neighbour's yellow townhouse.

But he found only the sea.

Afterword

SLIP ME A FIVER

"Where do you get your ideas?"

Every author has been asked that question hundreds of times. In fact, I remember being on a panel some years ago with authors Joe Haldeman, George R. R. Martin, Gardner Dozois, and Edward Bryant when that question was asked (yet again). Everyone tried to answer as best he could . . . you'll find that writers (this one included!) tend to get longwinded when trying to answer that question. But when Ed's turn came to answer, he just leaned back in his chair, nodded knowingly, and said, "Well. that's easy, folks. I just send five dollars a month to this little old lady in Duluth, Minnesota, and she sends me back ten brand spanking new ideas. That's all there is to it." He folded his arms over his chest, and the audience laughed. Nevertheless, several people came up to Ed after the panel and asked . . .

"Uh, excuse me, Mr Bryant, but could you give me the address of that old lady in Duluth?"

"Where do I get my ideas?" has always been a difficult question for me to answer because ideas not only come from my own personal experiences, books I've read, stories I've heard, etc., but they also take different forms. Some are narrative, while others are essentially visual; and it doesn't seem to matter whether the idea is for a short story, a novelette, a novella, or a novel.

The idea for "The Diamond Pit" came to me when I read F. Scott Fitzgerald's story "The Diamond As Big As the Ritz." After I read that story, I knew I would *have* to write my own story about the richest man in the world . . . a homage to Fitzgerald.

439

I saw the plot of "The Diamond Pit" rolling out ahead of me as if I was sitting in a locomotive and seeing the track twisting and turning as I whipped around this curve and that.

I glimpsed my protagonist, Paul Orsatti.

I "knew" he had been a mail pilot and a roustabout and played piano.

Although specific details might have been muzzy, the form of a rough plot and the cast of characters were all there. The rest was just connecting the dots . . . something akin to lucid dreaming.

In contrast, the idea for the title story "Jubilee" came to me as a single visual image some years ago when I was writing the novel *High Steel* with Jack C. Haldeman II. I saw in my mind's eye, as if the scene was really before me, crowds of people milling around on stone quays in a decaying city like Venice. One by one, men, women, and children jumped into the water and became transformed into sea-creatures. I had used the idea of genetically altered mer-creatures in *High Steel* as a throw-away; but the image of people being transformed by some unknown force in the water was so powerful that it seemed to burn in my memory. I would think about it every few weeks. Just that image, like a recurrent dream.

So too did my novel *The Memory Cathedral* begin as a powerful visual image. I was sitting in the lobby of the Algonquin Hotel in New York City and reading a biography of Leonardo da Vinci when I suddenly saw in my mind's eye a squadron of high-Gothic looking airplanes flying over Renaissance Florence. It was as clear and detailed and real as Giorgio Vasari's painting of Florence. I saw planes passing over the Duomo, saw them reflected in the mirror of the Arno River; and I knew, I knew then that I had to bring that image to life.

My story "Da Vinci Rising" draws on that same hallucinatory image (at least hallucinatory for me!), which became transformed in the writing.

Once I try to capture my original visual image in words, in a story, it changes. The image remains, informing the story, but the story creates its own demands and seems to rework the image according to its own needs.

It has been my experience that stories which begin with a powerful visual image become stories of discovery. I've likened the experience of writing them to being a sculptor working on a huge block of marble. He knows that the statue he's going to create is in there, but he has to find it in the material. One of the central scenes in *The Memory Cathedral*, an exorcism of Sandra

Botticelli, was not planned by the author. It *felt* as if the characters were leading me into the story, and I had to rework what I had written to accommodate them. I think that such discoveries give a story authenticity, a firm internal logic.

The structures of my "visual image" stories are often discovered in the writing. This was certainly true of my short story "Tea." I had an image of a woman who covered all the windows and mirrors in her apartment with aluminum foil. I knew that the apartment was in Sea Gate, the tip of Brooklyn, New York . . . my old apartment. I knew that she would have tea with a shadowy figure, that she was Jewish and would confront the Holocaust. That's all I "knew." But as I wrote, I could just hear Lorelei Lanzman whispering, musing. I could make out her thoughts, her daily routine of shopping and talking to the neighbours — and talking to herself — and line by line, the story evolved out of and transformed my initial image.

I should probably come clean and admit that sometimes the characters mutiny. They take over. They make up the dialogue. They create new and unexpected plot twists. When that happens, I always have the sensation that I'm simultaneously typing and watching a movie on the screen of my laptop. I feel like I'm just a conduit for the dialog and action.

While I'm working on a story, it does, in fact, feel like a live thing.

When I was a child, I used to believe that the fictional characters and imaginary places in books *were* real. I'd open a book, and the words and pictures would come alive. The characters would wake up and dance and play and have adventures. And when I closed it, they'd simply go to sleep.

In the quick of my subconscious, I still believe that.

After all these years . . .

Which is probably one of the reasons I keep writing.

Oh . . .

To answer that vexing question about where I get my ideas, I can only say, "Slip me a fiver, and I'll give you the address of this little old lady I know . . ."

About the Author

Jack Dann has written or edited over fifty books, including the international bestseller *The Memory Cathedral*, which is currently published in over ten languages and was No. 1 on *The Age* bestseller list. The *San Francisco Chronicle* called it "a grand accomplishment," *Kirkus Reviews* thought it was "an impressive accomplishment," and *True Review* said, "Read this important novel, be challenged by it; you literally haven't seen anything like it." His novel *The Silent* has been compared to Mark Twain's *Huckleberry Finn*; *Library Journal* chose it as one of their "Hot Picks" and wrote: "This is narrative storytelling at its best—so highly charged emotionally as to constitute a kind of poetry from hell. Most emphatically recommended." Dann's work has been compared to Jorge Luis Borges, Roald Dahl, Lewis Carroll, Castaneda, J. G. Ballard, Philip K. Dick, and Mark Twain. He is a recipient of the Nebula Award, the World Fantasy Award, the Australian Aurealis Award (twice), the Ditmar Award (twice), and the Premios Gilgames de Narrativa Fantastica award. He has also been honoured by the Mark Twain Society (Esteemed Knight). His latest novel, *Counting Coup*, has been described by *The Courier Mail* as "perhaps the best road novel since the *Easy Rider* days." Jack Dann lives in Melbourne Australia, and "commutes" back and forth to Los Angeles and New York.